Endless Water, Starless Sky

Endless Water, Starless Sky

ROSAMUND HODGE

BALZER + BRAY
An Imprint of HarperCollins Publishers

Balzer + Bray is an imprint of HarperCollins Publishers.

Endless Water, Starless Sky

Copyright © 2018 by Rosamund Hodge

ISBN 978-0-06-236944-4

18 19 20 21 22 PC/LSCH 10 9 8 7 6 5 4 3 2 1

First Edition

For Rebecca,
who gave aid and comfort

Come, gentle night, come, loving, black-brow'd night,
Give me my Romeo; and, when he shall die,
Take him and cut him out in little stars,
And he will make the face of heaven so fine
That all the world will be in love with night
And pay no worship to the garish sun.

—Romeo and Juliet, *act 3, scene 2*

Prologue

O my Juliet, my most beloved Juliet—
I have no right to call you "beloved" or "mine" any longer.

ROMEO HAD WRITTEN MANY LETTERS in his life, but none so important as this one. He had thought about it all day, but it was only now, after the sun had sunk beneath the rooftops, that he began to write slowly by the light of a lamp.

The first time he had written to Juliet, he had scribbled on page after page and thrown them all away as he tried to find the perfect words. But he was no longer the son of Lord Ineo, living in luxury; he was a fugitive presumed dead, hiding at the house of his friend Justiran, in the Lower City. And Justiran was only an apothecary; Romeo could not waste the pen and paper he'd been so generously given.

Slowly, he wrote another line.

If you thought me dead, know this: I am alive, and I deserve to die.

He'd been so proud of his letters once, how his words had won him Juliet's heart. But now there was no rhyme or turn of phrase that could ever set things right. All he could do was confess the truth.

I am alive because when we tried to make me into your Guardian—when the magic went so terribly wrong, and the land of the dead opened around us—I was dragged out by your kinsman, Paris Catresou.

Just thinking the name made the raw ache at the back of Romeo's mind start up again. That terrible, hollow sense of *nothing* where he had once felt the mind of Paris, with all his pride and his kindness and his prickly sense of honor.

Because Paris hadn't just saved Romeo from being dragged into the land of the dead. When his hand closed around Romeo's wrist and pulled him back, the magic that Romeo and Juliet had meant to use on themselves had locked around the two boys, binding their minds together with the same link that was meant to exist between a Juliet and her Guardian.

And now Paris was dead. Romeo had known it as soon as he woke up from his injuries, even before Justiran told him with sad eyes and a gentle voice.

Even when they had both been trying to block the bond as much as they could, Romeo could still feel that Paris was *there*, alive and just a heartbeat away.

Now he was gone.

Romeo stared at the page. He wanted to write more. To say, *Paris was loyal to you, he wanted to serve you, he was honorable and kind and the kinsman you deserved to have. And he deserved to have you know it.*

But this letter was not for making Romeo feel better about the loss of his friend. It was not even for honoring Paris as he deserved. It was for Juliet, and what she needed to know.

He began to write again:

> *I deserve to die, because I destroyed your clan.*
>
> *You have been told that your father, Lord Catresou, conspired with necromancers. It is true. Barely had Paris saved me when Lord Catresou came to the sepulcher with one of his men. We overheard them discussing their plans to use you in the service of a nameless Master Necromancer. We swore to hunt down this necromancer and avenge you.*
>
> *We could not find him. But we discovered where he was*

*about to conduct a ceremony with your father, one that would
open the gates of death and destroy Viyara.*

*This is how much they betrayed you: when they wrote the
spells on your back to make you the Juliet, they changed them.
They made you into a living key, able to open up the land of the
dead. After you disappeared, they found some relic they could
use in your place. But that power still remains in you, and you
must know this, because the Master Necromancer was never
caught. He might still try to capture and use you.*

Romeo stared at the paper a long time after writing those
words. Because he wanted to add: *I am going to find him. I am
going to stop him. I will save you.*

But he had promised her that they could be happy together,
and that had been a lie. He was done with making foolish promises out of his hopes.

So he wrote the truth instead.

*That is one of my sins: that I could not stop the man who
was the first author of all these misfortunes. But it is not the
worst. Because we did not think we could stop the Master
Necromancer alone. So we went to the City Guard.*

And Romeo couldn't stop himself from writing the next para-
graph; it felt like he would be slandering Paris if he did not.

Paris did not want to. He knew what it might mean for your people. But I was too naive, and in the end we were both too desperate.

We stopped your father's plot, though Paris died in the fighting. But it gave my father, Lord Ineo, the excuse he needed to destroy your clan. To force you to kill them.

And it was I who made it possible.

I am no longer the son of your enemies. I am the very worst of them, because first I swore to love you, and then betrayed you. And I am prepared to accept whatever punishment you see fit.

I meant to tell you this to your face, to kneel at your feet again and offer you my life. But you have been too often forced to take vengeance already. I will not do anything that could force you again. I will wait here, at the house of Justiran—the apothecary who helped us. If you desire justice, come here. Or send me your own letter, and I will come to you obediently.

With deep love and deeper remorse,

The one who no longer deserves to be called your husband,

Mahyanai Romeo

He put down the pen. His fingers were sore from gripping it, and he rubbed at his knuckles as he stared at the page.

It seemed like such a pitiful little thing. But telling her the truth was all he could do for her. He wished—

And then he heard the knock at the window.

It's Vai, he thought as he went to open the shutters. Because Vai, who had promised to carry the letter to Juliet, liked to travel across the rooftops more than half the time. And she had said she would come this evening.

He flipped up the latch, swung the shutters open—

And stopped.

Romeo's fingers were still gripping one of the shutters, the wooden corner digging into his palm hard enough to hurt. But he couldn't let go. Couldn't move, couldn't think, couldn't do anything except stare at the tall, dark-haired man crouched on the rooftop outside the window.

Even in the dim moonlight, he knew that face.

"Makari?" he whispered.

Mahyanai Makari. His tutor, who had raised him since he was ten, who'd been father and brother at once, more kin to him than anyone who shared his own blood.

Who was dead.

Makari was *dead*, murdered by Juliet's cousin Tybalt. Romeo had held him in his arms as he died, had smelled his blood dripping across the hot cobblestones, and then he'd gone mad himself. He'd picked up Makari's sword and killed Tybalt and doomed them all.

"Nothing gets past you," said Makari, in exactly the same tone of wry mockery that Romeo remembered, and he climbed in the window.

Romeo stumbled back a step, numbly thinking, *This isn't possible.* His head felt dazed and ringing, like somebody had struck him a blow, and then he remembered Makari's knuckles rapping him lightly on the skull to startle him out of a daydream, and—

And then he remembered that this *was* possible. That he and Paris had seen Tybalt summoned back to life by the Master Necromancer, and made into his slave. Tybalt had tried to kill them all, before they killed him again.

He remembered that Justiran was alone and defenseless downstairs.

He drew a breath, but before he could shout a warning, Makari had him pressed against the wall, an elbow to his collarbone and a hand over his mouth.

"Quiet," said Makari, his voice deadly calm. "Nobody can know I'm here."

He wouldn't hurt me, Romeo thought, heart pounding. *Makari would never hurt me.* But if Makari was living dead—a soul forced back into its undead body—then he would not have a choice.

"Can you be quiet?" asked Makari, still calm.

Romeo managed to nod fractionally, and Makari dropped the hand from Romeo's mouth.

"Who sent you?" asked Romeo.

"Well," said Makari, drawing out the word as he stepped back from Romeo and spread his hands, "you saw me die, so three guesses."

"The Master Necromancer."

"He told me to kill you and everyone you cared about." Makari shrugged. "I decided not to obey."

"You . . . *decided*," said Romeo.

Makari was making no move to attack, but the cold fear hadn't left Romeo's veins. He remembered Vai swearing to them that the living dead were slaves to the necromancers who raised them. He remembered the flat, lifeless tones of Tybalt's voice. Makari sounded nothing like that now, but—

"Yes," said Makari. "I decided. I disobeyed my master."

Romeo flinched. Tybalt had also said *my master.*

"It nearly broke my soul apart, but now I'm free. And if you don't believe me, well." He drew a knife, and held it out to Romeo, hilt first. "Finish this painfully dramatic scene and kill me."

It wasn't the knife that convinced Romeo, that made him fling his arms around Makari. It was the way he half rolled his eyes as he said *painfully dramatic*, exactly like he had when he read Romeo's poetry. Surely no necromancer's power could fake that.

"All right, enough," Makari said after a moment, sounding just as exasperated as he always did. He pushed Romeo away, muttering "spoiled brat" under his breath, but then he grinned and ruffled his hair. Just like always.

The next moment, the illusion shattered as Romeo saw Makari sheathe the knife.

"You said . . . the Master Necromancer sent you to kill me?"

Makari nodded. "Yes. Which is why you're going to leave this house *right now* and hide somewhere I can plausibly pretend I can't find you."

And that made sense, because Romeo couldn't bear to put Justiran in danger, not after all he'd done, but—

"Wait," said Romeo, "you're going *back* to him?"

"Yes," said Makari. "I'm going back to him, and I'm pretending to be his slave, so that he doesn't tear the city apart looking for you. Trust me. You don't want to fight him openly."

"But—Vai's people could help, we could go to the City Guard again—"

"Oh, because that turned out so well for you last time?"

Makari's voice was light, but Romeo still cringed as he remembered the rumors he had heard: blood running across the streets of the Catresou compound as an entire clan was destroyed.

"I . . ." Romeo faltered, searching for words. He'd never fought with Makari about anything before. Probably Makari would have told him not to court Juliet, but that was why he'd never told him about her.

"He hurt Juliet," he said.

"Mm, I think it was her own family that handled most of that," said Makari.

"I can't leave you with him!"

"It's not up to you to leave me anywhere," said Makari. "Unless you think you're ready to be *my* tutor all of a sudden."

Romeo's shoulders slumped.

Gently, Makari laid a hand on his shoulder. "Let me decide how I'll avenge my own wrongs," he said. "Just do me this favor, get yourself somewhere I won't be forced to hurt you."

"I can't leave yet," he said. "I have to wait for Vai. She's going to deliver my letter to Juliet. And the letter—it tells her to meet me here. If she wants vengeance."

Makari rolled his eyes. "Cross out that line, tell her to meet you by whatever fountain you like best, and I'll deliver it. And *go*."

Romeo hesitated.

"Do you trust me?" Makari asked quietly.

And there was only one answer he could give.

"Yes."

PART I

But Sad Mortality
O'er-Sways

1

SOMETIMES, IN THE FIRST MOMENTS as Juliet awoke, she could forget what she'd done.

She might hear Runajo's breathing, and think she was still hiding in the Cloister. She might feel the soft pillow under her cheek, and think she was still in her childhood bedroom at the Catresou compound.

She might open her eyes, look up at the whitewashed ceiling, and think for a moment that she hadn't killed anyone yet.

Not this morning.

She dreamed of blood running across the floors of her father's house. She woke, her heart pounding, her stomach churning with sick horror, and instantly remembered that the dream was true.

Juliet lay very still, controlling her breathing and blinking rapidly at the ceiling. She did not deserve tears.

Pale morning light glowed through the windows. She was alone in the bedroom, but as she thought this, she heard movement in the doorway. Juliet shut her eyes and slowed her breaths further, trying to mimic sleep.

Soft, light footsteps.

"I know you're awake," said Runajo.

Juliet didn't move. The voice of her former friend still left a cold weight hanging in her chest.

"Lord Ineo wants to see us," Runajo went on in the bored, polished tone she used whether she was discussing the weather or the eventual doom of the city. "Do you really think that sulking in your bed is going to prove a point?"

"I'm a prisoner," Juliet said flatly. "If you want something from me, you can order me to do it."

There was a short silence.

"Get up," said Runajo, and now her voice was low and ragged.

Juliet's eyes snapped open and her body rose in one swift, fluid motion. Her stomach pitched. Every time that the power of the bond between them seized her and forced her to obey, it felt like she was falling.

"Happy?" asked Runajo. Her arms were crossed, her lips a flat line. She was dressed in dark-green silk, with silver combs pinning her dark hair on top of her head. Except for the crimson tattoo on her chin—a round pattern of twisting briars—she looked like any rich and pampered Mahyanai lady.

"Are *you* happy?" asked Juliet.

Runajo looked away. It should have given Juliet at least a little satisfaction, but it only made her feel worse. Because she could remember when they had been in the Cloister together, when Runajo had been her ally, hiding her from the Sisterhood

When they had been in the Cloister, Juliet had still been a prisoner. She had still been enslaved to Runajo through the magic that had been meant to help her serve her people. She had just fooled herself, for a little while, into thinking that an enemy could ever be a friend.

Juliet dressed swiftly. She hadn't wanted any of the Mahyanai servants to touch her, so she had learned how to put on the wide-sleeved dress and tie the sash herself, how to twist up her dark hair and pin it in place with combs. In just one month, the style had grown hatefully familiar.

Lord Ineo was in the breakfast room, sitting on a cushion at the low table. He was a tall man with a proud, handsome face. His hair had started to gray at his temples, but there was no weariness or weakness to the way he held himself; even the way he reached for his cup of tea seemed to say how well he knew that he was leader of the Mahyanai clan and one of the most powerful men in the city.

He was also Romeo's father. Once, Juliet might have cared

about the obedience she owed to her father-in-law.

Now she bowed to him and said, "Anyone for me to murder today?"

Lord Ineo blew on his tea. Without looking at her, he said, "Runajo, tell your charge to be quiet."

"Kneel and be silent," Runajo said tonelessly, and a moment later, Juliet was on the ground, her neck bent, her palms flat against the floor.

One month since Runajo had offered Juliet's services to Lord Ineo, and he'd still gotten no respect from her that wasn't compelled. It was a cold comfort.

"I thought you'd have her better in hand by now," said Lord Ineo.

"I thought you understood how this magic worked," said Runajo, kneeling at the table.

"You can order her to stop sulking and eat, surely."

A hundred furious words coiled behind Juliet's teeth, and she couldn't say a single one, because Runajo had told her, *Be silent.*

Runajo sighed. "Consider yourself at liberty to sit up and speak."

Juliet was hungry. And all her fighting couldn't change a thing. The magic that bound the Juliet to her Guardian was absolute. There was no chance of escape.

But she didn't have to pretend to like it. Not until Runajo ordered her to.

So she remained kneeling, her head bowed. She listened to the clink of the dishes as Lord Ineo and Runajo ate their breakfast. She listened to Lord Ineo tell Runajo about the audiences he had been granted with the Exalted, the ruler of the city, and how the stolen Catresou children were learning the ways of the Mahyanai clan and would soon be part of it.

Juliet felt sick. She had helped drag the screaming children out of the Catresou compound. She had been the sword that Lord Ineo used against all of the Catresou clan, when he told them that they must renounce their ways and assimilate into the Mahyanai or die.

"I don't see how it's important to make them renounce," said Runajo, still infuriatingly calm. "What matters is that they abjure necromancy, isn't it?"

"Now of all times," said Lord Ineo, "we don't need dissension in the city. It was a mistake ever allowing the Catresou to become one of the three high houses, when they despised the magic that protected Viyara."

We despise you and your magic, thought Juliet, *because you murder people to keep the city walls alive.*

She said nothing.

At last Lord Ineo rose, bid Runajo good-bye, and left the room, his footsteps fading down the corridor.

There was a moment of silence.

"He's gone," said Runajo. "You can look up now."

Juliet stared at her hands, pressed against the ground, and wished that anything she did mattered.

"You know," said Runajo, "you could make things a lot easier for yourself if you just pretended to be obedient."

"What does it matter?" Juliet demanded, raising her head. "I have nothing left to fight for. You made sure of that."

Runajo flinched. But this time she looked Juliet steadily in the eyes as she said, "If we weren't here, if Lord Ineo weren't protecting us, we would be dead."

"*I* would be dead," said Juliet. "And I wouldn't mind that."

"We would both be dead," said Runajo, "because I would have refused to kill you in the Cloister."

She said the words with a flat, unsentimental defiance, as if there had been no friendship between them in the moment when Juliet accepted that Runajo would cut her throat open, and Runajo didn't.

I do not owe you for this, Juliet thought furiously.

Out loud, she said, "The world is *dying*. When we were in the Cloister together, you cared for nothing except finding a way to stop the Ruining. But now that you have Lord Ineo's favor and can put silver combs in your hair, suddenly it doesn't matter to you. Did it ever?"

And without waiting to hear Runajo's answer, she fled.

Juliet went to the shrine of the dead.

Unlike everyone else in the city, the Mahyanai did not believe in the nine gods. They did not think that anything awaited the souls of their beloved kin after death. But they did want to honor their dead. So in each household was a wall of wood paneling, carved with the names of all the dead members of the family.

Romeo's name was in the lower left corner. Juliet knelt and pressed her fingers to the swirling lines, still sharp and new.

He wouldn't be on this wall, except for her.

The Mahyanai reckoned inheritance through the female line; as Lord Ineo's son by a concubine, Romeo had not been heir to the clan. It was only after seizing the Juliet for his clan that it had become in Lord Ineo's interests to claim a connection with the boy she had tried to marry. So he had posthumously adopted Romeo, carved his name in the family wall, and declared their marriage valid.

If not for her, Romeo wouldn't be on this wall, because he would still be alive.

There was no one here for her to be angry at, and suddenly the feeling swept over her again: the cold emptiness that filled her every time she remembered Romeo. It wasn't like the grief she'd felt for Tybalt or her mother. She'd wept for them when they died, but she'd still felt alive.

Now Juliet felt like there was nothing inside her but the

infinite darkness and heavy stillness that waited in the land of the dead.

She had felt that way once before, after Runajo had dragged her out of the Mouth of Death. Juliet had hated Runajo for saving her from dying beside Romeo. But then she had discovered Runajo's dream of protecting the city—so like her own desire—and as they had plumbed the depths of the Sunken Library, faced revenants and reapers together, Juliet had become impossibly, treacherously *happy*—

When the Sisters of Thorn had discovered Juliet and condemned her to death, she'd been at peace. She had found a friend. She had done what she could for Viyara. She was going to meet her husband. It was enough.

But Runajo had saved her a second time . . . by handing her over to the Mahyanai. By twisting the spells painted on her back, so that she was compelled to avenge *their* blood, be *their* sword.

Now Juliet's people were dead, and she was left to wait for the rest of the world to die, because Runajo didn't seem to care about saving it anymore.

Juliet leaned her forehead against the cool wood.

Romeo, she thought, *I'm sorry*.

He had admired so much her determination to protect the whole city. He would be disappointed that she was giving up now. But she had been twisted and broken into a weapon for the Mahyanai, and she couldn't fight it anymore. There was no fire and no strength left inside her, just this cold, raw emptiness.

If Romeo were alive, if he were in her place, he wouldn't give up. After all, he'd looked at a Catresou girl who was more than half weapon and fallen in love with her. He'd talked his way into her heart, and brought hope along with him.

Juliet wasn't Romeo.

Juliet wasn't anything, anymore.

Juliet didn't know how long she'd been sitting there when she heard the sniffle.

She looked up. A little girl, perhaps ten years old, stood in the doorway. Her eyes were red and swollen; she wore a shabby gray dress. She was staring at Juliet with an anxious, wide-eyed expression.

"You're the Juliet," she said.

"Yes," said Juliet.

It was no surprise to be recognized. Juliet knew that her bright-blue eyes instantly marked her as a Catresou.

"They say you have to help us," said the girl.

A memory slammed into her: the Catresou children, when Lord Ineo had brought her to purge the compound. They had thought she was going to help them. They were all prisoners now, and most of their parents were dead at her hands.

She forced herself to take a slow breath.

"Yes," she said. "I serve you."

The girl bit her lip, clearly on the edge of fleeing. Then she said—words tumbling out on top of one another—"Will you come sit with me, please, just for a little, I'm all alone with her and I'm frightened."

"Who?" asked Juliet.

"My mother," said the little girl. "She's dead."

Juliet stared at her a moment before she understood. Like everyone in the city but the Catresou, the Mahyanai cremated their dead. It was the law. But perhaps they felt a little guilty at burning their family like so much trash, because they had a tradition of sitting vigil over the body for the first day.

"Show me," she said, standing.

She couldn't save anyone. But she could keep this little girl company.

Romeo would have liked that.

The girl led her through narrow hallways to a room in the servants' section. In the doorway was a little bronze incense holder, with three sticks of incense still smoldering.

It had been knocked over.

"Oh no," said the little girl, bending down to pick it up. "Who—"

Inside, the low bed was empty.

There was a feeling like ice from the back of Juliet's neck all the way down her spine. She was suddenly aware of every sound—her heartbeat, the little girl's gasp, an echo of voices from outside.

"How long was she dead?" asked Juliet.

"She's not—she can't be—"

Juliet dragged her into the room. *"How long?"*

"Since last night," the little girl gasped. "No more."

Ever since the Ruining began, all who died rose again as revenants, mindless and hungry for the living. But they did not rise until they had been three days dead. It was the only reason that the city of Viyara still survived: there was enough time to collect the bodies and burn them.

Something moved in the corridor outside.

"Stay here," said Juliet.

She didn't have a sword, but the knife never left her side. She drew it as she edged toward the door.

Her heart was pounding. She wanted to believe the body had just been taken—a mistake, a theft, anything less terrible than a revenant rising in only twelve hours—but she wasn't fool enough to trust in hope.

She leaned out the door.

From barely a single pace away, the revenant looked back at her.

Once, it had been a chubby, plain-faced woman with gray streaking her dark hair.

It was not a woman any longer.

It was not like the revenants Juliet had faced in the Sunken Library: shriveled, desiccated things, dead for a century. This one still had smooth cheeks and bright black eyes. But the horrible, moving emptiness in its face was exactly the same.

The revenant lunged.

Juliet dodged back, her knife coming up. She meant to slash its eyes, but then the little girl screamed, and Juliet was back in the Catresou compound, listening to the children scream as she dragged their parents away and killed them. She was fighting the magic that forced her limbs to move, she was wanting to die, she was—

Flat on her back, with the revenant on top of her.

Juliet slashed wildly. She didn't even get its eyes, just its face, but the revenant still recoiled and hissed at her. Juliet punched it, then grabbed it by the hair so it couldn't bite her.

She looked over the thing's shoulder and saw the little girl still huddled in a corner of the room, too afraid to run.

"Go!" she snapped. "Run to the yard, get someone with a sword!"

There were people out in the courtyard, practicing their sword work. She'd seen them earlier. A sword would make quick work of the revenant, so long as Juliet could keep it from running loose.

The girl whimpered. The revenant writhed against Juliet, trying to claw at her face. Juliet shoved its arm back and yelled, *"Go!"*

The girl ran, and Juliet was alone with a revenant.

Grimly, Juliet slashed at its throat with the knife. If she could cut enough, she might get its head off even without a sword.

She managed two deep cuts. The blood oozed instead of spurted: it had long since clotted. Then the revenant clawed at her face, and when she flinched, it broke free.

In an instant it was on its feet and running for the door. But Juliet launched herself after it; grabbed it by the neck—she felt the slick, bloody edges of its cut throat against her fingertips—and hauled it to the ground again.

She was on top of it now. The power of the Juliet—the magic that made her stronger and faster—was singing in her veins now. She cut and cut and saw bone and ground the knife down again.

The blade broke.

She seized the head and *wrenched*.

The writhing thing beneath her was still.

Juliet's heart was pounding in her ears, loud as a drum. Her breath came in great gusts. Her whole body felt numb and tingling and hot and cold at the same time.

She heard a noise, and looked up.

In the doorway stood a Mahyanai girl her own age. She held a sword—of course, Juliet had forgotten that the Mahyanai allowed their daughters to train in fighting—and she was staring at Juliet in wide-eyed shock.

The revenant's head was heavy in Juliet's hands. She dropped it, and flinched at the thump.

"Don't let her see," she said. "It's her mother."

The young woman stared at her a moment longer, then said, "She's out in the courtyard."

Juliet nodded. She wasn't sure what to say. Runajo was not giving her orders. Since the revenant was already dead, the magic of the Juliet had not compelled her to kill it.

She had never yet helped a Mahyanai when she was not compelled to.

"You should come out," said the young woman. "She was afraid for you."

Juliet nodded and rose. She followed the young woman out into the courtyard, feeling like a sleepwalker—the sunlight dazzled her eyes as if she had been asleep—and then the little girl slammed into her, clutching at her robe and crying.

Juliet knelt and took her into her arms.

She was aching and trembling with the aftermath of a battle. But for the first time in a month, the cold emptiness was gone.

I am the Juliet. I am the sword of my people.

She had known this ever since she could remember. Now she was the sword of the Mahyanai and the world was ending, and she had thought that made everything she was meaningless.

But the little girl was tiny and weeping and alive in her arms. Even if the walls fell tomorrow, right now she was alive.

Right now, Juliet had saved her.

Romeo had looked at a Catresou girl and loved her. He had

believed that Juliet was more than a weapon, and that it was worthwhile to love her, however little time they might have. He had died believing it.

Juliet had believed that once, too.

She couldn't free her people. She couldn't free herself. And she couldn't save the city from its doom.

But she could be like Romeo, and learn to love her enemies. She could protect these people around her for whatever time they had left.

It wasn't exactly hope, but maybe it could be enough.

2

THERE WAS A PECULIAR, MUSTY smell to the Catresou manuscripts. Whenever Runajo read them for more than a few minutes, she sneezed. If she rubbed her eyes after she'd been turning the pages, they'd start to water and itch.

But she couldn't afford to stop reading them, though the night was more than half over and her head ached with weariness.

The world was dying. Runajo was going to die trying to save it.

She was probably going to fail.

I could have saved us, she thought, and felt sick and shaky with rage and fear. Because she knew how to stop the Ruining. When she and Juliet went into the Sunken Library, where hordes of revenants roamed among the abandoned bookshelves, they had found a hidden text, bespelled to appear only when the world faced disaster.

Three thousand years ago, there had been another Ruining. The Ancients had tried to give themselves eternal life, and doomed the world to living death. Until the five handmaids of the last Imperial Princess had gone to the Mouth of Death, the black pool where souls walked into the land of the dead. They had written on their skin sacred words—the lost power of the Ancients—and one by one they had walked living into death. The first four all failed and died. The fifth died as well, but succeeded: she spoke to Death herself, and bargained to end the Ruining. When Death delivered the successful handmaid's body back to the princess, she had mourned and honored her friend— but she had also guessed that someday another Ruining might occur, and someone else might need to speak with Death. So she had carved from the handmaid's bones a key, to open the land of the dead; then she had founded the city of Viyara and the Sisters of Thorn.

Runajo had found that key kept in the Cloister, its purpose lost.

And then the ghost—necromancer?—who had been killing Sisters to raise himself from the dead had stolen it.

For the last month, Runajo had tried desperately to think of any way to reach Death without the key. She had written letters to the Sisterhood, begging them for help. But nobody had ever answered, and all she'd been able to think of on her own was going to the Mouth of Death and joining the procession of souls that she had seen when she sat vigil. Vima, the priestess of mourning, had told her that whoever joined the dead souls became just as dead—but there must be a little difference. Juliet, dragged into the procession by magic gone wrong, had kept her body, and been truly alive when Runajo pulled her out. Perhaps if Runajo walked into the procession alive and willing, it would be enough of a difference. Perhaps she would be able to speak to Death.

It didn't matter how slim the chance was. The only other choice was to lie down and wait for the whole world to die.

And that was why she was now reading the Catresou manuscripts, puzzling her way through old dialects and bad handwriting. Because she did not think that if she spoke to Death, she would come back alive. And if she died while bound to Juliet . . . well, some Juliets survived the deaths of their Guardians. But not many.

She had to dissolve the bond. Or better yet, make Juliet *not* the Juliet anymore, so that she could never be forced to kill again. But so far, no matter how many of the stolen Catresou records she read, she couldn't find any mention of anyone doing either.

She couldn't even find anyone who had *tried*. The Catresou had never, in all their history, desired to free a Juliet.

At least they had been considerate enough to keep exhaustive chronicles of every one. Sometimes she wished they had been a little less thorough; when they discussed how easily the Juliets had adjusted to the seals, how well they had been trained, if and how many children they had borne, she felt like she was reading the livestock records kept by the Sisters who guarded the city's small, precious supply of red meat.

There were records, too, of the girls who had died under the seals, unable to bear the weight of their power. All of them without names. When Runajo thought of that, she felt a cold, fathomless rage that she didn't have time for and didn't really have the right to. So she tried to ignore it, and she kept reading.

The nineteenth Juliet is now dead. It is my sad duty to write the record. She accepted all the seals without injury and received her full power. Three years she served us eagerly and well. Her Guardian, Andaros Ilarann Catresou, was widely considered a swordsman of great skill and honor, but in this, the common wisdom lied. For he was found to be a spy in the pay of our enemies, and when his treachery was discovered, he commanded the Juliet to sell her life protecting his flight. She was captured alive, but he escaped, and therefore she was left still bound by his orders. Two months we held her in chains, but Andaros could not be found nor killed, and all were moved to pity by the torment she suffered. In the end, the magi devised a desperate plan: to bind a second Guardian to her, that the newer seal might overpower the first, and free her from the traitor's orders.

Benario Valiet Catresou bravely volunteered for this task. May he find his way swiftly to the Paths of Light. For he died

in the attempt; the bond was made, but it destroyed him. The
magi believe that the Juliet, already having a Guardian, could
not shield another from the power of the seal. The Juliet herself
was driven mad, and in her rage slew nine of us before she was
brought down. We have permitted her burial in the sepulcher,
for it was only the treachery of her Guardian and then the
weakness of her own mind that turned her against us.

There was a line drawn across the page, and then under it, in
the same hand:

A girl, three years old, accepted the first two seals, but died
upon the third.

Runajo sat back, her stomach twisting. She'd already read several accounts of Juliets turning against their clan, and always
it was blamed on their Guardians, their families, or their weak
minds. Always the records said that they were *permitted* burial
in the sepulcher, as if they had not already paid more dearly for
it than anyone else. She wondered if this Juliet had really been
betrayed by her Guardian, or if that was just a lie to prop up the
Catresou pride.

One Guardian replacing another. Her first thought was of
Romeo, whom Juliet had tried to make her Guardian. But he
was dead. And even if he weren't—even if there were *anyone* left

alive whom Juliet could bear to have as a Guardian—there would still be the problem of the new Guardian dying. Runajo believed that part of the chronicle was true, for Juliet had told her much the same thing once: the magic that created the bond between Juliet and Guardian was too powerful for any normal human to bear. The Juliet could survive it only because her body had been trained since infancy to accept magic, and the Guardian survived only because the Juliet shielded him through the bond.

So it wasn't a solution at all. It hadn't saved that long-ago Juliet, and it wasn't going to save the Juliet that Runajo was so desperate to help now.

But it did mean that the rules could be bent. There might yet be some other way around them, a way to set Juliet free.

She just couldn't find it.

She wanted to scream, or maybe weep. She was out of ideas. She was out of time. Because three days ago, a revenant had risen before it was even a single day dead.

Runajo had hardly slept since.

The other Mahyanai had been terrified, of course. But now they were all sleeping in their beds. Runajo felt that this was on account of them being *idiots*, but she knew that really, it was because they hadn't spent time among the Sisters of Thorn. They hadn't been trained in the lore of the Ruining, and the magical walls that the Sisterhood wove to keep it out of the city.

They knew that a revenant rising after just one day was

frightening. But they didn't know what it *meant*.

A year ago, when Runajo had joined the Sisters of Thorn, she had learned that the walls around the city would not last forever. That the blood sacrifices would have to be offered more and more often to maintain the walls, and in the end no amount of blood would be enough. That they only had forty years left. The knowledge had made her desperate enough to break every law of the Sisterhood, looking for a solution.

If the dead were rising faster, that meant the Ruining was changing, growing stronger. They might only have months. Weeks. Who knew?

Juliet's life was not worth the whole of the city. Runajo knew this. She knew that Juliet would scream it at her, if given the chance. She knew that if the city were falling, she *would* do it, would sacrifice Juliet the same way that everyone else in her life had been willing to sacrifice her.

But she didn't want to. She was desperate not to.

Runajo stared at the page, her eyes watering, and tried to believe that if she kept reading, there would be an answer. But she was losing hope.

In her dream, she was trapped somewhere small and dark, her throat dry as she tried endlessly to explain something, but her words were never enough, and everyone was laughing at her, saying *Never forgive you—*

36

Somebody knocked on the door.

Runajo sat bolt upright, her head swimming. She was in her bedroom. She was not, at the moment, failing at anything besides all the things she had been failing at last night.

Juliet was gone.

The knocking kept on. "Yes?" Runajo called out, trying to clear her head.

The door eased open a crack. A young serving girl looked in at her.

"If you please," she said, "there's a visitor waiting for you. The blue room."

A visitor.

Hope and fear sparked in her stomach. Maybe somebody from the Cloister. Maybe somebody had finally, finally listened—maybe she was going to get help—

Runajo dressed as quickly as she could, ignoring the cosmetics and the silver combs. She all but ran for the sitting room painted with blue trim.

Waiting for her was a plump, pale girl with long dark braids.

Sunjai.

It took Runajo a moment to recognize her, because she no longer wore the plain gray robes of a novice. Nor did she wear—as she must have in her childhood, though Runajo hadn't known her then—the brightly colored dresses favored by the Mahyanai, with their wide, embroidered sashes. Instead, she was wrapped in the translucent white silks worn by the Old Viyaran nobility—the people who had originally created Viyara, long before the refugees of half the world arrived on their doorstep. A gold chain hung around her neck, and there were thick gold rings on her fingers.

Sunjai dimpled. "You've done well for yourself," she said, looking Runajo over. "A guest of Lord Ineo? Keeper of the undead Juliet?"

The smug, honey-poison tone of her voice hadn't changed a bit, and Runajo suddenly remembered that they had never been friends. That the last time they talked, Sunjai had called her a heartless monster.

She hadn't been far wrong.

"Juliet's not undead," Runajo said flatly.

"But the High Priestess said so. It *must* be true." Sunjai's grin was sarcastically wide. "Besides, you did drag her out of the Mouth of Death, didn't you?"

"Did you leave the Cloister and get a place at the Exalted's court so that you could argue with me about this?"

"No," said Sunjai, her smile draining away, "Inyaan summoned me. I obeyed."

"And did very well for yourself," said Runajo, looking at Sunjai's gold rings because she suddenly didn't want to look right in her eyes.

Inyaan was the younger sister of the Exalted. She had been a novice alongside them—a silent, expressionless girl. Runajo had thought Inyaan's blank stares were filled with pride and disdain. She'd thought that Sunjai had befriended her only out of ambition. She'd been wrong on both counts.

"Excellently well," said Sunjai. "But aren't you going to ask me why I'm here?"

Runajo swallowed, and then made herself look back into Sunjai's eyes. It was silly to feel humiliated now; she'd given up her pride five letters ago.

"I hope," she said, "you came here about my letters."

Sunjai's eyebrows raised. "Letters?"

Runajo felt like the worst idiot in the world. Of course the High Priestess would never have allowed any novice to receive letters from a girl who had been cast out of the Cloister in disgrace.

"I wrote you," she said. "Several times. About the Ruining. What I found in the Sunken Library—"

"That's why I'm here," said Sunjai. "None of us lowly novices were supposed to know what you said in the Hall of Judgment, but there are rumors." Her lips pressed together, and then she went on, "Have you heard what's happened in the Cloister since?"

Cold fear started to swirl inside Runajo. "No," she said.

But she remembered the hordes of revenants seething through the Sunken Library, far below the Cloister. She could imagine them pounding at the doors, breaking them down—if the Ruining was getting stronger, if the dead were rising faster—

"The Mouth of Death is dry. And the walls are failing."

The words were so unexpected that it took Runajo a moment to understand what Sunjai had said.

Then she stared.

"What?" she said.

She had known the walls were failing. That was not a surprise. But the Mouth of Death?

In her mind, Runajo could see the way it had been when she sat vigil. The little pool of perfectly still, perfectly dark water. The souls walking in silent procession, departing the world forever.

Every night for three thousand years, souls had walked into the dark water. It was why Viyara and the Sisters of Thorn *existed*. To guard the Mouth of Death.

"It's dry," said Sunjai. "I've seen it myself." She gestured. "Just a little hollow in the rock now. They still sit vigil, but nobody sees any souls. And meanwhile, we've been working the calculations. The walls will last another week."

One week.

Runajo felt dizzy and numb. She'd imagined so many terrible things in the past few days, once she realized the Ruining was changing. But she hadn't imagined *this*.

She hadn't imagined that she was already too late.

If the Mouth of Death was dry, she couldn't use it to walk into Death. Her last chance was gone. Runajo had braved the Sunken Library and learned the secret of how the first Ruining had been stopped three thousand years ago, and it didn't matter anymore.

She had destroyed Juliet's life, and it didn't *matter*.

"They're planning a great sacrifice," said Sunjai. "Twenty lives. They think it will keep the walls alive a little longer, but no one's sure how long."

If Runajo hadn't felt so sick with fear, she might have laughed at the understatement. It wouldn't be long at all. Not if the Ruining had become so strong it could crumble the walls in a week, and raise the dead in one day. They would have to offer again and again, and by the time the city finally fell, half the people might already be dead by a Sister's knife.

"So," said Sunjai, "if you really did learn anything about the Ruining, down in the Sunken Library, now's the time to share it."

We're all going to die, thought Runajo. *We're all going to die, and it doesn't matter that you have fine gold rings or Inyaan is the Exalted's sister,* nothing *will save you.*

"Nothing," she said. "There's nothing left we can do. That's what I learned in the Sunken Library."

Sunjai started back. "But—"

"Go back to Inyaan and tell her a comforting lie if you want," said Runajo. "But we are all going to die."

And then she fled the room.

3

THE NIGHT WIND SANG WITH the promise of sorrow and blood. The moon shone down, bright and pale as death.

Romeo crouched on the rooftop, watching the street below, and tried not to think of Juliet. But it felt like every stone of the city, every breath of the wind, was crying out her name: *Juliet, Juliet, Juliet.*

It was a month since Makari had delivered the letter. Romeo had kept going back to wait at the spot he'd told Juliet she could find him: the rooftop where he once asked her to marry him.

She never came.

It was only right that she wouldn't forgive him. It was more than he deserved that she hadn't come to kill him. But that meant he had to find another way to pay his debt.

His foolishness was the reason that the Catresou were now fugitives without allies. It was only right that he protect them.

Voices echoed from below. Romeo startled into readiness, his hand on his sword as he peered down into the shadows.

A girl was hurrying down the street, shoulders hunched, pulling her cloak tight. But the wind had blown her hood back, and her red hair whipped free.

There were people in Viyara who had red hair and weren't Catresou. But not many.

Two men were following her.

Carefully, silently, Romeo swung himself off the roof and onto a window ledge, then dropped to the ground. He landed in the narrow alley between two houses just as the two men overtook the girl. He heard their voices—loud, harsh, and laughing.

"Going somewhere, little girl?"

He strode out of the alley, drawing his sword. The men weren't touching the girl, but they had her crowded against the wall of the house, her shoulders hunched, her eyes darting back and forth as she looked for escape.

"Get away from her," said Romeo.

He'd done this a lot in the past three weeks. He still half expected them to laugh and call him a child.

One of the men flinched. The other one snarled, "You."

He knew why they stared: because he wore a Catresou mask,

painted blue and gilded at the edges, covering his face from forehead to cheeks. No Catresou dared to wear one now, but Romeo had donned one every night since he chose this way to pay his debt.

"Go home. Last chance." Romeo stepped forward, the cold tension winding through his body. There were only two of them. He could handle two.

One of the men started forward, and Romeo didn't even think. He whipped his sword forward to slice a thin cut into the man's cheek. Then he lunged and slashed the same shallow line of red into the other man's face.

They stumbled back, cursing. Romeo settled into a perfect dueling position, sword ready for the moment they would charge, and he would have to—

But they fled.

Romeo's heart pounded painfully. He noticed the sweat trickling down his neck, the cramp in his hand as he gripped the sword. There was a thin line of blood on the blade, but he hadn't killed anyone. He hadn't had to.

His hands shook only a little as he lowered the sword and turned back to the girl.

She still had her back pressed to the wall. "You," she said, wide-eyed. "You're real."

Romeo shifted from one foot to the other, his mask suddenly

a guilty weight. It was good for people to tell stories. That was half of why he'd donned the mask, so that people would think twice before trying to harm the Catresou. But he'd never expected the stories to spread so *fast*. In less than a month, he had become a legend.

"Yes," he said. "You need to get home. I'll walk with you."

The girl didn't move. "Is it true what they say?" she asked. "That you're going to punish the Juliet for what she did to us?"

The words bit at him like knives, and Romeo caught his breath. Because there was a time when he would have proclaimed that *they* deserved to be punished for what they had done to *her*. He'd said as much to Paris more than once.

But that had been when the Catresou were still one of the three high houses.

"I'm going to protect you," he said. "Come on."

The girl watched him a moment longer; then she turned and strode forward. Her home was only a few buildings away; Romeo hung back as she knocked on the door. When it swung open and she slipped inside, he sighed and stepped back to vanish among the shadows of the nearest alleyway.

He'd protected another Catresou tonight. He should be proud, or at least satisfied.

But his debt would never be paid. Juliet was still enslaved to the Mahyanai. Makari was still pretending to serve the

Master Necromancer. And Paris—

. A hand clapped him on the shoulder. Romeo whirled, his sword coming up.

"You know," said Vai, "staring sadly into the darkness is a lot safer in a locked room."

Vai was a lean boy in a long coat, with dark skin, dark braids tipped in bright-blue beads, and a smile like a curved knife. Vai was actually a girl, but she hadn't told him that until after Paris died. *Paris knew, so I suppose you might as well,* she'd said, and Romeo hadn't understood that logic, but he knew the two of them had been close.

Vai's only brother had died to necromancers, and the custom of her people dictated that she had to become a man in his place, so she could raise up heirs for his family. It had seemed like a cruel custom to Romeo, but it wasn't worse than what Juliet's people had done to her, and he knew what Juliet's duty meant to her; so he'd said nothing.

Romeo sighed and lowered his sword. "I could have hurt you," he said.

"I mean, theoretically you *could* have," said Vai. "You were pretty formidable that one time we dueled. But honestly, were you actually going to do anything except glare at me and think of how to complain about this in a poem?"

"I don't write poems anymore," Romeo muttered. That was something he'd done back when Juliet was free, and he'd thought there was a chance he could be with her.

"Probably why you're so sad," said Vai.

"How did you find me?" asked Romeo. He hadn't gone near Justiran again since the night a month ago, when Makari had appeared and told him to flee. He hadn't gone back either to the underground room where Vai held court as King of Cats, champion duelist of the Lower City.

"You're really not as stealthy as you think you are," said Vai. "And you've already got a reputation." She looked at the house. "So this is where the Catresou have taken refuge?"

"You *can't tell*—"

"—anyone, I know. Do you really think I'd sell them out?" And there was no laughter at all in her voice as she said, "Paris was my friend too."

But neither of them had been able to save him.

"It's just one family," said Romeo. "I've seen others in the streets, but I don't know where they live."

"Might be just as well that you don't," said Vai. "Secrets have a way of getting out."

"Why did you come find me?"

Vai shrugged. "Paris was my friend. I don't know if he'd be proud of or horrified by you right now, but he'd want me to protect you."

If Paris had been alive to see what happened to the Catresou, he'd probably want Romeo dead.

As he thought that, somebody screamed.

Romeo jolted into readiness, whirling toward the entrance of the alleyway and bringing his sword up, before he'd even realized where the scream had come from.

It was inside the house where the Catresou girl had gone.

Now there were more screams. Muffled thuds and crashes. Romeo bolted around the corner of the building. There were no windows facing the street, only the door. He rattled the handle: locked.

Another scream, suddenly choked off. Romeo slammed his shoulder against the door. The blow rattled his teeth and sent a spike of pain through his shoulders, but the door didn't give way.

"Get back," said Vai, and the next moment her foot slammed into the door, rattling it in its hinges. She kicked again, and then on the third kick, the door gave way.

They were too late.

The room was in shambles. The table had been knocked over, cups shattered. And blood was spattered across the floor and walls.

One body lay by the door: a man, his short hair tinged with gray. Romeo's stomach pitched with nausea, but he still made himself kneel and check.

The man was dead, his throat deeply cut. A few paces back was a young boy, also dead, blood pooling underneath him.

Footsteps echoed from above, and Vai charged up the stairs.

Romeo would have followed, but at the same moment, he heard a gasp from the corner of the room.

It was the girl. She was huddled against the wall, blood pooling at her feet.

The next moment he was at her side, hands trembling, hoping against hope.

"It's all right," he whispered. "Don't move. It's all right."

But in a moment he could see it was too late. She'd been stabbed six or seven times; her face was already deathly pale.

She looked at him. She started to lift her hand, and he caught it. Wrapped his fingers around hers.

"I'm here," he said. "I'm sorry."

He could hear thumps from upstairs, knew that Vai was probably fighting the murderer, but the girl was still looking at him and he couldn't leave her now.

"You're . . . here," she said.

There was no anger in her voice, but Romeo still cringed. "Yes," he said.

"Don't let them burn me," she whispered.

"What?" said Romeo.

The girl coughed and shuddered in pain, her fingers clenching around Romeo's. It was several moments before she quieted, and when she did, her eyelids were drooping.

Then she managed to look up at him. "Don't let them burn me," she said, and Romeo finally understood.

The Catresou believed that there was no peace in the afterlife for those whose bodies were destroyed. For a hundred years they had clung to the special permission that allowed them to embalm their dead and lay them to rest in chained coffins. Now they were outlaws and fugitives; their sepulcher had not yet been destroyed, but surely no more of them would be laid to rest in it.

All his life, Romeo had heard how the Catresou were superstitious fools for believing that a pickled corpse with its organs extracted and stacked in jars could preserve the soul after death. Now he could only think how this was one more harm he had done to Juliet's people.

"I promise," he said. "You will have a grave. I swear it."

The girl let out a long sigh.

"What's your name?" he asked.

But she didn't answer. She didn't answer because she was dead, and the smell of blood was clawing at Romeo's throat and making him shudder.

As if from a great distance, he heard Vai walk back into the room.

"Did you catch him?" asked Romeo.

"No," said Paris.

Once, that voice had been a part of Romeo's own thoughts. In such a short time, he'd become so used to it, that even now it took him a moment to realize that Paris had spoken out loud.

That Paris was here.

Then he knew, like lightning traveling up his spine, and he was on his feet and turning.

Paris stood in the doorway. *Alive.*

For one moment, Romeo couldn't feel anything except a desperate, burning joy. He'd seen Makari come back to life, but he hadn't dared hope or fear that Paris would suffer the same fate, come back to him the same way.

Then he realized that—unlike Makari—there was a strange coldness in Paris's face, and unfamiliar arrogance in the set of his shoulders.

There was blood spattered across his clothes, and he held a bloody rapier.

"You," Romeo said numbly. "You did this?"

Paris smiled. It was a hard, disdainful smile, utterly unlike the earnest boy that Romeo remembered. Then he moved, and the next moment he had Romeo slammed against the wall, blade to his throat.

"Don't move," he said quietly. "I'm trying to decide if I should kill you." He raised his voice. "If you step into this room, I'll definitely kill him."

"You do and I'll kill you," said Vai from the doorway.

51

Romeo could feel his heart pounding, but he didn't feel afraid. There was no room to feel anything, not when Paris was right here, and Romeo had one chance to reach him.

"I know you didn't want to do this," he said.

Everything was horribly clear. Paris had truly died, and then he'd been raised again by the Master Necromancer. And the living dead were the slaves of those who had raised them. Romeo had seen it with Tybalt.

But Makari had broken that binding. Surely Paris could too.

"I know you don't want to serve the Master Necromancer," he said. "Can't you remember me?"

Paris smiled. "Did you think you ever knew me?" he said.

Romeo had known him, Romeo *did* know him, and he knew this was a lie—but the words still sent an icy curl of fear into his stomach, because he remembered how Tybalt had been, when he returned as one of the living dead. He remembered the flat, lifeless intonation of Tybalt's voice, and Paris sounded nothing like him.

Paris sounded nothing like himself, either.

"I do know you," said Romeo. "And I know the Master Necromancer has made you a slave, and *I can help you.*"

"You know a lie," said Paris. "I served him of my own free will, even before I died. Like every good Catresou. Like every one of my kin."

It couldn't be true. But the words—the pitiless glee in Paris's eyes—still felt like knives between his ribs.

"No," he said. "That's not possible. I heard your thoughts. I saw your *heart*."

Paris pressed the blade closer—just a tiny fraction of pressure on Romeo's throat, but he still choked.

"That was Catresou magic binding us together," he said. "You think I wouldn't know how to use it against you?"

"Are you done talking?" Vai demanded. "Because I personally think it's time we got back to killing each other."

"Not yet," said Paris. The next moment he had seized Romeo by the arm and was throwing him away with terrible force. Romeo stumbled and lost his balance—Vai caught him—

And Paris vanished out the front door.

Vai snarled under her breath and bolted after him. Romeo knew he should follow, but now that there was no longer a sword at his throat—*now* he was shaking, and finding it hard to breathe.

Paris. One of the living dead.

He had believed in the ways of his people so desperately. He had wanted so much to be a proper Catresou, laid to rest in their sepulcher with all their traditional spells and prayers. Instead he had been raised again to be a slave and murder his kin.

Had Makari known?

Let me decide how I'll avenge my own wrongs, he had said, and Romeo knew that Makari had been trying to protect him, but he still felt betrayed.

"Still there?" Vai called through the doorway.

Romeo turned to look at her. "He got away?"

"It's not very fair, how fast the dead can run," said Vai, and her voice was light, but Romeo could see her fist clenching in frustration.

Romeo didn't have any comfort to offer, not when he was surrounded by the blood of his own failures.

"I should have died instead," he muttered, and instantly felt ashamed. He'd been saying that since the day he killed Tybalt, but what had he ever done to fix things? He had already thought, *Why didn't Makari tell* me *about Paris*—but if Makari had, would Romeo really have changed anything?

Vai snorted. "I can't deny I would rather have Paris alive, but then he'd want to die for *you*, and then you'd want to die *again*, and it would just be a pointless dance, really." She laid a hand on Romeo's shoulder. "We should leave. I'll cut the heads off the bodies if you don't have the stomach for it."

Romeo looked at the dead girl. He thought about all the promises he had made and broken. How little he had done, and how much he still owed.

Maybe it was time to make his own choices.

"No," he said. "They're Catresou. They deserve a Catresou burial."

"And how are you going to do that for them?"

Romeo squared his shoulders. "I'm waiting here. I know the

other Catresou come to check on them, and I'm done hiding. I'll tell them what happened, help them carry the bodies back, and then . . . I'll beg to join them."

Vai stared at him. "There are quicker ways to kill yourself, you know."

"I won't tell them who I am," said Romeo. "I'll keep the mask on. They know me as their masked warrior now, so maybe— maybe they'll trust me."

"That is a stupid idea and I doubt your intentions of survival."

Romeo shook his head. "No. I'm not trying to die. I'm keeping a promise."

Several promises. He had told the dead girl he would make sure she was buried. He owed her as well.

"The Catresou are being hunted because of what *I* did," he said. "They deserve to have my obedience, not just my protection at my own convenience. And . . . Paris said they were still working for the Master Necromancer. He might have been lying, but if some of their leaders are still conspiring—I have to know. I have to stop them."

Vai looked thoughtful. "I won't tell you not to do it, because it's not my business if you get yourself killed. But be careful. And tell me as soon as you learn anything."

"Right." Romeo nodded.

"Because if you learn something and die right after, that's pointless and annoying."

"To save Juliet's people, I would fight my way out of the land of the dead," said Romeo.

"But you wouldn't," said Vai, and for once there was nothing but quiet sadness in her voice. "You'd be back in your body in minutes, a slave to the necromancers."

Like Paris. Romeo closed his eyes against the sudden sting of tears.

"I'll be careful," he said.

Vai left, and he was alone with a dead girl.

He knelt down again beside her. His people were not like hers; they did not believe that elaborate ceremonies and spells could guarantee them a happy afterlife. They did not believe that anything awaited them after death at all. This girl, whose dead, blank eyes still stared at him, was already less than dust.

But the Mahyanai did honor their dead: all night, before the bodies were burned, they sat vigil.

He couldn't honor this girl like a Catresou should, but he could do this much for her, anyway.

So Romeo knelt beside the dead girl and waited.

4

HIS MASTER WAS PLEASED TO see him return.

"Did you do as I commanded?"

"Yes," said Paris, kneeling with his hands pressed against the floor.

The next question came silently.

Did you pity the ones you killed? his master asked, and the words crawled through his mind like cold fingers, feeling out the truth.

"No," said Paris.

He remembered the screams of the family very clearly. Their blood was still dried underneath his fingernails. But he had felt nothing except the dead, ashy certainty that he was following his orders.

And Romeo? Did you pity him?

"No," said Paris.

The grasp on his mind withdrew.

"Excellent," said his master.

And Paris was suddenly unsure. He hadn't felt any pity, because pitying the enemies of his masters was unthinkable. But he had felt . . . something like curiosity.

Everything he saw, when his master sent him into the streets on errands, was like a meaningless glyph in a dead language. Faces, voices. Blood and shattered bone. None of it meant anything, so none of it mattered.

Romeo hadn't meant anything, either.

But Paris felt like he could almost remember him meaning something.

"Did you do as I said?" his master asked.

Paris shuddered, revolted by how close he'd come to imagining something his master wouldn't want.

"Yes," he said. "Yes, I said everything that you told me to."

"Repeat what you said and Romeo said *exactly*."

And Paris did, and the treacherous half thoughts slid out of his mind, completely forgotten.

5

THEY CAME WHEN DAWN WAS barely starting to glimmer in the sky. They all recognized his mask. Some hated him, some admired him. None fully trusted him.

But when he offered up his sword, they agreed to take him to the new Lord Catresou.

Romeo had often wondered where the main body of the Catresou were hiding. He hadn't expected them to be in the worst slums of the Lower City—he guessed that most, like the family he'd failed to protect, had the money or connections to get themselves hidden in discreet houses—but he was surprised when they took him to one of the richest neighborhoods, where the streets were clean and the houses were brightly painted, and there were even lamps hung with orbs of white, glowing stone—the same kind that lit all the immaculate streets of the Upper City.

The house they brought him to was magnificent, painted in gold and red. Its hallways had floors of polished, multicolored stone that echoed under their boots.

They halted outside a door. The leader of the guards—a tall, angular man with pale hair and a scar that slanted across his nose, narrowly missing an eye—told them to wait, and went inside. Romeo heard the murmur of voices, but couldn't make out any words.

Then the door opened again. The guard hauled Romeo in by the shoulder and pressed him to his knees.

The room had once been a study, though it now seemed to be a meeting room of sorts—it was ringed with chairs, at which sat Catresou men, most of them with graying hair, all richly dressed. At the center was a desk.

Seated at the desk, leaning forward on his elbows, was Meros Mavarinn Catresou.

Romeo had never seen him before in his life. But he instantly recognized the wavy brown hair and the proud nose. Because this was Paris's older brother, who loved drinking and gambling and prostitutes, who had mocked Paris for his devotion to the Juliet and (much worse) mocked the Juliet herself—

Romeo took a deep breath, fighting against the rush of memories that weren't his.

But the worst memory was his own: Vai telling him what had happened at the Night Game while he was a drugged prisoner.

Meros had been there. He had helped Lord Catresou capture Paris. He might very well be the reason that the Catresou served the Master Necromancer still.

And now he sat at the center of them all—

"*You're* the Lord Catresou?" said Romeo.

"Take off your mask," said Meros, his voice low and angry.

The Catresou covered their faces before those they considered inferior, and took off their masks when they faced their betters. For Romeo to keep his on before the leader of the Catresou was a pointed insult.

But just as the Catresou didn't dare wear their masks now, Romeo didn't dare take his off.

"No," he said.

Meros waved a hand. "Gavarin, tear off his mask."

The leader of the guards wrenched the mask off.

Romeo could hear the gasps. He could see faces growing angry.

He knew he was about to die, and he wouldn't keep any of his promises.

"So," said Meros, his voice cold and venomous, "our hero is a Mahyanai."

Juliet, I'm sorry, Romeo thought, and waited for the killing blow.

But it didn't come.

"Tell me," said Meros, "why are you wearing a Catresou mask?"

"Because those who hate you," said Romeo, "should fear you."

"You think you deserve to protect us?" Gavarin demanded, fury in his voice.

But nobody had struck Romeo dead yet. He felt a sudden, terrible ray of hope. Perhaps he could persuade them. Perhaps he could still save them.

Perhaps he could, at least, speak the truth bravely before he died. The same way that Juliet would.

"Because I am Mahyanai Romeo," he said, looking around the room. "I loved the Juliet and I married her, and it's my fault that she is a slave to your enemies now. So I swore that for the rest of my life, I would serve and protect you in any way I could. If all you desire of me is my death, then for her sake, I will gladly die nameless and accursed. But if you have any use at all for a slave, then take me. Let me serve you."

There was a short pause. Even with Paris's memories to help him, Romeo couldn't read the cold expression on Meros's face.

"Where'd you find him again?" asked Meros.

"The Jularios household," said Gavarin. "They're all dead."

"I tried to save them," said Romeo. "But I wasn't fast enough. Their daughter—I don't know her name—she begged me to make sure she was properly buried. I promised her."

Someone in the room laughed—a harsh, skeptical noise.

"She was one of you, wasn't she?" Romeo snapped. "She deserves that. And—" He realized suddenly that they were actually listening to him, no matter if they planned to kill him. He

62

still might be able to save them.

"The Jularios family, they were killed by a servant of the Master Necromancer," he said. "One of the living dead. He told me himself, it was on his master's orders—"

"I know," said Meros. "He told me. That family was planning to sell us out."

For a moment the words didn't make sense. Romeo gaped at him, trying to understand.

It was the silence that brought it home. This was the assembled council of the Catresou lords. These were common Catresou guards holding him. And nobody was saying a word.

They all know, thought Romeo, and his heart broke as he remembered how horrified Paris had been when he learned about the previous Lord Catresou's conspiracy. But it was a conspiracy no longer.

"You can't do this," Romeo burst out. "You can't possibly work with the man who raises living dead and tried to end the world. Isn't this against *zoura*?"

Suddenly Gavarin's fingers gripped his hair. "Don't imagine you understand *zoura*," he said, his voice low and angry.

I know because Paris taught me, thought Romeo. It was the sacred Catresou word that meant "correct knowledge"—it meant their lore for embalming the dead, the charms they thought would protect them in the afterlife, but it also meant the knowledge of how to *be* correct. To live rightly.

63

It had been everything to Paris. To Juliet as well. But it seemed that now *zoura* was nothing to their people.

"Of course you're condemned to death," said Meros. "But since you know so much, the Master Necromancer may want to question you first. Gavarin, since he's shown such concern for our dead, lock him up in the quarantine room."

"Please," Romeo begged, "you have to listen. For the sake of your people, you have to—"

"No, I don't," said Gavarin, dragging him down the corridor. The other guards were gone; the Catresou seemed to have decided that Romeo was not a threat. Without his sword—and bound by his vow—that was true enough. He could never raise his hand against Juliet's clan, even if they had turned to evil.

But he could raise his voice.

"Doesn't it shame your clan to serve murderers?"

Gavarin looked back at him, eyes narrowed in scorn. "Which murderers? Seems the city is full of 'em."

"The Master Necromancer isn't just—"

"The Sisters kill someone every six months, and you Mahyanai call that noble." Gavarin's voice was soft and furious. "Your father made the streets run with our blood, and you call that necessary. But the Master Necromancer uses the lives given him in the Night Game, and *he* is too shameful for us to serve?"

It's not the same, Romeo wanted to protest. He understood now

64

why the Catresou hated the sacrifices so much, but they *did* keep the Ruining out of Viyara. He was horrified at what his father had done, but at least Lord Ineo had been trying to make the city safe from necromancers. Meros and the surviving Catresou—

Wanted to live.

As everyone in Viyara wanted to live.

Then he remembered the girl who had died in his arms the night before.

"And the Jularios family?" Romeo demanded. "Was *that* acceptable?"

Gavarin winced as he turned away. But his voice was flat and steady as he said, "We'd all be dead if they talked."

He dragged Romeo the last few steps down to the end of the hallway.

"That girl died begging for a Catresou burial," said Romeo. "I promised she would have one."

Gavarin laughed: a low, bitter sound. "Not yours to give," he said, unlocking the heavy bolt on the door in front of them. "Not exactly ours to give either, now."

"What?" said Romeo.

The door swung open. Gavarin shoved him inside.

There was nothing in the room but three cages—huge, heavy cages. Romeo had seen such cages before at the Night Game, where people brought prisoners for the Master Necromancer to sacrifice, hoping he would deign to raise their loved ones in return.

Something moved inside the nearest cage.

More prisoners, Romeo thought. It made sense—more people waiting to be sacrificed to the Master Necromancer's power, perhaps other Catresou who had resisted the bargain—

Then he heard the hissing. He saw one of the figures throw itself against the bars.

It wasn't a prisoner, because it wasn't a person anymore. It was a revenant. Once it had been a boy about Romeo's age, and it still looked like a boy, its pale skin smooth. It wasn't yet rotted or withered. But in its eyes was a hollow, absolute emptiness.

It clawed at the bars, still hissing. It could smell their living flesh and blood. It wanted them.

"You're . . . you're punishing them?" asked Romeo, sick with horror. He couldn't think of another reason to keep the dead in cages and deny them rest. "If you won't embalm them, at least *burn* them—"

"Embalming doesn't work anymore. None of our people can walk the Paths of Light."

Gavarin said the words without emotion, but Romeo's heart turned to ice in his chest. Because he knew what that meant. The Catresou believed that a realm of bliss awaited their clan after death, but that they could enter it only if their bodies were laid to rest with proper spells and prayers, embalmed with the brain and heart and stomach removed and placed in jars.

That embalming had always been enough to keep their dead

from rising again as revenants. It was why they, alone out of everyone in the city, had been permitted a sepulcher.

"The Master Necromancer can make them rest," said Gavarin. "But he makes us earn their entrance to the Paths of Light with our service. We've only bought peace for two so far. And there are more every day."

He nodded toward the nearest cage. Romeo looked, and realized that it wasn't empty like he'd thought: the dead in it just weren't moving. They lay piled together on the ground, blood soaked into their clothes and hair—

It was the Jularios family.

"Think on that, while you wait," said Gavarin, turning away.

"Wait!" Romeo called. He couldn't look away from the pile of motionless bodies, couldn't stop watching for the first twitch, but he had to ask. "The girl who died last night. You found me with her. What was her name?"

"What's it to you?"

"I made her a promise," said Romeo.

And if he had to watch her rise again as a mindless, crawling thing, the least he could do was remember her name.

"Emera Jularios Catresou," said Gavarin, and shut the door on him.

They left him there all day.

Romeo waited. And watched. Every time the revenants moved

in one of the other cages, he flinched, wondering if Emera was moving. He'd seen dead people before, and sat vigil for them, familiar faces turned still and empty. But he'd never seen them twisted into the Ruining's cruel mockery of life, and when he imagined Emera like that, he felt sick.

He didn't want to see her that way. The very thought seemed like a violation.

Right now, from where he sat with his back pressed against the wall, he couldn't see her face at all. But he could see several strands of her red hair, trailing across the floor of the cage. He remembered her voice as she asked if he was going to protect them.

She wasn't only her wounds and her dying request, either. She'd been a person, with her own loves and hates. Her own story.

Romeo just didn't know any of it except the ending.

He'd never bothered very much with wondering what happened to people after death. What did it matter if they were dust and nothingness, as the Mahyanai sages said, or feasting with the nine gods, as the Sisters of Thorn said? Either way, they were never coming back.

When he'd met Juliet, and she'd told him—her face alight with a defiant joy—about the Paths of Light, he'd thought it a beautiful story. But he'd also thought it unspeakably dreary, how the Catresou were shackled to spend their whole lives preparing for those paths. And he'd loathed their belief that the spells making

Juliet their protector would also keep her from the paths, and doom her to become a witless, nameless ghost that faded into nothing.

Then Juliet had died.

And when Romeo had been able to think again—when he'd been able to think of *her* again, without his thoughts splintering into a thousand bleeding shards of grief and shame—he still hadn't believed anything the Catresou said. But he had desperately *wished* that some part of Juliet remained somewhere still, and could be at peace.

He wished that for Emera now. And he finally understood why the Catresou served the Master Necromancer. If he had thought it the only way to save his loved ones from eternal darkness, he might have done it too.

"I'm sorry," he said quietly—to her body, to her *nothingness*, because the Catresou were wrong. There was nothing left of her but a name in his mouth and a memory in his heart. "Emera, I am so sorry."

Her fingers twitched.

Romeo shuddered. But he didn't look away. As she began to move, he forced himself to keep speaking: "I will stop the Master Necromancer. I will save your people. I will get you a Catresou burial."

All the dead in Emera's cage were moving now. They didn't seem to know how to walk at first, not even whether they should use legs or arms. They rolled into each other, crawled over each other, a writhing mass of limbs.

And then they smelled him.

They scrabbled their way to the edge of the cage, grasped the bars, and hauled themselves up. They slid arms out between the bars and clawed at the air, jaws yawning open and then snapping shut with desperate hunger. Emera's red hair was a tangled veil across her face, but Romeo could see her eyes, gray and sightless and inhuman.

The grief he felt was as dark and vast as the night sky. He grieved for Emera, and for Juliet, and for Paris—for everyone whose life had been shattered by the Master Necromancer—for everyone *alive*, and therefore doomed to die and become nothing. Like Emera.

"But none of that can save you," he whispered. "I'm sorry."

The bolt rattled. Romeo was on his feet in a moment; he turned and saw the door opening.

Paris stood outside. And Romeo's heart shattered in his chest again, because while the cruel smile of the night before was gone, now there was no life in his face at all. Just the grim, relentless obedience that Romeo had once seen in Tybalt's eyes, when the Master Necromancer sent him to kill them.

Makari had been living dead as well, but he remembered himself.

"Paris," Romeo whispered, "this isn't you, I know it, you don't *want*—"

"What's that you're saying about my brother?" asked Meros, stepping into view behind Paris. His voice was smug. "I'm afraid he understands his duties now. Death has a way of helping some people."

He ruffled Paris's hair.

You know he's a slave, Romeo thought, sick with sudden fury. *And you* like *it*.

"Anyway, it seems the Master Necromancer wants you alive a little longer," said Meros. "So we won't be putting you into a cage yet. If you give me your oath of obedience, I'll even let you out of this room."

He thought that Romeo was intimidated, broken by fear of the revenants. It was clear in the smug sneer of his voice, and it made Romeo want to defy him.

But he had come here to save Juliet's people. He couldn't do that locked away in a room full of revenants.

He couldn't save Paris while he was locked up either. And Paris could still be saved. Romeo believed that, he *had* to believe that.

"I will obey you on two conditions," he said. "Give Emera Juliaros a proper burial. And don't ask me to harm Juliet."

"You think you can make demands of me?" said Meros.

"I can tell you," said Romeo, "it is the only way I will serve you. I made Emera a promise. And rather than harm Juliet, I would lock myself in one of those cages and let the revenants tear me to shreds."

Meros snorted a laugh. "Really?"

Romeo's heart thudded. Then he strode back to the cage where the Jularios family clawed at the air. He slammed his back into the bars and faced Meros.

"Yes," he said.

His heart was beating very fast. His whole body crackled with fear. Nails scrabbled at his arm, trying to dig through his sleeve into flesh. A mouth closed on his shoulder, drooling and gnawing. A hand wrapped around his neck—he choked, but he wouldn't move, he *couldn't*—

Paris lunged, sword flashing.

The revenants shrieked. A moment later they had let go, and Paris was dragging him forward.

Romeo stumbled, all the strength going out of his legs, and fell to his knees. Suddenly he couldn't catch his breath; he could only gasp, and stare up at Paris's face—now blank of all expression—and think, *He saved me.*

Surely that meant something.

"I see you're just as foolish as they say." Meros looked down his nose at him.

"Yes," said Romeo.

It was true. He'd always been a fool. He was going to die one.

But at least he might die helping the ones he loved.

"If I agree to your absurd conditions, will you swear to serve me?" asked Meros. "As a true and loyal servant?"

And suddenly, Romeo was just as terrified as when the revenants had wrapped their fingers around his neck. Because if he took this oath, there would be no turning back. He would not be able to change his mind, to run away again and find another secret way to be a hero. If he couldn't persuade the Catresou to defy the Master Necromancer, he would have to serve along with them.

Romeo felt like he was falling. But he'd already made this choice. He had made it when he first put on a mask. When he had agreed to help Paris fight necromancers. When he had asked Juliet to marry him. When he had seen her for the first time, lonely and beautiful.

From the very first, he had belonged to the Catresou.

So he said, "Yes," and then he swore an oath.

6

THE NIGHT SKY YAWNED OPEN like the gates of death. The moon was down, but the stars pierced the darkness with a glitter like swords. All the world seemed to be holding its breath.

By now, Romeo was used to crouching on rooftops. He was used to keeping his head low, his breathing soft and steady as he watched the people below. He was used to the tension coiling tighter and tighter as he waited for the violence to begin.

He wasn't used to waiting with someone on each side of him.

He wasn't used to doing the errands of the Master Necromancer.

They weren't here to free the few Catresou prisoners that Lord Ineo kept on his personal estate. They were going to do that—Gavarin had all but demanded it, had insisted to Meros and the rest of the Catresou lords that it would be an excellent distraction, and their duty besides. But that wasn't why they had come.

There's a dead Catresou girl made living dead, and Lord Ineo keeps her for a pet, Meros had told them. *The Master Necromancer is sending us to bring her home.*

The other Catresou had been wild to rescue her. They hadn't asked who she was, or where she had come from. Romeo knew: she was the living dead girl who had once sat in a glass cage in Lord Catresou's secret study. He'd called her the "Little Lady" and used her to bargain with the Master Necromancer.

Paris had been horrified when they discovered her. Now he was living dead himself, and he would bring the Little Lady back to a Catresou cage—or worse. Romeo had no idea what the Master Necromancer might want her for, but it couldn't be anything good.

(He tried not to think about what the Master Necromancer might be doing to Makari right now.)

Romeo had wanted to go with Paris, but he wasn't trusted that far. He was to help breaking out the prisoners; there were fifteen of them, split into five groups. So there were only two people crouched on the rooftop with Romeo.

"Everything look normal to you?" asked Gavarin, his voice a barely audible rumble.

"Yes," said Romeo, his stomach tightening as he looked down at the empty courtyard. As a child, he'd been so desperately excited when he was allowed to visit.

He wasn't used to leading an attack on his own clan. But the Catresou prisoners surely deserved to be saved.

Ilurio snorted. "It's empty. Don't need any hero to tell us that." He was Romeo's age, and he'd imperiously introduced himself as *Ilurio Alabann Catresou*, as if it were an important name everyone ought to know. Maybe it was.

"Quiet," said Gavarin, still watching the courtyard.

"What's he ever done for us?" Ilurio muttered. "I don't see why everyone wants to treat him like a hero when he's one of our enemies."

Without looking, Gavarin reached over and cuffed the back of his head. "I said quiet."

Ilurio huffed indignantly, but held his tongue.

"Time to go," said Gavarin. "Masks on."

Ilurio pulled out his mask and started tying it on. Romeo, who'd already put on his, took a slow breath, trying to control his heartbeat. Now. He was going to start fighting his own people *now*.

Suddenly Gavarin seized Romeo's wrist. His grip felt tight enough to snap bones. He looked at Romeo, his gaze slicing through his mask.

"Wasn't my call to bring you with us," said Gavarin, voice still barely above a murmur. "Wasn't my place to choose. But you ruin this, and I will *gut* you."

Like the Jularios family? Romeo wanted to say. But he knew better than to pick fights on the cusp of a battle.

"I swore to serve your people," he said. "I will keep my oath or die."

The room was small and windowless and heavily bolted. Inside, on a little wooden stool, sat a girl. Her head was bowed, gold ringlets falling forward over her shoulders. Her face was pale and still as a wax doll.

She was living dead.

"I know you can speak," said Runajo, though she knew no such thing.

But the girl had walked into this room when they led her from the Catresou compound. She had settled into her chair and clasped her hands. She hadn't moved since, but she *should* be able to speak.

"The Catresou necromancers summoned you back. That means you know what Death is like. Have you talked to her?"

The girl didn't respond. But her laced fingers tightened. It was just a fraction of movement, but Runajo's heart jumped, and she took a quick step back.

The living dead girl was not turning into a revenant, mindless and hungry for the living. She had sat in the same locked room for a month, ever since the Catresou purge. She had been locked in Lord Catresou's secret laboratory for who knew how long before that.

She was not a soulless abomination; she was the abomination created when a necromancer summoned a soul back into a dead body.

"If I die," said Runajo, "will I see Death? If I walk out of this house and throw myself off the walls right now, will I be able to speak with her?"

The dead girl was silent.

The bitter irony was that Runajo knew what nobody had for three thousand years. She had read the manuscript written by the woman who helped end the last Ruining: *Death has a face. Death has a voice. Death will parley with those who unlock the gate, pass the reapers, and come to meet her.*

She had read those words, won out of the chaos of the Sunken Library. But they hadn't been enough.

"Do the dead care about the Ruining?" asked Runajo. "Do they hate it too? Because I'm trying to end it. But the Mouth of Death is dried up. The key to Death is lost. The walls are about to fail. *Nobody* knows how to fix this. You're the only one who possibly could."

The girl was utterly still, her blue eyes staring blankly into Runajo's.

The back of Runajo's neck prickled. Sometime while she was talking, the girl must have moved, because now she was looking straight at Runajo. Her head had been slightly bowed before.

Then she noticed the girl's hands.

They were still in the same position as before: loosely clasped, one lying on top of the other, with the fingers curled together.

But now her tendons stood out. Black liquid oozed between her fingers.

Blood. The black blood of the living dead.

For a moment, Runajo wanted to cringe. Then she lunged forward and wrenched at the girl's hands.

The girl was strong. It took several moments for Runajo to break her grip, and when she did, she saw that the girl's nails had ripped tracks into her palms as her hands were torn apart.

Runajo felt sick. She hadn't meant to hurt the girl. But this was all she did. She *broke* things.

"I'll get you a bandage," she said, rising, and then realized that of course there were no bandages in the room.

So she pulled off her sash instead. But when she knelt back down, she was surprised. There was still blood drying on the girl's hands, but the ragged edges of the wounds were gone. Gingerly, Runajo started to wipe at the blood, and found pale, unwounded skin beneath.

The Sisters of Thorn, among whom Runajo had once been a novice, had healing ointments for use after blood penance. They were a treasured, closely guarded secret because they could close cuts in hours.

This was perfect healing in moments.

Runajo looked into the girl's blank, helpless eyes and said, "I won't tell anyone. They won't study this."

The girl didn't respond. Her eyes were more or less directed at Runajo, but they seemed to be staring through her at something very far off.

"You don't have to be grateful," said Runajo. "You certainly don't have to forgive me for being the latest person to own you. But the world is *dying*. You could help us."

The girl didn't say a thing. She didn't even blink.

Of course she didn't. Runajo had been a fool to think anyone would help her. That anything she had broken could ever be fixed.

One step. Two. And turn.

Juliet moved through the sword form. She'd been practicing nearly an hour now, and her arms and legs had started to burn with exhaustion, but she didn't want to stop. She craved this moment, when all the thoughts were pushed out of her head, when there was nothing in the world but this movement, and the next.

It had been like that, kissing Romeo.

It had been like that, killing her father.

She stumbled on the turn, and the next swing of the sword came at a bad angle. With a heavy sigh, she lowered the sword.

"You do realize we're not going to beat you if you don't perform well enough?"

Nearby, on one of the low wooden benches, sat Arajo, leaning back on her hands—the girl who had come to help when Juliet was fighting the revenant four days ago. Since then, she had helped Juliet start learning Mahyanai sword techniques. Now she was watching Juliet with a sort of amused pity, as she so often did.

Juliet loathed that look.

"Nobody has ever beaten me," she said.

Nobody has ever hurt me more than your *people did,* she thought.

But she couldn't say that. She couldn't keep fighting these people, when she was trying to protect them.

As she thought that, she felt the death.

Rather: she felt someone become guilty of shedding Mahyanai blood.

It was as if the whole world shifted, reoriented, and suddenly the murderer stood at the center of all things and every heartbeat hurt because she wasn't there killing him.

Juliet could smell the blood. She could almost *taste* it.

"Arajo," she said. "Somebody just died. Go find the guards."

"What?" Arajo straightened, eyes widening. "How could you—"

"I have to go kill the murderer," said Juliet, and she did: the next moment she couldn't resist the pull any longer, and she was running across the courtyard, into the hallway, around the corner.

She smelled guilt. She smelled blood—real, physical blood—and then she spun around the last corner and she was upon him.

She could have made the stroke with her eyes closed. Every

bone in her body knew where the man's throat was and how to swing the sword in a clean slice that dropped him with barely more than a gurgle.

He hit the ground, and suddenly the pressure was gone, the world was right side up again, and Juliet could think.

She could notice that the man she had just killed wore a Catresou mask.

There was a shout. Then his two friends were on her.

Juliet didn't have to kill them. She didn't want to. But they were coming at her with swords and death in their eyes, and her body had learned every lesson of the past months too well. It wasn't the seals on her back that sent her sword lashing out; it was simple instinct, muscle and bone.

The end was just the same. Moments later, they were on the ground. One was already dead; the other was gasping and whimpering as he bled out.

Juliet couldn't breathe. Her knees gave out, and she sank to the ground.

They made me this, they made me this, Runajo made me this—

It didn't matter whose fault it was. The men were still just as dead.

Except the one who was still dying. Juliet forced herself to crawl to him. Through the slits in his mask, she could see his eyes focus on her.

"I'm sorry," she said. "I'm sorry."

He made a choking noise; his eyes were glazing over, and she wasn't sure how much he understood. One hand flailed, as if trying to strike her. She caught it, and then his hand squeezed hers, as he shuddered in pain.

She tried to remember the prayers for the dying.

"Go—go swiftly and in gladness," she said. Her voice was only a tiny whisper, but it felt like it was wrecking her throat. "Forget not thy name, in all the dark places—"

The man groaned.

"—forget not those who have walked before thee. Heed not the nameless, who crawl and weep, but carry thy name to the Paths of Light."

He was silent. His hand was limp in hers. She gently laid it down.

Slowly, she got to her feet. Her body dragged with exhaustion, but she knew she couldn't rest. Three Catresou breaking into Lord Ineo's home. Were they the only ones?

Farther down the corridor, she saw the body of the person they had killed. Slowly, she walked toward it: not a guard, but a servant. An old woman, with gray in her hair. She didn't have any weapons. She couldn't have hurt them, and for a moment Juliet felt sheer *rage* at the men she had killed. There was nothing around here except storerooms and sleeping people; they had come here for no reason but slaughter, to kill those who couldn't defend themselves—

Or they had come to cause a distraction, while their friends attempted to free the prisoners at the other end of the complex.

Juliet knew she could feel someone acquire blood guilt from that far away, even if the pull to avenge wouldn't be as strong at that distance. But she'd felt nothing. So there weren't any other intruders—*or they hadn't yet shed Mahyanai blood.*

Which meant she had a chance to help her people.

Juliet fled. The guards would arrive any moment, and there would be questions that she couldn't afford to be asked yet. She couldn't afford the slightest chance that Runajo would be with them, because then she would be given orders again.

As soon as she got out in the open, she clambered up onto the roof and charged straight across the compound. The night wind blew in her face. Her heart pounded against her ribs.

Runajo had ordered her not to release the prisoners or assist them in escaping. But Juliet was not going to do that. She was going to save the lives of the Mahyanai guards, and then she was going to fight the Catresou intruders.

Side effects of those actions were not her concern. At least, not enough to awaken the magic written on her back.

Runajo had thought she'd been careful with her commands. But she hadn't lived her whole life under obedience. She didn't really understand how to think about these things.

Juliet went more carefully as she got closer. She slipped down off the roofs and into the corridors again. She paused and listened: silence.

Most of the Catresou prisoners had been locked up by the City Guard. It was only those of interest to Lord Ineo, or those who had been deemed too old or too young for common prison, who were kept here.

So there were only a few guards.

Most of her training had been with the sword. But Juliet had studied unarmed combat as well. She knew how to choke someone unconscious.

The trick was doing it without the person seeing her.

The first guard went down easily. The next nearly saw her, and then nearly broke loose from her grip. She managed to slam Juliet against the wall before she went limp.

The noise brought the third guard running.

Juliet ducked back around the corner just in time to avoid being seen. She heard the steps pause, a soft exclamation—the guard was checking his fallen friend—and she darted forward.

Speed was her only hope. As he looked up, she slapped him across the eyes to blind him, and then she was safely behind him and getting a grip on his neck.

Then he was down.

Juliet stood, panting for breath. She had done it. All the guards were unconscious, which meant they were *safe*, which meant she could fight the intruders without any Mahyanai getting hurt.

In complete obedience to her orders.

And there were the footsteps of the approaching Catresou.

She drew her sword. She told her heart not to break. And she went to meet them.

There were three, all men, all wearing Catresou masks. When they saw her, they stopped dead. Two raised their swords.

Juliet didn't.

"You know how fast I can kill you," she said. "But I don't have to. None of you have shed Mahyanai blood yet."

For the first time in weeks, she was terribly aware of her naked face, and she tried to make it into a mask. Tried to ignore how the words hurt in her throat.

"But if you come forward," she went on, "I will have to fight you. I'm under orders."

The tallest of them—a pale-haired man, the oldest of the group and also clearly the leader—sighed.

"Well," he said, "we have orders too, Lady Juliet."

His voice was soft, almost polite, but the words burned like hot iron.

Her fingers tightened on the sword hilt. "The guards are unconscious."

One of the others—a boy, probably no older than her—sneered. "You want us to think you're *helping*?"

"I was protecting them," said Juliet. "I can't aid you. If one of you comes forward, I will have to fight him. *But I haven't been ordered to win.*"

7

SHE WAS FIRE AND DEATH and starlight. She was all the glory and all the terror in the world.

She was Juliet, and she was no longer his.

"The guards already found one of your squads," she said. "You don't have much time."

Romeo stared at her, this girl who had been so many times betrayed, and who was still trying to save everyone. He wanted more than anything else in the world to tear off his mask and say how much he loved her, that he would do anything to save her.

But he couldn't save her. And she no longer wanted his love. If she knew that he now served the Master Necromancer, she would surely want him to die.

All he could do for her now was fight for her people. And tonight that meant fighting *her*.

He didn't know if Gavarin would consent to the plan. He didn't dare ask for permission, because if Juliet heard his voice, she would certainly know. So he drew his sword and charged.

Her blade met his. For a moment they were caught, barely a stride apart, nothing between them but two swords and one mask.

Two swords. One mask. Two clans, two vows, and a river of blood.

Juliet broke the standoff, shoving his blade aside and dodging back. Romeo followed. She kept up a steady retreat, blocking his strikes but not returning them, until they were outside in one of the courtyards.

Then she attacked.

They had never crossed swords before. But they had met across the sword: on the Night of Ghosts, when she had performed the sword dance before her assembled people, and Romeo—wearing a mask for the first time—had caught the blade when she flung it up in the air, and danced with her.

They had danced, and when it was over, his heart, which had been hers, was twice hers. Perhaps in that dance, this duel had become inevitable.

That dance had been a game: sheer joy and delight, shared between enemies. For all that Juliet wasn't trying to win, this duel was no game. Her face—when stray lamplight fell on it—was grim. Romeo could see the grief and fury in every movement that she took, as she drove him back through the complex—she was drawing him away from the others, he realized, so that if they were seen, they would be a distraction from the raid. It meant he was more likely to be captured, but it also made the Catresou more likely to escape.

He didn't mind that.

He thought he could make it better.

The next time she lunged, he ducked backward, jumped up onto a low stone wall, and then hauled himself onto the roof. He turned to her, extending his blade in silent invitation.

She grinned.

And Romeo's heart broke. Because *that* was the joy he remembered, the ferocious delight that had been in her eyes, in her hands upon the sword, the first night they had danced.

He could only give it to her now in battle and deceit.

She followed him onto the roof. Now the alarm was beginning to spread. Vaguely, Romeo could hear shouts and clatter below. But he couldn't afford to pay attention, and it hardly seemed to matter.

Because the duel was still not a game, but it was starting to be a delight. Up here on the roofs, alone with the wind and the stars and Juliet—it felt like those moments they had once stolen together, just the two of them, creating their own secret world where love was possible and duty would not betray them.

Romeo's arms burned with exhaustion; he knew his strokes

were becoming slower and clumsier every moment. If this had been a fight to the death, by now Juliet would certainly have killed him.

But when he stumbled back, gasping for breath—when he stumbled, and started to slip off the roof—

She caught his flailing hand and pulled him up.

Her grip was warm and strong as he remembered, and when his feet were back under him, she didn't let go. She stared at him, her eyebrows drawn together, her lips half parted, and he knew she almost recognized him.

The world halted.

Nothing moved, nothing mattered, nothing except that she was looking at him and wanting to know him, and *Juliet, Juliet, Juliet*—

He thought, *I cannot stay silent,* and he opened his mouth.

Then she let go. All the life and wonder drained from her face, leaving it like a mask.

"I am summoned," she said.

For a moment Romeo didn't understand, because there was nobody there, they were still alone beneath the stars—

"I will have orders to kill you soon," she said, and turned away from him, and that was when he remembered that Juliet had a Guardian now, who could call her mind to mind.

Romeo had heard the stories from Justiran: that Lord Ineo had leashed the Juliet to a Mahyanai girl who was not only an orphan, but a disgraced former Sister. People called it a clever move on Lord Ineo's part, to choose a Guardian who owed him everything.

Romeo knew that Guardian had to be Runajo. Before Makari came to tutor him, she was the closest thing Romeo had to a friend. For years after, he had thought he was in love with her.

He'd been wrong about that. But one thing Romeo didn't doubt even now: Runajo was the last person in the world to obey Lord Ineo without question, no matter how much she owed him.

And Juliet had chosen to stay with her, when she could have asked Romeo for help.

So he watched Juliet go. He watched, and did not follow, because he no longer had any right to do more.

Juliet raced across the rooftops. Runajo's call still echoed in her head: *Get here at once,* surrounded by a flicker of images—a hallway, a door.

That was all. But there had been fear in Runajo's voice—Runajo, who hadn't spoken into Juliet's mind since she betrayed her. It was the only mercy she had shown her. If Runajo was desperate enough now—

She felt a sudden burst of pain in her arm, and she stumbled for a moment. The pain wasn't hers.

Juliet remembered the old serving woman, dead in the hallway.

She'd been an idiot to assume that there had been only one group of Catresou causing a distraction. She'd been so desperate for a chance to help her people, she had just stopped thinking.

Runajo had made Juliet a slave and a murderer. If Runajo died on a Catresou blade tonight, it would only be just.

And yet.

And yet Juliet was fleeing desperately across the rooftops, not looking for a single way to subvert this order. She had sworn by her soul that she would never forgive Runajo, and she didn't. She couldn't. But the thought of Runajo's blood spilling across the ground, like the blood of a hundred others who had deserved to live more—

Losing Romeo had robbed the sun from her sky. The thought of losing Runajo felt like it would scrape the last stars out of the night.

She was close. She dropped from the roof and a moment later was running through hallways.

There was the door. She slowed, drawing her sword and trying to catch her breath as she listened—

Paris Catresou stepped out of the room.

Sheer surprise caught her by the throat and held her still.

She'd met Paris only once, the day that Tybalt was buried. She had still been reeling from her cousin's death, from knowing that Romeo had killed him and soon she would have to kill Romeo in return. When her father had told her that Paris would be her

Guardian in Tybalt's place, she was already planning her escape.

But the awkward, desperately polite boy in her father's study had been nothing like the jailer she expected. At Tybalt's funeral, when grief overwhelmed her, he had been kind to her. Afterward, he had helped her slip away from the funeral feast, back to the sepulcher, where the sacred fire burned with the word *zoura* inlaid in gold on the wall above it. When she had told him how she had always only wanted to be correct, how she was afraid her father did not care about *zoura* at all, he had listened. And he had promised to serve her.

She had thought that, in another world, she could have been happy to serve her people with him.

The next day she had run away to make Romeo her Guardian, and destroyed him instead. She'd never seen Paris again; he hadn't been at the compound when she was sent there for the purge, and she'd heard nothing of him since. She had hoped that he escaped, and resigned herself to not knowing.

She hadn't expected to see him again.

To have *him* see her, holding a sword still smeared with Catresou blood.

Surprise held her. But only for a moment. The order Runajo had given her, *Get here at once*, still pulsed in her mind, and it dragged her a step forward—

As Paris attacked.

There was no warning: no shout, no spark of anger in his

blank face, no tensing of his shoulders. His sword just lashed out, fast and fluid as a whip, and Juliet barely saved herself from that first stroke, it was so unexpected.

But she should have expected it, she realized as she dodged back, parrying. Paris had wanted to serve his people. She was now their enemy. Of course he would try to kill her.

What had he done to Runajo?

That thought sent her attacking forward in a flurry of speed. She'd had the impression that Paris was not particularly good, and his technique was definitely not impressive, but he was moving with a speed and strength that matched hers.

And that terrible, empty calm on his face. She remembered when he'd looked at her with such *hope*.

"Paris!" she shouted. "I don't want to kill you!"

As she spoke, he tried to parry her stroke and failed. Her blade slid, and before she could stop it, sliced across his cheek. She pulled it away instantly, stumbling back a step, but blood was already welling up in a line across his face.

It wasn't red. It was black.

The living bled crimson. When their dead bodies rose again as revenants, their blood oozed in brownish clots, if it hadn't yet dried away entirely. But the living dead—whose souls were trapped by necromancers, so they could never find rest—they bled as black as night.

It was the very worst fate that could befall any Catresou.

Paris said, "My master ordered me not to kill you. But I have to complete my mission."

His voice was completely emotionless. Lifeless. It made Juliet's skin crawl.

"What's your mission?" she asked.

"Rescue," he said, and Juliet was about to reply, *But the Catresou aren't being kept here,* when she saw someone else stepping out of the room.

It was the living dead girl who had been pulled out of her father's secret laboratory. Juliet had only seen her once, when Lord Ineo was lecturing her on the depravity of the Catresou clan, and how grateful she should be that she'd been rescued from it. But she would know those golden curls and those dead eyes anywhere.

Runajo's order still burned in her mind: *Get here at once. Get here at once. Get here at once.*

"Get out," she said. "Now. I won't stop you."

Paris stared at her a moment longer. She thought of the dying man she'd tried to comfort, and she wished she could say the same words for Paris, but it would be no use. He couldn't walk the Paths of Light, because his soul was trapped *here.* He couldn't even understand the words, because the necromancer's power had shredded his mind.

In another world, he could have been dear to her. In this one, he was already destroyed.

Paris turned and strode away; he caught the dead girl's hand as he passed her, and dragged her with him.

Juliet ran into the room. Runajo was at the far end, huddled against the wall, terribly pale.

But alive.

Her eyes were squeezed shut, but she opened them as Juliet approached. "Did you stop him?" she asked.

"No," said Juliet, kneeling beside her. Runajo was cradling her right arm to her side.

"You should have stopped him," said Runajo.

"Then you should have ordered me to," said Juliet. She reached for Runajo's arm and then stopped, fingertips an inch from her skin.

She could see the faint, round scars from when the Sisterhood had forced Runajo to do penance for dragging Juliet back from the Mouth of Death.

"I don't think he broke it," said Runajo.

Juliet probed gently down the arm with a finger. Runajo's face screwed up, but she didn't wince or moan.

"Probably not broken," Juliet agreed. "Deep bruising, maybe."

Runajo glared. "He took the living dead girl."

"I know. She was already a prisoner, so I'm not sure how it matters."

"It matters because she could have helped me end the Ruining. She was the *last* thing that possibly could. And now she's going to be locked in a closet while fugitive Catresou mutter spells over her."

Runajo was alight with righteous fury, her pain momentarily forgotten. It reminded Juliet of when they were in the Cloister, and Runajo hadn't understood why Juliet was so furious to see her bleeding when they still had questions about necromancers and the Ruining to solve.

"No," said Juliet. "Paris isn't with the rest of the Catresou. He's living dead, working for a necromancer who wants me left alive. Probably the same necromancer who was killing Sisters in the Cloister."

Runajo looked surprised. "His name is Paris? You knew him?"

"Once," said Juliet.

8

IT WAS A LONG WAY back, through the clean, wide streets of the Upper City, the great gates, and the twisting alleys of the Lower City. By the time Paris had brought the girl back to his master's house, the sun had risen in the sky.

She walked silently, patiently, allowing him to lead her. She was dead like him, and Paris felt sure that she, too, had been raised by his master. She clearly understood the same inevitable truth: that they existed now only to serve him.

The girl's hand was small and cold in his.

Romeo's hands had been warm.

The memory was sudden and without warning, like a blade sliding between his ribs. Just before they left on the raid, Romeo had seized his hand, had said quietly and urgently, *Paris. Paris, do you remember me?*

Yes, Paris had said. *You are the enemy of my master.*

He didn't know why the memory was so vivid. It wasn't the only time that a living person besides his master had touched him. Meros especially liked to shove him by the shoulder and grab him by the hair. And since Meros was alive, surely his hands were just as warm, but Paris didn't *remember* them, they didn't seem real, not like—like—

Romeo pressed against the wall, Paris holding the blade at his throat, the stench of Catresou blood, and Romeo saying, I know you didn't want to do this—

Paris had done far worse things on his master's orders. He didn't know why he remembered *that* one.

His head throbbed with sudden pain. There was no "worse" when it came to his master's orders. That thought was vile. Absurd. Everything he had done in obedience, he had done right.

It was equally absurd to wish that his master's orders were different. But Paris almost wished that his master hadn't told him to keep Romeo alive at all costs. Because then he wouldn't remember pulling him away from the cage of seething revenants. He wouldn't remember—it wasn't a feeling, he couldn't feel things anymore—but he wouldn't remember that strange *unwinding* in his chest, almost like relief.

Paris realized he had stopped walking. The girl waited, unquestioning.

I am obedient, he thought. *I am obedient*, and he strode forward.

Once upon a time, a prosperous man had owned a large, well-maintained tenement. (His master had told Paris this, while laughing.) Then the man's wife had died, and he had come begging for favor to the Night Game. They were both dead now, and raised again to serve.

Paris knocked at the door. A stout, balding man answered it: the onetime owner of the house. When he saw Paris, he drew the door wide.

"Where is he?" asked Paris.

The man didn't ask who *he* was; there was only one possible person who could matter to either of them.

"The ballroom," he said.

Paris nodded, and led the girl inside.

Once, the tenement had housed men and women who were well-to-do. The large, high-vaulted room, painted in red and gold, had existed so that they could pay for the privilege of throwing parties in it.

These past three weeks, it had hosted the Night Game. The last one had been just the night before, and the room was not clean: there were scattered chairs, a few discarded masks. The cages of sacrifices still sat in the center of the room, and inside the cages, the bodies had begun to stir, hissing and gnawing at the bars.

Paris's master knelt by one of the cages, poking at a revenant with a stick. He rose and turned as Paris entered the room.

Instantly Paris let go of the girl's hand and dropped to his knees.

"I brought her back," he said, and he felt that rare, exquisite sunburst of joy, because his master *smiled.*

Not at him. But it didn't matter, because his master, smiling at the girl, was the happiest that Paris had ever seen him.

In two strides, he was before her, and he swept her into an embrace.

Paris, still kneeling beside them, found his head at level with the girl's still, limp hand. He wondered if he should go, but he had not been dismissed.

"I'm so sorry," his master whispered. "I understand everything now. I will make things right."

The girl's fingers flexed. Her hand began to lift—and then in one smooth motion, she had drawn the knife that hung from his master's belt.

In the next moment, she ducked out of his arms. She rammed the knife between her ribs, straight into her heart.

Paris's chest ached. He knew the peculiar pain of that stroke, even though now he was glad his master had inflicted it on him.

His master's cry ripped through Paris's mind, tore him apart. He had never heard grief like that before, felt grief like that before.

"No," said his master, falling to his knees before the girl, "no."

She stared at him expressionlessly. The knife sat buried

between her ribs, and black blood welled up around the blade, but she did not fall.

She was living dead, like Paris, and their master's power drove every pulse of her heart. Yet a knife driven straight *through* her heart should have killed her again, required her to be raised again, and Paris stared at her in puzzlement.

"I know what you need," said his master. "I will give it to you."

Slowly, gently, he pulled the knife free of her body.

"You know I can't kill you," he said. "Nobody can. But I'm almost ready."

He pressed his lips to the wound and kissed it. Then he raised his face to her and said, black-lipped, "I only need a few more Night Games to gather my power. Then I'll take the key, and open the gates of death, and you will be home. All the world will die, and you will finally know peace."

The girl looked at him. In the cages, the revenants hissed and writhed.

She raised her hands to his cheeks, slid them into his hair. And then she bent down and kissed him, again and again.

9

LORD INEO WAS NOT PLEASED with either of them. But he was especially not pleased with Juliet.

"The Catresou breached our walls, killed five of our own people, and absconded with nearly seventeen prisoners."

Juliet couldn't see his face. She was kneeling, head bowed, staring at the ground. But she could hear the flat, clipped tone of his voice, and she could imagine the sour look on his face. It was almost amusing.

"I had believed that your mission was to protect us," Lord Ineo went on. "Do you care to explain how this happened?"

His frustration wasn't amusing, not when he had the power to kill her or make her kill in retribution. But it was still *deeply* satisfying.

"I killed the first ones I found," she said, as meekly as she could. "Then I fought the next group, but before I could defeat them, Runajo summoned me to help her."

"Before you could defeat them," Lord Ineo said flatly.

"They also overcame your guards," said Runajo. "The ones watching the prisoners went down without a fight. I thought *they* were supposed to protect us."

"Oh, those guards will also be disciplined," said Lord Ineo. "I just want to know why our Juliet did not give her all to defend her people against a bloody, unprovoked attack. It makes no sense. Unless, of course, she is still confused in her loyalties."

Dread clutched at Juliet's throat. She could already imagine the next words: *Perhaps she needs a chance to prove herself,* followed by an order to kill Catresou prisoners in retribution for the attack. Runajo would relay the order, and the magic would strangle Juliet's will and send her walking out into the morning sunlight, out to the building where they kept the Catresou prisoners, and she would have to kill, and kill, and kill—

"Juliet," said Runajo, each word chilled and precise, "kiss his feet."

The order had seized her by the base of the skull and pressed her forward before she even knew what was happening. Then her lips were against his toes and she wanted to pull back in revulsion, but she couldn't. She could only let the magic move her to kiss his other foot before it allowed her to sit back, shaking with humiliation.

He had flinched. That was something.

"If you don't think she's entirely broken to our will," Runajo said impatiently, "you're a fool. And I know you're not a fool. You're very displeased that this happened, and you want us to be sorry. I assure you, we are. May we now discuss something important, such as how we're going to recover the living dead girl?"

There was a short, brittle silence. Then Lord Ineo laughed softly.

"I see I have no choice but to respect you," he said, and there was actually warmth in his voice. It turned Juliet's stomach, though she shouldn't be surprised. Of course he liked Runajo. She was ruthless enough. "Did they say anything, when they took her? Do they know what she is?"

Before Runajo could reply—before she could say that *they* had only been one boy, who had not been alive either—Juliet spoke up.

"When I got there, they were dragging her out. They were telling the girl that they were going to give her a proper burial, as one of their people deserved."

The worlds felt oily and unclean in her mouth. Juliet had never been a liar before.

But she'd never had such need before.

"Really?" said Lord Ineo. "Is that true?"

And for one agonized heartbeat, she could only wait and hope—

"Juliet," said Runajo, "tell him."

But she hadn't said to tell him *what*.

Juliet raised her head and looked Lord Ineo straight in the eyes. "I am telling you the truth, my lord. They were furious that we hadn't given her Catresou burial rites."

"They were shouting something like that when they attacked me," said Runajo.

Lord Ineo sighed. "Superstitious fools."

He didn't seem very worried at the thought. She'd given him the answer he wanted: that he had already nobly vanquished all necromancers in the city.

"But when are we going to get the girl back?" asked Runajo.

"When we round up the rest of the Catresou." He paused meaningfully. "It's not a thing to be discussed before your charge."

"Juliet," said Runajo, without looking at her, "go."

Her body rose and walked from the room smoothly and without hesitation. But the moment the door closed behind her, the order obeyed, she stopped. She thought she could still hear them if she strained—

Then Runajo spoke silently into her mind: *Do not find a way to spy on us.*

Again the order drove her feet into motion, carrying her down the hallway. When her feet were finally released, Juliet stumbled, then turned and slammed her palm into the wall.

For a few moments, as they talked to Lord Ineo, she had started to think that Runajo was her ally again.

But it seemed she was still determined to make sure that Juliet could do nothing to prevent the destruction of her people.

Because they would be destroyed over this, Juliet was very sure. Lord Ineo would not forgive nor forget the raid. He would hunt them down, and Juliet would be the one who killed them.

It was her duty. She was the sword of the Mahyanai.

She had decided to accept that.

So Juliet curled her hands into useless fists at her sides and went to do her duty by sitting vigil over the Mahyanai dead.

The Mahyanai did not keep vigil the same way, now. Lord Ineo was too careful for that. All five bodies were laid out together in a single large room, watched by three guards with polearms; they were to be taken away at noon, less than twelve hours after they had died.

Even so, not many were willing to sit vigil. Everyone knew how dangerous the dead had become.

So Juliet was surprised to find Arajo there. She was even more surprised to see her kneeling beside the old serving woman who had died first.

Without a word, Juliet knelt beside her.

"What are you doing here?" asked Arajo after a moment, her voice small and tightly controlled.

"You're my people now," said Juliet. "This is what you do for your dead, isn't it?"

Arajo drew a shuddering breath.

"Why are you here?" asked Juliet.

"She was my nurse." Arajo's voice wavered. "I loved her more than my own mother."

Juliet looked at the old woman's still, horribly pale face. If somebody had told her, the day before, that Catresou men would break into Lord Ineo's estate and kill a helpless old woman, she wouldn't have believed it. The Catresou weren't like other people in the city, who sent their women to join the City Guard; they understood that women were meant to be protected.

But they were desperate now. And angry.

"They said you killed them. The men who killed her."

"Yes," said Juliet. She remembered her sword slicing faster than her own thoughts, cutting them down in moments. And she remembered comforting one of the men as he lay dying, holding his hand and whispering the prayers to send him safely into death. "Yes. I avenged her."

"Good. I'm glad." Arajo's hands, resting on her knees, curled into fists. "Monsters like that deserve to die."

She was right. It was monstrous to cut down an unarmed woman, no matter how desperate you were.

It was monstrous to order an entire clan destroyed, just because the leaders had been practicing necromancy in secret, against the laws of the clan itself.

It was monstrous to live in a city whose walls were maintained by human sacrifice.

Once, in the Cloister, Juliet had told Runajo, *You live in a charnel house, and you're all guilty and dripping red.* She had only meant the Sisters of Thorn, because they poured out human blood in sacrifice. But it was true for everyone in Viyara, wasn't it?

She stared at the old woman, who had deserved and not deserved to die, and she wished that Romeo were alive. Because he would know the answer. He had known there was a way for Juliet to be more than a sword. Surely he would know of a way for Viyara to be more than a city of monsters.

Juliet only knew how to see guilt and render judgment.

She remembered, suddenly, the Catresou boy she had fought the night before. He had so terribly reminded her of Romeo. Not just the smile she had glimpsed in the darkness, or the impulsive way he had charged to attack. But when they had dueled on the rooftops, it had been like the sword dance where she first met Romeo: the way they had slipped into an easy, perfect rhythm without even trying, as if the whole world had come into being so that they could dance together.

For one moment, she dared to think, *I am here among the Mahyanai. Could he—*

But Juliet had seen Romeo die. When the magic they had tried to harness went out of control, it had dragged them both into the land of the dead. Runajo, sitting vigil at the Mouth of Death, had dragged Juliet back before she had been entirely lost. But there had been no one to draw back Romeo. He had truly died.

And there was only one way that dead souls returned to the land of the living: like Paris.

That boy she had fought on the rooftops was alive. So he was not Romeo: he was a Catresou boy who certainly wanted Juliet dead, and who probably would have been happy to help kill Arajo's nurse if he'd been given the chance.

"Teach me how to fight," said Arajo, startling her out of her thoughts.

"You have teachers already," said Juliet. "I've seen you practice."

"I know the sword forms," said Arajo. "But you've killed people. You know how it's *done*." Her voice wasn't wavering now; it was soft and dry and viciously determined. "The Catresou won't stop trying to kill us. I want to be ready next time."

"I'll protect you," said Juliet.

"I don't want to be protected! I want to kill them back. I want to be like *you*."

You shouldn't, thought Juliet. Arajo had a chance to be free, to be a girl instead of a weapon. She was absolutely guaranteed never to be enslaved to her enemies and forced to kill for them.

But the Mahyanai gave their women swords. Juliet supposed

that, as their Juliet, she couldn't try to stop them.

She couldn't tell Arajo not to want vengeance either, not when her own heart pounded with the need to kill every time Mahyanai blood was shed.

"I'll try," she said, and that seemed to satisfy Arajo.

So they sat together in silence for hours. The sun rose closer to noon, and more people came to sit brief vigils, and many of them stared at Juliet and whispered.

Juliet didn't listen. She stared at the dead woman, and thought of all the blood that had been shed, and dreaded what was still to come.

You live in a charnel house. You're all guilty and dripping red.

10

"YOU HAVE A PLAN TO hunt down the rest of the Catresou?" Runajo asked, once Juliet had gone.

Lord Ineo gave her a look of weary patience. "You don't need to pretend. I'm well aware of what your friend Sunjai must have told you."

Runajo's heart thudded. But there was no reason to hide what she knew.

"The sacrifice," she said. "You're really doing it?"

"I'd rather prefer the city *not* to fall five days from now," said Lord Ineo. "So yes. In three days, there will be a Great Offering the like of which this city has never seen."

Twenty lives, their blood running across the white stone dais in the grand court. The thought made Runajo feel sick, but what could she do? Lord Ineo would never listen to her if she said it was wrong. And if he *did* listen to her . . . everyone in Viyara would die. Because she had failed to find another way.

"You're not planning to tell the city how close we are to destruction, are you?" she said.

He shook his head. "Of course not. The people are already near enough to panicking, especially in the Lower City. We'll tell them the sacrifice protects them from the revenants, and they'll be grateful."

Runajo nodded. "And once it's done . . . then you'll hunt down the Catresou?"

She didn't want them to fall into his hands. She knew what Juliet would think of her urging him forward. But the living dead girl was her last hope. The sacrifice surely would not protect the city for long; Runajo had to find a way to talk with Death if she wanted the city to live. If she wanted Juliet to live.

"Oh, you've finally started to want justice for their crimes?" Lord Ineo half smiled. "Then rejoice. They're going to supply the victims for the sacrifice."

Runajo stared at him. "But . . . they won't volunteer," she said numbly.

The Great Offering that held up the walls of Viyara was meant to be a *free* offering. The three high houses had a duty to take turns providing victims, but those victims were supposed to be willing. True, it was an open secret that the Catresou sacrifice was usually somebody the clan didn't want, who had been told that "volunteering" was better than what life would become. But they at least followed the form of the law. The thought of anyone dragging out a prisoner in chains was . . . until now, it had been unthinkable.

The gods had offered their blood freely, and just as freely, men must pour out theirs. This was the ancient, sacred law of Viyara. Even when Runajo had come to believe that the offering was wrong, she still trusted in that.

Lord Ineo snorted. "No Catresou has ever been brave enough to volunteer," he said. "It's why they always sent a criminal to die. Now they're all criminals."

Her heart was pounding. "Simply because they are your enemies—"

"*Our* enemies."

Lord Ineo's voice was soft, and the look he gave her was mild. But ice slid down the length of Runajo's spine.

She hadn't come to Lord Ineo out of loyalty to her clan. She'd offered to serve him so that he would protect Juliet, when the Sisterhood had wanted to sacrifice her.

Juliet stayed safe only so long as Lord Ineo stayed pleased.

Runajo dropped her gaze and let her shoulders relax. "They attempted necromancy," she said, in the same meek voice she'd used when humoring her dying parents. "But we never proved that they managed to raise even a single person."

"They attempted more than simple necromancy, though,

didn't they?" said Lord Ineo.

The cold at the pit of her stomach got worse. Because it was true: the ceremony that the City Guard had interrupted at the Catresou sepulcher had been necromantic in nature, that was certain. But there had been no body or bones they were trying to raise. And while those who'd known the full plan had died that night or the next day—like Lord Catresou—there were still some left who had repeated confused rumors about *opening the gates of death.*

"And a month later, the dead began to rise faster," Lord Ineo went on. "I'd say it's clear they succeeded in tampering with death. After last night, it's clear that none of them will ever consent to obey our laws. Somebody must die, or else we all will; and I won't ask good Mahyanai to sacrifice themselves so that Catresou necromancers can continue to live."

The world is ending, Runajo wanted to say. *Why do you care if they defy you?*

But she already knew the answer, and it wasn't just his pride. The stronger the Ruining grew, the greater the danger of revenants and chaos and the walls collapsing, the less he could afford the risks of conflict in the city.

All her life, Runajo had argued and disagreed with everyone. Nobody had ever been able to persuade her.

She couldn't think of a single argument to use against Lord Ineo now.

"Why are you telling me this?" she asked.

"Because you're the Juliet's Guardian," said Lord Ineo. "I'm sure the renegade Catresou will try to stop the sacrifice. I mean to have her guard them. You're going to make sure that she succeeds at her duty." His mouth slanted. "I'm not fool enough to believe she failed last night by accident."

Runajo's body felt numb and dazed, but her mind was working perfectly and very fast.

If she didn't obey him, Juliet would die. Nobody else could protect them from the Sisterhood, and there was nowhere to run, because outside the city walls lay only death.

If she found a way to stop him, *everyone* would die. There was no more calculating risks; the equations had become unbearably simple. They must make this offering, or the city would fall.

She knew what Juliet would say: that it was better for them to die innocent than live as murderers. But Runajo had already become a murderer. Nobody in the city was innocent, because its very foundations were built on blood.

And she couldn't let Juliet die.

Runajo looked up into his eyes. "I would be honored to serve my clan," she said.

The Sisters of Thorn said that there was one governing concept to the world: *inkaad*, a word that literally meant "appropriate payment." It was the sacred mathematics, the holy law of bargain and exchange: life for life, price for price. It was how they justified killing someone every six months to maintain the spell-walls that kept the Ruining out of Viyara. The world had been created from the blood of the gods. It was now sustained by the blood of men.

Runajo had never believed in the nine gods. She had stopped believing in *inkaad* when the Sisters had told her to sacrifice Juliet, when Runajo had looked into her eyes and realized that her life was infinitely precious, and there was *no* appropriate payment to be given in exchange for it.

And if Juliet's life was that precious, then so was everyone's. Viyara and the Sisterhood were built on a murderous lie.

In one heartbeat, Runajo had come to believe that.

In the next, she'd become a murderer herself.

To save Juliet from the Sisterhood, Runajo had handed her over to the Mahyanai. She'd bound her to avenge their blood and ordered her to obey Lord Ineo. And Lord Ineo had used her to slaughter and capture the Catresou.

Now he was going to use her to kill the rest of them. And Runajo was going to help. Because for all her pride, she was no different from anyone else in the city. She wanted to live, and she wanted Juliet to live, and she would wade through blood to do it.

Runajo thought about this all afternoon. She knew that she had to tell Juliet—Lord Ineo was going to make his proclamation the next morning, and Juliet deserved to hear it from Runajo first—but she couldn't make herself say the words just yet. So she sat in the study and stared at a Catresou record of the ancient Juliets until her eyes ached and her vision swam.

Finally, when the sun slanted low through the windows, she went to find Juliet. She had ordered Juliet not to reach out to her through the bond—after she had tried to destroy Runajo with it—but though she could no longer feel Juliet's every emotion, she could still vaguely sense where the other girl was.

It was this sense that she followed through doors and around corners, until she stepped out into a colonnaded hallway that ringed a courtyard paved in red tiles.

Sunlight dazzled her eyes. Outside in the courtyard, metal flashed blindingly bright. Runajo blinked, and realized Juliet was holding a Mahyanai blade—long, single-edged, and slightly curved—while talking to a girl her own age. The girl had her own sword, and twisted it as they talked quietly.

Suddenly Juliet whirled into motion, dancing through the cuts and slices of a Mahyanai fighting form with the same speed and grace she'd used fighting revenants in the Sunken Library. Then she stopped, caught her breath, and looked back at the girl.

She was smiling.

A cold ache wove through Runajo's ribs. Juliet had never smiled at any of the Mahyanai before. She'd never been willing to forgive a single one of them for belonging to their clan before.

It was only fair. The girl might be Mahyanai, but she hadn't wronged Juliet the way Runajo had.

She strode out into the courtyard. Her eyes ached in the bright light.

"Juliet," she said, and instantly Juliet stiffened, her face turning back into a mask.

Runajo stopped a pace away. The girl was looking at her curiously, but she didn't matter now.

"Come with me," she said, "now," and instantly turned and strode away. Her skin crawled with the awareness she was being stared at, but it did not matter.

Nothing mattered, except what she had to do.

Juliet followed her into the cool shadows of the hallway. She said, "What are your orders?" and Runajo thought her heart was going to crack, because Juliet wasn't speaking in the same dead, obedient voice she'd used for the past month. She sounded wary but . . . alive.

Runajo turned to face her, but she stared at the wall behind her head as she started to speak.

"The Sisterhood has decided we must act to save the walls. In three days, they're going to offer twenty lives. Lord Ineo is going to use the Catresou prisoners for the sacrifice."

She heard Juliet's stuttering breath, but couldn't bear to meet her eyes.

"The adults," she added. "Not the children."

Silence. Runajo finally dared a look, and for the first time in weeks saw actual shock on Juliet's face.

"He can't—"

"You know he can."

Juliet closed her mouth, pressed her lips into a tight line. Her hands tightened into fists. Then she said, her voice low and controlled, "You could stop this. If you told someone outside this clan, he could be stopped. No Viyaran would accept it. Even by *their* laws, it's obscene."

Runajo had thought this herself. But only for a moment.

"Who," she asked bitterly, "in this entire city, would want to save the Catresou? Who isn't *terrified* of the dead rising faster? People will hate that he's offering prisoners, but they won't hate it enough until we run out of Catresou and have to start killing someone else."

"So you will help him," said Juliet.

"Yes," said Runajo. "And you will stand guard on the sacrifices, to stop any fugitive Catresou from interfering."

They both knew that wasn't the real reason. Lord Ineo wanted a show of power, of how totally he had destroyed his enemies. He was going to get it.

"This won't just destroy *my* people," Juliet burst out, suddenly passionate. "Don't you care what this will do to the Mahyanai? Do you *want* your clan to be murderers?"

"The walls are going to fall in five days," Runajo said bluntly. "The Sisters have worked the equations. There is no other way to save us. If your people don't die, somebody must, or we all will."

Juliet stared at her. And then she said in the dead, flat tones that had become so familiar, "Do you have any other orders?"

"No," said Runajo. "You can go."

This much of *inkaad* was true, in this way the Sisters of Thorn were right: everything was bought in blood. Nothing was preserved, except that something else was destroyed.

Runajo had decided to save both Juliet and Viyara, and now she was drenched in blood. Her whole clan was guilty was well. It wasn't right. But it was the only way there was.

Now she looked at Juliet walking away, and she thought, *I will change it.*

I will reshape the world. I will rewrite inkaad *itself if I must. I will make this killing not necessary.*

I swear it.

11

THE MORNING AFTER THE RAID, Meros went to see the Master Necromancer. When he returned, he said that as payment for their service the Master Necromancer would lay four of their dead to rest.

Romeo hated that he was grateful.

He hated how the rest of the Catresou were grateful, how there was an almost festival atmosphere among them as they prepared for the funerals. But he hated himself the most.

If Juliet knew that all her people served the Master Necromancer now, it would break her heart. If she knew that Romeo served him too, she would hate him even more.

If Makari knew—

But Makari had to know, surely, that Romeo willingly served the man who had enslaved him. Was that why he had never come to see Romeo again? Because he despised what Romeo had done?

But because of their service—Romeo's service—the Master Necromancer visited them in secret and laid four of their dead to rest. One of them was Emera. She was going to have a Catresou burial, as she had wanted. As Romeo had promised.

If he had broken that promise, surely Juliet would have hated him for that too.

Romeo had nothing left, except his faithfulness to her people. That was how he had ended up here, in the embalming room.

The stench was awful.

Romeo knew that the Catresou embalming process involved draining the blood from the body, then removing the heart, stomach, and brain. So he'd expected the place to smell at least faintly like blood and death.

What he hadn't expected was the smell of the embalming fluid itself—or at least, he supposed it must be the embalming fluid: an overpowering sweetness, so strong it made the air feel sticky, with a sour undertone that he could taste in the back of his throat as he breathed.

It must be so much worse in the old embalming rooms that the Catresou had used for generations. This was just a cellar in one of the Catresou safe houses, recently converted for use on the dead.

He didn't want to be here in this dim, crowded room—there were tables everywhere, and shelves filled with jars and metal equipment—but Ilurio had told him that he was needed. They wanted him to help carry out Emera's body.

"Who's there?" called out someone from behind a line of shelves. It sounded like an old man.

Romeo took a breath—his stomach pitched at the scent—and said, "I was told you need me to—"

Then he stepped around the shelves and stopped.

The old man was one of the Catresou magi. Romeo could tell, because he wore the golden full-face mask that the magi wore at all Catresou ceremonies. He'd never seen one before, of course, but he'd heard stories passed along by City Guards who had to stand watch at Catresou funerals.

The old man was also an embalmer. Romeo could tell, because there was a man's corpse laid out on the table in front of him, sliced open from neck to navel, ribs pried apart. The old man had his hands plunged into the middle of the corpse's abdomen.

Romeo stared. He couldn't breathe. He couldn't look away. He'd seen blood and death before, but not like this. The Mahyanai burned their dead cleanly; they didn't peel them open and cut out choice portions like slaughtered animals.

"What are you doing?" the man demanded. His hands must have moved slightly, because Romeo heard a very quiet, very distinct wet noise.

Romeo bolted. He managed to make it out of the room before he threw up.

"Oh, my," said Ilurio from behind him. "Did the brave warrior find something that he couldn't stand?"

Romeo was miserable enough that it took him a few moments to work out that if Ilurio was lurking in the hallway behind him, if he had followed him down here, then—

"If you were any younger, I would thrash you," Gavarin announced.

"I'm sorry," Romeo said quickly, straightening, and gulped as his stomach pitched again. He hadn't thought this moment could get more humiliating. "I—I just—"

"Not you." Gavarin had been holding Ilurio by the shoulder, as if he'd dragged him there, but he released him with a sigh and handed Romeo a handkerchief. "The young master here."

"I'm doing us all a favor," said Ilurio. "If he *deserved* to wear a mask and call himself Catresou, he'd be able to stomach a sacred rite."

"If you were a Catresou in *any* way except that your mother pushed you squalling out of her body, then you wouldn't have used the sacred embalming to play a prank," said Gavarin. "I'm going to apologize to the embalmer; *you* can start cleaning that mess up."

"We're not on the raid anymore," Ilurio said sulkily. "You don't have command over me."

"No," Gavarin agreed. "But I'm still first guard to the Lord Catresou, so it's up to *me* if you ever get to join in a raid again."

"How dare you," said Ilurio. "Don't you know I'm—"

"The son of illustrious dead parents, heir to a fortune that doesn't exist anymore. The world you knew is *over*, boy. Wake up and start earning your place in the new one."

"I'll clean it up," Romeo interrupted. He wanted to just escape quietly while Ilurio and Gavarin were arguing, but he knew that wasn't right. "I should be able to bear your people's customs."

There was a moment of fragile silence, as Romeo felt the yawning gulf between himself and anyone who had been born Catresou. Then Gavarin said, "Get to work," and vanished inside the embalming room.

Ilurio was still glaring at him. "Do you think you deserve to be our hero?"

"I never said I was."

"No, you just put on one of our masks and asked us all to worship you."

Romeo felt the heat along his cheekbones. The more time he spent around the Catresou, the more he was aware of how arrogant he'd been, putting on the symbol that they all had been forced to take off.

"I didn't *do* this for your worship," he said. "I only wanted to serve the Juliet."

Ilurio's laugh was harsh and ugly. "You think we'll respect you because you love that whore?"

The words seemed to slide straight down Romeo's spine. The next moment, he had shoved Ilurio against the wall, and his voice felt like it was coming from someone else as he said, "I killed the last man who called her that."

Ilurio's eyes were wide in actual shock.

Then the door opened. Romeo heard Gavarin's footsteps as he came out. He didn't say a word about *I thought you were cleaning up*. He didn't need to; Romeo could feel his gaze on the back of his neck, and it said everything.

Romeo let go of Ilurio and stepped back. "Where's—we need a cleaning cloth," he said.

"There's a storeroom down to the left," said Gavarin, in such a flat voice that it was impossible to tell if he was furious or trying not to laugh.

"Thank you," Romeo said, and marched down the hallway. Surprisingly, Ilurio followed him without a word. Maybe he was embarrassed too.

"I still don't believe you're a warrior sent by the gods," Ilurio grumbled, when they had gotten to the storeroom. Then he shot Romeo a sideways glance. "Did you *really* kill someone?"

Romeo remembered Tybalt's blood on the cobblestones. The shouts and the smell and the dizzying hot sun. If not for that one afternoon of loss and fury, Juliet would belong to her people still, and the Catresou would be safe, and Emera would be alive. So many people would be alive.

"Yes," he said.

Romeo had heard all his life about the exotic, sinister pageantry of Catresou funerals. He supposed that the actual ceremonies in the sepulcher would be more elaborate, but even so, it was far simpler than he would have imagined.

The Catresou had obtained a house built over the ruins of another, which meant there were several underground rooms. They didn't bother with individual coffins or graves; they had just carved a pit out of the floor and lined it with bricks and then a white cloth. The four bodies lay in it nestled side by side, each wrapped in a shroud. If Romeo could ignore the nagging awareness that the bodies were going to be left there forever, he could almost pretend that they were simply performing a normal Mahyanai vigil.

He couldn't really pretend, though, because there was a magus in the traditional gold mask. And a row of jars, three for each body.

Meros was there, dressed and masked in somber black—all the Catresou were masked for the occasion. The magus went to each of the bodies, touching their eyes, mouths, hands, and feet with a golden seal as he muttered prayers in an undertone. The soft whisper of his voice, like fluttering moth wings, made the back of Romeo's neck prickle with uneasiness.

Emera had wanted this. She had thought it holy. Just as Paris had, as Juliet had.

It was this "holy" Catresou magic that had twisted the spells on Juliet, that had tried to rip the world open and end it. Romeo stared at the magus and wondered if he had been part of that plot. If he was working with the necromancers now.

After the magus, Meros went to each corpse and laid one jar at the head and another at the feet: the embalmed stomach and brain. Romeo reminded himself that this was enough to keep them safe. The chained coffins in the Catresou sepulcher were only a precaution; no body could rise as a revenant with so many organs removed.

Then it was time for the final jars to be laid: the embalmed hearts of the dead.

Romeo had been given Emera's. It was small, a cheap little unglazed jar that had probably once held oil. It was light in his hands, and he tried not to think about the tiny object inside it.

Emera's face was very pale, but peaceful. Her wounds were covered by the shroud, and so too were the seams from the embalming. Romeo still felt nauseous when he looked at her; his mind kept skipping back to the bloody embalming room, and the way she had clawed at the bars of the cage—and that was *wrong*, because she was more than a corpse, more than a monster.

She was a person, and Romeo had never really known her, and he didn't deserve to stand at her funeral.

But there was no one else. So he did.

12

RUNAJO CAME UP WITH THE plan late that night.

But then she couldn't figure out how to make it *work*.

She squinted at the paper where she had been trying to do calculations. The numbers seemed to be wiggling. It was nearly dawn; her eyes felt swollen and gritty, while her head ached and felt too light at the same time.

She could hardly think when she was this tired, but she didn't have time to sleep. The Great Offering was in three days. Two days, now, because it was nearly dawn. And Runajo still couldn't get the numbers right. She'd always been good at the sacred mathematics, but this calculation was more complex than anything she'd ever tried before.

The plan itself was simple: shrink the city walls. Viyara was huge. The Upper City—the original city, which had stood guarding the Mouth of Death for thousands of years—was built upon a vast spike of rock, with the Cloister at its top. Carved into that spire were the underground chambers where the Sisters grew the food of Viyara. At the base lay the Lower City, built a hundred years ago when refugees from the Ruining arrived. Only the Catresou and Mahyanai had negotiated a place for themselves in the Upper City; the rest built a sprawling, overgrown labyrinth of buildings that went right out to the edges of the island.

The city walls—the invisible sphere of magic that surrounded Viyara, keeping the deadly white fog of the Ruining out—didn't even touch the land. They rose out of the surrounding water. They were so vast, no wonder they were failing.

Runajo was sure that if the city walls were shrunk to the base of the city spire, it would take much less power—much less *blood*—to maintain them. It wouldn't be an easy way to live. They'd have to evacuate the people of the Lower City, and whether they went into the Upper City or the inside the city spire, it would be hard to fit them all. It would be hard to keep the peace.

But it had to be better than a perpetual bloodbath. Surely she could convince Lord Ineo to see it that way.

If she had the numbers worked out, to prove it could be done.

And that was the problem. She had to design a new set of walls for the city, and she had to design a plan for shifting from one set of walls to another, without the walls having a deadly reaction. And she had to do it without really knowing how the walls worked. That knowledge had been lost in the first days of the Ruining, when over half the Sisterhood died protecting Viyara, and the Sunken Library was overrun by revenants. Now they only knew how to keep producing the walls; Runajo had to extrapolate from that how to create new ones.

She groaned and rested her head on the table. Time to face the truth. She wasn't going to finish in time. She might not be able to do this alone at all.

And Juliet would have to guard the sacrifices.

Cold nausea dragged at her stomach. Juliet wouldn't do it without orders. So Runajo would have to look her in the eyes and tell her to stand guard as her people were slaughtered one by one.

She didn't want to hurt Juliet anymore. She didn't want to get people killed anymore.

She wasn't going to have a choice.

Runajo let out a slow breath, and admitted another truth to herself: she was not going to make this plan work on her own. She needed help.

And the only way to get it was to wait, and pretend she was obedient, and go to the palace of the Exalted.

Runajo had never been inside the palace before. Like all the Upper City, it was carved of white stone, alive and glimmering with the power of the Sisterhood. But it felt like a different world.

She was used to smooth white walls, to lamps carved of

glowing stone in the shape of flowers, to the occasional stray spark of light running down the floor. Here, every surface was carved with swirling lines, with birds and flowers and tiny dancing figures. There were no lamps; light glimmered and pooled in the crannies of every carving. Veins of light glowed in the floor, ever-shifting. In every room were pools and fountains, their inner surfaces tiled in gold or bright blue.

When Runajo had come to the gates and told the guards that she needed to speak with Mahyanai Sunjai, she hadn't expected to be allowed in. She had thought that she would be left in one of the outer courtyards and made to wait until Sunjai came to her. She had written a note, in case she wasn't allowed to see Sunjai at all. She had thought she might have to beg and plead, and she'd brought her best gold earrings in case she had to bribe.

But as soon as she told the guard her name, he nodded, and said, "Come with me."

He led her through the glimmering rooms and corridors to a little walled garden with three pools where huge carp glittered dimly from under the lily pads. Between the pools was a stone bench, and on the bench sat the younger sister of the Exalted: Inyaan, who had once been a novice beside Runajo and helped weave the walls with her.

Once, Runajo had hated her.

Inyaan had the dark skin and white-gold hair of all the Old Viyaran nobility, but she didn't look like the child of a dynasty descended from the gods. She was a short, scrawny girl, neither pretty nor impressive. Now that she was no longer a novice, she wore gauzy white silks and glittering gold chains, but they hung on her like weights, not adornments.

Her face was like a mask, fixed in a blank expression that looked both bored and disdainful. That was just the same as in the Cloister. It had taken until the very end of their time together for Runajo realize that the blankness had actually always been fear.

The guard bowed low. Runajo did too.

Inyaan didn't blink.

Well, Runajo hadn't expected getting permission to see Sunjai would be easy. She stepped forward, opening her mouth—

She gasped in pain as the guard caught her by the hair. "May she approach, Sister of the Exalted?"

Runajo felt unbearably stupid. As a novice, Inyaan had been treated almost the same as all the other novices; but here in the palace, she was due the same courtesies as the Exalted.

For a moment Inyaan was silent. From a nearby pond came a *plop* as one of the carp gave a sudden wriggle.

"Allow her," said Inyaan, her voice soft and dull.

The guard released Runajo's hair. She stumbled slightly, and then—feeling the guard's eyes still on her—dropped to her knees.

"Leave us," said Inyaan. As the guard retreated to the doorway of the garden, she finally looked Runajo in the eyes. "Why are you here?"

Runajo was painfully aware of the fact that they'd never been friends in the Cloister, and that she'd loathed Inyaan until nearly the end.

"I need to speak with Sunjai," she said. "I need her help."

"She serves the family descended from the gods," said Inyaan. "What has she to do with you?"

"She served the gods themselves in the Cloister," Runajo snapped, "and wasn't too grand for me then."

But that was a stupid thing to say, when Inyaan could have her thrown out with a word—and wrong, because Inyaan had never been as proud as Runajo thought.

"Please," she said quietly. "I know she's your friend, but—"

"She is nothing to me," said Inyaan, instantly.

The words were a lie: they had been friends. Runajo had worked at weaving the walls with the two of them every day, so she knew this for sure.

The words were clearly a lie, but also a reflex. Runajo felt sick as she remembered discovering that Inyaan's proud stares had always masked fear, as she wondered now what Inyaan was hiding.

"I'm not trying to make trouble for either one of you," she said. "But I need her help. I need *your* help. No one else outside the Cloister knows enough about weaving the walls."

Inyaan drew a breath. Her fingers flexed as if preparing to unclasp, but didn't.

"Why should I help you?" she asked, and the little bit of resentment that had crept into her voice was comforting. At least she sounded alive now.

"I got you out of the Cloister," said Runajo. "Out of that room."

The last time she'd seen Inyaan, she had been locked in a room for "ascetic seclusion" by order of her brother, the Exalted. That meant having tubes of the Cloister's living stone burrow into her arms every day and drain her blood to feed the city. When Runajo had brought Juliet to Lord Ineo, one part of her bargain had been that he'd use his influence with the Exalted to get Inyaan out.

Inyaan's lips stretched into a flat grimace. "For what part of that should I thank you?"

She twisted her arms, tilting the insides up. Runajo barely kept herself from recoiling. Inyaan's skin was livid with half-healed cuts and scars.

She remembered now what Inyaan had told her the last time they spoke in the Cloister: that the royal family of Viyara, being of divine blood, were required to offer their blood every day. That while they could use the same ointments to speed healing, they were not allowed the drugged bloodwine that the Sisters drank when they needed to dull the pain of sacrifice.

Inyaan had been so desperate to escape the seclusion, Runajo hadn't thought of anything else.

"I am out of that room," said Inyaan. "But I am still in seclusion. Except now my brother laughs at me as I bleed."

Runajo swallowed. She was so tired of hurting people.

"Then don't thank me," she said. "Plan out a way to punish me. You won't be the first, and unlike some, you *do* have the power. But don't ignore me."

"Why?" asked Inyaan.

Why does nobody ever want to listen? Runajo thought.

"Because this city is dying," she burst out, "and right now, Lord Ineo and the High Priestess are going to turn it into a slaughterhouse. You have heard, haven't you? The offering of Catresou prisoners? That's blasphemy by your own laws—and it's not going to fix the Ruining, just slow it down. There will be open war with the fugitive Catresou, and of course we'll win, but when they're all dead, what next? Start slaughtering the rest of the city?" She drew a trembling breath. "I think I have another way to strengthen the walls and buy us time without death, but I can't work the calculations by myself. Not nearly fast enough. I need help."

Inyaan stared at her. "So?"

So you have to help me, Runajo wanted to scream. *You have to help me or you're as good as a murderer.* But Inyaan wasn't going to care. It was so easy not to care, after all. To pick one thing you wanted—power for the Mahyanai, prestige for the Sisters of Thorn—and let the rest of the world burn for it.

Hadn't Runajo done the same?

And then she knew what to say.

"Because this city is dying, and Sunjai is in it. Are you ready to let that happen to her?"

Inyaan was very still except for her hands, twisting at each other. Then she said, "No."

The room Inyaan took her to was modest, compared to the rest of the palace: the walls were decorated only with simple, shallow spirals, and the little wooden table was unadorned.

"Wait here," said Inyaan, and left.

Runajo waited. It felt like forever before Sunjai strode into the room, her smile just as obnoxious as ever.

"So I hear you finally need someone's help," she said. "I'll remind you that when *I* asked for help, you told me we were all going to die."

"Did Inyaan tell you anything?" asked Runajo, straightening up.

Sunjai crossed her arms. "Maybe. But I wasn't listening too closely. It was time for me to give her the daily dose of healing creams."

Runajo felt a sick pang as she remembered the half-healed cuts on Inyaan's arms.

"You think she was better off in ascetic seclusion?" she asked.

"At least her brother wasn't there," said Sunjai, her voice low. "And I think you had no right to do as you willed with her, simply because you fancied it."

It was true, wasn't it? Runajo had wanted to help Inyaan, so she had simply done as she pleased, without a thought for the consequences. The same as she had done with Juliet.

"Well, right *now* what I fancy is keeping the city alive," said Runajo. "And stopping Lord Ineo's sacrifices."

Sunjai's mouth flattened. "I still haven't agreed to help you."

"You will," said Runajo, "because Inyaan sent you."

But then she remembered Sunjai saying, back in the Cloister, *We're comrades, aren't we?*

There had been a time when Sunjai thought they were friends, or something like it. Runajo hadn't ever realized it until it was too late, just like she hadn't realized . . . anything, it seemed.

She never learned, until she had hurt people.

"I'm sorry," she said. The words were soft, but still hurt in her throat. "I was never kind to you or Inyaan. And I'm sorry."

Sunjai rolled a shoulder. "You don't need to be kind to *me*." She paused. "I'm going to help you, but I want to know: why did you get yourself thrown out for that Catresou girl?"

Runajo wasn't sure how she could even begin to explain that.

"Why did *you* spend all your time following after Inyaan and wiping her tears?"

It was something she had actually wondered about. Once, she had thought Sunjai just wanted the prestige of being the only friend of the Exalted's younger sister, but she knew now that she had been wrong.

"She's the blood of the gods," said Sunjai, deadpan. "I owe her all that and more."

Runajo rolled her eyes. "No, I mean, truthfully. Can you even explain why she's your friend?"

"She's the blood of the gods," Sunjai repeated, and suddenly Runajo realized that her voice was quiet not with deadpan sarcasm but absolute sincerity. "She deserves all my loyalty and worship. But she's kind enough to call me her friend."

"You . . . believe in the gods," said Runajo.

Mahyanai didn't believe in the gods. Everybody knew that. It was something they were all proud of: that while the rest of the world might cringe and beg before imaginary masters, might require the dream of a second life in order to face death, the Mahyanai were brave enough to bear the truth.

"Why do you think I joined the Sisterhood? The pretty clothes?" Sunjai's voice was bitterer than Runajo had ever heard it. "Our people are parasites who mock the holy rites that shelter them. I wanted to make recompense. To please the gods with my penance. I'd pour out every drop of blood in my body for that."

Runajo's skin crawled. Because while she didn't care what Sunjai chose to do with her own blood—if she believed in the nine gods, if she longed for penance, then she believed the sacrifices were holy. She didn't think they were a tragic necessity, she thought it was *holy* and *right* when the High Priestess cut someone's throat before the face of Ihom.

And then she realized: this was why Sunjai was going to help her.

"Then," she said, "you surely don't like that Lord Ineo has taken the sacrifices into his own hands."

Sunjai made a noise of disgust deep in her throat. "I'd like to see *him* led out to pollute the sacrifices with his unwilling blood."

"Good," said Runajo. "Because I know how to make it stop. Do you want to help?"

Sunjai looked her up and down, and her mouth curved up as she said, "Yes."

13

ONE DAY LEFT.

Juliet woke, and remembered instantly: the next day, the sacrifices would begin. Her people would die and she would safeguard their slaughter, so the rest of Viyara could live.

Runajo wasn't there in the bedroom. She was never there now, and Juliet reminded herself that it didn't matter if she never slept, because she was only paying for her own choices.

At the breakfast table, Juliet forced herself to eat, barely noticing what, until Arajo burst into the room and sat down beside her.

"Just look at that," she said, dropping a little square of paper on the table, and yawned.

Juliet stared. Two lines were written on it, in rather wobbly script:

I saw the stars through the window,
But they were not as lovely as you.

"What is it?" she asked.

"Karu," said Arajo, as if Juliet should know who that was. "He was delightful in bed, but that poem? That *handwriting*? Ugh."

Juliet's mind was still clogged with the sacrifice. It took her a moment to put together the slip of paper—so like the ones Romeo had given her—and Arajo's words, and realize that this was a morning-after poem.

She knew what the Mahyanai permitted their women to do, but it still sent a hot flush crawling across her face.

Arajo giggled. "Of course, I *say* that, but I'm not too good for him. I'll send him a reply and pretend his poem was lovely. I just had to tell someone first." Then she looked at Juliet. "What, you're blushing? You're not a virgin either, you know."

Juliet couldn't help flinching at the word *virgin*. That remark would have started a duel among her own people.

"And I've heard Romeo was terrible at poetry too," Arajo went on, "so I hope he made up for it in other ways."

"Don't," Juliet snapped. "Don't talk about him that way. He was my husband."

Arajo gave her a pitying look. "Husband, lover, truest of all true loves. You do realize it doesn't matter anymore? You're not still among those monsters who'd cast you out just for kissing him."

They would have. There probably was not one Catresou who would have forgiven Juliet for kissing Romeo, let alone taking him to her bed in a ceremony they would not have acknowledged as marriage.

They were still *her people*.

And she was going to help kill them tomorrow.

"I'm sorry," said Arajo, the laughter melting from her face. "You loved him and he's dead, and—and I'm the worst. I think a thing, and I can't help saying it. Ask anyone."

She was genuinely sorry. That was the worst part. Arajo didn't want to hurt Juliet. She just couldn't imagine that Juliet having to slaughter her own people might *hurt*.

The Master Necromancer didn't want them to stop the sacrifices.

Romeo could not believe that the Catresou were going to accept it.

"There will be a better revenge soon," said Meros. "When he has gained his full power, he will drive the Mahyanai from their homes and slaughter them as they meant to slaughter us."

But meanwhile, twenty of the Catresou prisoners would be killed, and they would have no Catresou burial. Romeo was furious at the injustice of it, and he wasn't even one of them. He was baffled when he saw the other Catresou lords nod in agreement.

"It's not right," said Romeo. "They'll burn the bodies—"

"Paris," said Meros, "silence him."

The slap across Romeo's face was precise, stinging; the next moment, Paris's cold hands were wrapped over his mouth, muffling him.

Romeo couldn't help begging silently, *Paris, please*—but he knew that Paris couldn't hear him. The bond had been broken when Paris died.

"Don't imagine that obeying our orders once gives you the right to tell us what to do," said Meros, and Romeo felt like a fool. He'd only made sure that the other Catresou would want to obey Meros so they could spite the enemy in their midst.

But later that day, when he was cleaning weapons under supervision, Gavarin said to him, "What's it to you, if our people don't get buried?"

"Don't you need it to rest?" said Romeo.

"Don't tell me you believe in the Paths of Light."

"No," said Romeo. "But Juliet did. You do. And I swore to serve your people."

"What does your obedience mean to you?" asked Gavarin.

Romeo went still, his hands halted on polishing the blade. "What do you mean?"

"We Catresou, we live under obedience. To the Lord Catresou, but to *zoura* first of all. And our lord has told us to obey the Master Necromancer and leave our people to die. Some of us would rather obey *zoura*. How about you?"

If he disobeyed Meros's orders even once, he would be killed.

Romeo had no doubt of that, and he was not unafraid. Even now, after everything, he did not want to die.

He also didn't want any more Catresou to die while he could do anything to stop it.

"Yes," he said.

Half a day left.

"Supervising sacrifices is not my usual duty," said the sub-captain to Lord Ineo. She was a tall woman; her white-gold hair wrapped around her head in a six-strand braid, marking her as not just an Old Viyaran but an aristocrat.

"Nothing is usual about this situation," said Lord Ineo. "And who better than you? After all, you helped bring the Catresou necromancers down to begin with. The Exalted greatly desires you to have this honor."

The subcaptain tilted her head slightly and regarded him. She didn't seem the least bit impressed by his status as the Exalted's right hand. Juliet would have liked for her that, if she hadn't been preparing to assist in murder.

"I'm told you have an extra weapon for me," said the subcap-tain, her gaze sliding beyond Lord Ineo to Juliet and Runajo.

"Several. I'm sending eight of our best guards, and also the Juliet." Lord Ineo reached back, laid his fingertips on Juliet's shoulder, and drew her forward. "Juliet, this is Subcaptain Xu. She will command all the guards at the sacrifice, including you."

"Is this also the will of the Exalted?" asked Xu, studying Juliet the way outsiders always did: like an exotic artifact.

Juliet stared back at her. The woman at least met her eyes, which was more than many did.

"Yes," said Lord Ineo, proving that he didn't lack for either nerve or influence. "We must show the city that the Catresou will never be a threat again."

"The Exalted is wise and glorious," said Xu. "But I'd prefer to command soldiers who follow orders."

"That won't be a problem," said Lord Ineo. "She can't disobey her Guardian, and Runajo will command her to obey *you*."

"We both saw that girl kill two men," said Xu, "one of them against orders and the other her own father."

Juliet was aware of Runajo flinching behind her. But her own heart didn't skip a beat. She'd lived with that memory every day: the moment she'd looked in her father's eyes and felt the power of his blood guilt seize her. The moment after, when her hands inevitably gripped his head and snapped his neck. She'd remembered it so often, she no longer flinched from it.

Of all the blood on her hands, her father's was not the worst. At least he had actually been guilty.

So Xu was the subcaptain who had been there on that terrible morning. Juliet remembered that she had protested Lord Ineo seizing a Juliet for himself and claiming the old Catresou right of swift vengeance. She might be as vile and murderous as all the

Old Viyarans, but at least she cared for the Accords.

"Keep the Mahyanai guards alive," said Juliet, "and I won't be a problem. I don't need to avenge any of *your* blood."

Xu's eyebrows rose; then one side of her mouth turned up slightly, as if reluctantly pleased. "I'll see what I can do."

He was having trouble with his name. Some days he knew it, but not today.

He could remember hearing somebody say it. Somebody calling it, voice alight with desperation.

That boy. The one he had seen when he killed the traitor family. There had been a speech that his master wanted him to deliver.

Had he killed that boy, or left him alive? He could remember seeing him among the main body of the Catresou, but he now he couldn't remember if that had happened before or after.

The question bothered him more than it should have. Whatever he had done, it had been his master's will. He told himself he could be sure of that, and that was all he needed to know. That was the only real thing.

Now his orders were to guard the Little Lady, and stop her if she tried to harm herself again. His master had been very firm about that, as if it were likely to happen. But she had sat in the chair for hours, not a single golden curl moving.

He thought he understood what drove her. Sometimes the

cold weight of his flesh and blood and bones was almost too much, pressing him down with the helpless desire to be forever still. If he had thought that tearing open his veins would make that happen, maybe he would try it too.

No, he *wouldn't*, he *couldn't*, his master wouldn't want it. Nothing was real and nothing mattered except for making his master happy, and he couldn't understand why the Little Lady would ever try to displease him.

His hands were shaking, his dead heart frantically pumping.

The doorknob rattled, and he was on his feet in an instant. But it was only his master, come home at last.

"Anything happen?" his master asked.

"No. Nothing."

His master turned to the Little Lady. She finally moved, raising her eyes to meet him; he took her hand and drew her up out of the chair.

"There's going to be a lot of death tomorrow," he said gleefully. "Not at my hands. I'm still going to need a final Night Game. But the Catresou are dying. They're going to pay for everything they did to me and you."

He cupped his hands around her face, and kissed her. She kissed him back greedily, her fingers tangling in his hair, drawing welts down his neck.

"Master," said the dead boy.

His master turned and looked at him. "Yes?" he said.

"What's my name?"

His master shook his head. "You really are stupid."

This was true.

"Your name is Paris. You used to be a Catresou, but now you help me control them. Sometimes you kill them. That's really all you're good for."

"Oh," said Paris.

"And right now, you're going to leave me alone with my lady."

"Yes, master," he said, and was out of the room in the same breath.

But as he walked down the hallway, he found himself thinking about his name again. Trying to patch together the memory, and hear that strange boy's voice as he said, *Paris*.

The night was endless.

Runajo waited in her room, but Juliet never came back to sleep. When the last light had drained from the sky, she panicked and went looking for her, terrified that somehow she had found a way around Runajo's order not to kill herself.

But she was kneeling in the shrine of the dead, staring at the wall where Romeo's name was carved. Runajo saw her through the doorway and didn't dare go inside, didn't dare make a sound.

What right did she have?

She went back to her room alone. She thought, *In seven hours, I will have to give her the order.*

Sunjai hadn't sent any message. The calculations weren't finished. Lord Ineo believed he was doing his best for clan and city.

There was no way out.

She didn't sleep. She tried for a little while, but then she got up again.

Runajo wasn't afraid. Her mind was completely calm. She knew what she had to do, and she knew that she would do it.

But her body was afraid. Waves of cold-hot fear washed through her stomach, and if she sat still for too long, her hands started shaking.

She tried to calm herself. She took deep breaths, and she told herself what she always had when she was afraid: *I can pay any price. I can renounce any love. I can bear any terror.*

But it had been one thing to tell herself that when she was entering the Sisterhood, when she was scheming to risk her life entering the Sunken Library. Now, she wasn't the one paying the price.

Your heart is stone, she told herself savagely, remembering how she had abandoned her mother's dead body to sneak into the Sisterhood before the rest of her family could stop her. *You are pure obsidian inside your chest.*

But it wasn't true. Perhaps it had never been true.

Sometime in the trackless middle of the night, she finally started crying.

She couldn't do this. She couldn't *bear* it.

She wasn't the one who would be holding the sword or the knife; how could she pity herself for this?

All her life, Runajo had been terrified of dying: the silence and the ending. The absolute, utter *nothing*—because she had always believed that her people were right, that her parents had ceased to exist the moment they died and that someday she would too. She remembered lying awake at night, sick with fear over it.

Now she imagined it: her heart slowing. Her breath stopping. Choking, infinite darkness. Nothing, nothing, *nothing* forever, and it still had the power to make her heart flutter in fear.

If she could pretend that she was already dead, that she no longer existed, maybe she could get through this.

When the sky began to pale with approaching dawn, Runajo stood up. She washed and dressed herself as carefully as the morning she had gone to the palace of the Exalted.

The walk to the shrine felt like it took forever. The morning sun seemed very bright; every line of the building, every pebble on the ground scraped at her eyes, razor-sharp. Her mind skittered through every link in the chain of logic that had brought her here, and she couldn't find a break, couldn't find a place where she could have changed things.

Unless she had cut Juliet's throat when the Sisters of Thorn ordered her to. Unless she had dared to walk into the Mouth of Death when she had the chance.

When she opened the door of the shrine, Juliet looked up at

her. She hadn't moved from her place on the floor. Her face was pale, her eyes bloodshot with exhaustion.

There were a thousand things that Runajo wanted to say: *I'm sorry* and *I have to* and *Run, just run, I order you to run away from us all.*

But she opened her mouth and said, "Juliet. I order you to go with Subcaptain Xu, obey her orders for the length of today, and protect the sacrifice."

14

JULIET KNEW THE FIRST PRISONER, when Xu's guards brought him out into the narrow white hallway of the garrison. She wasn't sure that she'd ever exchanged ten words with him, but she knew him at a glance: Amando Mavarinn Catresou. Lord Lutreo's second son, and Paris's older brother.

He would have been a guest at the ceremony where Paris became her Guardian. If she had stayed.

The few times she'd seen him before, he'd always been lurking a step behind his older brother, Meros, smirking at something he'd said. Now he was thinner, and paler, and not smiling at all as the guards dragged him out, hands shackled together.

"You—you'll pay for this!" he shouted, struggling against them. "My brother will see you all punished! He'll tear you to pieces, he'll—" He wrenched against the guard holding him and nearly broke free; then the guard slammed a fist into his gut and he sank to the ground.

"Don't hit him," Xu said sharply. "Why don't you already have the bloodwine here?"

Juliet looked at Amando. Their gazes met, and his eyes were wide with panic, but he found the strength for a sneer.

The compulsion hummed in her spine, cold and unforgiving. She would see him dead. She would not be able to stop it.

"Let me do it," she said, and snatched the flask of drugged wine from the guard who had just come running.

She knelt in front of Amando. "I'll say the prayers for you," she whispered. "I promise. Just drink this and it won't hurt."

"Traitor," he panted. "You're not one of us. You—"

"Enough," said Xu. With one hand, she gripped his head by the hair and tilted it back; with the other, she pinched his nose shut. Juliet poured the wine; Amando struggled and choked, but in the end he had to drink it.

"Hate you," he said when they released him, his voice already starting to slur. In another minute he was completely docile, his pupils huge, his mouth slack. The guards hauled him to his feet and he went obediently, swaying but not struggling.

"Bring out the next one," said Xu.

One by one, nineteen more prisoners were brought out— women as well as men, because the Mahyanai had no honor, of every age from barely adult to doddering on their feet with the weight of their years. Some fought the bloodwine like Amando; others clutched at the cup and gulped it down, desperate to escape the pain that waited for them.

All became the same: wide-eyed, wordless, stumbling, and obedient. Like dumb animals led to slaughter. Fury strangled Juliet, because this was what the rulers of Viyara did, what they thought holy: human lives reduced to cheap fodder for the walls.

"Good," said Xu, when all twenty prisoners had been drugged. "Let's get this over with."

She didn't sound like she thought she was preparing for a sacred rite, but Juliet doubted the subcaptain had any real guilt. She was clearly Old Viyaran through and through; she probably just hated Lord Ineo's meddling.

"What are your orders?" she asked, under her breath.

Xu looked her up and down. "Guard the sacrifice and don't run mad."

Juliet had been to the Great Offering twice a year as long as she could remember. It was required of all who held rank in the three high houses—Mahyanai, Catresou, and Old Viyaran. They came, and they took turns bringing the victim for sacrifice.

The Great Offering was a festival. It was held in the grand court at the center of the Upper City; it was begun with songs and dancing, attended by vast crowds. Many held feasts afterward, though the Catresou never did.

This sacrifice was still held in the grand court, where the vast obsidian face of the god Ihom grew out of the wall, looming over a dais of white stone. There was still a crowd that had gathered to watch.

But it was no festival. There was no singing, no dancing, no ranks of white-robed Sisters of Thorn. Only three Sisters had come, with red bands on their sleeves and knives in their hands. The Exalted was not there, and neither was Lord Ineo; and of course, there were no Catresou at all.

Except Juliet.

And the prisoners.

Amando was first in line, and Juliet walked beside him. He stumbled as they led him forward, and nearly fell; the guards had to hold him up. His eyes were still wide and sightless with the drugs. Juliet tried to comfort herself that at least he wouldn't suffer.

It was no comfort.

Go swiftly and in gladness.

She breathed the words, barely moving her lips, barely more than thinking them. Amando wouldn't hear the prayer anyway; the important thing was that it be said. That in the middle of this obscene ritual, one thing be done right.

Forget not thy name, in all the dark places.

The altar was ten steps away. Then nine. The prisoners were not afraid, but Juliet was: with every step, the cold dread hung heavier in her stomach, and her heart pounded with the need to run, run, run—

But Runajo's orders sang coldly in her blood, driving her toward the altar.

Forget not those who have walked before thee.

Eight steps away.

She could see sunlight glinting on the knife.

Seven. Six. Five.

Heed not the nameless, who crawl and weep—

And that was when the Catresou attacked.

She would have seen it earlier if she hadn't been staring at the Sister's knife. Instead, she didn't notice until they burst out of the crowd, swords glinting. And she felt one heartbeat of hope as she thought both, *That's a bad strategy* and *Maybe they can do it anyway.*

Then the whole world narrowed down to Runajo's order: *Protect the sacrifice.*

Juliet seized Amando by the arm, hauled him the last few steps, *four-three-two-one*, and flung him onto the altar all in one motion, before vaulting it to stand sword out on the other side.

"Kill him now!" she yelled at the Sisters, and then two of the Catresou were upon her with swords. They were both tall, well-muscled men, and they moved with the grace and confidence of those who had survived serious duels.

But they weren't the Juliet.

It took her only moments to drop them.

She heard shouts, and at the edge of her vision she saw bright white lines flare across the ground. She knew that meant the Sister had managed to cut Amando's throat, but there was no time to think about it. She was already turning to meet the next opponent.

There was blood on his sword, but she didn't feel the awful drive to kill him; if his last opponent had been one of the Mahyanai guards, he hadn't killed him.

But her heart still pounded against her ribs. Because it was the boy she had fought on the night of the Catresou raid. She knew him instantly from the line of his jaw, the way he held his sword, and her heart wrenched within her because here in the sunlight, he looked so like Romeo, who was dead and never returning to her.

It felt like a mockery of the dead.

She had to unmask him.

This time when she attacked, she was actually trying to win. But he was just as good as she remembered, maybe even better, and though she drove him back, he was still countering all her strokes. He didn't have her strength or speed, but he had a terrifying intuition for how she would move.

As if he knew her, as Romeo had known her.

Traceries of light flared along the ground again—another successful sacrifice—but Juliet didn't care about anything now except stopping this treacherous boy. With a snarl, she lunged forward, and this time she got inside his defense, pressed her sword to his throat.

He went still. She was close enough, she could see his eyes widen through the slits in his mask.

Then she ripped the mask from his face.

The world seemed to stop.

Romeo looked back at her. Romeo, who was dead, who was not Catresou, who had no desire to fight, *who was dead.*

And could not possibly be standing before her.

"Juliet," he said, and it was his voice. She would know that voice, though they had been parted a thousand years.

"You were dead," she whispered, and for one instant, one horrible instant, she thought that perhaps he was like Paris, raised again as a mindless slave—

But Romeo's eyes were too alive and too haunted as he whispered, "I nearly was. I thought *you* were, and then—when I found out what my people had done, that you wouldn't forgive me—"

"You fool," she said. "You utter and absolute fool."

She lowered her sword from his throat, and one-handed, dragged him into a kiss.

This was the truth at the heart of the world: Romeo was hers and she was his. Even now, with battle around them and blood on their swords, both of them exhausted and panting for breath—when their lips touched, the world melted and reformed around them. There were no clans and no feud. She wasn't a weapon, bloody and guilty. He wasn't her enemy. She was nothing except his, every part of her, and this boy, this dizzying delight, was all *hers*.

For one moment.

Then she tasted blood on his tongue.

Smelled it.

Fire seared through her veins, and it wasn't desire, it was the need to *kill, kill, kill*.

She shoved him back. She was gasping and shaking and she didn't understand, because he hadn't been guilty a moment ago—

Then she saw the Mahyanai guard lying too still on the ground. The blood on Romeo's sword.

He had already dealt the stroke when he kissed her.

Romeo met her eyes.

"Run," she whispered, and then her throat closed up as she fought against the power inside her, fought as she never had before, not even when it had been driving her to kill her own father.

But she was losing. In another heartbeat, she knew that she would move, she would hunt Romeo down and kill him, and she could not, she *would* not survive it—

A blow to her face sent her staggering back. She blinked, saw

Subcaptain Xu, and the next moment Xu was behind her, arms wrapping her neck in a choke hold.

Juliet only had time to think, *She knows how to use a blood choke*, and then the world was dark.

PART II
How with This Rage

15

TWICE NOW JULIET HAD KNELT before Lord Ineo, listening to his fury. But this time, his fury was not directed only at her.

"Do I understand what you are telling me?" His voice was cold and remote. "Rather than subdue these rioters, you subdued one of the guards who might have stopped them?"

"You gave me a guard who was going to run mad at the sight of blood," said Xu. She stood at attention, her back perfectly straight, her voice clipped and contemptuously polite. "Yes. I choked her out. I don't allow any of my guards to disobey orders."

Juliet could still feel Romeo's lips against hers, could still taste the blood that stained him now. If she'd attacked him sooner, before he could hurt that guard—if she'd realized who he was the night of the raid—if he had only *told her* that he was alive—

And now there was no hope.

Romeo had escaped. She had learned that from Runajo. And now that he was far enough away, hidden in the Lower City, the compulsion didn't drive her to search him out and destroy him. But if she ever saw him again—

"If you hadn't stopped her," said Lord Ineo, "she could have destroyed them all."

"She could have." Xu nodded. "I, for one, don't trust battle frenzies created by Catresou magic, and I was the authority in that situation. You are the Exalted's right hand. But you have no rank in the City Guard." She bowed to him. "I'll see you when you fancy another holy sacrifice. Good day, my lord."

She turned crisply and strode out of the room.

Lord Ineo sighed, then looked to Runajo, who stood like a bloodless statue behind Juliet.

"May we go?" asked Runajo, her voice quiet and lifeless.

"There's one other thing first," said Lord Ineo. "People are already talking about the attack. They say that the Juliet kissed one of the attackers. Order her to tell me the truth about this."

"Tell him," said Runajo, again leaving Juliet free.

But this time, she *wanted* to tell him the truth.

She looked him in the eyes, and said, "I did. It was my duty to greet him with a kiss."

Lord Ineo's mouth flattened. "Explain."

"He was Romeo," said Juliet. "My husband. Your son. He's alive. And now it's my duty to kill him, my lord."

For the first time Juliet could remember, Lord Ineo looked actually taken aback. "That's not possible."

"I don't know how he survived," said Juliet. "But he fights for the Catresou now. He killed one of your kinsmen today. So I will assuredly kill him in return. That's what having a Juliet means. Did you think—"

"Stop," said Runajo.

Juliet's mouth snapped shut. She knew taunting him was dangerous and she didn't care; she was shaking from sheer satisfaction that finally, *finally* he was helpless.

Did he think the Juliet was a tool forged only for his convenience? He would find he was wrong.

Lord Ineo looked down at her, his face expressionless.

"I consider it very likely that, in your grief for Romeo, you are confused," he said finally. "And anyone who has joined with the Catresou is no son of mine. Runajo, order her not to tell any of our people this fancy of hers."

"Do not tell anyone that Romeo is alive," Runajo said tonelessly.

"Good," said Lord Ineo. "Runajo, we will talk later." Then he swept out of the room.

They were alone together.

"Is it true?" Runajo waited a moment, then sighed and rubbed at her forehead. "You can speak. Was Romeo really there?"

"Yes," said Juliet.

They were the only truths left in her life: that she loved Romeo, and she was going to kill him.

"I don't understand," said Runajo, and she sounded . . . brittle. Tired, in a way that Juliet had never heard before. "You said he died—"

"I was wrong," said Juliet, and a harsh laugh ripped out of her. "He was alive, all this time. I would have gone to him, if I'd known. I would have cut my way out of the Cloister and waded through a river of blood to find him, and none of this would have happened. *None of it.*"

Everything had nearly been so different, and they'd never known. She had nearly saved Romeo from his fate of dying at her hands, and she'd never *known*.

Runajo drew a shuddering breath. Juliet remembered that she had known Romeo since she was a child, that they had been something like friends. That Runajo, too, had regrets.

But her heart was too exhausted and broken to care. Seeing Romeo had torn open all her wounds, and it was like her first days in the Cloister: dazed with grief, unwilling to believe that everything had gone so terribly wrong, unable to accept surviving it.

"Is this what you wanted?" Juliet demanded. "Was it for *this* that you saved me?"

"No," Runajo whispered, looking haunted, and that only

made Juliet angry, because what right did she have to mourn what she'd done, when she was not the one who suffered for it? When she'd done it for such *little* reasons?

"I always knew you were a murderer," she said. "That you watched the sacrifices every year and called them holy. But I thought at least you wanted to stop the Ruining."

"I do," said Runajo.

'Then *do* it," said Juliet. "Find out where the necromancer hid that key, walk into the land of the dead, and bargain with Death. Make the death of my people worth something. Or is it so delightful bowing to Lord Ineo, that you haven't even tried?"

"I can't," Runajo burst out. "It's too late. The Mouth of Death has dried up."

Juliet had thought herself beyond all shock, all fear. But Runajo's words still stunned her.

"Dried up," she echoed.

Runajo's arms were wrapped miserably around her middle. "There's no way to walk into the land of the dead anymore."

"You could die," said Juliet, fighting the traitorous wish to lay a comforting hand on her shoulder. "I've even got a knife, if you need it."

Runajo snorted. "Who knows in what state the normal dead meet Death? If such a one could bargain to end the Ruining, somebody would have managed it already. All we can do now is try to delay the end."

That wasn't enough. That was *no excuse*. Runajo had never, ever been content with what was possible; what right did she have to give up now?

"If we're all doomed anyway, then what is the point of this slaughter? What is even the point of your sins?" Juliet's hands were shaking, and she clenched them into fists as she leaned forward. "I had to be broken and enslaved before I would help Lord Ineo slaughter people. What's your excuse?"

"I loved you," said Runajo. Her voice was dazed, helpless, as if the words were bleeding out of her. "You were my friend. I wanted you to live."

And Juliet knew that, she *knew* that, it didn't change anything that Runajo was saying it with eyes like the nameless dead—

"If you had ever loved me," she said, "you would have killed me when the Sisters told you to."

Then she turned and fled. She couldn't bear this knowledge any longer, that each breath took her closer to the moment she faced Romeo and slid a sword between his ribs—the moment when the walls died and the last city fell—

"Juliet. Juliet!"

She turned and saw Arajo behind her, eyes wide with concern.

"Are you all right? What happened?"

Juliet swallowed. She could feel Runajo's order around her neck like a noose.

"There was a sacrifice," she said. "The Catresou tried to stop us, and they failed."

Arajo looked unhappy, her eyes darting uneasily side to side before she said, "People are saying—there are these rumors, but I know they can't be true—"

"Yes," said Juliet. "I kissed one."

Arajo must have been expecting that, but she flinched. "Why?" she breathed.

The pure, heartbroken horror in her voice snapped Juliet's anger back to life, and she realized that this order, too, had a way around it.

(Every order did. Every order but the one she most wanted to disobey.)

"If I were allowed to speak, I could say that I kissed my husband. I could say that Romeo is alive, and fights for the Catresou. But Lord Ineo has forbidden me to say that."

Arajo looked dazed. "Why . . . would Romeo do that?"

"He married me," said Juliet. "By your own customs, that made him part of my family."

"But you're one of *us.*"

"Not when I married him," said Juliet. "You had not yet captured me."

"Captured you?" said Arajo, and there was the beginning of anger in her voice now. "You were a slave to those monsters. We *saved* you."

"No," said Juliet, "you took me, because I was a weapon and you wanted to use me. I was a slave to the Catresou too, but at least they never sent me to kill my own kin."

She was shaking with anger; she felt as if she might actually strike Arajo, and she whirled and fled before she could.

How dare she. How *dare* Arajo be upset that Juliet, for one moment, had not pretended to be grateful.

At least the Catresou had acknowledged that the Juliet was a sacrifice, her life and her death forfeit for the good of her people. The Mahyanai wanted to pretend they had done her a favor.

She realized that she was running back to the shrine of the dead. Numbly, she walked inside and knelt where she had so many times before, looking at Romeo's name.

Once, she'd sworn to be more like him. To love his people, to protect them and make peace for them. It had seemed like the only way left for her to honor him.

Once, he had convinced her that if they simply loved each other truly, the world would change to allow that love. Now she knew that was a lie.

And there was no honoring the dead who were not dead.

She leaned her forehead against the wall and wished that she were Romeo. Maybe he would see another path out of this maze. Maybe he would know what to do.

But Juliet was only a weapon. All she knew was blood and obedience.

She had never really known anything else. She had dreamed, once, of being more. Of protecting the whole city, and not just her clan. But now that dream was dust and ashes twice over: she was bound to the Mahyanai, to the will of Lord Ineo. And the city itself was dying, and there was no way left to save it.

Once, Romeo had told her that the Mahyanai thought things beautiful even as they perished. It had seemed a lovely thought, kinder and truer than the Catresou's insistence that only their clan mattered, because only they would live on after death.

Now all Viyara was perishing. Juliet thought of the shimmering white streets of the Upper City, and the twisting, grimy maze of the Lower City. The quiet halls of the Sisterhood, the still sepulcher of her people, the mangy cats ranging wild through the streets.

It was all still beautiful to her.

Suddenly, without meaning to at all, she imagined Runajo's voice: *Well, what are you going to do about it?*

She wanted to give up. She wanted to throw everything away except her love and grief. She wanted to destroy the world that was so cruel and senseless, or else destroy herself so she wouldn't have to face it.

But that was unworthy of a weapon. It was unworthy of the Juliet.

And it was unworthy of the girl that Romeo had loved.

So she would have to kill him. She swallowed, and thought dizzily but very clearly, *I will kill Romeo.*

The world was far too small for him to escape her forever. If she didn't kill herself now to avoid it, then sooner or later she would see him again, and have to kill him. There was no longer any other possible ending to their story.

All she could do was try to make that death worth something.

16

ROMEO HAD BEEN HERE BEFORE, on his knees before the assembled Catresou, ready to die.

It seemed less terrible this time.

He was still afraid. He still, after everything, did not want to die. And he was still a failure: they had saved none of the prisoners at the sacrifice, the Catresou would be hunted even harder for this attack, and if Juliet ever saw him again, she would have to kill him.

But Juliet had kissed him.

She had kissed him, and when he had said that she couldn't forgive him, she had whispered, *You utter and absolute fool.*

He hadn't realized how much the whole world had become suffused with his despair, how the shadows of his grief had clung to everything he saw. But now that he knew Juliet still loved him, that she had impossibly decided to *forgive* him—

Now the whole world had become luminous, shot through with glory and delight. He stared at Meros and the other Catresou lords, these people who had bargained with necromancers and wronged Juliet and were going to kill him—and all he could think was that he loved them, he loved them, because Juliet had loved him first, and this clan was part of her.

"This was all my fault," said Romeo, "I was the one who—"

Gavarin, kneeling beside him, cuffed him lightly in the head. "Don't believe him. I started it. Don't regret a thing."

Meros leaned forward, raising his eyebrows. "You disobeyed the orders of the Lord Catresou. You know the penalty."

Gavarin shrugged. "All of us knew what penalty we'd face."

"But he was trying to save your people!" Romeo protested. "We all were! You can't—"

"You don't understand a thing," said Gavarin.

"I understand that they want to *kill* you for trying to save Catresou lives, when the only reason that nobody else would save them is the orders of the Master Necromancer!" He stared around the room. "Is that really what your clan's become? Servants of a necromancer, who won't save their own kin if it displeases him?"

"*You*," said Meros, "are not even one of us. And you would die for this, but it seems the Master Necromancer wants you. So that's how we'll dispose of you."

Romeo's heart pounded with fear and regret. He wanted to

rage against Meros, against what he was doing to Juliet's beloved people, but he knew that nobody would listen.

So instead he looked at Gavarin and said, "Thank you for letting me help you."

Then Paris seized him by the arm and dragged him away.

It felt appropriate, to go to his death with Paris. He'd been prepared to die when they went to the Night Game together.

Paris had been prepared to kill him, when they first met.

"Juliet said that she forgave me," said Romeo as Paris dragged him down the hallway. "And if she could forgive me, I'm sure she would forgive you too."

He knew that Paris didn't care anymore, but when he was alive, Paris would have cared so much what Juliet thought of him.

Paris would have helped them try to save the Catresou prisoners, when he was alive.

Now Paris was leading him to meet the Master Necromancer. They hadn't left the house, but they were in a small, narrow corridor; Romeo guessed it connected two different buildings.

Had the Master Necromancer, all along, been living next door? Here in one of the rich neighborhoods of the Lower City that people called safe?

If Romeo had known that earlier, he might have been able to free the Catresou. Maybe he still could. If he could just manage to kill the Master Necromancer—well, the Catresou would still be fugitives, and Paris would still be living dead, and Romeo would still be facing death by Juliet's sword, but at least he would have done *something* to keep his promises.

The thought steadied him. He just had to watch for his chance, and take it when he could.

He had nothing to lose by trying. Not anymore.

Then Paris hauled him through another doorway, and Romeo was face-to-face with Makari.

He wore the same simple clothes he had when climbing in Romeo's window. He had the same affectionately exasperated expression on his face as he said, "Well, you have made a mess of things, haven't you?"

"Makari," Romeo said blankly.

He supposed he should have expected this—he'd known that Makari had gone back, after all—but he'd still been imagining that he would be alone when he faced the Master Necromancer.

"I'm going to end this," he said. "I can stop this, if you help me. If we work together."

Then he remembered that Paris was listening, was still a slave, and he gave him a fearful glance. But Paris didn't seem to be paying any attention to him. He was staring at Makari, his face utterly blank of everything except respect, and he said, "Master, did you want me to—"

Makari made a sharp motion with his hand, and Paris fell

silent. He was still looking only at Makari.

"You . . . command him," said Romeo.

Makari heaved a sigh. "I suppose I had to tell you sooner or later. There's little enough time left, anyway."

"You have to set him free," said Romeo. He felt dizzy, numb, like all the world was sliding around him. "You have to set him free *now*."

"I can't, you idiot. If he were free, then he'd be dead."

"*You* got free," said Romeo.

"I'm special," said Makari. "Come with me. I'll take you to meet the Master Necromancer."

He strode forward, out the far door.

Romeo followed him, and halted two steps over the threshold. Outside the door was a hallway, and lining the hallway were men and women. He thought, for a moment, that they were statues—they were so still—but then their heads turned in unison to watch Makari walk down the hallway.

On every face was the same quiet, mindless obedience that filled Paris.

They were all living dead.

Horror seized Romeo and he couldn't move. He was standing in a hallway filled with the living dead, and Makari—

Makari was at the other end. Casually, he looked back and said, "Paris, bring him."

The next moment, Paris had seized Romeo in a grip like iron, and was dragging him down the hallway.

Romeo felt sick. None of this made sense. Makari was living dead himself; he couldn't possibly think that it was good to keep those like him as slaves—perhaps he didn't have a choice—

Perhaps he does. Perhaps he chose.

Romeo wanted to silence the thought, wanted to unthink it, but he had learned too many horrible truths in the past two months, had watched Paris learn too many as well. He couldn't stop himself thinking, *maybe*, and though he wanted to flee and forget everything, he let Paris drag him after Makari because he needed to know.

"I thought for quite a while about how I should introduce you to her," Makari said conversationally, as they turned the corner. "I mean, for a long time, I didn't plan to introduce you at all. I just meant for you to die along with everyone else. Or not die, however you want to define it."

"Who?" Romeo asked, his throat dry and his heart beating fast.

"But you know what?" Makari stopped before a door and turned back. He smiled, just the same wry smile that Romeo remembered, and ruffled his hair. "I'm glad I met you. Come in."

He opened the door.

Inside was a small sitting room, and seated on a chair with cushions was a short, pale girl with golden curls.

Romeo knew her instantly. He had never seen her so closely

with his own eyes, but Paris had been so indignant that the image had passed clearly through the bond: the living dead girl, kept in a glass cage in Lord Catresou's secret laboratory.

"Is *she* the Master Necromancer?" asked Romeo.

Makari laughed. "Of course not."

"Then who is she?"

"When they kept her as a prisoner, the Catresou called her the Little Lady," said Makari. He walked forward, then dropped to his knees before her. "In truth, she's *my* lady and always was." His fingers caressed the girl's cheek. She leaned forward—her eyes still blank—and kissed him.

Despite all the terrifying, strange things that Romeo had seen in the last few minutes, this was what seemed most unsettling: the worshipful delight on Makari's face as he looked at the girl. A thousand times over, Makari had rolled his eyes and muttered about *those fools who think they love*. Romeo had always believed it was part of who he was, to sneer at love and those who fell in love—and if that had always been a lie—

"Makari," he said, *"what is going on?"*

Makari swung his head back to give him a patient look. "You really haven't figured it out by now?" He stood. *"I'm* the Master Necromancer. This is my lady, for whom I am going to tear down the gates of death. And you are lucky enough to be my friend."

It felt like there was ice spreading through Romeo's stomach, through his lungs and his fingers and his whole body. He knew what Makari was saying. On some level, he'd known it since Paris called him *master*. But he just couldn't believe—

"No," he said. "You wouldn't."

"I don't know why you're so shocked," said Makari. "Your friend Justiran's a necromancer too. Or was. Paris, don't let him leave the room. I've got a story to tell."

Paris's hand landed on Romeo's shoulder again. Romeo shuddered at the steady, implacable grip.

He suddenly remembered how shattered Paris had been, when he learned that the old Lord Catresou was conspiring with necromancers. Romeo had pitied him, but not really understood that pain. Had even thought him foolish for being so desperate to deny it.

Now he understood.

"I was once a love-struck young idiot like you," said Makari. "I was sixteen years old and I lost my heart to a Catresou girl. That clan hasn't improved in a hundred years, I assure you."

"A hundred years?" Romeo said blankly.

"Oh," said Makari, his mouth slicing up into a grin, "didn't I mention it? This was before the Ruining. But not before the Catresou became utterly insufferable. They forbade me from meeting her, of course. I didn't intend to listen. I had an entire plan for us to flee together, to a place where neither of our clans could bother us. But then *her own father*—your dear friend Justiran—told her that I was dead. And she killed herself."

Slowly, absently, the Little Lady raised her hand to rub at the base of her throat. Makari caught the hand and kissed it.

"From the way he carried on, you'd think no one in the world had been bereaved before," Makari continued, his voice thick with disgust. "And because he was a Catresou, he thought he could master death. We made an alliance, the two of us, and for five years stole ancient books and crossed the world looking for answers. Then we raised her back to life. And the Ruining started."

The words were too huge, too horrible to comprehend. Romeo stared at Makari, and he tried to think of a response—a question—he desperately tried to convince himself that Makari was lying under orders, just like Paris.

But Makari looked like *himself*, as Paris never had.

"How did you cause the Ruining?" Romeo finally asked.

"Well, if you see Justiran again before I kill him, he can explain the theory. I don't care. Do you know what it's like, to see the girl you love open her eyes after five years of death, and immediately beg to die again?" Makari's smile was like an open wound. "The dead want to stay dead. It's the only thing they wish. But that first necromancy, the one that split the world open? It was too strong. She couldn't die again. Until at last she threw herself into a furnace, and we thought that was the end of her."

Very gently, Makari laid a hand on the top of the Little Lady's head and stroked her hair. She didn't move.

"Justiran and I both ended up in Viyara, because though it's hard for us to die now, the world outside is not a pleasant place. I killed myself sometimes, but I never could find my lady in the land of the dead, so I always came back. I thought it was enough to wait for the end, and watch the Catresou slowly die. But twenty years ago, do you know what I discovered? She didn't die, not even in the furnace. The Catresou found her and brought her with them, and kept her as an *interesting artifact*."

"And that's why you tried to open the gates of death," said Romeo, finally understanding.

"She can't find peace in the living world," said Makari. "And she can't leave it. But if I open the gates of death and make this the land of the dead as well, then perhaps she'll finally smile again. For Juliet, would you do anything less?"

Romeo thought of Juliet, of the look in her eyes when she talked about justice, about her ferocious courage and dedication.

"I would do even more," he said. "But not this."

"Then you're not as in love as you fancy yourself. Don't worry, I've enough love for the whole world."

"Makari, this is *wrong*," Romeo burst out. "All those people—how could you do that? And . . . wait, if you only decided to end the world twenty years ago, why were you running the Night Game before that?"

"Well, it was really amusing," said Makari. "Especially when the Catresou got desperate enough to defile themselves with my magic."

Romeo thought of Vai, her grief for her family and her brother. He thought of the girl he and Paris had met in the Lower City, keeping her father as a revenant in her room because she hoped the Night Game might save him. He thought of the people he'd seen drugged and locked in cages, as they waited to be sacrifices for the Master Necromancer.

He could understand—not forgive, but he could *understand* wanting revenge on the whole clan that had killed his beloved. He couldn't understand spreading that revenge to the whole world.

"Why are you even telling me this?" he asked quietly.

"Because you're my friend," said Makari. "And I want you there with me, after the end of all things. I told the Catresou a lot of lies when I got their help, but one part of it was true. Whoever opens the gates of death *will* have power afterward. We can be like a family together."

Romeo remembered sobbing as Makari had died in his arms. He didn't quite understand why he had no tears now, but one thing was exactly the same: this feeling that the entire universe was ripping apart, and reforming itself into something incomprehensible.

But he'd already seen his world torn to pieces several times over. He knew how to bear it.

"I'm going to stop you," he said.

Makari sighed.

"Paris," he said, "guard Romeo. If he tries to escape, kill him." Then he shrugged at Romeo. "Sorry, but rest assured that I *will* raise you promptly."

Romeo's heart was pounding against his ribs. "Then why not do it already? You know I'll be more obedient."

"Mm, yes," Makari allowed. "But honestly, it's depressing when everyone in the house is a mindless slave."

"If you won't kill me now," said Romeo, "it's because you know in your heart that this is wrong. It's because you don't want to kill and enslave more than you must, and you don't *need* to—"

Makari flicked two fingers at his forehead. "Which one of us has been through the Ruining and the collapse of a whole world, you or me? I assure you, I know what it takes to accomplish my will."

"I can't let you do this," said Romeo.

"You really don't have a choice, do you? But don't worry. I will give you Juliet, when I'm done using her as a key and everything is over. The four of us will be together, forever." He ruffled Romeo's hair. "Won't that be nice?"

17

RUNAJO WAS NOT AFRAID.

She didn't *feel* much of anything, not in her heart, not since Juliet had come back from the Great Offering two days ago.

But her body didn't seem to agree. Nauseous, fear-like waves passed through her stomach as she knelt at the table, flipping through another old Catresou book.

There's a solution, she told herself. *There has to be a way to set Juliet free.*

Sunjai and Inyaan were still working on the calculations for the new walls. Between the three of them, they would surely have an answer soon. So right now, the real problem was Juliet being bound to kill Romeo the next time she saw him, and likely to die when Runajo walked into Death.

Somebody knocked on the door of the study.

"Yes?" Runajo called out.

The door opened, and a serving girl peeked in. "Lord Ineo wants to see you."

"Of course," said Runajo, rising. Another fear-like pang cramped her stomach, and she told herself that it might not be anything terrible. There were many reasons that Lord Ineo might want to talk to her.

But she wasn't surprised when he handed her a cup of tea and said, "I have word from the High Priestess. The sacrifices have helped, but not enough."

Runajo gulped a mouthful, and felt the too-hot liquid slide down her throat.

"Maybe they weren't offered properly," she said.

"You doubt your own Sisters?" Lord Ineo raised his eyebrows.

"They're not my Sisters anymore," said Runajo. "Surely by now, I have proved myself a Mahyanai?"

She could almost hear Juliet saying, *Of course, because you're a murderer.*

"Your loyalty is admirable," Lord Ineo said dryly. "What I wonder at is your effectiveness."

Runajo's heart thumped. "I will do whatever you command of me."

"I commanded you to make sure the Juliet protected the sacrifice." His voice remained gentle, but Runajo still had to repress a flinch.

"She did. All twenty prisoners died, and several of the attackers as well." Runajo set the cup down, keeping her voice calm but determined. "And you cannot blame me for giving her no orders about Romeo. We all thought him dead."

"He *is* dead," said Lord Ineo, and Runajo couldn't help her shoulders hunching a little as she remembered the grief twisting Juliet's face.

Remembered, too, the earnest boy who had badgered her with poems but who had also—long ago—been the closest thing she had to a friend.

"What do you want of me?" she asked.

"An obedient Juliet," said Lord Ineo.

"I already promised you that." And she had never, in her whole life, regretted anything so much.

"There's to be another sacrifice tomorrow," said Lord Ineo. "Just two prisoners, but we're going to keep offering as many each week. The High Priestess says that will be optimal for maintaining the strength of the walls."

The High Priestess had a whole Cloister of Sisters to calculate the sacred mathematics for her. Runajo just had Sunjai and Inyaan and her own wits, and it wasn't enough. She still believed they could solve the problem—but not before the next day. Not before she had to give Juliet the order to assist again in the slaughter of her people.

If you had ever loved me, you would have killed me.

Runajo looked up at Lord Ineo and said, "She will be obedient. I promise."

The next morning, she found Juliet in one of the courtyards, practicing sword work alone. Runajo wondered why that other girl—Arajo, had her name been?—was not there with her, and then put the thought aside. She didn't have the right to wonder.

Juliet lowered her sword as Runajo approached. She turned to face her, but kept her eyes meekly fixed on the floor.

She knew already why Runajo was there. The news had been flying through the clan the night before.

"Juliet, I order you to go with Subcaptain Xu, obey her orders for the length of today, and protect the sacrifice."

The words felt like dust and ash in Runajo's throat. But she had to say them. Lord Ineo was going to have Juliet killed if she didn't. And she knew, she *knew* this was wrong. But she didn't have anything left, except this desperate attempt to keep the girl who had once been her friend alive.

Juliet didn't look up. She didn't give Runajo one single glance as she walked away.

Runajo went back to her room. She took out the papers on which she had worked on her share of the equations for the new walls. She tried to check them over, but her mind felt numb and the calculations were dead on the page.

Sunjai hadn't sent word yet. Maybe she had abandoned the

project. Maybe Runajo was all alone in her quest—and she'd been like that before. She remembered when facing down the entire Sisterhood had only made her more determined.

But she couldn't remember how to be that girl anymore. She tried to imagine being that strong and that sure, feeling anything except this dull, miserable weight inside her chest, and she couldn't.

Runajo stared at the scribbles on the paper and thought, *Why am I even fighting?*

She had wanted to save Juliet, and she had only destroyed her. She had wanted to save Viyara, and she'd found it was only a charnel house of blood and guilt. She had wanted, once, to understand the secret truth of the world. And the only truth she'd found was that everything existed only by murder, and that she didn't care as much as she thought she would.

If Viyara fell to the Ruining, if they all died now, what did it even matter? In another year they would have all killed each other anyway.

Runajo stood and walked numbly to the little garden outside her room.

It was a beautiful place; she could recognize that. Carp glittered in the murky green depths of the pond. Rushes bent in the breeze. A dragonfly hummed as it hovered near the surface of the water. The warm, humid air smelled of growing things and hot water on stone.

A long time ago—when she was just a child, before anyone she knew had died, before she'd known the world was dying—Runajo had sat in her family's garden and watched the light and the shadows dance beneath the trees. The sky had dazzled blue above her, the cool breeze had caressed her face, and for one moment she'd felt as if the world was peeling open, and she could glimpse its secret heart.

This garden now was just as beautiful. But beauty no longer seemed to have any meaning.

Runajo knelt by the edge of the pond. Her eyes stung and her throat ached. She thought that maybe all her life, she'd been trying to catch at the beauty she'd seen on that long-ago morning: by joining the Sisterhood, by stopping the Ruining, by saving Juliet. She'd thought she was so clever and so brave every time, but all she'd ever done was ruin everything that she grasped at, and learn she was just as weak and foolish as every other person in the world.

She thought, *I don't want to do this anymore.*

She thought, *I don't want to* be *this anymore.*

But there was no way out, and nobody to help her.

The sun beat down on her hair. The air was a warm weight on her shoulders. Before her, the dragonfly droned lazily as it wove between the rushes, its dark body shimmering iridescently in the sunlight.

And the world changed.

The shapes and colors, sounds and smells, were all exactly the same. But Runajo experienced a sudden conviction that every splash of a carp's tail, every bright-green hue of the rushes, was not itself only, but a word spoken into silence. A bell tolling the night hours, or the string of a lute plucked with urgent intent.

Sunlight drenched her, thick as honey, and the warm air in her lungs was like wine. Runajo's eyes were watering in the brightness, or maybe she was actually crying, because she felt absurdly small and worthless of the dazzlement around her.

Worthless, yet comforted. The world had been dying for a hundred years, torn apart by deadly magic and human foolishness. The city was tearing itself apart now, festering with cruelty and pride and revenge. Runajo and Juliet tore each other to pieces at every opportunity.

And yet, and still, the dragonfly's giant, bubble-shaped eyes glittered in the sunlight. It droned low over the water, then landed on a water violet, and the long stalk of the flower bowed under its weight. Something fathomless and inexhaustible welled up through the cracks of the world, drenching it with glory and making it more than she could ever destroy or create or even, perhaps, comprehend.

Runajo closed her eyes. Sunlight glowed red through her eyelids. For a trackless time, she was still.

Then she thought, *I can't fix this.*

Later—perhaps very soon—she would despair over that again.

But here, now, the thought couldn't hurt her. She could imagine she was like Viyara, like the whole world, cracked and ruined and broken, but still able to shelter the jewel-like glitter of a dragonfly.

She could believe that any least, little thing she might do to amend that breaking was worth it.

And when she stopped thinking of everything she'd done wrong, it was very clear. There was only one thing that she could and must do.

Juliet returned in the late afternoon. She stood before Lord Ineo, her head obediently bowed, as Subcaptain Xu reported that the sacrifice had been accomplished and the fugitive Catresou hadn't even tried to attack.

Lord Ineo smiled and said, "Well done."

"I am pleased to serve the Exalted," Subcaptain Xu had said with the barest and most regal of nods, and left.

Runajo was silent. But after Lord Ineo had dismissed them, she told Juliet, "Come with me."

And silently, Juliet followed her, back to her bedroom.

Runajo realized that her heart was beating very quickly. That she was afraid. Because she had no idea what would happen next. This might be the last moment she was alive. Or that *Juliet* was alive.

There were a thousand things she wanted to say first. But

most of them were some form of *I'm sorry*, and she no longer had any right to say that.

So she turned to face Juliet, who still was not meeting her eyes, and said the words that she had shamefully held back for so long.

"Juliet," she said. "I release you from all the orders I ever gave you."

18

FREEDOM FELT LIKE DEATH: A vast, dark emptiness all around her, and the whispering of a thousand voices. Juliet stared at Runajo. She thought *murderer* and *traitor*—and, yes, she remembered *friend*.

She thought, *My people are dead because of her,* and also, *She saved my life.*

"What are you doing?" she asked, her voice low and unsteady.

Runajo's chin lifted slightly. "Setting you free," she said. "As much as I can."

Juliet didn't know what this glittering, white-hot feeling was.

"Why," she said breathlessly, and then her voice found strength and the words ripped out of her, *"why didn't you do that earlier?"*

She realized that the feeling was rage, that she had seized

Runajo by the shoulders and pressed her against the wall.

"Now you're going to set me free?" she demanded. "When my people are destroyed, and I am a murderer, and Romeo must die by my hand? Now, when all the world is doomed and I'm *one* of you?"

Runajo said nothing. She was very pale, her lips pressed together, and she stared over Juliet's shoulder at nothing.

Juliet wondered, *Does she expect me to kill her now?*

Runajo deserved to die. It was something Juliet had thought often enough, from the first day they'd met. But this was the first time she'd had the power to do it—because while the bond still existed, she felt sure that Runajo would give no order to stop if Juliet decided to kill her.

If she chose to be the killer that everyone wanted to make her.

Juliet let go of Runajo and stepped back, trying to collect her scattered wits. She was still the Mahyanai's Juliet. She still could never return to her people, and she was still bound to kill Romeo as soon as she saw him.

The world was still dying, and there was nothing she could do to stop it.

Her freedom meant nothing except that she might be able to kill herself before killing again, and that thought was so bitter that for a moment it threatened to swallow her whole.

Then she thought: *if there is nothing I can do, then I may do as I wish.*

And she wished for a thousand things, but there was one she might still possibly accomplish: to send Romeo a letter. To tell him, before one of them died, the ten thousand ways she still loved him.

She had no idea where he was hiding. But she knew of somebody who might.

"There's an apothecary in the Lower City," she said. "A friend of Romeo's. I need to talk with him, which means I need your help."

"To talk with him," Runajo echoed. There was a dazed look on her face.

"No, I need your help getting out of here," said Juliet. "And if I run into Romeo in the Lower City, I need you to give me orders. It won't stop me for long, but it might give him a chance to run."

Runajo stared at her.

"Will you help?" Juliet asked.

She didn't say, *You owe me*. She didn't say, *I can make you*. They both knew that. And besides—

Juliet realized that her whole body was tensed like at the start of a fight. Her heart was pounding against her ribs. She could tell herself that she only wanted this plan to work, but she knew that was a lie.

Runajo had enslaved her and destroyed her clan. Juliet had sworn a vow never to forgive her. She didn't intend to break her word.

And yet she desperately wanted Runajo to help her willingly.

"Yes," said Runajo.

The last time Juliet had gone to the Lower City, she had been with Romeo. He had kissed her as they sat on the rooftops together, and he had asked her to marry him.

It was very different now, and not just because Runajo walked silently at her side. The streets were the same seething, chattering chaos of people. The buildings were the same maze of dead stone, no glowing traceries lit by the power of the city, painted bright colors or covered in grime or both.

But there was a tension now to the people as they bustled through the streets. There were City Guards standing at corners. When a corpse wagon rolled past, people shrank away from it.

The Lower City was afraid. Lord Ineo, with all his sacrifices, couldn't stop the dead from rising faster than they ever had before, and people were *afraid*.

They were also, possibly, starting to resent those sacrifices. Juliet had seen some of the looks that people gave Runajo, who might be wearing a threadbare tunic she had stolen from the laundry, but who still had clearly Mahyanai features and the briar tattoo of the Sisterhood.

Suddenly, above the din of the crowd, Juliet heard the strumming of a lute, and a voice raised in song. It was a street musician, sitting on a corner and singing to passersby for coins.

"O mistress mine, where are you roaming?
O, stay and hear, your true love's coming,
That can sing both high and low:
Trip no further, pretty sweeting;
Journeys end in lovers meeting,
Every wise man's son doth know."

For a moment, she couldn't move. Her throat ached. She had heard another musician sing this song once, but she hadn't been able to make out the words, and Romeo had sung them to her.

"What is love? 'Tis not hereafter;
Present mirth hath present laughter;
What's to come is still unsure.
In delay there lies no plenty,
Then come kiss me sweet and twenty;
Youth's a stuff will not endure."

She had kissed Romeo after he finished singing, kissed him twenty times over, until she was breathless and drunken with delight. It was the first time she had truly, truly felt that she was only a girl in his arms, and he was only a boy, and all the walls their families put between them didn't matter.

She was wretchedly homesick for that sunlit afternoon, for that easy peace. But she had kissed him, and sealed their journey's ending, and now she had to pay the price.

"Juliet?" Runajo asked softly.

She meant to say, *It's nothing*, but what came out instead was, "Romeo sang that to me."

Runajo stiffened, dropping her gaze as if she were ashamed. Juliet felt abruptly sick, because for once she hadn't meant the words as a rebuke or punishment.

"Come on." She seized Runajo's hand. "We haven't any time to lose," she said, and dragged her forward down the street.

Justiran's house was in one of the better neighborhoods of the Lower City, where the streets were mostly clean and the houses were carved from a warm, golden stone. Juliet didn't hesitate as she strode to the door and knocked sharply.

Justiran answered the door. His eyes widened.

"Is Romeo in this house?" Juliet demanded. She hadn't felt anything, but she wasn't sure, this long after his crime, how easily she could sense him without seeing him. She had never before gone so long without killing somebody who was guilty.

"No." Justiran was still staring at her as if she were the dead come back to life—and Juliet supposed that she was, but she had been no secret for the past month. Surely he'd gotten used to the idea by now.

"I need you to give him a letter," said Juliet. "Will you let me come inside and write it?"

She had brought paper and ink with her; she hadn't dared

write the letter out in advance, in case she got searched.

"Come inside," said Justiran, pulling the door wide as he gave the street a worried look. "Who's this?"

"I'm her Guardian," Runajo said flatly.

"She's helping me," said Juliet, stepping into the house.

Then she stopped. Because Justiran hadn't been alone: there was a boy sitting at his table, leaning lazily back in his chair. He wasn't Mahyanai or Catresou; he dressed in the style of the Lower City, and his dark hair was in braids, decorated with blue beads.

He was looking Juliet up and down, much too carefully.

"Well," said the boy. "I suppose that answers whether I've ever accidentally killed a Mahyanai."

Juliet had appeared unmasked at two public sacrifices now; it wasn't impossible for the boy to recognize her, but her skin still prickled with unease.

"Who are you?" she demanded.

He grinned as he stood. "I'm Vai dalr-Ahodin, captain of the Rooks and King of Cats."

"You can trust him," said Justiran. "He's a friend of Romeo."

"Romeo would befriend anyone," said Runajo.

"Very true," said Vai, stepping forward.

The next moment, he had Runajo shoved against the wall, a knife at her throat. "I can gut you before you get a word out. Juliet, did you bring her for us to kill?"

It had happened too fast for Juliet to react and now—her heart was pounding with the need to *move, move, move,* but she didn't know if she could pull Vai off Runajo before he cut her throat.

Looking over Vai's shoulder, Runajo met her eyes, and Juliet knew they were thinking the same thing: that she wouldn't *have* to move until Runajo was already dead. Then she would have to kill Vai, and then she would probably go insane as so many Juliets did when they lost their Guardians—but she would be free. Truly free, not just without orders as she was now.

It would be a really excellent plan.

Juliet was still carefully not touching Runajo's mind, but she was absolutely sure that Runajo was thinking this, and approving.

"Vai," said Justiran, in an infinitely calm voice, "what is this?"

"Either a rescue or a really amusing story to tell later. I know what a Guardian is, so I know what that means she's done, and I don't mind shedding her blood."

"No," said Juliet.

"Are you sure?" asked Vai, not moving his knife.

"I am a Mahyanai now," said Juliet. "And I don't want her dead."

The second part slipped out before she was aware of thinking it, and her hand went to her mouth as if she were still a child who thought covering her mouth could make people forget what she'd said.

At the same moment, Justiran reached out. His hand touched the side of Vai's throat for barely a moment—she saw his thumb trace some sort of pattern—and then Vai fell to his knees, barely managing to catch himself with his hands so his face didn't hit the floor.

"There will be no killing under my roof," said Justiran.

"What did you do?" Juliet demanded. Her knife was out, she wished she had brought a sword, and her heart was pounding as hard as when there had been a blade at Runajo's throat.

"That was *obviously* magic," said Runajo, sounding breathless and annoyed at the same. "What, was that more of the sacred words?"

Justiran knelt beside Vai. "Ready to behave?"

"He's not the first person to put a knife to my throat," said Runajo.

Justiran laid three fingers against Vai's forehead. And Vai, whose face had been blank and slack, stirred and straightened.

"That was a little more than necessary," he said.

"*You* were a little more than necessary," said Justiran.

"That's what everyone always says. But I was waiting for the Juliet's word."

"What," said Runajo, "are you a friend of the Catresou?"

"No," said Vai. "The Juliet's nothing to me and so are the Catresou. But she was everything to Paris, and he was my friend." He grimaced. "And I might have opinions about people who force other people to slaughter their families."

"Well," said Runajo, "she's already sworn to have her revenge on me, so you don't need to worry about that."

"Enough," snapped Juliet. She looked at Justiran. "What was that?"

"Magic, obviously," said Runajo.

"I have read an ancient book or two," said Justiran.

Juliet snorted. "Don't take me for a fool. That was nothing like the art of the Catresou magi. What is that power you used, where did you learn it, what have you done with it, and do you know anything about the necromancer who's still loose in the city?"

Justiran's eyebrows raised slightly. "I am not calling you foolish," he said gently.

Juliet crossed her arms, and Runajo felt a sudden ripple of frustration from her. An echoed memory of the Catresou elders who had liked her but thought she asked too many questions. Juliet had let them silence her, had hidden her doubts away and confessed them to no one but Romeo and—just one time—to Paris.

Now Juliet crossed her arms and looked Justiran in the eyes.

"The walls of the city are failing. The dead are rising after only one day. There is a necromancer turning others into the living dead. My people have been slaughtered, imprisoned, or forced into hiding. If you still want to keep secrets now, then *you* are a fool, and Romeo was a fool too for ever trusting you."

For a moment, Justiran stared at her. Then he let out a laugh that was half a sigh. "You remind me so much of her."

"That is not an answer," said Juliet.

"It's the start of one," said Justiran. "You remind me of my daughter. I loved her very much. And then she died."

"She wasn't the first or last," said Juliet.

"You might say she was both," said Justiran. "She died a hundred years ago."

19

THERE WAS A MOMENT OF silence. Runajo turned the words over in her head—*she died a hundred years ago*—and yes, Justiran had really said that, and it sounded impossible but he had no reason to lie, and if it was true—

Numbly, she thought, *He saw the Ruining start.*

He had to have helped cause it. How likely was it that somebody, for some unrelated reason, would become immortal at the exact same time the nature of death changed?

"Did you start the Ruining because you wanted to live forever?" she asked.

"You jumped to that conclusion quickly," said Justiran.

"I've done research," said Runajo, bristling—*Because nobody would help me learn,* she thought.

"—so I happen know that there was another Ruining three

thousand years ago, that it destroyed the Ancients, and it was begun when they used the sacred words in an attempt to live forever."

And the amusement drained out of Justiran's face. "I researched that too," he said, and looked at Juliet. "I didn't want to live forever."

"Then what did you want?" asked Juliet.

Justiran shrugged and smiled sadly. "I told you. My daughter died."

Runajo remembered her mother kneeling beside her dying father, and kneeling herself by her mother's deathbed in turn, and she felt a strange, sharp pang of fury.

Her mother had wept so much. People had told Runajo they felt so sad for her. As if there could have been *any* other ending.

"That was a stupid reason," she said. "Didn't you know she was mortal?"

"I did," said Justiran. "But you see, I killed her."

He looked at Juliet again. "She was very like you: she fell in love with a Mahyanai boy. Our peoples were not friends even then. I could see no future that would give them any joy. So when his family called him away, I told her that he was done with her. That he'd told me he was no longer in love. But she couldn't believe me. She demanded to know the truth, so finally I . . . I told her that he was dead. Murdered by our kin when they caught him trespassing. And she killed herself. She left me a note saying she would not accept any world that could be so cruel to one whose only crime was loving."

Justiran's voice remained soft but steady, as if he'd told the story a thousand times before. And maybe he had, in the privacy of his own mind at least. Runajo could have recited the tale of how she bound Juliet to the Mahyanai in just such a voice.

She didn't want to think she had anything in common with the selfish idiocy of someone who would start the Ruining to heal his private grief. But she had destroyed a clan and betrayed a friend to save herself from bereavement. She was just as bad.

"It was my fault," said Justiran, "so I sought to change it. I learned from the Catresou magi, and when they would teach me no more, I sought other teachers. I found the boy my daughter had loved and got him as my ally, and together we tore the world apart, looking for secrets. Until at last we found it: the sacred word for life."

The same that the Ancients had tried to use, when they destroyed themselves. A chill ran down Runajo's spine.

"We broke into the sepulcher and stole my daughter's body. We wrote the word over her heart and raised her back to life. But she never smiled. The only thing she would say was that she wanted to die. She tried to kill herself, again and again, but the power of the sacred word was such that she could *not* die, no matter what she did. Until at last she climbed into a furnace and burned herself to ash."

Justiran stared blindly at the ground, and for a few moments he was silent. Then he sighed and went on. "What else is there to tell? By that point, the fog had already crawled across half the continent. We fled, as so many did. We discovered that we were no longer mortal. And in the end, we came to Viyara."

"Why are *you* immortal?" Runajo asked curiously. "There were no sacred words written upon your skin, were there?"

Justiran shrugged. "When we raised her from the dead, we broke the balance of life and death. It is my theory that, being at the center of such powerful magic, we were also changed."

"So you came back here and set up shop as an apothecary," said Juliet.

"There was no way I could amend what I had done. I thought at least my skills might help someone." Justiran looked her in the eyes again. "I dared hope for nothing more, until Romeo brought you to visit me. And I thought that I might set one thing right, by helping you to be with him."

Runajo's fury was a sudden, white-hot thing. And then she realized that it wasn't just her revulsion that she felt; it was Juliet's, spilling through the bond unbidden. She saw what Juliet was remembering: the first time she had met Justiran, when she was drunk on the freedom of walking the city without a mask, and all the world seemed fresh and new, because nobody looked on her as anything except another girl.

With quiet intensity, Juliet said, "I did not fall in love and nearly die for it so you could feel better about your daughter. I was not born to give you peace."

Justiran's eyes widened, and then he dropped his gaze.

"If you had really wanted to make amends, you could have gone to the Sisterhood and compared notes," said Runajo. "Do you have any idea how desperately we need this sort of information?"

And that was when someone knocked on the door.

The curtains were drawn, but Runajo could tell with a glance that it didn't matter, because the window didn't have the right angle for seeing who was at the door.

"It's probably just a customer," said Justiran, but Runajo barely heard him because she was overwhelmed by the stark rush of fear she felt from Juliet. There were no words, but she knew why Juliet was afraid: because Romeo was quite likely to come here. Because if he was here, she would have to kill him.

"Order me upstairs," said Juliet.

"Go," said Runajo without hesitation. As Juliet bolted up the stairs, Runajo called silently after her: *Stop your ears and do not come down until I tell you. If Romeo is here, do not kill him.*

"It's probably not Romeo," said Vai, getting to his feet. "But that's a clever precaution."

Justiran opened the door.

And Runajo found herself staring at Romeo's tutor, Mahyanai Makari.

His *dead* tutor.

Beside him stood the living dead boy who had attacked Runajo a few nights ago. Paris.

"You," said Justiran, sounding weary and sad.

Runajo was too stunned to move. Vai was not. He lunged forward, drawing his sword. Instantly Paris counterattacked, and for a few moments they fought, swords flashing. At first they seemed evenly matched. But Paris was too fast, too relentless. In a flurry of strokes, he drove Vai back against the wall, and held a sword to his throat.

"Stop," said Makari.

And Paris went still.

"If you keep fighting, King of Cats," Makari went on, "Romeo dies."

"I'm going to kill you," said Vai with a strange intensity, but did not struggle.

Runajo's head was whirling. If Makari could command the living dead—if he had been dead himself and come back, but was not bound to obedience—

She remembered blood spattered across the floor of the Cloister.

"You're the Master Necromancer," she said.

He smiled. "Yes. And you are Romeo's friend Runajo, the girl who stole the Juliet from me. You're going to give her a message."

"What is it?"

"I need the Juliet for my purposes. She must deliver herself to me by sunset. If she doesn't come, Romeo dies, I bring him back as living dead, and I send him to fetch her."

"That seems a very poor bargain," said Runajo. "She's going to kill him as soon as she sees him, and then he'll be a revenant anyway."

"You seem to believe that you're negotiating," said Makari. "Allow me to assure you, the only choice you have is how gracefully you submit."

"Zaran," Justiran said softly.

Makari rounded on him. "That's not my name anymore."

"I know you're angry at this whole world," said Justiran, his voice still gentle. "You have every right to be. But do you think *she* would want this?"

Makari laughed. "Oh, I *know* she does. She told me so."

Justiran shook his head. "My dear boy—"

"I don't mean in my dreams or any such idiocy. Your daughter's alive. I have her."

"That's—not possible." Justiran sounded shaken.

"Oh, yes, it is. Do you know where she's been, these past hundred years? Locked up in a Catresou laboratory." Makari stepped closer, smiling viciously. "I leave it to *your* imagination, what your own people did to her."

Justiran buried his face in his hands.

"You're coming with me," said Makari. "Now. Tonight. I want you to make your apologies to her before the end."

"Here's an idea," said Vai. "Don't."

Justiran was very pale. "I have to," he said. "If she's there—I have to go."

"This is your amends?" said Runajo. "Submitting to the enemy?"

"I'm sorry," he said. "She's my daughter."

Makari grinned at Runajo. "Tell the Juliet, go wait by the face of Xinaad. The little King of Cats can show her if she doesn't know the way. Remember: this evening, or a living dead Romeo comes looking for her."

The door slammed shut.

I release you from my orders, Runajo said silently. *You can come down now.*

Juliet was down the stairs in a moment. "What happened?"

In a few words, they told her.

"You can't go," said Runajo, when they had finished.

Juliet turned. "Can't I?"

Runajo's heart jumped as she thought her words over, reversed them—and then she relaxed as she realized that they were not an order. Juliet was not staring at her with a face like a mask because she was under compulsion.

She was remembering the last time that Runajo had tried to save her life.

Runajo swallowed, feeling a hundred possible, half-formed

speeches in her throat like broken glass.

"It's your business if you want to die," she said carefully. "But he said that he needed you. Whatever he's going to use you for—"

"Do you not know?" Vai demanded.

"I've been captive to the Mahyanai for the past month," said Juliet. "I was a little busy learning *their* purposes."

Vai made a sound of disgust in his throat. "You never got Romeo's letter, did you?"

Runajo felt a sudden flash of grief from Juliet, quickly stifled, but she still caught a glimpse of Romeo with a bloody sword in his hand.

"No," said Juliet.

"He asked me to deliver it for him, and then he vanished before he gave it to me. He must have given up on sending it. If we get him back, I suppose we can ask him why he was such a fool." Vai crossed his arms. "I should have just gone to tell you myself, because it's important enough. The Master Necromancer got the Catresou to tamper with the invocations they wrote on your skin. You're not just the Juliet, you're the key to the gates of death. You were his first plan to destroy the city walls."

Juliet is the key.

The thought stole Runajo's breath away. It felt outlandish, but as she unraveled it in her head, everything made sense. Makari couldn't have planned to be killed by Tybalt in a duel, so he hadn't planned to be a ghost in the Cloister. He might not have even known that Vima's key existed until he was there, working the blood-magic to resurrect himself. So he must have decided to make his own key.

When Juliet had tried to make Romeo her Guardian, the ceremony had gone wrong, and the land of the dead had opened around them.

Everything made sense.

And if Juliet was the key . . . the Mouth of Death was dry. It still might be too late for them to find Death and bargain with her. But at least they might have a chance.

If Makari didn't destroy Viyara tonight.

"You can't go to him," she said, looking at Juliet. "If you ever meant anything about protecting people, you can't let him use you this way."

"She's got a point," said Vai. "I'd rather not see the city destroyed, especially after I went to such trouble saving it a month ago."

"I'm going to Makari tonight," said Juliet.

"But—" Runajo started.

"You're forgetting the same thing that he's forgetting," said Juliet. "He said to come alone."

And that's impossible for me, she added silently.

Runajo's heart jumped. Even now—when she knew that Juliet could never forgive her—when there was so much danger waiting for them—she heard Juliet's words and her first thought was *She trusts me*, with a dizzy thrill of excitement that slid all the way down her spine.

"I'll tell you where he takes me, and you'll follow," Juliet went on out loud, and then looked at Vai. "Do you know about—"

"Oh, yes, we used that trick with Paris and Romeo," said Vai.

"Romeo?" Juliet echoed.

"Right," said Vai, "you don't know anything. What you and Romeo did at the sepulcher? It bound him and Paris together, the same way you're bound to that Mahyanai girl. Very convenient for using Romeo as a lookout while we broke into the Lord Catresou's study. Less convenient when it made the pair of them act like idiots protecting each other, which was always." He let out a huff of air. "And yes, I will help you destroy Makari and save Romeo. On one condition."

"Name it," said Juliet.

Vai had been slouching back, hands against the table, but now he straightened. "I get to kill Paris."

"Why?" asked Juliet.

"Because he was my friend," said Vai. "And he died because he saw Makari, and thought he was only a slave, and tried to free him for Romeo's sake. I don't know exactly how Romeo got captured, but I would bet anything that he went after Paris. Even though I told him not to." Vai's mouth twisted. "I'm ending it. I'm killing him. I won't let anyone stand in my way."

"You don't want to save him?" said Juliet.

"I know the living dead." Vai's teeth flashed in a bitter smile. "My brother was one. He slaughtered my family until I killed him. The living dead have no will but that of the necromancers who made them. There's no way to save them except to kill them. Romeo didn't understand that, but I thought you might. Wouldn't you have rather died than slaughter your people?"

Runajo felt the raw surge of pain in Juliet's mind, and it drove her forward a step, fists clenching with fury that this boy would dare throw that in Juliet's face.

Juliet held up a hand. *No,* she said silently.

To Vai, she replied, "Yes. But little though I knew him, Paris is the only one of my kin who never betrayed me."

"You won't be party to his death," said Vai. "You just won't be flinging yourself in front of my sword, as I'm sure Romeo would have tried to do. Because you never knew him, did you? So you can't be that desperate to save him."

"No," said Juliet. "He was nothing to me. But he is my kin, and he never betrayed me. And I do not want to destroy anything that is dear to Romeo."

Her face was calm, her voice serene. But Runajo could feel the rage and grief beneath the surface, leaking through the wall between their minds, and she felt rage herself. Because Juliet had already been forced too often to accept death and murder, at her own hands or someone else's, and it was Runajo's fault. It was the fault of all Viyara. And yet there was no one to punish, no one to give recompense, and *she wanted to change it*.

"But you're right," said Juliet. "I know what it means, to be under orders. So I will not stop you."

And in a heartbeat, Runajo remembered the ancient record she had read: the Juliet whose Guardian had betrayed the clan, and whom they had tried to save by giving another Guardian—

"I have an idea," she said.

Juliet and Vai both turned to her.

"I've spent a lot of time reading records stolen from the Catresou," she said. "There was one record—a Juliet whose Guardian betrayed the clan and fled. They tried to free her from his orders by giving her another Guardian, but it didn't work, because he didn't have a Juliet of his own to shelter him from the power of the bond. But I have *you*. If I write the sacred word on Paris and make him mine—I might survive it. And I might set him free of Makari." She drew a breath. "But I know that bond is sacred to your people. And I don't know if it would be worse than death for him. So tell me: Should I try?"

Juliet looked at her. It felt like it went on forever, the moment that she looked at her.

Finally she said, "Romeo wants him to live. And I give my permission. So if you think you can, then try."

20

"PLEASE," SAID ROMEO. "MAKARI LOVES you. Can't you make him listen?"

The Little Lady stared at him, her blue eyes expressionless, and the back of Romeo's neck prickled with unease.

Makari had summoned Romeo to eat breakfast with him and the Little Lady—he still wouldn't give a straight answer on her name—and then he had left them together, guarded not by Paris but by another of the living dead: a man with receding gray hair and a potbelly who had still lunged as fast as a whip when Romeo tried to get to the door. There was a bruise on his arm where the man had grabbed him.

So for hours, there had been nothing for Romeo to do but sit at the breakfast table, stare at the wall and the empty teacups, and try to coax the Little Lady into talking.

"He's going to destroy the world," he said. "Is that what you want?"

Her head tilted just a fraction. She stared at him still. And then she said, quietly and distinctly, "I want to die."

And Romeo couldn't speak, because in that soft voice was all the despair of the dying world, and he understood why Makari was willing to tear all things apart for her.

He understood. But—

"I know a girl who was also captive to the Catresou," he said. "They took away her name before she ever had a chance to know it. They tried to take her heart away as well, and she won it back with so much courage. And then she lost everything. Because of *me*, because I thought I could help her but I made everything worse.

"I know that I have to die soon. I'm ready to face it. But this girl, no matter how she was wronged, she never stopped loving the world that had wronged her. I just want her to have a chance to live in that world." He swallowed, the grief an ache in her throat. "She'll have to live in that world without me. But she's stronger than me. She can do it."

The Little Lady looked at him, her forehead creasing slightly, and he waited, but she did not reply.

"If we're going to die together," he said finally, "then please, at least tell me . . . what's your name?"

She started to open her mouth—

And the door slammed open, and Makari strode in.

"I have a wonderful surprise for you," he said, smiling at Romeo.

It was a familiar smile. Romeo could remember exactly how delighted he'd once been whenever Makari smiled at him, and he felt sick.

"Are you going to let me go?" he asked.

"Obviously not. No, your true love's coming here. Everything ends tonight."

"Juliet?" Romeo was on his feet in a moment. "No—please, you *can't*—"

Makari paused to tilt the Little Lady's chin up and give her a kiss. Then he looked back at Romeo and said, "I definitely can. If she loves you as much as you think, that is. I told her what would happen to you if she didn't come."

"It won't work," Romeo said desperately. "I've got blood guilt, she has to kill me as soon as she sees me, and then she'll be free to kill you."

"That's why you're getting locked up in the attic. Paris, take him."

Paris stepped in the door, his face as terribly blank as ever, and seized Romeo's arm in a grip like steel.

"Don't worry, you'll have the Juliet in your arms soon enough," Makari went on. "Once she's under my control, she won't be able to hurt anyone unless I will it."

"Please," said Romeo. "You can't really want this. Don't you remember—"

The slap across his face left his head ringing for a moment.

"I remember," Makari said quietly, "things you cannot imagine."

And for a moment he did not look like Romeo's tutor at all, but an ancient, furious undead thing that had cast the world into ruin and would ruin it further still.

Then he sighed, and said to Paris, "Take him upstairs, lock him up. And *do* kill him if he tries to escape."

She's coming here because of me, Romeo thought, sick with terror. *Because of me.*

He wanted to believe it was a trick, that Juliet would never throw her life away because of him. That Runajo would never let her. But he knew how brave Juliet was, and how kind, and in all honesty, he had never truly understood Runajo. And Makari had been so sure.

What it all came down to was this: Romeo should have died already. He should have died long ago, and then none of this would have happened—but if he had at least died at the sepulcher, or on Juliet's sword when she unmasked him, then he wouldn't be causing this disaster *now*.

Romeo glanced uneasily at the window. The narrow, dusty attic had only one; the shutters hung open, letting in a wide shaft of golden, late-afternoon sunlight.

He was at the very top of the building. If he jumped from there, he would die.

His stomach lurched at the thought. He could face that death, if he had to—but it wouldn't really help Juliet, would it? Unless she happened to be in the street at the very moment he jumped, she wouldn't know he was dead, so Makari would be able to continue threatening her.

Romeo had to escape. And then either he had to stop Makari, or . . . he had to find Juliet and die at her hands, so that she could stop Makari.

She might never forgive him for that. But he didn't mind that, if only *she* would be all right, and the rest of Viyara.

So he had to get out. Now.

He looked at Paris, who stood by the door of the attic, watching him without blinking.

Kill him if he tries to escape, Makari had said.

"This room is a terrible mess," said Romeo. "I'm going to organize it, for Makari's sake. So it can be the kind of attic he deserves." He smiled at Paris. "Will you help?"

He kept smiling as he waited anxiously. The lie would have fooled nobody alive, but Makari had said again and again that the living dead had little wits left—

"For my master's sake?" Paris said slowly.

"Yes!" Romeo declared, his heart jumping as he realized this plan might work. "Don't you think he would be happy to come back and see it set to rights?"

Without waiting, he leaned over and started shoving at the boxes. He had no idea what was in them or what he was doing, but it didn't matter: the important thing was to get Paris away from the door.

If he asked Paris to come over and help him, would he say yes? Romeo was right next to the window; with surprise on his side and a lot of luck, he might be able to push Paris out. The fall wouldn't kill him, and that would *definitely* give Romeo time to run.

Then the box Romeo was lifting slid out of his grip, and it fell open.

Inside was a sword.

A shiver of excitement ran up his spine. If he had a sword, then—well, he would still probably have to die tonight, but he might be able to take Makari with him.

He looked up again, and saw that while Paris had barely moved from the door, he had leaned over to poke at a pile of clutter.

There might not be another chance.

Romeo laid his hand on the sword hilt. Took a breath. Then grasped it, and bolted for the window.

He'd already gotten plenty of practice in climbing houses

with a sword. He was out the window and hauling himself up onto the rooftop in moments.

But Paris was even faster than he'd thought. Romeo was barely on his feet when Paris clambered up behind him. If it hadn't been for that month fighting in the alleys of the Lower City, Romeo might not have gotten his sword up in time.

"Don't—" he started, and then Paris attacked.

Romeo had never dueled Paris when he was alive, but he'd watched him fight Vai, and he'd seen snippets of his training in his memories. He knew that Paris was not a terrible swordsman, but not particularly good either.

Now . . . his technique was barely better. But he moved with such speed and strength that Romeo could barely keep up. He was driven back, slowly, across the rooftop—and he was still trying not to actually strike Paris, but it was gradually dawning on him that Paris would not tire. He could spend all night wearing him down, while Juliet died below.

He had to stop Paris.

That meant truly fighting him.

Romeo lunged. This time his blade slid past Paris's guard and stabbed straight between his ribs—

And Romeo knew this feeling, the exact way that flesh resisted steel and then gave way, and the scrape of the blade against bone. It was just like Tybalt, just like the Mahyanai he had killed, but *this was Paris*, and even though Romeo knew he hadn't struck close to Paris's heart, the horror of what he was doing rolled over him in a wave and choked him. Stilled him.

For a moment, they stared at each other.

Then, quite calmly, Paris reached down with his bare hand and pulled the black-smeared blade out of his side.

He tried to hold on to the sword, but Romeo jerked it free and staggered back. Not without slicing open Paris's palm: he saw the black blood dribbling onto the rooftop.

His stomach turned over with nausea. He tried to raise his sword, to ready for the attack, but his hands were trembling.

Paris was living dead. Romeo could practically slice him into pieces, and so long as he didn't cut off his head or stab him through the heart, he would live. He would never flinch either, and maybe that meant he wouldn't feel pain—but as Romeo stared at his blood, as he remembered how the blade had felt going in, it didn't matter how little it might hurt. It didn't matter if there was nothing left in Paris's head of the boy who had been Romeo's friend.

Paris was still Paris.

And Romeo might be able to fight him for someone else's sake, to stop him from killing another innocent like Emera—but slicing him open to save his own life?

Forgive me, Juliet, he thought.

But she would have been angrier if he died at her hands. And she could vanquish Makari without him. He believed that. He had to.

Just as he had to believe that there was still something left of his friend.

And as he thought that, he threw the sword away, arcing into the darkness between buildings.

"Paris," he called out. "You're my friend. I won't fight you, even if I die for it. But please, can't you remember me?"

Kill him if he tries to escape.

The order thrummed in his head, and Paris wanted nothing more than to obey. There was nothing else in all the world for him to want.

But as he looked at Romeo—as he stepped toward him—the sword felt strangely heavy in his hands.

Romeo's eyes were very wide. "Paris," he said. "I *know* you remember me. You told me about *zoura*. You told me I was an idiot. You saved me at the Catresou sepulcher."

"No," said Paris.

The word was faint, barely more than a breath, but it made Romeo break out into a desperate smile.

"You wanted to protect your people," he said. "You did protect them. *We* did. Together. We stopped Lord Catresou from opening the gates of death. Don't you remember?"

His head ached. He did not remember those things. If he *did* remember them, it didn't matter. He still belonged to his master, walked and breathed and felt his dead heart beat because of him.

But he realized that he had stopped moving.

His body felt infinitely heavy, like in the first moments after he had been raised back to life. He could hear his heart pounding, quick and desperate, like it wanted to escape.

"Please," said Romeo. "You're my friend, and I need you."

"I belong to him," said Paris.

But with a feeling of cold nausea, he realized that he wanted to spare the boy in front of him. He wanted to disobey his master.

He was dead. He wasn't supposed to want anything.

But he did, he *wanted*, and that horror would have made him weep if he had any tears. He had failed his master so completely.

Then he realized his hands were raising the sword.

"I have to obey," he said.

Something was terribly wrong with him, but his hands could still serve his master, and there was peace in that.

"I agree that his poetry is terrible, but you don't have to kill him for it."

Paris whirled around, and saw somebody new on the roof: the girl he had fought just hours before, in the apothecary's house.

She grinned at him now and his mind buzzed with confusion, because he had to kill Romeo now, he had orders, but she was the enemy of his master and she had to die for it—

"I'm going to kill your master and then I'm going to set his twitching corpse on fire," she said. "Ready to attack me now?"

And the world became simple and made perfect sense as Paris lunged for her.

The moment Runajo heard the noise of swords on the rooftop, she knew what Vai was going to do. It was the logical strategy.

She still couldn't believe it when she saw the two figures silhouetted against the evening sky, and saw Vai land a solid kick on Paris that sent him falling over the edge of the roof. She flinched when Paris crashed onto the cobblestones, barely a pace away from where she stood.

He didn't move. And for one sick moment, Runajo thought, *Vai killed him after all.*

But then Vai yelled down, "Get him while you can!" and Runajo remembered that Vai, of all people, would know how much the living dead could survive. So she lunged to Paris's side and dropped to her knees.

Paris was still for now, black blood oozing from his forehead, but she knew it wouldn't last for long. Her hands shook as she tried to uncork the ink pot. Maybe she should have written the mark on her hand already, but she wasn't sure how fresh it had to be.

She got the jar open and jammed the brush inside. Then she dropped the ink pot, not caring about the black splash on the ground, and traced the symbol on her left palm, twin to the swirling symbol on her right: the sacred Catresou word for *trust*.

She grabbed Paris's slack hand, raised it to hers, and pressed their hands together.

Nothing happened.

Nothing happened, and Runajo's heart thudded in icy horror as she realized she had been wrong, in a moment Paris would wake and kill her, then probably kill Juliet and Romeo and Vai and it was *all her fault—*

Then she felt heat between their palms.

For one moment it was simple warmth, like the outside of a cup filled with hot tea. Then it flared hotter and hotter until it seared her skin with a heat so intense it felt like being stabbed with ice. A choked-off scream shuddered in her lungs, and tears started in her eyes.

And then it was done. As suddenly as it had begun, the pain was over. Runajo was doubled over, panting for breath, still clutching Paris's hand—

Paris's eyes blinked open.

In a moment she was on her feet, saying breathlessly, "I command you to be free of the Master Necromancer."

If he hadn't already overwritten his loyalty, then an order probably wouldn't make a difference. But she couldn't help herself.

Was there a bond?

Runajo couldn't feel any emotions from him, any sense of

another mind touching hers. But he wasn't making any move to attack her; as she watched, he sat up slowly, gingerly, still staring at her.

"Tell me if you're free of him," she said.

"Yes," Paris said instantly, in the same dazed, obedient voice that Juliet had first used when Runajo asked her questions.

She could never hear that voice again without sickness, and yet relief rolled through Runajo in a dizzying wave. Because they had done it. *She* had done it, had finally made *something* better, and for a moment her eyes stung.

Juliet, she called silently. *Juliet, it worked. He's free.*

There was no answer. Juliet had walled off her mind again as soon as she had arrived at Makari's house and didn't have any more directions to give them. Maybe she hadn't wanted to be distracted; maybe she had wanted to face her death alone, without the girl who had wronged her.

Runajo couldn't blame her. But even after such a brief conversation, the inside of her mind felt strangely empty.

Paris said, softly, roughly, "What did you do?"

Runajo remembered that while Juliet had consented to this plan, he had not. She drew a breath and knelt down, making herself meet his eyes.

"I put a bond on you. To make me your Guardian. I'm sorry, I know it's blasphemy, but Juliet gave me permission."

"Juliet," he echoed.

"Yes," said Runajo.

His eyes were very wide. "You—you should have—" He rubbed a hand over his face, finishing the thought silently: *You should have killed me.*

And then she did feel his mind: a horrifying cascade of guilt and memories, screams and blood and driving a blade between someone's ribs. The scrape of a blade against bone. The sound of a final breath choking out, and the sick smell of blood dribbling out on the ground.

Runajo cringed, choking on the memories.

"Stop," she whispered, and then added immediately, "that's not an order."

The wave of memories ceased, but she could still feel his guilt and misery bubbling on the other side of the wall between their minds.

He stared at her, and he asked, "Why did you save me?"

Runajo stared at the Catresou boy who was nothing to her—who had been forced to kill the same way that she had forced Juliet—and felt unutterably weary.

"Because," she said, "I love a girl who loves a boy who loves you. And this is all I can do for her."

He stared at her, and she walled off her mind as best she could, but she didn't need any bond to tell that he was utterly confused.

She didn't really understand it either.

"Paris!" she heard Romeo shout from behind her—he and Vai must have finally gotten down from the rooftop—and a moment later he rushed forward to pull Paris into an embrace.

And then she heard Juliet's voice call, *Runajo?*

21

"YOU SHOULD BE GRATEFUL," SAID Makari. "You might say that I'm doing this for you." He flashed a bared-teeth smile over his shoulder.

Juliet looked at the ballroom: the high vaults painted red and gold, the polished floor, the cages of weakly hissing revenants.

"*You* might," she said. "I wouldn't."

Along one wall, servants stood to attention; from the blank, obedient look in their eyes, she guessed they were living dead.

At the center of the ballroom, with an air of infinite loneliness, sat a Catresou girl—Juliet's own age—with eyes just as blue as hers, but golden curls. Juliet recognized her because once Lord Ineo had taken Juliet to look upon her, that she might understand the depth of her people's evil. It was the living dead girl who had been locked inside Juliet's father's laboratory. She sat now in a wooden chair, free of any visible bonds.

She met Juliet's eyes. There was intent in that gaze, without any hope.

"But you haven't met my lady yet," said Makari.

Juliet looked at him. She recognized his mocking smile from Runajo's memories and Romeo's words. Runajo hadn't cared about him and Romeo had thought the sun rose and set on him and they had both been terribly, terribly wrong.

"Does she have a name?" she asked.

"No," said Makari. "That's why I hate your people." They stood before the dead girl now; Makari grasped her hand, raised her to her feet, and kissed her slowly, passionately. The girl returned the kiss just as hungrily, her fingers grasping at his sleeves, but when he loosed her—she swayed, and said nothing.

"She was the Juliet once," said Makari, turning to her. "She feared to die, because *your people* taught her that there was no hope for her."

Juliet crossed her arms. "If she was ever the Juliet, she would hate you for destroying her people. But that doesn't matter to you, does it, when you've made her living dead and a slave."

Her voice was calm, measured, but her heart was beating very fast. She wanted to attack now, to snap Makari's neck in one clean motion the same way she had her father's. But Runajo and Vai had probably just reached the house. They must be looking for Romeo and Paris right now. She wasn't sure what power

Makari might call on when attacked—if, seeing he was going to lose, he might silently order Paris to kill himself or Romeo—so she had to wait as long as possible. She had to buy them time.

It was lucky that Makari was so in love with talking about himself.

"Oh, she is nothing like the puppets I raise," said Makari.

"And yet she is silent," said Juliet, and looked into the other Juliet's dazed blue eyes. "Is this what you dreamed of, when you were a child suffering the pain of new seals? Is this the price you wanted to pay for loving him?"

The girl looked at Juliet. Then she said, softly but distinctly, "I want to die."

And for a moment, Juliet felt her heart shudder within her. Because she knew the sound and the shape and the taste of those soft, dead words; they had been all her own heart said, when she woke in the Cloister and believed Romeo dead for nothing.

"Those are all the words she has left," said Makari. "And I will grant her wish."

He snapped his fingers. Another door to the ballroom opened, and two more of the living dead dragged in another prisoner: Justiran. His face was bruised, and his right sleeve was soaked with blood, but his eyes were alert as they brought him to Makari and shoved him to his knees.

"I've got one demand," said Makari.

Justiran looked at Juliet, and then at his daughter.

"I am so sorry," he said quietly.

"Listen to me." Makari's voice was cold and clipped now. "Your daughter wasn't newborn when you handed her over to the magi. You must have given her a name."

"Zaran—"

Makari's hand cracked against Justiran's face. "I told you not to call me that."

"Then you can't need to know her name that badly," said Justiran, his voice soft and tired.

There was rage in the set of Makari's shoulders, in the white knuckles of his fingers as he gripped Justiran's hair and tilted his head back, and Juliet felt a thrill of hope. Because Makari was definitely distracted now.

"Listen to me, old man," said Makari, "I am giving you a chance to make one *minuscule* reparation to your daughter. Because once, long ago, she told me that she wished she knew."

There were no weapons nearby except Makari's sword. It would be a fitting way for him to die. Juliet shifted her weight a fraction, readying herself to spring.

"I would have told you," said Justiran, "if you had asked before you broke another Juliet."

Two thoughts flashed through Juliet's mind, swift as lightning: *I am not broken*, and *Now Makari's going to look at me*.

She thought, and she didn't even decide, she simply acted: pivoted and slammed the side of her foot into the side of Makari's knee. He staggered, pulling Justiran off-balance, and then the two of them went down together.

Juliet was on him the next instant—her hands found the hilt of his sword—

And Makari's fingers closed around her wrist and the world went white.

There was no pain. There was only a cold hum that severed her mind from her body. She was kneeling on the floor—she realized this after few moments—and she could feel the cold tiles against her knees, and the breath moving in and out of her body, but she couldn't control the slightest movement.

"Brave of you," said Makari. "But stupid. It seems to be a Catresou trait."

Juliet tried to speak, to tell him that another Catresou trait was destroying those who defied *zoura*, but all she could do was puff air between numb, half-open lips.

"Paris was like that, when he was alive," said Makari. "Trying to save me, like I could be some sort of present for Romeo. I admired that ambition, I must admit, but I had to crush it."

He stroked the top of Juliet's head once, twice. She wanted to shudder, but she still didn't have enough control over her body.

Justiran sat up. "Makari," he said, his voice raw. "You deserve your revenge. But take it on me. Why do you need to hurt this girl?"

"Honestly," said Makari, "haven't you been listening to anything I've said? She's a tool just as much as my lady was, and I'm

239

going to wield her to give my lady freedom."

Juliet flexed her mouth. She wanted to howl, *Have you* asked her *if she wants to pay this price?* But all she could force past her lips was a soft moan.

She thought, *I will die speechless,* and the idea set her stomach shaking with fear in a way that revenants and reapers hadn't.

She didn't fear death, but she feared dying without a fight, and speaking was fighting: Romeo had taught her that.

"Tell me, love," Makari called out, "do you want your father to live?"

Juliet was able to lift her head, just a little. So she saw the girl's face. She saw the girl tilt her head, and look at Justiran, and then look at Makari.

And say nothing.

He is your father, she wanted to cry. *Even if he were evil as mine was evil, you would mourn his death.*

But she could speak no words, only harsh gasps.

Makari leaned down and said to Justiran, "You see how it is. You see what she wants."

Justiran ignored him. He looked past Makari, straight to his daughter, and he said with a terrible serenity, "I love you. And I'm so sorry."

Makari drew a knife and plunged it into Justiran's throat.

He drew the blade out again swiftly, and though it hadn't been a wide slice, blood still gushed from the hole. Justiran choked and convulsed; Makari knelt, and dipped his hand in the pool of blood.

Then he stepped to Juliet, and with a bloody finger, traced a symbol on her forehead. Faintly, under his breath, she heard him whispering words that she couldn't quite make out, but that made her skin buzz with trembling wrongness.

The world seemed to shiver around her. Juliet's vision blurred for a moment; she felt like she was falling or perhaps shooting up in the air very quickly.

Darkness fell, and Juliet recognized this: the same unearthly darkness that had surrounded her and Romeo when they tried to create the bond and everything went wrong.

She heard the song of death: a rippling murmur like a thousand voices whispering to themselves. Light clung about her—and Makari, and Justiran, and Justiran's daughter—but otherwise they seemed to stand on an infinite, empty plain filled with darkness.

She knew what would happen next: she would be drawn all the way into the land of the dead, and Makari would go with her, and use her to wrench its gates open and make all the living world dead. She would have failed everyone she had ever tried to protect.

No, she thought.

"It's time," said Makari. He held out a hand, beckoning to his lady. "Come, darling."

She stepped toward him, her golden curls strangely bright in the darkness. She took his hand and leaned into his chest.

No, thought Juliet, *no, no, no—*

"No," she whispered aloud, her voice barely more than a breath.

Once more, the world shivered.

Makari started. "What's that?" he demanded, turning on Juliet.

She wasn't sure. But she knew that she had felt the power of his magic running through her body, across her skin.

She knew that it had changed when she said *no*.

"No," she said again, and her voice was stronger now. The world itself seemed to change her; she felt warmth curling at the bottom of her stomach, felt her fingers start to stiffen and clench with her own anger, and she said, *"Stop."*

And the song of death grew quieter, and the darkness began to fade. There were still inky, unnatural shadows everywhere, but the air had lost that cold, sweet sense of blowing across an infinite expanse; faintly, Juliet could see the walls of the room. She could hear the hissing of the revenants in their cages.

Makari grabbed her hair. "What have you done?"

"You made me the key," said Juliet, her lips still numb but curving in a grin. "You made the living *Juliet* the key."

"The Juliet is only a weapon—"

"—forged for a single purpose, and *that is protecting my people.* What did you expect?"

He slammed her to the ground and knelt over her. He dipped a finger in Justiran's blood and wrote a word on his palm. She knew that it was the sacred word for *trust*, which the Catresou used to form the bond between Juliet and Guardian.

Makari pressed his palm to her forehead. "Open the gate," he said, his voice shaking with rage.

Juliet could feel the sign he had written burning on her skin, but it had no power over her.

"No," she said.

Juliet was helpless, pinned to the ground, and would likely die in a moment, but her body thrilled with defiant exultation.

"I *order* you," he snarled.

"You're not my Guardian," she said. "You don't own me, Runajo does. You're not Catresou, not Mahyanai. You are *nobody* I have to obey."

Makari stood, his face becoming cold. "I will kill Romeo," he said. "I will kill him and raise him again and again, as many times and as painfully as it takes until you obey."

"No," said Juliet.

She was not afraid. There was no room left in her for fear, not when every last scrap of her will was focused on defying him, on silently whispering *no, no, no* to the power that still rippled through her body.

She didn't think she could move yet, but it didn't matter. All she had to do was refuse.

"Romeo loves this world," she said. "I will not destroy it to save him. I can watch him die if I must, but I will not break him."

"*I* will break him," Makari snarled, turning away from her, and then fear did stab through Juliet's heart, because he was surely going to do it now—

And then Makari gasped and halted, shuddering.

From where she lay on the floor, Juliet couldn't quite see what was happening. Makari fell to his knees with a thump, and gasped, "*You.*"

His lady stood over him, holding a bloody knife, and then Juliet understood.

Makari pitched to the side, gasping for breath. But he must have been stabbed straight through the heart—his shirt was already drenched with blood.

His lady sat beside him and gently lifted his head into her lap.

"Why?" he asked. "I would have—"

She muffled him with a kiss.

"I want to die," she said when she raised her face. "I want to die."

Makari shuddered and gasped. Then he was still.

And Juliet felt his power leave her. She sat up—her vision swayed a moment in sudden dizziness—and she looked at the other Juliet.

"Thank you," she said.

The other Juliet stroked Makari's forehead. "I want to die," she repeated quietly, calmly.

Juliet got to her feet. She was still a little unsteady, but she made it the few steps she needed to kneel by Justiran's side. His face was pale, his sightless eyes wide open; his skin was still warm, but he was very clearly dead.

I was not born to give you peace, she had told him, but that wasn't quite true. He had been Catresou once, and the Juliet created peace for all her people.

"Go swiftly and in gladness," she said quietly. "Forget not thy name, in all the dark places. Forget not those who have walked before thee. Heed not the nameless, who crawl and weep, but carry thy name to the Paths of Light."

There was a thud behind her, then another. Juliet bolted to her feet and whirled, nearly lost her balance, and then saw what had alarmed her: the living dead were falling.

It was surreal. Horrifying, and yet almost comic. One by one, Makari's servants—dead still, but living dead no more—collapsed to the ground and were still. They didn't cry out, they didn't flinch or gasp. They toppled like puppets with their strings cut.

The sight was so bizarre that for one moment, Juliet didn't think anything of it.

Then she thought, *Paris.*

The next moment she was calling silently, *Runajo?*

Yes? said Runajo after a moment.

Did you find Paris? Is he—

245

Yes. He's free.

But there was a restraint to Runajo's thoughts; Juliet could tell that she was trying to hold something back, some memory or emotion from what had happened.

Is he alive? she demanded. *Right now?*

I'm watching him hug Romeo this moment, said Runajo, and the confusion in her voice sent a wave of relief down Juliet's spine.

Are you *all right?* Runajo asked after a moment, strangely hesitant.

Yes. Makari's dead. His servants too. The hissing of the revenants grew louder—

The hissing was from all around her.

Her body knew before her mind had finished comprehending: she dived for Makari's corpse and wrenched the sword away from him.

She turned and raised the blade just in time to meet the first revenant.

Juliet? Juliet! Runajo's voice was desperate in her mind; something must have slipped through the bond.

Revenants, Juliet snapped, dodging and then lashing out with her sword. But this revenant was new, not rotted away; the sword wasn't sharp enough to slice all the way through the neck. Its head wobbled, and it lunged at her again.

Juliet grabbed it by the hair and wrenched.

One unspeakable moment later, the thing was dead, and she

called to Runajo, *Ballroom. First floor.*

Not all of Makari's servants had risen yet; of those that had, most were still moving slowly, not yet fully awakened. Juliet knew she might have only moments left before the whole crowd was upon her, and then her speed and strength and sword would not be enough; they would pile on her and tear her to pieces. All her instincts screamed at her to run, but she had to kill them before they escaped into the rest of the city—

She had to make them come at her one by one.

She seized the other Juliet by the arm and hauled her to her feet. Makari's corpse tumbled to the floor with a thump; Juliet ignored it, already dragging the other girl to the nearest door.

There were several doors into the ballroom. But revenants were too witless to use strategy; they would run to the nearest living human, and that was Juliet.

"I want to die," said the girl.

"Not now," said Juliet, shoving her out into the hallway. Then she turned and planted herself in the doorway—just in time to meet the next revenant.

She killed it. And the next, and the next.

There were still more.

Juliet's arms burned with exhaustion, and her breath rasped in her throat. She couldn't remember how many living dead had been in the room when she entered it. She only knew that she had to stop them from leaving.

She hoped desperately that she had been right, and none of them were going for the other doors.

"Need help?" Vai called out, and the next moment slid through the door under Juliet's sword. Somebody followed: Paris.

Juliet charged after them, and the three of them made short work of the remaining revenants.

When they were done, for a few moments, all Juliet could do was gasp for breath. She was near the center of the room; Makari's corpse lay near her. He hadn't moved once; whatever magic had bound him so closely to the Ruining had also stopped his body from coming to life once his soul had fled.

All around her lay the heads and bodies of the slaughtered revenants.

They had not been living when she killed them, but they had been new; there were wide pools of black blood all across the floor, and suddenly Juliet remembered the pools of blood in the Catresou compound, when Lord Ineo gave the order and she killed and she killed and she killed—

She rubbed a shaking hand across her face. *It's over,* she told herself. *It's over. He can't give you orders anymore.*

She forced herself to look around the room again—to notice that the foul smell of the black blood was *different*—and she saw, standing only a few paces away, Paris.

One of her kin, who had actually been saved.

She walked toward him. "Paris," she said.

He turned to her, and for one moment his face was blank and empty, so close to how he'd been attacking Lord Ineo's house that for a moment she feared—

Then he dropped to his knees. "Lady Juliet," he said, his head bent low. "I have sinned against you and our people."

She swallowed past the ache in her throat. She remembered how carefully respectful he had been when they had met, how it had touched her even in the midst of her grief for Romeo.

"I have as well," she said, and laid her hand on his head. "Rise and serve me."

He seized her hand and kissed it. "I will," he said, and got to his feet.

"Is Romeo safe?" she asked.

"Yes, and waiting nearby," said Vai, sauntering up beside her. "Did you have a plan for what to do next about him, or were you counting on dying first?"

"I . . . thought I would probably die," Juliet admitted.

Vai snorted. "Well, it's obvious why you two belong together."

"Of course *now* I'm going to—" Juliet broke off when she saw Runajo standing in the doorway. "What are you doing here?"

"Coming to your assistance," said Runajo, sounding cross. She wasn't looking at Juliet; she was staring at the carnage of the revenants.

"You are *useless* in a fight," said Juliet.

She knew that, had even one of the revenants escaped, Runajo probably would have been dead anyway. But it still filled her with a peculiar, helpless fury to know that Runajo had been standing just outside while they fought—a revenant could have gotten to her, and Juliet might not have even known until it was too late.

"I'm the only one who knows anything about magic," said Runajo. "Where did they all come from?"

"His servants," said Juliet, and couldn't help glancing at Paris. "They all died when he did, and rose again after."

"That's not normal," said Runajo.

"What part of the attempted necromancy and massive carnage tipped you off?" asked Vai.

"No," said Runajo, "it's the dead who turned to living dead in seconds."

Cold fear seized Juliet's heart. When the dead had started rising in one day instead of three, it had meant the walls were almost destroyed. If they were rising instantly now, did that mean—

"They were living dead," she suggested desperately.

"No, she's right," said Vai. "I've killed living dead before, and none of them rose so fast. Something's wrong."

The revenants in the cages were still hissing and clawing at the bars. *We have to kill them before we leave,* Juliet thought distractedly.

"How far did Makari get with his ceremony?" asked Runajo.

"I stopped him," Juliet protested. "The land of the dead started to open around us, like it did with Romeo, but I stopped him."

But she already knew what Runajo was thinking: that opening the doors of death might have gone no further than with Romeo, but that had been before the Catresou attempt. The walls were already weakened now. The *world* was weakened.

The world shivered.

It was the same unearthly movement-that-was-not-movement that Juliet had felt when Makari tried to open the gates of death. Her whole body was tensed up with pure and simple fear, the need to run or fight, but there was nothing to fight and nowhere to run, and *she had stopped Makari.*

"Something's happening." Runajo licked her lips. She was very pale, and there was a strange emotion rolling off her in waves. It wasn't exactly fear; it was too numb and sick and all-encompassing for that.

"It's the Ruining," said Paris. "It's getting closer."

"How can you tell?" Juliet demanded.

Paris looked at them, and in this moment there was nothing awkward or hesitant about him, only a terrible, cold calm.

"I'm still dead. Those he raised? Death still calls to us. It's closer now. I can hear it." His voice grew softer. "We're going to rest soon."

Vai smacked the side of his head. "Not yet," he said, and a very human half smile flickered across Paris's face.

Runajo said, "I have a plan."

22

WHEN THEY FINALLY REACHED THE Exalted's palace, it was the middle of the night. Runajo wasn't at all sure that she and Juliet would even be allowed inside, let alone that Sunjai would come see them. But she had forgotten that not everyone followed the strict nighttime rituals of the Sisters. The palace lamps were alight, and as they were led to the receiving room, they heard music and laughter drifting down the hallways.

Everyone said that the Exalted would amuse himself with dancing girls at the very edge of doom, and now it was true.

After several minutes of waiting silently in the little receiving room, staring at the ivory whorls and curlicues sculpted into the wall and trying not to think about the way the revenants had hissed and screeched, the door swung open and Sunjai walked in. Her hair was loose from its braids, which meant she had probably been hauled out of bed, but she seemed awake enough.

"Do you know, Lord Ineo was here earlier?" said Sunjai. "He seemed convinced you would have told me where you were taking the Juliet."

So they were already being hunted for. Runajo was not surprised; it was why Juliet had decided to come with her instead of going back to the Mahyanai compound.

"Lord Ineo doesn't matter now," she said. "You'd better have finished your part of the calculations or we're all dead."

In the moment of silence that followed, it occurred to Runajo that now was probably not the best time to antagonize Sunjai.

On the other hand, Sunjai had already agreed to help Runajo even though she had never been anything *but* unpleasant to her.

"Did something happen," asked Sunjai, "or were you just reminding me of the situation? Because one of us has seen the Mouth of Death standing dry, and it wasn't you."

"We found the necromancer and killed him," said Juliet. "But he got too close to opening the gates of death. The dead are rising in moments. We think the walls are coming down."

"Which means we need the new walls up *now*," said Runajo.

"She means tomorrow," said Juliet. "After the people from the Lower City get inside."

Sunjai raised her eyebrows. "That fast? It's going to take some doing."

"We'll do it," said Runajo, horribly aware that they were not going to get everyone inside. A lot of people were going to die very soon, because they didn't have enough time. But the only alternative was everyone dying.

That had always been the way of Viyara.

"We have a plan," said Juliet. "Can you do your part?"

"I never knew the sword of the Catresou was this talkative," Sunjai said musingly, looking at Runajo.

"Yes, well, none of you people know anything about the Catresou, do you?" said Juliet.

Sunjai grinned. "I'll wake Inyaan. We can start the preparations."

Juliet had given Paris two orders before they parted.

"Help Vai spread the word," she said. "And find Justiran's daughter, if you can."

It wasn't until halfway through their planning that they had realized she had slipped away. They had tried to find her at once, but without success. Runajo still believed that she might help them finally end the Ruining, and Juliet trusted Runajo; so as Paris and Vai ran through the streets, he kept looking for the Little Lady, straining to sense any remaining hint of Makari's power that might reveal her.

But he caught no glimpse of her, and he was afraid that he would fail his duty again.

"I *think* it's her night to patrol this neighborhood," said Vai, turning a corner. And there, learning against the wall by a fountain, Paris could see the shadowed form of Subcaptain Xu, the woman who had brought the City Guard to help them stop Lord Catresou.

She had also helped stand guard at Lord Ineo's sacrifices. Now that Paris's mind was his own again, not continually shattering under the weight of Makari's power, he could remember that.

He didn't want to ask her for help, but he knew they didn't have a choice. And he had certainly shed more than enough Catresou blood himself.

"How do you know her schedule?" he asked.

"I'm clever," said Vai. "Have to be." And she strode forward, shoulders back, chin up.

"Haven't seen you in a while," said Xu as they approached. Then her gaze fell on Paris. "I heard you were dead."

"It's catching, but not always permanent," said Vai. "And not important right now. A necromancer weakened the city walls before we could stop him, and the whole Lower City is going to be covered in the Ruining very soon. You've got to start an evacuation. There will be walls around the Upper City."

There was a short silence.

"Really?" said Xu.

"Well, to be honest, I don't know the chances that the smaller walls will *work*," said Vai. "But if they don't, we're all dead anyway, so it doesn't much matter if you've wasted your time, does it?"

"You've got proof of this?" asked Xu.

In answer, Vai whipped out a knife and sliced a short, shallow line across Paris's cheek.

"He's living dead now," she said. "Listen to him."

Paris hadn't had time to react to the cut. But now swift, cold dread pounded through his chest, because Xu belonged to the City Guard, and she would—she would—

Part of him still wanted to die. Part of him always would. But the Juliet had given him orders. He had never thought that he would be lucky enough to serve her again. And he didn't want to abandon Romeo or Vai, either.

But though Xu's hand dropped to her sword, she did not draw and cut him down. After a moment she looked at Vai and said, "Still you find ways to surprise me. *This* is your idea of persuasion?"

"It's about to be your idea, because you're going to realize I'm right and do what I say." Vai paused. "Probably."

"You are insane," said Paris. He looked at Vai. "It's true. I was killed and raised by a necromancer. His plan was to destroy the walls and open the gates of death."

"Popular plan," Vai muttered.

"He nearly succeeded. We killed him, but he got too far first. The Ruining has changed, I can feel it. If you don't start an evacuation, a lot of people will die."

"Also," Vai put in, "quite possibly anyone who dies will rise instantly now."

Xu's eyebrows went up. "'Possibly'?"

"Saw it happen with a crowd of living dead we slaughtered. Did not choose to test it on a crowd of innocent living folk." Vai shrugged. "But I would call it *very likely*."

Xu pinched her nose. "It's a terrible night for this."

"There's a good night for this kind of thing?" Paris asked in disbelief.

"No," said Xu. "But this night, there are a lot of things afoot. You're lucky you caught me now. I was about to leave my post."

"You're here until dawn," said Vai.

"That's what's in the schedule," said Xu. She sighed. "Get on with talking to your friends who won't talk to me because I'm the City Guard. I will spread the word."

"Please," Romeo yelled at the door, "you have to listen to me. The city is going to fall."

No one answered. No one had, for the last few hours.

Once more, he struggled against the ropes tying him to the chair. But it was useless. They were too secure.

Romeo was going to die in this little room, and he wouldn't even die because the Catresou executed him. He was going to die because they hadn't listened, they had tied him up and locked him away to deal with later while they examined the dead bodies left in the Master Necromancer's lair, and before they came back to deal with him the Ruining would kill them all.

Maybe he should have asked Paris to come. They might have listened to him.

But Romeo knew, as soon as he had the thought, that Meros would never have let anyone listen to Paris. He would have rather killed him a second time.

He would never have listened to Romeo, either. This had always been a fool's errand.

Gavarin might have listened, but he hadn't been there when Romeo had arrived back at the main Catresou safe house. Probably he was still locked away in disgrace somewhere, if he had been allowed to live at all.

Juliet, I'm sorry, he thought. *Emera, I'm sorry.*

They had both wanted him to save their people, and he had failed both of them.

The door opened. Romeo caught his breath, looking up with wild hope—

It was Ilurio.

For a moment they stared at each other in silence. Romeo couldn't imagine that Ilurio had been sent there, which meant he was probably . . . here to mock him. Because Ilurio wasn't a murderer, Romeo was sure of that; he hadn't come here to kill him.

"They said you'd come back." Ilurio looked down his nose.

"Yes," said Romeo.

"They said you killed the Master Necromancer."

And despite everything Romeo had learned, despite everything Makari had *done*, Romeo's heart still clenched in grief.

"No," he said. "Someone else did that. But I did choose to fight him. Because he was against *zoura*, and he was going to destroy us all. He tried to open the gates of death, and we managed to stop him, but he weakened the walls of the city. Very soon, nowhere outside the city spire will be safe. You *have* to get your people inside before that happens."

Ilurio stared at him another moment. Then he darted forward and started tugging at the ropes.

"You . . . believe me?" Romeo said slowly.

"No!" Ilurio blurted out, before he looked away and muttered, "Yes. It doesn't matter."

"Why?"

"You saved my life," Ilurio mumbled, the words so low that Romeo could barely make them out.

"I did?" said Romeo. He couldn't remember anything like that on the raid, unless Ilurio was just thinking of when Romeo had dueled Juliet, but that hardly seemed—

"Weeks ago! Before you came to inflict yourself on us! I wouldn't expect an ingrate like you to remember." Ilurio gave the ropes another useless tug, made a noise of disgust in the

259

back of his throat, then pulled out a knife. "Catresou pay their debts."

He cut through the ropes quickly, then hauled Romeo out of the chair. "Come on. There's a meeting going on now. They're questioning Gavarin. They think he conspired with you."

"Take me to them," said Romeo.

Ilurio made a noise deep in his throat. "If you had any honor, you'd ask to be punished in his place," he said, but there was worry in his eyes.

You don't really want me dead, Romeo thought, but didn't say it out loud.

Ilurio led him quickly through the corridors, back to the same room where Romeo had first been questioned by Meros. "In here," he said, and turned away.

"Ilurio," said Romeo, catching at his arm.

Ilurio looked back over his shoulder, his expression poisonous and reluctant.

"*Thank you,*" said Romeo, and meant it. "I am in your debt. And please, *please* get yourself and as many people as you can to the Upper City. There isn't much time left."

He saw Ilurio's mouth tighten, and saw him nod once.

Then he turned and threw open the door.

It was like he remembered: the Catresou lords gathered together, Meros at the center. This time, the one who knelt before them under guard was Gavarin. His head was held high, his back straight, but his face was ragged with unshaven stubble, and there were shadows under his eyes.

Romeo knew this because Gavarin had turned to look at him, along with everyone else in the room.

"You have to listen to me," he said.

"*You,*" Meros began.

"The Master Necromancer is dead. You can stay here and die in the ruins of his folly, or you can get your people to safety in the Upper City," said Romeo. "There's not much time left. Please, for the sake of your people, evacuate now."

Meros scoffed. "You want us to walk through the gates of our enemies and give ourselves up? Better for us to die down here."

"Half the Lower City is making their way through those gates already," said Romeo, desperately hoping it was true. "Haven't you looked out your windows?"

He saw uneasy glances exchanged between some of the Catresou lords, and felt a flicker of relief. Maybe they had seen the evacuation start. Maybe he could still convince them.

"You can lose yourselves in the crowd if you go now," he said. "It's a risk, but it's the only way your people live."

"I know I'm under sentence of death and all," said Gavarin, "but I'd advise you to trust him. The boy's a fool, but he's not stupid."

Meros's face was pinched and white with anger. "I will not be given orders by the son of Lord Ineo."

He won't listen, thought Romeo with a wave of despair. But in the same moment, he realized something: nobody had seized him yet.

There were guards in the room. Some of the Catresou lords were not so old and weak. Yet none of them had laid a hand on him.

They were not all determined to destroy him yet. Some of them were *listening*.

"You'll be advised by the husband of the Juliet, if you want to live," said Romeo. "Anyone who wants to live—who wants his family to live—needs to follow me now."

He turned and strode out of the room.

And after several heart-stopping moments, some of them followed him.

They brought Gavarin with them, and he fell into step beside Romeo. "You know the Juliet will kill you if she sees you."

"Yes," said Romeo. "She'll kill you too."

Gavarin chuckled. "Nobody should take up sword for the Catresou without being prepared to die for them."

"I tried to die for you," Romeo said bleakly, thinking, *If only I had succeeded.*

Gavarin's hand dropped to his shoulder. "You haven't done so badly, boy."

The Ruining began with the dawn.

Probably.

Paris didn't know exactly, because he was still with Vai, pounding on doors, telling people to leave, to grab what they could and start the trek toward the Upper City.

But he heard the screaming start. The wild, helpless screams of people who saw the white fog creeping through the alleyways and knew that the Ruining was here, it was happening, there was no more safety.

The streets were suddenly crowded then with people screaming, shouting, trying to escape.

He still didn't see the Little Lady.

But when he saw a narrow tendril of white fog winding between the houses near them—Paris grabbed Vai by the shoulder and hauled her back around the corner.

"You have to get inside," he said.

Vai shook her head. "There are still people to get out. And we still have to find the Little Lady. Didn't you hear the Mahyanai girl?"

"Yes," said Paris. "But you're not going to help anyone if you're dead." He took a shaky breath. "You should go back. I'll keep looking, because I'm . . . I think the fog might not kill me."

"You don't know that," said Vai.

"No," said Paris. "But it's worth a try, isn't it?"

Vai looked at him silently, then said, "I've always liked your courage."

She seized his shoulders and pressed her lips to his in a swift, warm kiss.

It lasted only a moment, but when their lips parted, she didn't let go of his shoulders. She held on to him and gave him a smile like sunlight on swords.

"Come back alive," she said, "and I'll be a woman for you."

Paris stared at her. He didn't know how anyone could be so fearless, so alive. He didn't know how she could stand to touch him.

"Vai," he said. "I'm already dead."

"And I'm already a man, but you don't see me giving up."

There were a thousand things he could say about how hopeless it was, how the blood was still cold and black inside his veins, how his dead heart still ached for death.

But he wasn't entirely dead yet. And the whole world was dying around them. And in this moment, perhaps the last he'd ever speak with her, he only wanted—

He kissed her.

He kissed her and didn't stop, because this was the only time he'd be able to touch her, the only chance he would have to learn the shape of her mouth when it was smiling into his. To feel this warmth, so bright and beautiful that it hurt.

Vai kissed him, and kissed him, and laughed as she stumbled

back until she was pressed against the wall. Paris kept kissing her, but slower now, less desperately, as her body relaxed against his.

When they finally stopped, they were molded to each other, forehead to forehead, hip to hip. He could feel her swift heartbeat, her breath in his ear, and it felt like she was living and breathing for both of them.

She would have to.

He thought, *I love you*, but he didn't want to say it when he had nothing to offer, nothing he could promise.

So he let go.

23

"YOUR EQUATIONS LOOK CORRECT," SAID Runajo, peering at the paper—she hadn't known that Sunjai had such terrible handwriting—"but why did you resolve this part *that* way?"

"Because I assumed we'd be in the Cloister," said Sunjai. "Really, did you think the walls were going to come out of anything *except* the sacred stone?"

Runajo thought of the wide, round room at the heart of the Cloister, and the dark, lumpy stone that some said had fallen from the sky, some said had been thrust up out of the land of the dead. She remembered the column of bubbling light that flowed up from the stone, the raw material that she had once daily woven into the walls around Viyara.

"But they won't let us in," she said.

The High Priestess had never once believed anything that

Runajo said, and in the Cloister, her word was law.

"They won't let *you* in," said Sunjai. "They'll obey the sister of the Exalted."

Runajo looked at Inyaan. The girl had been standing quietly in the corner of the room, her arms crossed, her face blank.

"The High Priestess—" she started.

"I am no longer a novice," said Inyaan. Her voice was quiet, but steady. "I am the one who outranks her, now."

Inyaan had always been silent and biddable. Runajo wondered whether now she would have the will to make the High Priestess comply . . . but she didn't think she still had the right to question her.

And Sunjai's calculations were correct. Their only hope of remaking the walls was inside the Cloister, and Inyaan was their only hope of getting in there. Runajo had no choice but to trust her.

Instead, she turned to Juliet, who waited silently by her side.

"I wouldn't advise you to go back there," she said.

"I wouldn't consent," said Juliet. "And I'm not free to go, anyway. The world is ending. I must be with my people."

Runajo's heart lurched with dread. "But the Catresou will kill you—"

"I mean the Mahyanai," said Juliet. "Don't you remember writing their name on my back?"

Her mouth curved. For once the smile wasn't bitter, but guilt still seeped through Runajo's body like acid.

"You do not owe us anything," she said quietly.

"No. I do not. But I am the Juliet. I was born to protect my people."

Juliet was serene, like a marble statue carved for duty and acceptance, and Runajo almost choked on her own rage. "We *are not your people.*"

For a moment Juliet stared at her, unreadable. Then—gently—she took Runajo's hand.

"You were right about one thing," she said. "My family wronged me. They made me a slave. But you never understood this: I chose to love them. I choose to love your people now."

Runajo's throat ached, and she couldn't speak. She wasn't sure she could ever find words.

But she remembered what she had seen Paris do, and she did the same: she sank to one knee and pressed her lips to Juliet's knuckles in a kiss of wordless repentance and loyalty.

Juliet pulled her hand free and laid it on Runajo's forehead. "I made a vow," she said. "So I cannot forgive you. But I wish that I could."

The heart of the Cloister was almost the same as as Runajo remembered: a huge, round room where glyphs and patterns shimmered as they swirled ceaselessly across the stone walls. At the center lay the sacred stone, a dark hulk of rock. The raw material of the walls still rushed up from it in a pillar of bubbling light that disappeared into a round shaft in the ceiling.

But the light was no longer a glowing white-blue. It had become dimmer, yellowed; there were gaps in the pillar as it rushed up into the ceiling.

The High Priestess stood before them, her aristocratic face a mask.

"Is this the will of the Exalted?" she said.

And Inyaan—who had always, for all the time that Runajo had known her, mumbled and refused to look anyone in the eye—raised her chin to stare down the High Priestess.

"By the blood of the gods that runs in my veins," she said, "I claim the ancient right to offer at the stone."

The High Priestess let out an angry breath, her nostrils flaring. For one moment, Runajo's heart jumped in fear, even though they had already been let so far into the Cloister: there was no one except the High Priestess to stop them, but that meant there was no one to see if she refused.

But the High Priestess bowed her head and said, "As the blood of the gods wills it."

She bowed gracefully and walked away with her head held high, equally graceful. And reluctantly, Runajo understood: the High Priestess might have longed to have her killed—she might think now that the three of them were no more than foolish children—but she believed in her duty to the gods and the royal house.

Against her will, she would allow them to save Viyara.

"You know your part?" asked Sunjai, circling the stone.

"Yes," said Runajo. She trailed a finger across the surface of the light, felt it fizz hot-cold against her skin. "We can't start till the last moment." It had taken them hours to get from the Exalted's palace to the heart of the Cloister—it must be dawn or later in the world outside—but that was still hardly enough time for the Lower City to be evacuated.

"That might be now," said Sunjai. "Taste it. You tested the wall the most, didn't you?"

That was true. Runajo leaned forward; she took a breath through her nose, then gently opened her mouth and touched her lips to the stream of light.

She felt the bubbling light swirl into her mouth, and for a moment she could imagine she was standing on the peak of the Cloister again, tasting the walls in the morning sunlight, planning how to save Viyara and never imagining how terribly wrong her plans could go.

Then the light curled around her tongue, and it wasn't anything like the bright, mineral taste she remembered. It was sour, buzzing against her teeth, a taste of cracks and shards and ending. She coughed and spat out the light; it spiraled away from her mouth and slid back into the column.

Runajo ran her tongue over her teeth. The taste still lingered in her mouth, dissonant and wrong.

"How long do we have?" asked Sunjai.

Runajo grimaced. "Not long. We'd better start."

Then she heard footsteps echoing through the doorway: many footsteps, a whole crowd of people. Runajo whirled, heart thudding with the fearful thought: *The High Priestess changed her mind. She's going to stop us.*

It was indeed the High Priestess who strode into the room, all the high-ranking Sisters of the order behind her. But there was no anger on her face; she did not call out for them to stop, and the women behind her did not rush forward to seize them.

Instead, the High Priestess halted a respectful few strides away and said, "If the blood of the gods is to be shed tonight, it is fitting for us to shed our blood as well."

Beside her, Miryo, the novice mistress, glowered at Runajo. "You'll need all the help you can get."

"Hush," said the High Priestess. "Take your places."

At her command, the Sisters spread out around the room in a ring, one stopping at each of the mouths of the city: the little stone bowls carved into the white stone floor of the chamber. And Runajo understood. They were here to offer penance, granting the walls what little extra strength they could.

The Sisters dropped to their knees. Runajo's stomach turned as she watched Miryo draw her knife and cut a thin line into her forearm—as the Sisters did the same, and all of them dripped blood into the mouths of the city.

The rims of the mouths were carved from solid white stone. But here at the center of the Sisterhood's power, the very stone was alive; as Runajo watched, the rims uncoiled into little tendrils of stone that curled up through the air, searching for the source of the blood.

Then she had to turn away and stare at the sacred stone, her stomach churning—because she knew what was happening now, to Miryo and all the Sisters in the room. The little strands had burrowed into their wounds, and the white stone was blushing pink as it sucked out the blood from their arms.

Runajo had offered penance only once, and the cold, foreign tendrils jammed into her arms had terrified her as knives never could.

"Time to start," she said, hoping her voice didn't shake, and drew her own knife.

She didn't hesitate making the cut in her own arm: she'd gotten plenty used to *that* in the year she'd spent as a novice. The pain was a strangely comforting thing, because it reminded her that she had trained for this. Once, she had been one of the best at weaving the walls, and she had sat in a room above this chamber every day.

There were three Sisters sitting in that room right now, still weaving. It was time for Runajo to change the walls they wove.

She reached into the stream of light—shivered at the cold, bubbling sensation across her skin—and let her blood drip onto the sacred stone. Sunjai and Inyaan did likewise.

Light sparked around the drops of blood. Runajo looked at Sunjai and Inyaan, saw them nod in readiness.

She reached into the pillar of light. It parted easily into strands, curled around her fingers like the tail of an affectionate cat.

Runajo started weaving.

The problem was not just constructing a smaller version of the wall. It was also killing as few people as possible while they constructed it. If they simply undid the former walls and then built new ones, there would be a time—however brief—when all Viyara was completely unprotected.

It might be that the white fog of the Ruining would not move fast enough, that the city could survive a few minutes naked before the power of living death.

None of them had been willing to take that risk. The pattern that Runajo and Sunjai had hit upon would shrink the walls in stages, surrendering more and more of the Lower City to death.

It had been a clever plan when they worked it out on paper. It was simple, now, to weave the strands of light in the rhythms they had planned.

But Runajo couldn't help remembering when she had walked through the Lower City with Juliet, seen the bustle in the marketplaces, heard the musicians on the street corners.

There had been so many people. They couldn't all make it

into the Upper City. She tried not to think of it, because regrets changed nothing, and this was a bargain she had to make—but each time the walls shrank, the light shuddered between her fingers, and she wondered who was dying. Who was screaming as the white fog wound between the buildings, and a heartbeat later would be silent ever after.

They were not any of her kin, dying down there in the Lower City. But that didn't matter. They were all of them as infinitely precious as Juliet. She had seen that once, had understood it, and the knowledge haunted her as she wove their deaths.

They would die anyway, she reminded herself. *I am buying life for the rest.*

But she couldn't stop the cold trickle of doubt, that this bargain might be as horrible and unclean as all the sacrifices of the Sisterhood.

They wove the walls. They brought them down to the width they had planned, tightly girdling the base of the city spire. It only remained to make the walls take their new form and keep it.

They wouldn't.

The pattern shuddered in Runajo's hands, striving to be larger and smaller at the same time. She was weaving as fast as she could, but it wasn't fast enough.

"It's not strong enough," said Sunjai.

"No," said Runajo. "We can make it work." Her hands moved faster, twisting the light into the new pattern, but it kept sliding out of her grasp, returning to its old form. They were, all three of them, twisting the new shape into the walls as fast as they could, but it was too eager to keep its old pattern.

"We need blood," said Sunjai.

"We've *got* blood," Runajo snapped. "We need"—she lunged to catch a strand—"another pair of hands—"

But all the hands in the room except theirs were held in place by the greedy stone tongues of the city.

"You promised me," said Sunjai, and Runajo was about to ask when she had promised Sunjai anything, but then she realized that Sunjai was looking at Inyaan.

And she knew. She knew what was going to happen, and she couldn't stop it. Because the spell had to be maintained. When Sunjai lowered her hands, Runajo lunged forward to grab the strands of light that she had dropped. When Inyaan also lowered her hands from the light—Runajo couldn't grab any more strands.

She could only weave as fast as she could and watch.

Watch as Inyaan drew her knife, as Sunjai threw herself back onto the stone, dark hair fanning out, eyes closing. It was the same position as the sacrifices at the Great Offering, but Sunjai wasn't drugged; the dazed smile on her face was sheer, idiot reverence, and Runajo's heart was helplessly beating faster and faster—

"No," Runajo said desperately. "Don't."

Inyaan was expressionless as she touched Sunjai's cheek gently, briefly. Then her knife flashed with the reflected light of the walls as it struck.

Runajo had attended the Great Offering every year of her life. She had seen many throats cut before. But she had never—even as a novice—been so close. She had seen the spray of blood, but she had never felt any of the warm droplets spatter across her face and hands. She had never heard the strange, gurgling gasp of the air escaping from the torn throat, and she hadn't realized how long the body would shudder and twitch.

She couldn't breathe. She couldn't think. Her throat was clenched and her body was numb with horror. But her hands kept moving, weaving the new pattern into the walls, because if she stopped now they were all dead.

Inyaan laid the knife down on the stone beside Sunjai's still-twitching body. The neat little *thunk* it made against the stone sent a shudder through Runajo. Then Inyaan put her bloody hands back into the light and started to weave it again.

Suddenly the light shivered around them, and Runajo felt a wave of power sear over her skin. The color of the light changed from a dull yellow to a pure white-blue.

Runajo thought, *Sunjai bought this,* and she hated the thought, utterly hated it.

Murder should not buy safety for gentle, helpless lives. It was wrong. It was *obscene.*

It was the only reason she was alive, and weaving the wall between her hands.

At last the pattern was strong and steady. She dropped her hands then—her arms ached with weariness—and flexed her fingers. Half-dried blood made her palms sticky.

Inyaan's and Sunjai's faces were equally dead, their eyes equally sightless as they stared at her.

"You killed her," said Runajo. "You planned this."

"Yes," said Inyaan, for once looking back at her.

You made me part of her murder, Runajo thought. *I had a choice and no choice and I will have to remember her blood forever.*

As Juliet remembered the blood of her people.

"I will never forgive you," she said.

Inyaan shrugged. "That is no matter to me," she said. "I am the blood of the gods. Her life was mine to sacrifice."

24

PARIS COULD STILL HEAR THE screams, but they were very faint now.

It was partly because of the fog, which muffled sounds. His boots made only a soft patter against the cobblestones even when he ran. When he called for the Little Lady, his voice did not echo; the sound was tiny and fell short.

Mostly, it was because this far out, there was nobody left alive.

A revenant that had once been an old man shuffled past him on the street. It didn't look at Paris: the living dead, he had quickly found, were of no interest to revenants.

He was doubly glad now that Vai had gone back. He hoped that she had made it to the Upper City in time.

Paris turned the corner of the street, and found a marketplace. The place was a shambles: stalls overturned, skinned rabbits and broken cups and a rainbow of scarves scattered across the ground.

Wisps of fog drifted across the sky but did not blot out the sun. In the early morning light, all the colors looked pale and raw and dreamlike.

The square was completely empty. All the new-made revenants were gone, drawn toward the base of the Upper City, where they could smell the living flesh and blood. Perhaps nobody was left out here but Paris and the Little Lady.

He drew a breath and called again, "Lady Juliet! We need you!"

He had no other name to call her. He wanted to believe that she would remember that name, that it would still mean something to her, as serving his Juliet still meant something to him.

But there was only silence in reply.

The hairs stood up on the back of his neck. Paris didn't understand, at first, why he felt such sudden dread clutching at his chest.

Then he realized: at the far end of the marketplace, he couldn't see the buildings anymore. Only a curtain of merciless white fog.

It was everywhere in the Lower City already. But so far the fog had only been in stray clouds and banks, easily avoidable. Paris hadn't let it touch him yet, hadn't yet tested his guess that he could survive it.

He realized, suddenly, that he was at the edge. That beyond this point, there was only the fog, no gaps, no spaces to hide.

And it was coming closer. White tendrils of fog slid across the ground, reaching like greedy fingers to touch the dead rabbits, the abandoned scarves.

Paris couldn't move.

The fog was death. He knew that. He could *feel* it. And one part of him yearned to crawl toward it, drink it down, let it embrace him.

One part of him was desperate to escape.

He remembered Vai laughing as she kissed him. And Romeo throwing an arm over his shoulders. And Runajo saving him for no reason. And Juliet letting him kiss her hand, trusting him with a mission even though he was now living dead, an abomination who would never find the Paths of Light.

And slowly, he walked forward.

The fog came to meet him, rushing forward like a friend. One tendril reached out to meet his hand, twined around his fingers— he shuddered—and then it was all around him.

It was icy-cold against his skin, and burned like acid. His eyes watered with pain and his heart stuttered in his chest.

But a moment and a moment later, he was still alive. And still dead, but still himself.

He opened his mouth, breathed in the fog. It burned in his lungs.

Paris could hardly see now. But as the fog trickled into the hollows of his ears, suddenly the muffling was gone. He could hear ten thousand voices and footsteps and heartbeats; he could hear the shape of the city around him, and the screaming crowds still trying to force their way through the gates to the Upper City, and the relentless crowds of revenants following.

And before him—not near, but not too far—he could hear one quiet set of footsteps, and one quiet heartbeat.

The Little Lady.

"You deserted us," said Lord Ineo.

Juliet knelt before him in one of the wide courtyards of his house. Several guards stood beside him. People crowded around the edges of the courtyard—she thought she saw Arajo's face—the whole city was already awake for the disaster.

"I was in the Lower City, killing a necromancer," said Juliet. "But it's true, I left the Upper City in defiance of your will."

Lord Ineo frowned. He was silent a moment, and in the distance, Juliet could hear the faint clamor at the gates.

"Did Runajo go with you?" he asked.

"Yes," said Juliet. "Now she is at the Cloister. They are remaking the walls to keep the Upper City safe."

"Did Runajo order you back to us?"

"No," said Juliet, meeting his eyes, and she knew that *he* would understand these words, even if no one else watching did. "She released me from all the orders she ever gave me. I came back of my own accord."

It was a testament to Lord Ineo's courage that he stared her down, barely flinching. The seals on her back still kept her from shedding any Mahyanai blood, but he had to know exactly how much destruction she could find a way to inflict, if she chose.

"Why did you come back?" he asked.

"It is the end of all things," said Juliet. "I must be with my people."

She didn't quite hear—she *felt* the way that the people watching shifted, breathed out, listened. She knew without looking that they were all looking at her as she said to Lord Ineo, "You are the lord of my clan. You have the right to punish my trespass. I am here to submit to your judgment."

And then she waited, heart pounding, for him to reply.

Obedience was the one thing that nobody could take from you.

Lord Ineo's faint sigh was endlessly weary. But his voice, when he spoke, was calm as ever. "Rise. You will tell me everything about the walls. And then you will atone by standing guard at our gates."

The fall of Viyara did not last much longer.

Juliet should not have been surprised. She knew quite well how quickly destruction could be accomplished. And yet she was surprised by how soon the screaming at the gates fell silent. There were still crowds trying to break in from the Lower City— she heard this from the people who passed by the gates of the

Mahyanai compound; she did not see it herself—but they were silent. They climbed over each other as desperately as the refugees once had, their hands reaching and pounding; but as they scraped and crushed each other, as they tried to beat their way into the Upper City, they were absolutely silent, every one.

A young guard told her that, his eyes haunted, before he went in to make his report to Lord Ineo.

Juliet stared at the street before her—the immaculate white stone, gleaming in the morning sunlight—and wondered if the walls would hold, and tried to comprehend what had happened.

It was Makari who had broken the walls. He was the one who had twisted the adjurations on her back, who had threatened Romeo to make her come to him, who had worked the final spell. She knew this, and hated him for it. And she knew that she had fought him in every way she could.

But she hadn't expected him to be so strong, there in his lair, and she couldn't help thinking—if she had never gone, if she had let him kill Romeo—

The walls had been breaking anyway. This would have happened soon, anyway.

That horrible thought was her only comfort.

Then she heard screams again.

A moment later, she saw people fleeing down the street. Two of them—a man and a woman—bolted toward the gate she was guarding.

"Revenants!" the man gasped as he shoved past. "Here! Summon the guards!"

For one horrifying instant, Juliet wondered if the gates had broken, and the revenants were surging through the Upper City.

But if that had happened, there would be far more commotion. It must be someone who had died just now and not been noticed.

"Get back!" said Juliet, drawing her sword, and she charged forward.

Then she turned the corner, and she saw what had found its way into the Upper City.

It was Paris.

He was deathly pale. His veins were swollen and visibly black through his skin, and black blood oozed out of his eyes.

He was a monster, and Juliet's heart turned over as she thought, *I sent him to become this.*

But he wasn't trying to attack anyone. He was stumbling forward, leading a girl with a perfect, doll-like face.

Justiran's daughter. The other Juliet.

Then Paris saw her. His mouth made something like a smile.

"Lady Juliet," he said. "I found her."

Juliet lowered her sword. "Everyone stay back!" she called out.

Paris let go of the girl's hand and stepped forward to meet Juliet. She thought he was still himself—he was certainly no revenant—but the sight of him still set her stomach churning with instinctive fear, the knowledge that this was a dead thing walking in broad daylight—

He stumbled.

Juliet caught him. The movement was unthinking, and then he was in her arms, coughing up black blood. Her throat tightened in revulsion, but she couldn't thrust him away.

Paris sighed and went limp in her arms. Juliet staggered under the sudden weight and sat down heavily.

"I found her," Paris whispered. His eyes squeezed shut and opened again; she didn't think he could see anything. "Did I—did I—"

"Yes," Juliet said. "You did."

It was tears that made her throat hurt now, but she couldn't let herself weep. She was the Juliet, she was *his* Juliet, and there was only one thing left she could do for him.

"You were very brave," she said, "and you have served me very well. You can rest now."

She pressed her lips to his cold forehead.

"Rest," she said, and he did not move again.

25

THERE WAS A STRANGE EMPTINESS to the world, now that half the world was gone.

Juliet gave Paris's body to the City Guard for disposal. She took Justiran's daughter by the hand and led her back to the same room where she had sat before. She explained obediently to Lord Ineo what had happened.

And she went back to her post at the gate. She watched, and waited, and wondered if Romeo was still alive.

Runajo came back at sunset. She told Lord Ineo that she had been attending the funeral of a Sister who had given her life for the wall. Her face and voice were faultlessly calm as ever, but Juliet could feel grief and guilt oozing through the cracks in the wall around her mind.

When they went back to the study together, where the other Juliet waited, Runajo didn't even try to study. She slumped to the ground, hugging herself, and didn't move. Her face was still perfectly calm.

Juliet waited beside her.

"Paris is dead, isn't he?" asked Runajo finally.

"Yes," said Juliet.

"I thought so," said Runajo. "I felt it."

The bond. Of course. Juliet hadn't thought about that part of it; she'd been shielding her mind from Runajo's for so long.

"He didn't suffer at the end," she said, remembering the peace that had been on his face, despite how horribly deformed it had been.

She remembered cutting his head off—she *had* to, just in case—and then she hoped desperately that Runajo hadn't seen that memory.

"He was nothing to me," said Runajo. "But I felt him die."

Juliet sighed, and decided that she could at least sit beside Runajo. That didn't count as forgiveness.

"He was hardly anything to me," she said. "But he was my kin. And he wanted to serve me." Her throat tightened with a sudden spike of grief—because Paris was dead, and if he hadn't been much to her, that was only because of her family's wickedness and cruelty. Because of all the people who had died today, he was one whose face and name she had known, whom she could mourn at least a little.

"He served me very well," she whispered, hands clenching as she bowed her head.

There was a moment of silence, and then she felt Runajo, very gently, lay a hand on her head.

Accepting comfort was not forgiveness, so Juliet let her.

After a while, Runajo spoke, her voice low. "The Sister who died—she wasn't really a Sister anymore. It was Sunjai. You met her, briefly."

Juliet nodded. "Your friend."

"She was *never* my friend," said Runajo with sudden fury, drawing her hand back. "I never liked her. I *hated* her. But she—she lied to me about her half of the calculations. There wasn't enough power for the spell. She let Inyaan cut her throat to make it work, and I had to stand weaving over her body as her last blood spilled out. I *hate* her."

Runajo's voice cracked on the last words. Suddenly she stood, and strode over to where the other Juliet sat in a chair, staring impassively at the both of them.

Runajo took the girl's hand, turned it over, and examined the wrist. Then she did the same with the other one. Juliet couldn't tell what she was looking for.

"I suppose it will help fulfill your vow," she said, her voice calm and polished once more, "that I was forced to help kill someone."

And Juliet knew her heart was fully traitor, because she hadn't even thought of it.

"I suppose it does," she said. "But it's not so amusing as it would have been once."

Lord Ineo sent for them early the next morning.

Runajo looked calm as they walked to his sitting room together, but Juliet could feel the worry coiled tight inside her.

Juliet herself was not afraid. Lord Ineo surely wanted revenge for what she had done yesterday. He surely also wanted a way to control her now. But the very worst that could happen . . . was that Romeo waited in that room for her to kill. Juliet was not sure that even Lord Ineo would willingly kill his own son, and even if he would—she was already doomed to kill him.

There was little more Lord Ineo could do to her.

But Romeo did not wait beside Lord Ineo in his room hung with exquisitely embroidered wall hangings.

Instead—blue kerchief garishly bright in the morning light— Vai stood, his arms crossed, before Lord Ineo. Beside him was Subcaptain Xu.

"Well," Vai was saying, as they walked into the room, "if you didn't want us in here, you should have locked us out to die."

Then he turned to look at Juliet, and grinned. "Good morning."

Juliet bowed as gracefully as she could and said, "What is your will, my lord?"

Lord Ineo's face twitched slightly. "It seems your former clan has infiltrated the Upper City."

"If you want to call sitting with the other refugees in the Great Court that," said Vai. "They're also under my protection. Over half the refugees are wearing my colors, and by the way, that puts me in the same position that your ancestors were a century ago, when you were important enough to sign the Accords."

"That's an interesting line of argument," said Xu, her voice faintly amused.

"To be debated another time," Lord Ineo said flatly. "However. It might be inadvisable to instigate a full-scale hunt for them at this time."

"The City Guard cannot allow that kind of chaos," said Xu.

"And however much the Catresou have betrayed us, the power of their necromancers is broken," said Lord Ineo.

He doesn't know that, Runajo said silently, her voice wrathful.

He knows it's no longer convenient for him to hunt them, Juliet replied bitterly.

"So I am prepared to offer the Catresou a mercy," said Lord Ineo. "Don't your people have a custom of trial by duel? I will allow them to send a duelist against you, and if he wins, I will consider the remaining Catresou innocent of necromancy."

Juliet stared at him. He must not have told Xu or Vai his plan before, because they were staring at him too.

This makes no sense, Runajo said furiously into her mind. *I have read your records; the Catresou haven't practiced trial by duel since—*

It doesn't matter, said Juliet. *He knows you released me from his orders. I'm a weapon he can't depend on anymore.*

And she felt Runajo's sick dread as she understood what was happening: if Juliet won, he would have an excuse to drive out the Catresou. And Juliet herself would have willingly destroyed her kin; he must be counting on that to finally break her will.

If Juliet lost . . . at least he would be rid of her.

"That kind of trial has no place in the laws of Viyara," said Xu.

"The Catresou have forfeited their place before the laws," said Lord Ineo.

"It's still not—"

"I am the Right Hand of the Exalted," said Lord Ineo. "Have you heard him to complain about me?"

Xu looked at him expressionlessly. "Not yet," she said, and was silent.

"I'm not sure how you think—" Vai started.

"I will fight," Juliet interrupted.

Vai looked at her, met her eyes. After a moment, he nodded.

What are you doing? Runajo demanded silently.

Winning, said Juliet.

All she had to do was fail.

It was a terrible gamble. They might send her someone with blood guilt upon him, and if that happened, she did not know if she could restrain herself long enough for him to kill her.

(They might send her Romeo, if they were very cruel, if he was very brave. And she knew how brave he was, and how cruel her people could be.)

But this might be the best chance she'd ever had to set things right. To save both her peoples.

You can't die yet, said Runajo. *You—you're the key to death, I need you—*

You have the girl who saw the Ruining start, said Juliet. *You have time. And you are very clever.* She could feel Runajo's icy desperation rising like a wave, but she couldn't let it drown her.

It's not mathematical to die now, she said. *But I am done with reckoning lives against each other. Will you forbid me?*

Runajo was silent a moment, and then she said, *No.*

Vai managed to catch Juliet quietly in the corridor before she left.

"Did Paris come back?" he asked.

"No," said Juliet. She didn't want to speak of it again, but she knew Paris had cared about Vai; she owed him this much. So she told Vai the story.

Vai listened without interrupting. When she was finished, he let out a slow breath and said quietly, "Thank you."

"For killing him," said Juliet, "or for telling you about it?"

"For letting him die in your service. I know what that meant to him." Vai paused. "Do you have a message for Romeo?"

Juliet's heart pounded against her ribs. She remembered, suddenly, holding her sword to Romeo's pale throat, the night after he killed Tybalt. She had nearly taken vengeance in that moment.

Instead, she had pressed her lips to his, and then taken him to her bed. That had been their third night together, the night that had made them husband and wife by Mahyanai custom—if not Catresou.

She could no longer offer any such mercy.

"Tell him," she said, "not to fight me."

"I will," said Vai. "And you don't know how much it means, that I am actually prepared to tell the truth. But you might want to consider exactly which man it was that you married."

"I must fight her," said Romeo, to the remaining high lords of the Catresou—because not all of them had made it out of the Lower City.

Including Meros.

Remeo heard the rustle of whispers: he wasn't alone with the high lords this time. The Catresou had been luckier than many of the refugees—Vai had managed to wrangle them a few abandoned houses to shelter in—but they were still crammed together; there was no room for private audiences.

"You'd claim the right to fight for us?" said one of the lords.

"Enough of your people have died already," said Romeo.

"You think you can *win* for us?" a man called.

Romeo turned, looking about the room. "I killed Tybalt," he said.

The hush that fell on the room was slightly shocked.

"He was your best, wasn't he? I defeated him. I think that's proof enough. And if I can't win—at least he's finally avenged." He turned back to the Catresou high lords. "Don't you think that's fair?"

"You do realize," said Gavarin from the corner, "that to win this duel, you'll have to kill the Juliet?"

"Yes," said Romeo, his heart breaking for the thousandth time.

"*Can* you kill her?" asked Gavarin.

"I took an oath to this clan," said Romeo. "Yes."

He knew Juliet. He knew that she wasn't planning to live at the cost of her people. He didn't see any way he could prevent that fate.

But if he could be the one who met her in battle—if they could somehow manage to *both* die on each other's swords—

That was something he could accept.

26

THE DUEL WAS AT SUNSET, before Lord Ineo's house.

The Catresou champion did not come alone. Vai was with him, and five of his men, as well as several Catresou.

He came masked, but Juliet knew him even before he bowed and removed his mask. Now that she knew he was alive, she didn't need to see his face.

It felt like her heart turned over in her chest with dread—but no surprise. Since the instant she had agreed to the duel, she had half known she would face Romeo.

Perhaps she had always known.

They had met on the Night of Ghosts, when Juliet had performed the sword dance before her people, and Romeo had caught the sword from her hands and danced with her. Perhaps

from that instant, they had been doomed to end this way, dancing with swords.

Lord Ineo was saying something, but Juliet didn't hear it. The
moment Romeo cast aside his mask and she saw his face, the rest
of the world ceased to exist. There was only him, and her, the
blood she could smell on him.

And her endless, furious need to kill.

They met in the center of the courtyard. Romeo had a
Catresou rapier, Juliet a Mahyanai sword. Unfamiliar weapons
for both of them, but the whisper of steel through air, the clash
as their blades met—that was all too familiar.

Juliet could have killed him in that first exchange. She saw the
opening in his defense. But she fought the compulsion burning
in her veins, forced her sword to slip, to let him catch her blade
and push it aside.

For a moment they were caught together, blade to blade, fingers almost close enough to brush.

Romeo's eyes were wide and dark. "I can't lose to you," he
whispered.

"Then *why did you come?*" she snarled, and wrenched herself
back. In another instant, she would have lunged forward and
killed him—but he attacked instantly, sword moving swifter
than she had ever seen him fight. For a few moments, he actually
drove her back.

This was the boy who had killed Tybalt Catresou, and now he

was pouring all his skill into fighting the Juliet herself—not so he could defeat her. Not so he could escape. So that he could give her these last moments to say good-bye.

So that he could kill her in the same moment that he died upon her sword.

She didn't doubt for an instant what he planned. It was exactly what she would have done had their places been reversed, and she hated him for it as fiercely as she loved him for it.

And nothing she felt mattered next to the terrible power driving her sword.

In the next moment, her sword slashed forward, and she barely turned the killing blow into a shallow slice of his cheek. Then he parried, and his rapier slashed her arm.

Her own was the only blood she had never been bound to avenge. The pain steadied her, gave her a moment of control where her sword wavered and their eyes met.

Then she kicked him solidly in the ribs and sent him sprawling to the ground. The next moment she was kneeling on top of him.

I love you, she thought desperately, *I love you, I love you, I—*

"I judge you guilty," she whispered, pressing the sword against his throat, every muscle trembling with the effort of holding it back, not killing him *yet* as she lowered her head and pressed her mouth to his in a desperate ghost of a kiss.

And she knew what she was about to do, knew exactly how it

would feel to push her sword that last inch and shed his blood across the white stone of the courtyard, knew it so well she almost thought it was happening—

His palm slammed into the side of her head with a deafening clap, rocking her to the side, and then he was out from under her, grabbing his sword.

"I love you," he said.

And as Juliet lunged for him again, she remembered the song he had once sung to her: *Journeys end in lovers meeting.*

Runajo shuddered as Juliet lunged again at Romeo. She wanted to look away, but she couldn't. Because she didn't deserve to look away.

She had put this fate on Juliet. She had no right to find it too horrifying now.

But even as she thought that—as she helplessly braced herself for the moment that she would feel Juliet die, the same way she had felt Paris die—her mind was still scrabbling for a way out.

There *had* to be a way to countermand the Juliet's killing. It was the only thing that made sense. Why would the Catresou create a weapon they couldn't choose how to wield?

Romeo was bleeding from his arm, but he was still on his feet, still moving quickly. Runajo didn't know anything about sword fighting, but even she could tell that they were drawing this out. Juliet couldn't stop herself from killing, but she could make everyone watch, make all the Mahyanai know what they were doing.

What Runajo had done. Because this was all on her, and her sudden, *brilliant* idea to save Juliet from dying by making her a killer.

Maybe it was just as well that she couldn't find a way to free Juliet. It might turn out just as terribly as when Runajo had handed her over to Lord Ineo. She had been so sure of herself then, sure that she was doing the right thing, but when had she ever known what she was doing?

The thought caught, shivered, and repeated: *When did you ever know?*

She hadn't known there was an answer in the Sunken Library. She hadn't known there was a way to end the Ruining. She had guessed, and gambled her life and Juliet's—the same way she'd gambled all Viyara when she and Sunjai and Inyaan bullied their way into the Cloister to remake the walls.

And maybe it was foolish to gamble again, but what did she have to lose?

The moment that Paris had died, it had felt like the air was gone from Runajo's lungs. She had staggered, the world dimming in her eyes, for several endless moments unable to separate herself from his death. Unable to realize that her heart was still beating. The gap where he had been still yawned in her mind.

Even though they had been bonded for no more than a day,

and their minds had barely touched ever, and he had been nothing dear to her.

If she lost Juliet—

Runajo was moving before she finished the thought, pushing her way to Lord Ineo's side, where he stood watching the duel.

"You have to stop this," she said quietly, rapidly. "Do you want your son to die?"

Lord Ineo gave her a look of weary disdain. "No traitor is a son of mine."

But she noticed the tendons in his tightly clasped hands. He wasn't as calm as he pretended.

"Do you want to be known as the man who had his son killed? Because that will be your legacy. *That's* what they will remember, not his treachery. Not even that you saved the Upper City."

"There's no way to stop her," said Lord Ineo. "You know that."

Runajo knew nothing. She only had a wild guess, and a hope that it could be true.

"Yes, there is," she lied. "If you pardon him, and declare his people kin. I read it in one of the records we stole from the Catresou. The Juliet enforces justice, but she must abide by the treaties of her clan. Do you think they'd want a weapon they couldn't control?"

Somebody shrieked. Runajo looked back to the duel, and her heart thudded. Because a Mahyanai girl—it was Arajo, the one she'd seen hanging around Juliet before—had bolted into the middle of the courtyard and flung herself between Romeo and Juliet, arms outstretched.

"Stop!"

And even through the walls between them, Runajo could feel the sudden spike of Juliet's fear, because this was an innocent, but the compulsion to kill was driving her nearly mad—

"You can't kill me," said Arajo, very pale. "I'm your clan."

"*No*," Romeo shouted, and tried to pushed his way forward between them, but Arajo threw herself forward at Juliet, grabbing her arm—and more people ran forward—

Runajo looked at Lord Ineo. "Your people will do it if you don't," she said.

He knew it; she could see it in the way his mouth twisted. "Stop," he called out, his voice ringing across the courtyard. "He is my kin and I pardon him."

For one heart-stopping instant, Runajo thought, *What if it doesn't work?*

And then she felt Juliet's dazzled wonderment as the need to kill was gone.

Her hands.

That was the first thing Juliet noticed, in the dazed moments after Lord Ineo called out the pardon and left her head ringing like a bell.

Her hands weren't moving. They felt hollow, at once heavy weights and lighter than air. Nothing drove them, twisted them, gave them power.

Then she was shaking and then she had fallen to her knees. She stared at her hands—braced against the ground—and she wasn't killing, she *wasn't hurting anyone*, and she didn't know if she could breathe through this much joy.

"Let me go!" she heard Romeo shouting, and she managed to raise her head and see him kneeling in front of her. His hands hovered beside her face, just barely not touching, as if he were afraid—

"Juliet," he whispered. "Are you all right?"

Because Romeo had never been afraid of her, only afraid *for* her, even when she'd been about to kill him. Juliet smiled and found she couldn't stop.

"Yes," she said. "Yes." And she reached out and touched his cheek—the unbloodied one, that she hadn't cut. They were both still bleeding from the wounds they had put on each other, their peoples were still at war and the whole world was dying, and none of it mattered because of this. This: the warmth of his cheek under her thumb, the cautious, steadying pressure of his hand against the back of her head.

What did you do? she called silently to Runajo, because she knew there was only one person who could have found a way.

I persuaded Lord Ineo to pardon him, said Runajo.

That was enough? How did you know? Another time, Juliet would rage or weep that she had never known it could be so simple, but not now. Not when Romeo's forehead was pressed against hers and she could feel his breath against her face.

I didn't know, said Runajo. *I guessed. And then I lied.*

Thank you, said Juliet, and did not care that she hadn't forgiven Runajo, could not forgive her. *Thank you.*

Wait until we've finished negotiating with Lord Ineo, said Runajo.

But Lord Ineo was not a problem. Juliet had just found the strength to rise, to lead Romeo by the hand before Lord Ineo—but she hadn't yet had time to speak—when there was a commotion at the gates. It was Subcaptain Xu, but over her uniform was hung a new gold chain. She strode through the courtyard without looking to the left or right, straight up to Lord Ineo, and said, "I must speak to you. And the Catresou."

"About what?" asked Lord Ineo.

"The Exalted desires peace among her people."

Lord Ineo's eyebrows went up. "*Her* people?"

"Yes," said Xu. "The Exalted *you* served was so distressed by the ruin of his people, he poured out his lifeblood in sacrifice to honor them, and beg the gods for mercy. His younger sister now sits upon his throne, she has appointed me as her right hand, and she has sent me to settle this feud."

So that was that. Vai went to fetch the Catresou leaders— Romeo would not let go of Juliet's hand, would not leave her side for an instant—and they held their negotiations in his study that night.

This was the agreement that they made, under Xu's watchful eyes: that all the necromancers were dead. That there was to be peace among the four houses—because Vai's followers were numerous and unified enough now to be considered one of them. That, to make sure Juliet's power would not drive her to kill again and restart the feud, the Mahyanai and Catresou were to be considered allies.

And to seal that alliance, Juliet would be given to Romeo in a Catresou wedding, so that both clans would recognize the marriage.

After it was all over—after Romeo had finally left with the Catresou, so that he could give them his own account of what had happened—Lord Ineo looked at Juliet and said, "You've won yourself a very great concession."

Anger shuddered at the pit of her stomach. "I wasn't forced to kill your son," she said. "That's what you call a *concession*?"

"Do you want revenge for that?" he asked flatly. "Because you won't find it easy."

Juliet stared at him and thought wearily, for the thousandth time, of Catresou blood spilling under her blade, her father's neck snapping between her hands.

But she thought also of Arajo smiling, and the silence in the family shrine where the names of all the Mahyanai dead were written.

"I was made for revenge," she said. "But the world is very small now. Too small, I think, for me to take it."

"You were made for *obedience*," he said bitterly. "Or so I was told."

And Juliet could not hold back her weary, triumphant smile.

"I was born under obedience," she said. "Did you think I wouldn't know how to use it?"

27

THEY WEREN'T MARRIED FOR ANOTHER three days.

A year ago, that would have been a foolishly short time to prepare for a wedding. Now it seemed to Romeo like an outrageous
delay. There was no such thing as a proper ceremony anymore,
not when all the Lower City was dead and filled with revenants,
and the walls around the Upper City had only barely survived.

But the wedding was still part of the peace between the clans.
Lord Ineo wanted it to be celebrated as well as the desperate
circumstances would allow, and so did Lord Indarus, who had
become the new Lord Catresou. And that took time to arrange.

"We're already married," Romeo had muttered rebelliously
when he heard the news.

Gavarin had given him a hard look before saying, "So far as

you're a Catresou, you're not. Take the time to restore the girl's honor the right way."

"She lacks *nothing* of honor," Romeo had said hotly, but he didn't complain any more. He knew that this wedding was for the clans as much as it was for him and Juliet.

And even though the Catresou had been granted their old rights and homes again, there was still much to be done. In some parts of the compound, there was still blood dried onto the floor.

The day before the wedding, Romeo realized that he had been so busy with preparations, he still didn't know exactly what the ceremony would entail. He meant to simply ask Gavarin about it, but he hadn't found him yet when he ran into Ilurio, and let slip why he was looking.

Ilurio's explanation was delivered in extremely smug tones, but it was easy enough to understand, and it sounded much simpler and less exotic than Romeo had feared. For one thing, there were no organs in jars.

"Is that all?" he asked when Ilurio finished.

"Well," said Ilurio, "then you have to bed her—"

Romeo glared at him. "I know about that."

"—in front of witnesses."

"What?"

"Ancient custom," said Ilurio. "To ensure that the marriage is properly consummated."

"She is already my wife," Romeo snarled, his face hot and cold at once, because he couldn't imagine asking Juliet to undergo that—but if this was her people's tradition then she must expect it—

"What's this?" asked Gavarin, who walked into the room, looked at the pair of them, and then slapped the back of Ilurio's head.

"I was just telling him what to expect," Ilurio muttered. "With the bedding."

Gavarin sighed and turned to Romeo. "The wedding party takes you to the bed and witnesses you unmask each other, to be sure there's been no trickery. *Then* we lock the door on you."

"Oh." Romeo relaxed. "Do people really try to switch places?"

Gavarin shrugged. "There are stories of it."

"It's more to make sure nobody can dispute the dowry by claiming the marriage wasn't consummated," said Ilurio. "Though I suppose you don't have to worry about *that*."

There wasn't nearly the same scorn or venom in Ilurio's voice as there used to be, but the words still rankled. Romeo opened his mouth to protest—

"Ignore him," said Gavarin. "He's jealous because he's never yet kissed a girl." And while Ilurio sputtered, he went on, "We've got more important things to discuss."

"Yes?" said Romeo. Gavarin was looking at him with a grim concentration that he hadn't seen since he was threatening

Romeo with death at the start of their raid.

"Listen, I know marriage isn't the same thing among your people," said Gavarin.

"I would *never* take a concubine," Romeo said earnestly. "I promised her that already." And no matter how many people he'd heard say that the heart needed room to roam, he couldn't imagine loving any woman but Juliet.

"Good," said Gavarin, "but that isn't what I meant to tell you. I know the Mahyanai like to send their women into the Guard, but that isn't our way. You're a Catresou now, and that means you protect your wife."

Romeo thought of the way that Juliet's sword had danced through the air when they dueled, and he almost laughed. But then he looked at the grim set of Gavarin's face. He thought of how lonely Juliet had been when he had met her, the girl without a name, reverenced by all her people and befriended by none.

He had thought, *I can save her,* and he'd been terribly wrong in every way. He'd broken her heart and left her alone and nearly destroyed her.

Except . . . he had made her less lonely, for a little while. And after everything went wrong and they were parted, she had found Runajo—and it hadn't been any of his doing, but it wouldn't have happened if he had never seen a girl alone in a garden, practicing her sword work, and wanted to talk to her. If he hadn't asked her to marry him, one sunlit afternoon as they sat on the rooftops of the Lower City.

He thought, *Maybe I can protect her now.*

This time, maybe I can give her happiness that lasts.

"I don't care what the Mahyanai have done to her," said Gavarin. "The Juliet is still one of us. So you take care to do right by her."

"I will," said Romeo.

It was not unknown for Juliets to marry. But it was rare. Few men wanted wives who were living weapons. Though Juliet had attended several weddings in her childhood, she had never dreamed she would be at the center of one herself.

"That's an ugly mask," said Arajo, puckering her mouth at the wedding mask resting on the table. It was a full-face mask, gilded all over, with curling red designs painted around the eyes.

"It's traditional," said Juliet.

"Well," said Arajo, "you belong to *us* now, so you can at least wear a proper wedding dress."

"I didn't know your people cared so much about weddings," said Juliet.

"Just because we don't lock up our women before they're wed, doesn't mean we don't care," said Arajo. "My mother has found a dress you can borrow."

It wasn't a single dress: it was three silk dresses, layered on top of each other, so that the inner colors showed only at the hem and neck and sleeves. The outermost was gold, the middle layer was white, and the third—silky against her skin—was deep crimson.

"I know a handmaid who is splendid with cosmetics," said Arajo, examining her critically, "but it would just be smeared all over your face when you put that mask on, so I won't bother."

Our women are beautiful enough without painting, Juliet thought. But she supposed that if she was Mahyanai now, she would need to learn their beauty.

That was not something she had ever expected. Even when she had planned to make them hers, when she had turned all her will to learning their ways—even before she had known that Romeo was alive, and she could only avoid killing him if she died—she had never imagined herself *living* with the Mahyanai.

She had never dreamed that she might be happy among them. That she might ever look forward to sunrise or sunset because it was going to bring something better.

The world was dying still, but at sundown, she would be in Romeo's arms again. Every day that remained to her, she would be with him.

Suddenly she was very aware of her heart fluttering against her ribs. The shiver in her stomach.

"You don't have to wear the mask," said Arajo, looking at her with concern.

"If I don't," said Juliet, "I'm saying that everyone in the room is my better, and deserves to rule me."

Arajo went very still. "Is that how you felt when you came here?" she asked.

Juliet hesitated a few moments, trying to find the truth.

"Yes," she said finally. "But at least you were all shaming yourselves along with me."

"Hm." Arajo fiddled with the hair combs on the table, and then set them down. "You should have something gold, not silver. I'm going to go check my mother's jewel box."

"Arajo." Juliet caught her hand before she could leave. "Thank you for saving Romeo."

Arajo's hand did not grip her back, but she didn't draw it away either. The look she gave Juliet was . . . *caught*.

"I was ashamed," she said quietly, after a few moments. "When I stopped being angry, I was ashamed of what we did to you. Whatever your people are like, *you* are—" Her mouth snapped shut and she stared at the ground. "I don't understand how you forgave me."

I never said I did, Juliet nearly replied, but she stopped herself just in time. She realized with a sudden, heartsore pang that Runajo would grin at the words but Arajo wouldn't.

"You saved my husband," she said instead, and Arajo smiled weakly before she left.

Juliet looked at the table, piled with discarded ornaments.

Silently, she called out to Runajo: *Am I going to see you at all tonight?*

She had hardly seen Runajo at all the past three days. She had either been talking with the Sisterhood—helping restore the city's walls had put her back in their favor—or she had been studying the dead Juliet.

Do you want to? Runajo asked, and her silent voice was rawer than Juliet had expected.

I'm going to see all my other enemies at this wedding, she replied.

Runajo was there barely a minute later. "A Mahyanai dress and a Catresou mask," she said. "You will look atrocious to everyone."

"Except Romeo," said Juliet. "And he's the only one I have to please."

Runajo remained standing just inside the door. "And Lord Ineo," she said bitterly.

Juliet grinned. "Not in bed."

Runajo clapped a hand to her mouth, covering her laugh as if it were a sick cough.

"I thought Catresou girls were supposed to blush at these things," she said.

"Yes," said Juliet, "but I'm almost a married woman."

And the memory welled up between them, so sudden and overwhelming that Juliet couldn't tell which of them it came from: the last time that Juliet had been unashamed to speak of Romeo in her bed. When they had been prisoners in the Cloister together, and the High Priestess had given Runajo a knife and told her to sacrifice Juliet, and Juliet had believed she would.

When Runajo—

Juliet caught the thought, stopped it and the flood of bitter, hateful memories that went with it. Because Runajo had set her free. Because today was her wedding day. Because, very soon, everyone in the world would die anyway.

(She suspected *that* thought had sidled in from Runajo's mind.)

She looked up at Runajo and said, "I don't forgive you, but I am glad that I lived until today."

"That makes no sense at all," Runajo muttered, but she was almost halfway smiling.

And so, before both their peoples, Juliet Catresou was married to Mahyanai Romeo.

They joined hands, and the wedding scroll was wrapped around their wrists: a long strip of silk on which the magi had embroidered seals and sigils that invoked fertility and faithfulness. It was plainer and simpler than the wedding scrolls Juliet had seen as a child, but it was the only one that had survived the purge and the Ruining.

Juliet felt dizzy when Romeo's fingers squeezed hers. When

he looked into her eyes, and she told herself, *This is real, this is real,* as he swore aloud that he would love and cherish her, honor and guard her. When she replied with her vow to give him her life and her children, to honor him with breath and body, as two clans listened and she thought, *They cannot take us apart now.*

There was a feast afterward—though little more than a dinner, given the circumstances. Juliet hardly tasted the food. She did not have to wait long, anyway: the custom was that the bride and groom were escorted to their bed early.

It felt like a dream when they were led in procession to the bedroom: like a vision, something that might come to pass but was not yet real. But then Juliet sat on the bed, and she felt the mattress shift as Romeo sat down beside her. She felt his fingertips brush the side of her face as he undid her mask and lifted it away; and then she lifted his mask away, and she didn't care that one of the magi was still droning the traditional blessing. She leaned forward, as easily and inevitably as breathing, and kissed him.

Somebody laughed, but she didn't care either.

With that, the wedding was over. The crowd filed out of the room.

The door closed.

They were kissing still. But then Romeo's hand drifted down the side of Juliet's face to rest on her shoulder, and landed on the spot where he had wounded her. She flinched, her breath hissing in, and he jolted back.

"I'm sorry," he said desperately. "I'm sorry."

Juliet flexed the shoulder. "It's not bad," she said.

Runajo had managed to obtain some of the Sisterhood's healing ointment for both of them; the cut on Romeo's face was already gone completely. But deeper wounds took more time to heal.

Rome still looked haunted; he raised a hand, then snatched it back. "I don't want to hurt you."

Juliet put a hand on his face, and rubbed her thumb against his cheek, in the spot where her sword had once cut his skin open.

"I have hurt you," she said. "I have hurt a lot of people. I can't forgive myself. But I can forgive *you*."

Romeo smiled, and he was the one who kissed her next. Kissed her, and did not stop.

Juliet remembered their first night together, how it had felt like they were the only people in the world. How she had pressed her lips to his and forgotten her name, forgotten her clan, forgotten everything but the boy in front of her and the cascading joy of his touch.

It was not like that now.

She could still hear the ragged echo of Catresou wedding songs. When Romeo slid off the first layer of the Mahyanai wedding dress, she felt another twinge of the wound in her shoulder. She knew that each touch, each kiss was hers only because of the alliance they had forged. That it was *part* of the alliance, as fragile and fierce and dearly bought as the walls girdling the city, holding back death for one more day.

In all her dreams, Juliet had never imagined she might have this gift: that this joy might be not just for her, and not just a secret to be shared with Romeo. That it could be part of her duty as well, a payment of debts and a promise for the future.

That here in this bed, they could be making peace between their peoples.

28

JULIET WOKE IN THE ARMS of her beloved.

She had greeted three dawns in Romeo's arms before. But every one of those mornings she had woken a dozen times before dawn, twitching awake each time Romeo shifted or she heard a noise from elsewhere in the house. In half-awake snippets, she had watched the sky grow pale until it bloomed with cold morning light, and she had pushed Romeo out of her bed in her haste to get him safely away.

This morning, she woke once before dawn, her heart pounding with sudden, nameless fear. But Romeo was sleeping beside her, and she remembered that she was his wife. That she did not have to fear discovery. That she was *meant* to be in his arms. And she lay back down beside him and slept until the risen sun was bursting through the chinks in the curtains.

When she opened her eyes again, Romeo was already awake. Morning sunlight danced in his dark eyes as he gazed at her with delighted reverence.

"I married you," he whispered.

Juliet smiled, and reached to touch his face. "You did."

But the world was dying still.

And those who lived had to pay the price.

Juliet had barely finished breakfast when Runajo, white-lipped, came to give her the news: Inyaan, the new Exalted, had decreed a weekly sacrifice.

"They have worked the equations," said Runajo. "It's the only way to maintain the walls."

Juliet's mouth felt dry and sour. "Even after Sunjai's sacrifice?"

"Of *course* even after," Runajo said bitterly. "Did you think we'd live another way?"

Her pain ached through the bond between them.

"Then we end it," said Juliet.

The words hurt. She had never had so much to lose, in all her life. But she was the Juliet and she was the key to death and now that the Mouth of Death was dry, she was the only hope to stop the Ruining.

And she had always, always mattered less than what she could do for her people.

"When do we go?" she asked.

"I don't know if *we* have to go anywhere," said Runajo. "You might just need to open the way into death and let me go through. And not yet. Now that the Sisterhood will talk to me, I want to try some more research. We only get one chance at this. I need to be *sure*."

"Is it safe to wait?" asked Juliet. "When the Ruining is so strong?"

Runajo laughed bitterly. "Inyaan's pouring out enough blood to keep us alive another month at least. You can't imagine how the Old Viyarans love her. They're lining up to offer themselves for sacrifice. I think we can wait a little longer."

But Juliet could tell that Runajo thought the time they had left was more *little* than *longer*. She thought of this when she watched Vai argue down Lord Ineo, negotiating on behalf of a new-forged clan than might not last another year. And when she walked the streets, and saw mothers caring for children who might never grow up. And when she leaned against Romeo, and listened to his heartbeat, and wondered how soon the final end would start.

On the third day after her wedding, Lord Ineo dismissed her before she had expected. She meant to find Runajo, to ask how her research was going—but then a servant told her she had a visitor waiting for her in one of the sitting rooms.

It was Vai, holding a gleaming, straight-edged razor.

"I hope that's not a challenge," said Juliet.

"No," said Vai. "I'm here to ask a favor."

"Why?" asked Juliet, genuinely curious. They had never been friends or enemies.

"Well, I hear you're a woman."

"Romeo tells me you are too," said Juliet, eyeing her cautiously. She knew there were a lot of strange customs among the various peoples in the city; she couldn't say she felt at ease with this one, but she had learned to live with the Mahyanai, after all.

"There he's wrong," said Vai. "I'm definitely a man. I have the braids and a dead brother and a vow to prove it. Did he tell you that, too?"

"Yes," said Juliet. "Romeo thinks it's very touching."

Vai grinned. "Not you?"

Juliet often needed to watch her tongue these days, but after a moment's hesitation, she decided that Vai was not one of the people who preferred her quiet.

"I think it's an utterly abhorrent custom," she said. "Demanding that your girls renounce their womanhood so they can raise up bastard heirs to their families?"

"Says the woman who wields a sword," said Vai. "Not to mention those spells on your back. At least I was given manhood before I was compelled to fight for my people."

Juliet crossed her arms. The words cut closer than she would have liked.

"And you?" she demanded. "Do you thank your family for what they did to you?"

Vai was silent a few moments. Then: "My grandfather was also born a girl," she said, very softly. "He died when I was nine, but I still remember him. He told me once that he was never so happy as on the day his mother declared he would be her son." She sighed. "It's a finer thing to be a man than a woman, or so my mother told me. I should have found it easy to be just as delighted as my grandfather. But I never could."

"You didn't come here to tell me that," said Juliet.

"No." Vai pursed her lips. "Did Romeo tell you that there's no one left of my people but me and my mother and my grandmother?"

"Yes," said Juliet.

"I made a vow to be a man so long as my family needed heirs. If my father were still alive, and got a son on my mother, then I could stop. It's a very traditional loophole. But my father's dead. I'm the man of the family, and that means my word is law. Or should be; I'm not sure my grandmother has ever quite accepted that. But if I declare that our women can pass down an inheritance—well, *she* won't accept it, but my mother might after we bury her."

She held out the razor to Juliet.

"I'm not helping you kill your grandmother," said Juliet.

Vai rolled her eyes. "As if I would suggest such a thing."

"I don't actually know you well enough to be sure you wouldn't," said Juliet, but she couldn't help smiling.

"I'm asking you to help shave my head," said Vai. "That's what the women of our people do: shave our heads when we turn thir-teen, and never let a single hair grow after. And it's meant to be a thing that women do for each other, but . . . my mother won't while my grandmother lives. My grandmother won't *ever*."

"And I'm not your kin," said Juliet.

"No," said Vai. "But you're a woman. And kin to Paris, who was going to be mine. And you know what it means to pick and choose the duties that you pay to your family."

I didn't get to choose those duties, thought Juliet, but that wasn't true. She had chosen to love Romeo and try to make him her Guardian. She had chosen to help Runajo in the Cloister. She had chosen to win the Mahyanai's loyalty.

Even in her childhood, when she had done nothing but what she was told—she had *chosen* to be so scrupulously obedient. (And she was uncomfortably aware that even if she had a chance, now, to find her way back to being that girl—she wouldn't want to.)

She took the razor. "I've never done this before," she said. "I will probably cut you."

"Well, don't try to shave me," said Vai. "I can take care of that myself. Just cut the braids off. That's the part that's ceremonial."

Slowly, carefully, Juliet began slicing off the braids one by one.

"Thank you," Vai said quietly as she worked.

"Paris cared for you and he was mine for a little while," said Juliet. "These days, I think that makes us close enough to sisters."

It was strange, for Romeo to wake without desperation.

He could hardly remember what it was like. He'd been desperate to save the Catresou, to atone for his sins—before that, to find the Master Necromancer, to save the city and avenge Juliet—before *that*, to find a way to be with Juliet—

Now he could wake in her arms and fear nothing.

There was also nothing for him to do now. The Catresou might count him as kin, but he could do nothing for them, besides exist as Lord Ineo's son and Juliet's husband.

That was how he found himself going back to the Little Lady.

"I don't think I ever properly thanked you," said Romeo.

The Little Lady stared back at him with empty blue eyes. Romeo knew now that she had once been a Juliet, but he couldn't stop thinking of her by the first name that he'd known for her.

But that wasn't really a name, was it?

"You saved Juliet," he said. "You saved us all. I know you probably didn't do it for my sake or hers, but . . . thank you."

She was silent.

"What's your name?" he asked. "They tell me you were once a Juliet, but . . . is that what you want to be called?"

Still she didn't reply.

"You don't have to tell me," he said. "But I've heard Juliet and Runajo talk. I know we're all going to die soon. And when I'm dying . . . I want to remember the name of the person who let me live long enough to marry Juliet."

"I want to die," she said, and the back of his neck prickled.

He knew that he was very ignorant about necromancy and the land of the dead. That Runajo was the one who should be questioning the Little Lady. That Juliet should be the one deciding what to do about what she said.

But she looked so lonely and so lost, and he remembered how they had sat together locked in the room where Makari placed them, and it had felt like they were prisoners together.

He remembered what Makari had never asked her.

"What do you want me to do?" he asked. "I owe you my life. I will help you any way I can."

For several silent moments, he waited, and he started to think that she wouldn't answer and that it had been a useless question—

"Take me back," she said. "Open the door."

She still spoke in the same soft, dead tones. But now she was looking *at him*, directly into his eyes, and his heart jumped and thudded against his ribs.

"How?" he asked.

"I can't find the way," she said. "I can't go back. But you could lead me. You are the key."

29

My dearest Juliet,

I will not beg you to forgive me. I do not have the right, when I do not regret. But I will beg you to understand.

The Little Lady—Justiran's daughter, the other Juliet—spoke to me. She told me what I think you know: that if she is to rest, somebody must open the doors of death and lead her in. But she told me something else: when Paris and I broke the bone key with a knife covered in my blood, its power passed to me.

We are now both of us the keys to death.

And that means one of us must take her to rest. And I do not think the one who goes will return.

I know you are angry, and you have every right. I have wronged you greatly; I should have told you, and let you make this choice. But you are the peace between our peoples. You are *the one who can protect us. So that means I should protect you.*

And I am selfish, and I cannot bear to live without you
again.

The Little Lady says that if I lead her back to rest, the
Ruining will end. I hope she is right. But if you read this letter
and the world is not healed, you may still need to follow after
me, and do what I could not. So know this: the Little Lady
told me that for the two of us, opening the door is as simple as
spilling blood and calling on Death.

I do not know what waits for me in that darkened kingdom.
But I know that whatever I may find, if there is any way, then I
will wait for you.

With deepest love and resignation,
Romeo

JULIET, STILL SITTING IN BED, stared at the page. At the graceful handwriting she knew so well. Her body felt numb and cold, her fingers like weights, her heartbeat like falling stones.

He had left her. He had *left* her.

And now he was dead.

She did not doubt that he had managed to open the gates of death. Romeo had his weaknesses, but he had never, ever failed to do the impossible. And since she was alive and breathing, she knew he had not destroyed the world by doing so.

She did not know if he had saved them.

She did not know if she could ever forgive him. She thought this, and knew even as she thought it that it was a lie. Nothing could make her hate him for being too kind and too brave—for doing what she would have done in a heartbeat, if she had been given the chance.

Last night he had whispered into her hair, *Do you know how much I love you?*

She had laughed as she replied, *Of course I do: a little more than reason.*

And you, he had asked, *how much do you love me?*

A little more than vengeance.

And now he was gone. A death she could never avenge.

She realized that she had been waiting to weep. But her eyes were still dry. So she got up, and dressed herself, and went to find Runajo. She had fallen asleep over a stack of ancient books, her dark hair loose and tangled.

Juliet shook her awake. "Has anything changed?" she demanded.

"What?" said Runajo, sitting up. Then she looked at Juliet's face. "What happened?"

"Romeo discovered that he's also a living key to death. Because when he broke the bone key, his blood was on the knife. So he's taken Justiran's daughter and gone."

The words felt jumbled and meaningless in her mouth.

"*Romeo* went into death?" said Runajo. "But . . . he didn't read any of the records, he doesn't have any idea how to talk to Death—"

"You don't either," said Juliet. "He wanted to stop me from going first."

Runajo grimaced. "Of course he did," she muttered.

"We need to find out if he stopped the Ruining," said Juliet. "Because if not, I've got to go after him."

"Well," said Runajo, "I suppose we'd better find someone who's just died, and see what happens."

"People don't die on command."

"You have a knife," said Runajo, running a hand through her hair. "*Or* we could check the gates into the Lower City. If the Ruining is ended, the revenants should all have died again."

As they walked through the streets together, Juliet strained her ears with every step, twitching at every tiny noise. If the Ruining had ended, would there be a commotion? A terrible silence? Would anyone have noticed yet?

Without the Ruining, what would the world look like?

But she wasn't going to find out. Because when they got to the gates, and looked down into the Lower City, they saw the mass of revenants still pawing at the doors. They saw the white fog swirling among the houses, despite the dazzling morning sun.

Juliet sat down heavily on the cobblestones. A moment later, Runajo sat beside her.

"It might not happen at once," she said gently.

"You let me read that manuscript," said Juliet. "You know how fast it happened last time."

The sun was so very bright. It didn't seem right, when Romeo was dead.

She remembered Justiran's daughter saying, *I want to die*, and she thought viciously, *I hope you think your death was worth it. I would have lived ten thousand years without rest, rather than be his death.*

I have been his death.

Gingerly, Runajo laid a hand on her shoulders.

And then, at last, Juliet started to weep.

"I won't take you with me," Juliet said that evening.

"That's ridiculous," said Runajo. "I was the one who read the manuscripts—"

"And told me what they said. 'Death will parley with those who pass the reapers'—tell me, which of us has killed reapers?"

"Which of us," demanded Runajo, "has been trained in that lore?"

"That girl who bargained with Death," said Juliet, "she wasn't a trained Sister, was she?"

"She was one of the Ancients, a servant of their Imperial Princess," said Runajo. "She probably knew a lot more of magic than you."

"Or *you*," said Juliet. "And if I don't succeed, you can read my father's notes, make a new key to death as he made me, and have a second chance. You know it's logical."

"But—"

"Mahyanai Runajo." Juliet stared her down. "You owe me a life. Many more than one, in fact. So consider this my vengeance: you will not go with me. You will live, and do what you can to protect our peoples."

Runajo's face was very pale, her hands clenched into fists. For a moment, Juliet thought she was going to protest again. Then her breath sighed out as her shoulders slumped.

"I don't have the right to tell you no," she said.

You could forbid me, thought Juliet, but—with a sort of dazed wonder—she realized that until now, it hadn't even occurred to her that Runajo might.

Then she felt the sudden stab of Runajo's guilt, and realized that she had let that thought pass through the bond between them.

"But I trust you won't," she said out loud.

Runajo smiled faintly. "You were always stupid," she said, but gave her no orders.

Runajo insisted that they go to the Mouth of Death.

"I thought it dried up," said Juliet.

"Yes," said Runajo. "But it's still the place where somebody succeeded three thousand years ago. It might help you now. And

I can get you there. The High Priestess owes me a favor."

Romeo had not needed to go there before he walked into death. But then, he had not succeeded in ending the Ruining. And Juliet thought that Runajo needed to do something to help her. So she followed her back to the Cloister, and finally saw the spot where Runajo had once saved her, when her attempt to make Romeo her Guardian had gone wrong, and she had nearly been dragged into the land of the dead.

The Cloister sat at the very top of the city spire, and the Mouth of Death sat above the rest of the Cloister, in a tiny round valley of smooth, dark rock. The Ancients had been the first to make it a shrine, and they had inlaid glowing green glyphs around the rim of the walls. Juliet recognized none of the glyphs—Runajo told her that nobody knew what they meant anymore—but some of them looked hauntingly familiar.

At the far end of the little valley was a small, round dent in the ground.

"That's it?" asked Juliet.

"Yes." Runajo's voice was very quiet, her eyes distant. "That was the Mouth of Death."

Juliet approached it slowly. She knelt and pressed her palm against the bottom. The stone felt cool; prickles ran up her arm, but perhaps that was only because she knew what she was touching.

Once, this little dent in the earth had been a bottomless pit of inky-black water that flowed straight from the land of the dead. Juliet had heard about it all her life; Runajo had seen it, when she sat vigil one night months ago, and dragged Juliet out of the procession of dead souls.

She stood, and turned to face Runajo. "Thank you," she said. "I'm ready now. You can go."

Runajo's lips pressed together. Then, with an ungraceful thump, she sat on the ground.

"No," she said.

Juliet took a step forward. "You are *not coming with me—*"

"No." Runajo shook her head. "I will obey you. I will stay alive. But I will sit vigil for you until you come back."

"That won't be any help to me," said Juliet. "And I likely won't return. You'll be sitting here forever."

Runajo glared at her from the ground. "Then you'll just have to drag yourself back, won't you?"

And Juliet couldn't help it: she smiled, one final time.

Then she drew her knife and cut a tiny line into her wrist. Blood welled up and dripped to the ground.

She heard a deep, noiseless ringing: the gates of death opening.

She thought, *I am the key. Let me in.*

She heard the song of death, murmuring with many voices.

She saw dark, endless water, and dark, starless sky.

She thought of Romeo and Runajo, of everything she had lost and was about to lose. She thought of the chants of the Catresou magi and the Mahyanai poems that Romeo had whispered to her. She thought of sunlight and hot tea and the mangy little cats wandering the Lower City.

And she walked forward, across the water. She followed Romeo into death.

PART III

Unless This Miracle Have Might

30

AT THE END OF ALL things, there was dark, endless water and dark, starless sky.

Beneath Juliet's feet, the surface of the water was cool and firm. In her ears, the song of death echoed over and over: a chorus like the rippling of many waves, insistent with meaning like a thousand voices.

The song drew her forward. It wasn't like the last time, when she hadn't understood what was happening, when she'd been helpless to escape her fate. Now, she knew what the song meant, why it felt so familiar and inevitable. Now, she stepped forward freely.

Then her foot sank into the water, up to the ankle.

Though she was walking into death, her heart could still pound with terrible, mortal fear. This was farther than she had gone before.

Juliet thought, *Romeo braved this too.*

And if she did not follow him, then all of Viyara would die. They would rend each other apart, first in sacrifices and then in panic, and then the Ruining would roll into the city and kill the last few survivors.

She could not allow it. The Juliet could not allow it.

So she walked forward. The song of death was in her ears, humming through the air in her throat, and there was water up to her knees and then her hips. Her chest, her shoulders, her chin.

The cold water kissed her lips. It slid between her teeth. She was sinking, she was drowning, and the song was gone as she slid down into the darkness, clutching the sword to her chest.

Juliet sank forever.

Down, and down, through the dark waters, and she began to fear that death was only this: forever sinking, forever falling, the memories of life growing fainter and fainter, until she dissolved into the water and was nothing but darkness and currents. Until she was nameless, and hopeless, and could not love or protect anyone.

The water began to change. It was warmer now, softer somehow. She saw bubbles: no, tiny floating lights all around her, like unborn stars in the womb of the sky.

She drew a breath of sudden wonder and realized that she was breathing air again. That she could think and remember herself again, and her heart flooded with sudden hope. *I have not failed yet,* she thought.

And then she settled on her feet.

In the land of the dead.

She could not see far. She could see this: she stood on a hill that sloped away downward before her. The ground was moss and pebbles at her feet, and thin, threadlike vines studded with little bell-shaped white flowers. Farther down the slope were thickets and low, twisted trees. The sky was black as night, but there were no stars overhead; the light came from the multitude of tiny glowing points floating in the air, shivering slightly as if stirred by a breeze, though the air was still against her cheeks.

It was a beautiful place. And yet fear wove itself through her ribs, because this was not the death she had learned about as a child, sitting beside her mother. It was not the Paths of Light that good Catresou were supposed to walk in joy and peace. It was not the howling, ghost-filled darkness that was supposed to take all outsiders (and the Juliet).

She could have faced that darkness with courage and with honor.

But this gentle, flowering slope?

It meant the lore of her people was wrong. That the prayers she had learned as a child were useless to defend her. That any danger could await her.

All she knew for sure were the words of the last woman to

speak with Death, three thousand years ago: *Death will parley with those who unlock the gate, pass the reapers, and come to meet her.*

Juliet had killed reapers in the world above. But what kind of power might they have here, in Death's own kingdom?

She thought of Romeo walking into this silent realm, with not even Catresou lore to guide him. She thought of Runajo waiting for her in the world outside, despairing and yet faithful. She thought of the crowds huddled in the Upper City, with no hope but the bloody sacrifices of the Sisters, which could not protect them for long.

The fear ebbed a little. She had nothing to rely upon except what she'd always had: the people she needed to protect.

Juliet drew her sword. She took a deep breath. And she called out, "I have come to speak with Death. I want to make a bargain."

She waited, heart thudding. But the slope remained gentle and empty and still. No reapers formed themselves out of the dark air to attack her. No revenants crawled out of the ground to devour her—

And Juliet's breath huffed out in almost-laughter, as she realized there was one danger that could not exist here.

In the land of the dead, she was safe from the Ruining.

And if the reapers would not come to her, then she would have to find them.

So Juliet began to walk down the slope.

And she walked.

She walked.

It was easy going, but weariness began to drag at her. There was no tracking time in this eternal midnight, but it felt as if she had been walking for days. No matter how she tried to keep in mind her duty, her desperation—even her fear—slowly the weariness drained them away. The tiny lights drifted about her, and she kept pausing to stare at them, entranced by the tiny, gentle movements.

Her eyelids felt heavy.

I cannot rest, she thought. *Runajo is waiting for me. Paris and Romeo trusted me. My people need me.*

Slowly, the undergrowth had become heavier. There were thickets all around her now; she no longer walked an open slope, but followed a path. Here and there to the sides, she saw lone, crooked little trees.

Before her lay a forest.

The trees grew close, branches twisting together. The path she was on ran right through the center, and she paused. There was something ominous in the way the trees huddled together, and she wondered what might hide in their shadows.

But the lights still drifted ahead of her, glimmering against the slick, knobby bark. And she had a mission.

She stepped beneath the leaves.

It was just as silent outside the forest. But here the air was closer, warmer, almost thicker; it tasted of dust and spices. She kept feeling little gusts of air, almost like breaths against the back of her neck, but there was no one with her and the leaves did not stir.

The path twisted again, and then there was a wide, round clearing.

At the other side sat a woman clothed in white. Her back was turned; her dark hair flowed to the ground and wound away among the fallen leaves.

Fear chilled the back of Juliet's neck, lifted the weariness from her eyelids. Because she had expected the land of the dead to be filled with dead souls, but it was not; and if she could not see other dead souls here, then this woman had never been alive; and perhaps that meant that already, without having faced the reapers, Juliet had found—

"I have come to speak with Death," she said. "I need to make a bargain."

She had pitched her voice to carry, trying to sound brave, but in the close hush of the wood, her voice was small and muffled.

"Death wears the face of whoever comes to her," said the woman. Her voice was low and sweet, but there was a strange, alien note to its music.

Then she rose and turned. "Do I look like you, little girl?"

Juliet flinched back, hand dropping to her sword.

"No," she whispered.

There were seven eyes in the woman's forehead, each a

different color. In each of her palms gaped a wide, red mouth, lined with little pointed white teeth.

And Juliet recognized her.

"You're the Eyes and the Teeth," she said.

The Catresou magi told stories of many monsters who roamed the land of the dead, hungry for anyone who had not yet found the Paths of Light. The most fearsome of them all was the Eyes and the Teeth, who entranced dead souls with lullabies before she ate them. Not even good Catresou could escape her unless they knew one particular spell, and Juliet had never been taught. It was not considered fit for her to learn, when she had no real name, and would turn into a mewling ghost regardless.

Juliet knew this, and yet she was still a little comforted. Because her people had known at least one thing. In this strange, dark world of death, there was one creature that might follow rules she understood.

"Look," said the Eyes and the Teeth.

And Juliet saw.

There were people in the forest. The people *were* the forest. Their bodies were tangled among the roots, half covered in dust and moss; they were wound into the trunks, eyes and mouths blindly gaping among the tree knots; branches and twigs grew in and out of stretching hands and fingers.

Juliet had grown up hearing tales of the nameless ghosts who forgot they had ever been human. She had never imagined anything so horrible as this.

"Don't be afraid," said the Eyes and the Teeth. "They long for this rest. Don't you feel it?"

And Juliet did. The forest was not silent now: there was a soft, droning song in the air, like a hundred thousand sleepers humming, and her heart began to slow and beat in time to the gentle thrum.

Here there was no more striving. No more weeping, no more waking. An end to hate and anger, an end to fear and pain. To laughter and to longing, to love itself and all the chaos it could bring.

She was on her knees. Her palms pressed against the soft, soft earth. Her lips felt numb. She knew that she was not supposed to sleep, but it was hard to remember why.

"Can they be woken?" she asked breathlessly.

"Oh," laughed the Eyes and the Teeth, "you are not the first to hope that."

Fingers stroked through Juliet's hair; she shivered, but then leaned into the touch. When she had still been a child, but her mother was already dead, she had longed so often for someone to touch her hair again, to hold her with gentleness.

"Consider the two who lie beside you," said the Eyes and the Teeth, and through dimming eyes, Juliet saw them: two ridges of roots and arms and legs, braided together in an endless embrace.

"Once they were both alive, and then only one of them was."

And as the Eyes and the Teeth spoke, Juliet saw the story, as if it were a dream:

There was a girl and there was a boy, and they loved each other as everyone does: as no one else has loved before. But the girl died and the boy, he was lost and good as nameless without her. So he sought and he learned and he found secret ways, and at last he walked into death while still alive, his heart pulsing with mortal blood and hope.

And he found her, here in the grove where seeking ends: her lovely limbs tangled with the earth and roots, her fair face cradled by the leaves and dirt. He called to her and wept for her and he begged her. But she did not wake, and he would not leave her.

At last he sang to her, a song of all his love and longing. "Wake, my love, I came so far to find you, I cannot rest without you." Oh, there was never such a song in this land before.

And her eyes did not open but her lips did part, and she sang to him: "I am dead, I am silent, I am still. I will never wake again."

He sang, "But kiss me once, and then I'll be content to go."

She sang, "Kiss me but once, and you'll lie here with me forever."

So he pressed his face to the earth and kissed her sleeping
mouth, and he took root, and fell asleep. And now he lies beside
her, who sought so long to find her, and he knows her not, nor
loves her, and though they lie here for eternity, he will never kiss
her once again.

Juliet could see no longer. She was cradled by the earth, lulled
by the fingers in her hair. All about her, the forest hummed with
endless peace.

This was death. This was the whole of death: the silence and
forgetting. There was no use trying to save Viyara with bargains.
No one had ever bargained with Death and won, because to bargain was to sleep, and to sleep was to forget.

Here in the grove, where all seeking came to an end.

But the fingers were gentle in her hair, and they were like her
mother's: her mother who was long, long dead, but once stroked
her hair as she lay drowsing.

Her mother, who once whispered charms that she should not
have wasted on a girl without a name: *In darkness, may thy feet not*
fail thee. In silence, may thy name not desert thee. In death, may the Eyes
and the Teeth not find thee.

Juliet forced her eyes open. She wasted two breaths, puffing
them out between numb lips, before she was able to move her
tongue and ask, "Then what . . . are *you*?"

If death was nothing but sleep, what need had the grove for a guardian?

The Eyes and the Teeth laughed, low in her throat. She took away her hand, and Juliet shuddered as feeling crashed back into her body. She raised herself back to her knees, gasping still and trembling.

I nearly gave up, she thought. *I nearly gave up and betrayed everyone.*

"I am the eater of names," said the Eyes and the Teeth. "Those who bury themselves here, who send roots into the silence, they bear fruit. Look."

She reached a languid hand toward one of the nearby bodies: a young man, mostly buried, whose head tilted back over a thick lump of root, his dark hair trailing among the leaves. She stroked his face, and he did not wake, but his mouth dropped open, and inside—something like a little round fruit, crimson and glowing bright.

The Eyes and the Teeth plucked the red globe, rolled it down her fingers and around the rim of her palm, before letting it slide into the hand's mouth. She made a fist, and all her eyes closed at once.

Then she opened them and smiled at Juliet.

Already, bark had grown over the man's face.

"What did you do to him?" Juliet asked, revolted.

"I ate his name."

Juliet, who had lived all her life without a name, and known how it doomed her, felt nauseated.

"It would be kinder if you had—" she said, then stopped.

The Eyes and the Teeth smiled. "If I had killed him?" she asked mockingly. "That is already done."

Again Juliet felt the terror of this alien place, with its unknown laws and prices. Here in the land of the dead, there was no death to limit anything.

"What happens to them?" she asked.

"Some heal, and rise, and namelessly walk farther in. Others decay. None ever remember who they were." The Eyes and the Teeth shrugged. "It's not particularly my concern. I eat their names and guard their sleep." She looked at Juliet, and now her seven eyes were not mocking, but full of compassion. "I tried to trick you first, but I'll ask you fairly now. Would you like to sleep?"

No, thought Juliet, but though she could hold her head up now, she was still tired, and for a moment—for a moment she imagined sleeping. Imagined peace, imagined rest.

She remembered the first night she spent with Romeo. Not when she had first kissed him, all fear and longing and hope; and not when he had first kissed her bare shoulder, and turned all her longing into fire; and not when they had made love, and she thought her heart might break from so much bliss. But after, when she was his, and drowsed in his arms, and she felt like the whole world drowsed with them in sleepy delight.

She remembered that peace. And the price she paid for it, all the people who paid and bled and died for it, and she *was not* done with striving.

Not until Viyara was safe.

"No," said Juliet, and rose to go.

31

WHEN JULIET LEFT THE FOREST of terrible sleep, she found the same dreamlike, flower-studded slope on the other side. The same dancing motes of light in the air.

This time, though, she felt a little less afraid as she continued her march downward. She still didn't understand this strange world; she had no idea if she could find the reapers, let alone Death—

But she had faced one danger, and survived.

Surely that meant she had hope.

Then she heard far-off voices. And a roaring, as of water.

Suddenly, there was a dim, warm light before her: the edge of the sky was heated pink and gold, as if with sunset.

And she stood on the bank of a river.

It was vast: she could hardly see the other edge. It roared and steamed and bubbled, for it was boiling hot—a wave of heat struck her face, and she took a step back. For a moment, she thought it was the ruddy sunset light that made the river so red, but then she noticed how thick the ripples were, how heavily the waves fell.

Then she smelled it.

The river was made of blood.

The stench was overpowering, and Juliet choked as she remembered blood on the altar of the Sisters, blood in her father's house, Romeo's blood on the edge of her sword—

You killed them all, the river sang to her. *You killed them.*

"Come away!"

Hands grabbed her arm, pulled her back a few steps. Juliet wobbled and blinked, gasping for air. A cool breeze hit her face, and suddenly she could breathe again.

She was shaking. She didn't know how the river had unstrung her courage, and she didn't dare to look back at it.

So she looked at the person who had saved her.

It was a girl about her own age, with a heart-shaped face and sleek black hair. She looked human—she wore the same style of tunic that Juliet had seen on a hundred other girls in the Lower City—but Juliet remembered how the grove had looked harmless at first.

"Who are you?" she asked.

"My name's Xanna," said the girl.

It was a common name in Viyara. She spoke with the accent

of the Lower City, and a little of Juliet's uneasiness faded.

"Come away from the river," said Xanna. "If you look at it too long, you'll have to wade in. And if you wade into it, you'll never come back. That's why we made our festival here."

She gestured, and suddenly Juliet saw, farther up on the slope to the left, a crowd of brightly colored tents. Strings of lamps hung glittering from every tent, crimson and gold.

They made her think of the glowing red orb that had been the man's name, and she wondered if *this* place stole something from the people who trusted it.

"Join us!" said Xanna. "There's food and dancing for everyone."

Juliet knew that she should refuse. Viyara was dying. There was no time for a festival.

But when she thought of facing the river again, she felt sick with fear.

There was no way that she could ford or swim it. Perhaps in the festival, she would find somebody who could tell her another way around.

So Juliet followed Xanna up the slope, into the crowd of tents.

It was filled with people and life. She saw a woman cradling her baby, and a man laughing with his friends, and two lovers exchanging kisses in the shadows between two tents. She could hear chatter in a thousand tongues, the beat of drums and wild song of pipes.

Everywhere, people were eating the same thing, a fruit she had never seen before: large, teardrop-shaped, with a pale golden skin and moist, crimson flesh. It smelled salty and sweet at the same time, and her mouth watered.

Juliet remembered the Eyes and the Teeth swallowing up the man's name, and she wondered what the fruit really was.

Perhaps it didn't matter. She wasn't here to feast.

"I must speak to Death," she said to Xanna. "Is there a way to get across the river?"

"Oh, no," said Xanna. "But they say if you are good enough at the dancing, a reaper will come and speak to you, and perhaps grant you a wish."

"A reaper?" Juliet echoed, filled with sudden hope. Could this be the first of the reapers she was supposed to face before Death would speak to her?

"Oh, yes," said Xanna. "They can't harm us here. They come to watch the dancing."

Juliet supposed that was no stranger than anything else in the land of the dead.

"Where's the dancing?" she asked.

"This way," said Xanna, and led her into a wide open square. People clustered around the edges, laughing and clapping. The music sang loudly, though Juliet could see no musicians.

Suddenly a great cheer went up. The person at the center had finished dancing—it was a sword dance: she saw the glint of the blade—and then Xanna gave a delighted shriek and ran forward, pushing her way through the crowd. Juliet followed.

The dancer stood with his back to her, but Juliet knew him even before he turned. She knew him by the proud set of his shoulders, by the tilt of his head. She knew him because he was Tybalt, her cousin, whom she once loved more than anyone else alive. Who she once thought loved her.

Xanna ran to him, and he took her in his arms and kissed her soundly.

Then he saw Juliet.

Their eyes met, and the world stopped as memory seized her, made her live the terrible hour once more:

Romeo kissed her again, again, and then she pushed him away to the window before he could kiss her for the hundredth time.

"You must go, it's already dawn," she said. "You'll be back tonight."

"I will die a thousand times before tonight," he said, and she laughed as he kissed her palm and pressed his poem into it, before climbing out the window.

She had slid back into her bed and started to drowse when the key rattled in the lock. The door flung open, and Tybalt strode into the room and ripped the covers from the bed. He stared down at her through the slits of his mask.

"Someone climbed out your window," he said, and there was a terrible coldness to his voice she had never heard before. "Who was it?"

Fear was a vise about her heart. But he was her most beloved cousin, and she had never been a liar. So she stood and she told him of her love, of the secret wedding two-thirds complete.

"He slept with you?" Tybalt asked, and his low voice made the words unclean.

Her cheeks were aflame with blushes, but she met his eyes. "The third night makes it a marriage," she said. "It's the custom of his people. He promised me—"

The slap to her face stung, but the words that tumbled out of Tybalt's mouth were worse: whore and slut and traitor.

"I'll kill him," he said, and shook her by the arm. "I'll kill him, and when I'm your Guardian, I will govern you as you deserve."

Then he shoved her away and strode from the room.

She sank to the floor and hugged herself, thinking, He doesn't really mean it. He wouldn't really do it. *But she was too afraid to follow him.*

She never saw him alive again.

She saw him now. There were no masks here in the land of the dead, so she could see the derision that curled across his face as he recognized her, as he sauntered forward. The same mix of shame and fear and rage curled in her gut.

She did not want to be a coward. She waited, and tilted her head up to meet his eyes when he stood before her.

"I bled for you," he said. "I died for you. I was raised a slave and I died again. Because of *you*, my lady."

Romeo would have words for this bleeding, breaking feeling in her chest. Romeo, perhaps, would be able to weep. She stared up at Tybalt dry-eyed and said nothing.

"There are a hundred others here," he said. "Good Catresou men who died because you wanted to warm your bed with Mahyanai filth."

This was a worse trial than any reaper. But Juliet stood her ground, and stared him in the face. She had a mission that left her no time to surrender to her guilt and her shame.

"If none of them found the Paths of Light," she said, "then none of them were good Catresou."

Tybalt barked a laugh. "Dead, and you haven't realized? There are no Paths of Light. There is nothing here in death but blood and memories."

The light grew redder at his words, or perhaps it had already changed and only now she was noticing.

If you say that, you are no Catresou, she thought, but she couldn't say it, because the same dread had been gnawing at her own heart ever since she came to this place.

This place, so like and unlike everything her people ever believed.

Xanna peered around Tybalt's shoulder. "Who is she?"

"Don't you know?" Tybalt's voice rose. "Hasn't anyone guessed?" He threw up his hands. "Gather round, all you noble dead, and take a look! This is the notable whore who fancied herself the wife of Mahyanai Romeo."

There was a muttering from every direction, far vaster than the size of the crowd. Juliet saw faces, Catresou faces, and some that she recognized. They were pushing their way through the crowd toward her. They were molding themselves out of the air.

They were her reckoning. They were the blood she had shed, the fate she deserved, but *she had a mission.*

The music still played on, and her heart was as fast as the drumbeat.

Tybalt turned back to her. "Tell us, who died for you," he said, "what joy did you get of him, that was worth our blood?"

She met his gaze and said, "It's not modest for a wife to speak so of her husband. But I'll show you the arts I used to ensnare him."

And she drew her sword and began to dance.

The crowd pressed closer, but Juliet's blade flashed and whirled in a circle around her. She was dizzy with fear and regret and fury, but she had known this dance since she was ten years old. It uncoiled itself from her bones and danced itself with her limbs, and there was nothing left in the world but the sword and her hands and her feet, the beat of the music and her drumming heart.

The sword and its dance had always been her language. She had loved Romeo first because he had caught the sword from her, had used those words to speak to her.

The music ceased. She realized she had closed her eyes, and she opened them.

Darkness was all around her, but she stood in a pool of light.

Before her was a reaper.

But it was not like the monsters she had seen in the world above. It was terrifyingly strange, but it was *beautiful*: a tall, lithe creature whose two golden eyes were alight with intelligence. Dark hair cascaded from its head. Its fingers were longer than human fingers, and tipped in claws; its mouth was a crow's beak; little feathers dusted its cheekbones. But all that strangeness seemed only a kind of ornament, like the dizzying curlicues of an elaborate jeweled necklace.

And it had wings: huge wings of soft, dark feathers that beat the air in a slow, graceful dance.

"Why are you here?" asked the reaper. Its voice was low and sweet, neither male nor female.

"I am looking for Death," said Juliet, and her heart beat fast with fear and exultation. Because she might still fail, the reaper might kill her, but she would not wander lost forever in the land of the dead. She was on the path to finding Death.

"Are you indeed?" The reaper tilted its head. "And what will you say to her?"

"I will beg her to stop the Ruining."

"And what will you offer her?"

"Whatever I must," said Juliet. Her fingers tightened on the hilt of her sword. "Whatever trial or test you want to give me, I am ready."

"You are very brave," said the reaper. "But you are not the first one to be so brave, and to beg a favor of Death."

And the reaper's voice fell into the cadence of a story, and Juliet saw it happening before her, as if in a dream:

There was a warlord, so ruthless and so terrible that all the world lived in fear of him. Whatever he wanted was his for the taking. Until one day he saw a sad-eyed slave girl singing to herself in his garden. In that moment, he loved her, and found himself wanting what could never be had by force. Long he courted her and long her heart was dead to him, until at last he wept at her feet, renouncing his sword and his armies and his pride. Then she raised him up, and kissed him, and they fled together into the wild.

But the warlord still had enemies. In the end they found him, and shot him with arrows as he rested in the girl's arms. She screamed, and she wept, and she walked the whole world until she found a path to the land of the dead. There, in a field of poppies, she found Death: and Death wore her face, and smiled at her.

"Tell me," said the girl, "where is the one I love?"

"He lies in a river of boiling blood," said Death, "remembering all the blood he shed on earth. Tell me, why do you come here?"

"I wish to have him back," said the girl. "I wish to have him live again. I wish only to kiss him one more time."

"Those are three wishes," said Death.

"I tell you," said the girl, braver than any warrior, "I will suffer any torment, I will serve you any length of time, I will become any terrible thing, if you will only let me see him again."

Oh, she was noble and terrible as the clash of arms. And Death loved her, as she loves all the dead. So this is the noble and terrible fate that she gave her: as the girl spoke, feathers grew from her face, and her fingers twisted into claws. Her sweet, soft lips turned into a razor-sharp beak, and she became a reaper. Death sent her up into the world, and tirelessly she still walks through plagues and battlefields, guiding lingering souls to the world below.

Once every hundred years, she approaches the river of blood. She wades into it, up to the knee and up to the neck and farther in: and there, beneath the boiling blood, she finds her lover. She

draws him out to the shore, and for one hour she is human, and
they may comfort each other. Then she changes back to a reaper
in his arms; and she herself must lead him back to the blood and
torment for another hundred years.

When the tale released her, Juliet was shaking. She thought she could hear the roar of the river again, and the muttering of the Catresou dead. She could not imagine another fate than being rent apart for her sins.

But Romeo and Runajo had trusted her. Viyara needed her. She could not let the sacrifices continue; she could not let the city fall.

"Still," she said. "Still I must try." She lifted her chin, and tried to steady her voice. "Did my dance please you? Then grant me a wish. Take me across the river. Or show me another way to Death."

"Your dance was lovely as spilled blood," said the reaper. "But if you wish to speak with Death, you must ford the river. There is no other way."

The next moment, the darkness and the silence were gone. Juliet staggered, overwhelmed by a pandemonium of light and sound. She was back at the festival, back in the center of the crowd.

It was different now. The crowd still surged, but they were not dancing, they were running. The voices were not laughing, they were shouting and screaming. The music still played, but fiddles wailed high and desperate.

The light was from the tents burning.

She whirled, trying to find the source of the chaos. And then she saw them, among the crowd: people who did not have the faces of people anymore.

For one instant, she thought of the fanciful animal masks that the Catresou would sometimes wear at parties. But these people were not masked: the fangs and tusks, the scales and dripping fluid, the elongated mouths and extra eyes—they were real, and they made every face a different nightmare.

Juliet had fought armies of revenants, and yet this sight closed her throat in horror.

She ran.

Everyone was running, all around her. Some ran back up the slope, into the darkness. Some ran down, toward the river.

Juliet was running that way too, before she realized it. Her feet hungered for that direction; she only paused when the heat and the smell struck her across the face.

Then she saw the people plunging into the river. They screamed as they broke the surface; then they sank back down. Those on the bank wailed as well, but they were too close. They could not seem to stop themselves as they rushed forward into the boiling blood.

Above the chaos, pipes and fiddles were shrieking still.

Something shrieked behind her. She whirled—

It was not Tybalt anymore. And yet it was still Tybalt, this hissing creature with claws and a forked tongue. She saw the ruins of his face among the scales and the bony knobs.

She saw, but not in time. Her sword was already moving, and it slashed across his throat, cutting deep and releasing a rush of blood.

Tybalt staggered, and she cried out because she never wanted to kill him, never, not even when he hated her—

Then he raised his head.

Of course, she thought with numb horror. *He is already dead. We are all of us already dead.*

Tybalt lunged forward and slammed her to the ground. Juliet was only barely able to hold him off as they wrestled, his jaws snapping at the air an inch from her throat.

She flung him to the side for a moment, found her dropped sword. When he sprang again, she slashed it across his eyes; as he howled, she kicked him to the ground, then plunged her sword down through ribs and spine and earth, pinning him in place.

He writhed, and whimpered, but the steel seemed to sap his strength. He did not rise.

The screams were silent. All the other people had disappeared, into the darkness or into the river. The fires had died among the tents.

The music was very soft now, a slow dirge for the end of all things.

"It's brave and beautiful," said the reaper, "the festival that they built here."

Juliet looked up, and saw the reaper standing beside her, wings gently flexing, feet not quite touching the ground.

"It was not wrong of them to build it. But those who linger here too long begin to rot. Eventually they overwhelm the festival, and force the rest into the river, however much they fear it."

Her throat felt dry and raw. It took her a few moments to speak.

"But Tybalt—he's only been dead two months. He was speaking to me just *now*."

The reaper looked at her and Tybalt with infinite, heartless pity. "The dead keep their own calendar."

Juliet remembered how his face twisted when he ripped the covers from the bed, when he tried to shame her in the festival. He had been rotting, perhaps, for a very long time.

"What is the river?" she asked.

"All the blood that's shed on earth," said the reaper. "All must wade through it, to remember what part of it they shed."

"Or sink beneath it forever," said Juliet, remembering the story of the warlord.

The reaper shrugged. "For some, it's a very wide river."

And she had to cross it, if she was to find Death and save her people.

"The people who have already changed into monsters," asked Juliet, "if they go into the river, will it help them?"

The reaper considered this awhile before it said, "Yes."

Juliet looked down at Tybalt. The music was silent. The air at her back was still, no longer stirred by wings, and she knew without looking that the reaper was gone.

She remembered his cruelty as she knelt beside him. He was still now, his eyes wide and dazed. She looked into those eyes, remembered when they were dearer to her than all the world.

"You wronged me," she said. "You and all our clan. You *wronged* me when you made me Juliet, and every day thereafter. I do not know if I can ever forgive you."

She swallowed, feeling dizzy and lost. "But half the blood in that river was shed by me. So I do not know if I have the right to forgive you."

She drew the sword from his body.

He didn't spring at her. He didn't make a sound. But he let her take his hand, and pull him to his feet.

And she drew him, step by step, into the river of boiling blood.

32

THE NIGHT WAS DARK, AND silent, and very long.

Runajo did not move from her place, kneeling before the dry remains of the Mouth of Death. Her back ached and her eyes felt gritty with exhaustion, but she did not lie down. She did not close her eyes. She watched the spot where Juliet had disappeared, and she waited. Because there was nothing left in the world that she could possibly do, except keep her promise, and wait.

Alone.

She had thought she knew loneliness before. But ever since Juliet had vanished into darkness, and the bond had broken—

It felt like the close walls of her own mind were going to smother her. Even when they had both been doing their best to close off the bond, Runajo had still felt Juliet's presence in every moment, endless and unquestioned as the sky overhead.

Now that sky was gone. Was *forever* gone, even if by some miracle Juliet returned. Runajo was locked up forever in her own mind, with no company but her own thoughts endlessly circling.

Juliet is dead. You should have died in her place.

That was true.

You destroyed her clan and became a murderer to save her, and she's still dead.

That was also true. The thought burned, but it was a familiar pain now.

She will never come back.

Runajo's clasped hands tightened. She had promised to wait. She had promised to hope. She did not want to be faithless to Juliet again.

But as the night wore on, she knew that waiting was the only part of her promise she could keep.

It wasn't that she doubted Juliet. If courage and will could let anyone walk into the land of the dead, defeat the reapers, bargain with Death herself to end the Ruining, and then walk back out again—Juliet surely had enough of them.

But she remembered how desperately her mother had willed her father to live. How bravely they had both borne the pain of their illnesses, never complaining. It wasn't enough to be willful or brave, any more than it was enough to be good and kind.

The Ruining had covered the whole world except Viyara. Surely somewhere on one of those continents had been Juliet's equal. And that person had saved no one.

It was done before, Runajo told herself. *There was another Ruining once, and a mortal woman ended it. Juliet can do it now.*

But the woman who ended the last Ruining had not come back alive. It seemed scarcely likely that Juliet would do better.

And if Juliet did not come back—if the world was saved, but Juliet did not come back—

Runajo realized that her eyes were stinging with stupid, foolish tears. Because she knew what was going to happen. There had been so many moments like this, so many long nights like this, as she waited for her father and then her mother to die. Kneeling in silence, telling herself that a happy ending was still possible.

But it never was. She had said as much to Justiran: *Didn't you know she was mortal?*

If Juliet did miraculously come back, she would only have to leave again. No matter what Runajo did, no matter how much she learned or how desperate she became, she would lose her in the end.

There was no other ending to anyone's story. It was why she cut her parents out of her heart even before they died. Because she had seen the truth, that she was inevitably going to lose them.

She couldn't do that to Juliet. There were tears running down Runajo's face now, as she realized that she couldn't *do* that. She could bear the death of her parents, she could bear becoming a murderer, but she couldn't harden her heart against Juliet's death.

And she couldn't, here alone in the darkness, believe that Juliet was ever coming back.

But she could keep the other half of her promise.

She could wait.

For the first time in her life, on this one terrible night, she could not cut the person she was losing out of her heart. She could not try to scheme a way to escape the loss. She could wait, and know what was going to happen, and still wait.

It was all she could do now.

So she waited.

The night was very long.

33

JULIET MEANT TO BRING TYBALT with her, out the other side. No matter how terribly they had wronged each other, she owed him that much.

But the moment the blood touched her, she forgot him, forgot everything but the pull of the river. The scalding pain couldn't stop her. She rushed forward, wading into the boiling blood up to her neck and up to her lips and until it flowed over her head.

She did not drown. The currents wrapped around her, dragged her down, down into a merciless crimson light that picked through her soul, finding each life she ended and saying, *This one. This one. And this.*

She saw each one. *Knew* each one. When she crawled, choking, onto the far bank of the river, she could barely remember that she existed; her mind was full of those she had killed or helped kill.

Her fingers scrabbled at the ground and clutched at the little pebbles that covered the riverbank. Her breath came in whimpering little gasps.

My fault, she thought, *my fault, my fault,* and shuddered with grief over the wrongs that could not be righted.

Slowly—very slowly—she remembered those she had no part in killing, yet had to watch die. And those who were yet alive, and hoping for her to succeed.

Juliet rose.

Then she did remember Tybalt, and looked back. But the smooth, glowing surface of the river was unbroken; no one else stood upon the bank.

Her heart twisted as she wondered if he suffered still at the bottom of the river. But perhaps he had already climbed out, and found his way farther down. In the end, he might have killed fewer than she had.

There was nothing more she could do for him, either way.

She still remember his twisted, animal face—his anger when she told him about Romeo—but she tried to think of the times she was a child, when he was the only one who hugged her and made her laugh. That part of him had been real too. She could mourn that much of him, even if she couldn't forgive the rest.

"Farewell, cousin," she whispered.

Then she turned, putting the dim glow of the river at her back.

Before her lay a city.

The buildings were made of stone and steel and ivory. Some were small, little cubes with one door and one window; some were huge, jumbles of rooms and gates and towers piled upon each other. Some were smooth and plain, while others were adorned with steel filigree, ivory arches carved so finely they looked like foam, statues jutting from every corner.

All of them were moving, some swift and others slow, across the flat stone plain of the ground.

A moment before, the only sound had been the rushing of the river and her own ragged breaths. Now all she could hear was the groan and scrape and clash of the city, as buildings plowed into each other. Some crashed thunderously, others settled to a halt, but none ceased to strive. Stairways unfolded from windows, statues moved and scaled walls, arches extended themselves and planted pillars. Two buildings would try to eat each other until one succeeded, wrapping its walls around the other, and then it resumed its course.

It was not fear that Juliet felt, gazing upon the city, so much as a terrible smallness. This city had not been built for human comfort. It would crush her in an instant without caring, and for a moment, she could almost believe it had the right. What was she, to challenge such relentless majesty?

She told herself, *I am the sword of the Catresou. For the sake of* zoura, *I can challenge anyone.*

Defiantly, she straightened her spine, and cried out, "I am looking for Death."

But her voice was small and muffled by the din, and there was no reply.

She had forded the river of blood. The reaper had told her it was necessary. If it had not been enough, then she simply had more reapers to face before she found Death.

So she marched forward.

There was a sharp line between the pebbles of the riverbank and the slick stone of the plain. When she stepped over the line, the air seemed to thicken and cling about her for a moment.

Then the ground swelled beneath her feet, birthing a small, flat stone. When her other foot landed on it, the stone trembled and then slid free, carrying her forward. It didn't move quickly, but the motion still caught her off guard, made her bend and wave her hands for balance. And that's how she discovered, in those first few, dizzy moments, that cupping her hands one way turned the little stone raft to the left, while the other way turned it right. Beckoning gave her speed, holding up her palm slowed her down, and flexing her fingers just like *so* made little walls start building themselves up around the rim of her raft.

At first it was dizzying and frightening, trying to control the tiny, half-made house and dodge the vast, hurtling buildings on either side. But soon it grew easier, and then it was like a game:

dancing between the buildings as she once danced between the swords of the men who trained her.

And then she saw him.

He was very high up—she only glimpsed him for a moment, silhouetted in a window—but she would know the shape of her father's shoulders anywhere.

The sight distracted her, and then his house crashed down upon her. Strings of bricks whipped about her head, and she crouched; walls clattered, chattered triumphantly as they built themselves around her.

The chaos ceased. The roar of the city was muffled now; there was only a slight vibration beneath her feet. Carefully, she rose. She was in a room made from the rubble of other rooms— windows were embedded in the floor, half-formed flights of stairs ribbed the ceiling, and flower-shaped lamps glowed from the walls.

She had to find a way out.

The building was an impossible jumble. Stairs wound and climbed their way straight up into the ceiling. Windows opened to reveal flat, featureless walls. Rooms were turned on their sides, or nestled inside each other. Statues hid in corners, their cold, marble faces too lifelike for her to be easy looking at them; she remembered the statues on the outer walls, which moved and climbed.

At last, she found a stair of polished ivory, and at the top a room paved in black and white tiles. There was a great bay window, looking out on the city, and before the window stood her father.

As she stepped into the room, he whirled, one hand rising, his face contorted into a snarl of fear. It was an expression she had never seen on him before, and she flinched from it.

Juliet remembered when she loved her father, when she was so proud if he was the least bit pleased in her. It seemed so long ago.

She remembered breaking his neck, and it felt only a moment past.

Then he recognized her. His face smoothed.

"It's only you," he said. "Well, then."

And he turned away from her.

Juliet had braced herself for rage, but the simple dismissal was like a knife between her ribs.

"Father," she said weakly, but he did not turn.

Never, in her whole life, had he cared when she needed him.

"Father!" she called again, striding toward him.

He whipped his hands up in a violent motion, and the building surged forward. She stumbled, nearly losing her balance.

"If you must be here," he said, "you might as well make yourself useful and guard the door."

Juliet swallowed dryly, wondering if he remembered that she had killed him. "Against what?"

"The statues," he said. "Haven't you learned *anything* since dying? Some of them rebel, and find their way inside. They move more slowly in here, but they're still troublesome to stop."

She glanced at the doorway, but it was empty.

"What are you doing here?" she asked. "What is this place?"

He laughed harshly. "When I'm done? The closest thing to the Paths of Light."

The old, bitter disappointment twisted at her heart, and she demanded, "Did you *ever* believe in them?"

There was a vast thunder of colliding stone, and the floor shuddered beneath them. Her father's house was eating another.

"No," he said, and the word was soft, but it rocked her back on her heels, because it was an admission she knew he never would have made while alive.

"When has there ever been a place prepared for us?" he demanded. "A peace we did not buy with our own blood? All other peoples hate us, and death claws at the doors of our city, and yet still the magi tell us to trust in *zoura*. What has *zoura* ever given us, but death and silence? I'll trust in what I can build. I'll make a palace for our people right here, and invite them all home."

Juliet knew, with a knife-edge clarity, that he was at last speaking truth. That this was his heart and what he desired, and it was almost a noble ambition. It was almost like something Runajo might have said.

She could almost forgive him for it. But she knew what he had done for that ambition—and still, *still* he did not look at her.

"You can try to drag him out," said a voice from behind, "but you'd have to build a house to do it. And then you'd just make him into a statue."

She whirled. A reaper stood in the doorway, watching her with calm, golden eyes.

"He can't see me," said the reaper. "I'm surprised he can see you. He must not have been here very long."

"What is this place?" she asked.

"You're a clever child," said the reaper. "Do you want to hear a story about what happens to clever children when they face Death?"

And as the reaper told her the story, she saw it as if in a dream:

There was a boy so clever he could talk the stars into his
hands. He had a brother, and he loved that brother more than all
the stars in the sky.

Of course the brother died.

And this boy, he decided he was clever enough to get his
brother back. He found his way through the chinks and crannies
of the world, down into the land of the dead. He tricked the Eyes
and the Teeth into eating a cake of poppy seeds that put her to
sleep. He charmed the reapers into carrying him across the river
of blood. And finally, beside a pool of still, black water, he found
Death waiting for him, wearing his face.

The boy smiled and said, "If you love me so much already,

I'm sure we can come to an agreement."

Death did not smile in return, but she loved him for his cleverness. "I can't give you something for nothing," she said. "But do me a favor, and you can have your brother back."

"I'll do anything you like," said the boy, "and I'll make you laugh while I'm at it."

Death took him by the hand, and led him to an endless plain of stone. "I would like to have a palace here," she said. "The stone of this plain has a special power: it can be shaped by a single thought—but only a thought from a human mind. Fill this plain with a palace from end to end, and I will give your brother back."

"Is that all?" said the boy. "Prepare for your kingdom to be one soul smaller."

He threw up his hands. Arches and columns and walls sprang out of the plain. Room by room, tower by tower, he built Death a palace, and oh, it was very fair. But the plain was as wide as thought is quick, and no matter how swiftly he built, he came no closer to filling it.

And still he builds, endlessly clever and devising, surrounded by all the clever souls who think they can devise a way to rule death; and Death, when she visits him, laughs.

The vision released Juliet at the same moment that the building shuddered again. She staggered, then fell to her knees.

Despair was like a heavy weight in her heart. Because she had seen what happened to the brave, and now she had seen what happened to the clever.

She had trusted in her own bravery. She had trusted in Runajo's cleverness. If neither could save her—

"Juliet!" called her father. "Juliet, listen to me!"

Her head ached. Slowly, she turned to look at him.

"Yes, Father?"

"Stand up. You're a child of mine. Guard my house with pride. Stay."

He still did not turn to look at her. But he wanted her. He wanted her, and in his voice was the promise of meaning and purpose.

She had believed in that promise so long. And what else did she have any hope of? If she tried to challenge Death, only ruin would follow.

Her hands felt stiff and heavy. Juliet looked down, and saw paper-thin traceries of stone winding around her fingers. She flexed them, and the stone crumbled. But she could still feel the heavy weight of obedience at the pit of her stomach, dragging at her like an iron weight.

Stay. It was like a voice in her ears, like a drug in her veins. *Stay with him. Obey.*

But she had made her own promise.

Slowly, painfully, she turned to the reaper.

"Is Death on the other side of this plain?" she asked.

"For you, she is," said the reaper.

"If this plain is as wide as thought," said Juliet, "how can I get across it?"

"How did you come to this land?" asked the reaper.

"I sank into the water," said Juliet. Then she looked at the window and started to understand. "I fell," she said, more softly. "It felt like I was falling forever."

The reaper smiled. "You will need to fall much farther still, to speak with Death," it said, and vanished.

Juliet remembered buildings crushed to rubble against the heartless plain, and she was afraid. But here in the land of the dead, she could hardly die *more*.

Slowly, she walked forward. She thought of Tybalt, whom she loved. She had not loved her father in a long time, but she was his daughter still.

"Father," she said dutifully, "this is not the place for you."

He sighed—the spare, dry sound that made her shudder as a child.

"You are only a Juliet," he said. "What would you—"

"*Look at me,*" she demanded, stepping in front of him.

And her breath stopped.

His eyes had turned to pure white stone. Dust hung on his mouth and his fingers; he stood on bare feet, and they too were made of stone.

Her stomach twisted with something sick and unfamiliar. She realized it was pity.

"Don't try to distract me," said her father, twisting his hands. The building jolted and started to slide in another direction. "Be quiet and do as you're told."

She wanted to stay, and the wanting took her breath away. She didn't think it was just the power of this place.

If she stayed, if she knelt beside him and let stone crust over her fingers and eyes and face, if she begged and pleaded for a thousand years, perhaps he would listen. Perhaps she could save him.

She wished that she could.

But there were too many people waiting for her, relying on her. She couldn't throw herself away and become a statue just to save her father.

It was a calculating thought. Runajo would approve. In another world, where her father was a better man, perhaps he would too.

"Father," she said. "I'm sorry that I killed you. I wish I could have obeyed you."

She backed up until she felt the edge of the windowsill against the base of her spine. Her father stared past her with colorless eyes, saw the chaotic surge of the city. But not her.

"I did love you once," she said, and then she flung herself backward, out the window.

She fell.

For one instant, she feared that she guessed wrong. But then she was falling still, and falling, down into darkness.

When the crash came, it hurt as if it was splitting all her bones apart. But when she raised her face from the ground, the city was gone.

34

ROMEO HAD LIVED HIS WHOLE life expecting that death would be nothing but darkness and forgetting.

Even when he spilled his blood, and took the Little Lady's hand, and saw the land of the dead open around them—he more than half expected that all he would know was a swift, eternal silence.

As he and the Little Lady sank down into the dark waters, he had thought, *Juliet,* because he wanted it to be his last thought.

But as they sank, he remembered her, and then his feet landed on solid ground, and he loved and remembered her still.

He was Romeo still.

He looked about him, and wondered, *Did we succeed?*

There was nothing in the gentle, flowering slope to tell him yes or no. He could not even feel sure if he was dead: he felt the blood pulse in his throat, the breath move in his lungs. Was that an illusion? Was he so different from all the other dead, having walked here without dying?

He turned to the Little Lady. She had dropped his hand; she was looking about the landscape, her chin lifted, her face half smiling and alive, as it had never been before.

"Did we do it?" he asked. "Did we end the Ruining?"

She shrugged gracefully. "I do not know."

"But—you knew this would help, so surely—"

"It is no more concern of mine," said the Little Lady. "I am dead. I have only one purpose now."

And she strode away from him, down the slope.

After a moment, Romeo followed her. He had no idea where else to go. He had no idea what he should *do*.

He had planned, many times and in many different ways, to sacrifice himself. He had never thought what might come after.

And he was not sure that his sacrifice was done. If more was required for him to save Viyara—to save Juliet—then he had to know, and following the Little Lady seemed the likeliest way for him to find out.

So together they walked down the slope for what seemed like hours. They were not always completely alone—Romeo saw other shadowy figures walking down the slope, sometimes in twos and threes, sometimes by the dozen. But they were always far away; Romeo could not make out their features clearly, and their voices were no more than a mutter on the soft breeze.

"Do you know where we're going?" Romeo asked finally.

"I know the one my heart loves," said the Little Lady.

Romeo's own heart suddenly pounded against his ribs.

"Makari?" he said, halting. "You *killed* him."

"I loved him," said the Little Lady, not pausing in her slow, graceful stride.

After a moment, Romeo started walking again. "Was it . . . meant to be a kindness, when you killed him?"

The Little Lady looked over her shoulder, and in her face there was an echo of Juliet's exquisite scorn. "I was the Juliet. To punish him was my duty and my joy." She shrugged. "And I wanted him with me, when I rested. I am that selfish still."

She turned away from him. Romeo stared at the back of her shoulders and imagined his Juliet bereft of friends, bereft of comfort or joy or a lover who could love her people.

He thought, *I cannot blame her,* and he followed her.

The slope seemed to go on forever. But then the moss began to dry out; the vines grew sparser, and the flowers wilted. At the same time, the slope began to ease, until at last they were walking on flat, raw earth. But the little sparks of light drifting through the air remained, the only thing in the world besides them, and the ground, and the starless sky.

Then Romeo saw shadows, outlined against the glow of the lights. A moment later, they drew closer—the lights shifted—

And he stopped, his heart thudding in fear and wonder.

Before them stood—no, floated, their toes barely a handspan off the ground—a line of reapers, their eyes closed, their huge wings beating the air with dreamlike slowness.

Dark, crow-like beaks. Long, pale fingers tipped in claws. Romeo knew them from stories that he had never believed. Juliet had told him that she had faced them, and he had believed her—but he had still never imagined that he would see any himself.

The Little Lady continued to walk peacefully toward them.

Juliet had told him of how ruthlessly the reapers desired to kill.

Romeo lunged forward and grabbed the Little Lady's arm. "Wait," he whispered, shoving himself in front of her. "They might—"

The reaper before them opened its eyes. They glowed bright gold.

"We have no need to kill the dead," it said in a low, sweet voice.

"We do not kill in the world above," said another reaper, opening its eyes.

"Except those that have refused death," said a third.

"Or when the necromancers force us," said a fourth.

And more eyes opened, more and more, a line of glowing eyes stretching endlessly in either direction.

Romeo didn't dare move. He hardly dared breathe. And yet, as he stared up into the faces of the reapers, he couldn't see them as monsters. They looked like Juliet once had, the first time he saw her: alien and perilous and lovely.

"Why are you here?" he asked.

"We guard the ruination of our kingdom," said the reaper before him.

"The rot must be prevented from spreading," said another.

"We have at last made the great ruiner captive in it—"

"But we cannot pry loose the souls he has taken."

"Until what is lost returns."

"Until his sin returns."

"I am here," said the Little Lady, pushing Romeo aside.

There was a vast rustling among their wings as all the reapers turned to look.

"I am his dearest sin," said the Little Lady, "and I seek him, for my heart loves him. Let me pass."

Slowly, reverently, the reaper bowed to her, wings crossing over its head; then the wings were a puff of smoke and then it was gone. The other reapers vanished likewise.

Before them lay a plain of boiling mud: a bubbling, gray-brown ocean studded with white stones. Before them, the stones grew close enough together to form a twisting road. Clouds of white mist drifted across the surface.

The Little Lady strode forward. With every step she looked more determined, more alive.

Romeo followed. He feared the ocean of mud as he had not

feared the reapers. He kept thinking he saw an ominous pattern in the bubbles and ripples. The soft muttering of the ocean was like a thousand secret, resentful voices.

But he kept walking forward, because Makari was here. Makari, and some of the souls he had raised—and Romeo wanted to think that they had freed Paris from him completely, but if not—

"He is here," said the Little Lady, and knelt.

Romeo halted suddenly, looking around. He nearly said, *Where?*

But then he saw.

The mud before them was alive. It seethed with swimming, writhing figures just below the surface, and with those who broke the surface, but who were coated still with the gray-brown slick and so looked like part of it.

At first Romeo thought it was a simple chaos of writhing figures, but then he realized: the disturbance had a center. The swimmers clustered around one person, who could not swim, but whom they held up, so that his mouth could break the surface and gasp air.

Makari.

Even with his face half submerged and slicked with mud, Romeo recognized him. How could he not? He had known Makari since he was ten years old. Makari had been more than father, more than brother to him. Makari had been everything

388

to him, and then everything except Runajo, and then everything except Runajo and Juliet and Paris—

But he was still half the world to Romeo, and dearer than his own soul.

And yet he was upheld by the suffering of his slaves. Romeo felt sick as he looked at the swimmers. He couldn't make out any of their faces; it felt like they had no faces, no identities left but their obedience.

"It is righteous," said the Little Lady. "He deserves to suffer."

"His victims don't," said Romeo. "Can we help them?"

"*You* can do nothing," said the Little Lady.

That had always been true. But Romeo couldn't help stepping closer to the horrifying tangle of bodies in the muck. He could do nothing to help them, and yet it felt wrong to look away. He could at least *try* to see their faces.

And then his heart banged against his ribs as he recognized one of those faces.

He called out, "Paris!"

It was only after those eyes turned to him, only after he realized Paris was *here* with him, that Romeo truly felt ready to destroy Makari.

Because Makari was half the world and dearer than his own soul, but Paris was one-half of his heart, and in the moment their eyes met, Romeo knew that he would do anything, *anything*, to set him free.

"Paris!" Romeo called again. "Can you hear me?"

But his heart was cold within him, because he remembered what had happened when they dueled, when he had begged Paris to remember him, and all the love and friendship in his heart were not enough.

Then Paris turned to look at him.

Paris looked, and in the next moment Romeo was kneeling at the edge of the path, reaching out his hand, and Paris grabbed it.

Romeo hauled him up onto the path. Paris fell to his knees, gasping and coughing for breath. The mud that had coated him was already dry, falling off him in flakes and clouds of dust. When he stopped coughing and looked up, his face was already clean.

"Romeo," he said, sounding dazed, and then Romeo pulled him into a hug.

"I'm sorry," said Paris. "I'm sorry. You shouldn't be here—you shouldn't have to save me—"

"You're my *friend*," said Romeo. "I will always try to save you. And you brought the Little Lady back. You saved us all."

He supposed he still didn't *know* that bringing her into the land of the dead had ended the Ruining. But he had to have faith it would.

"But you're dead," said Paris.

"Yes," said Romeo, his heart twisting with grief. He had no

idea how much time had passed, or if time even meant anything in this world. But surely Juliet had found his letter by now. He hoped that the world around her had changed, that she had seen the Ruining ended, but he knew that right now she was abandoned.

She was strong enough to bear the grief, he was certain of it. But he hadn't ever wanted to make her feel it.

"I didn't die for you," he told Paris, looking straight into his eyes so he could see that Romeo was telling the truth. "I died to end the Ruining, and to keep Juliet from being the one to sacrifice herself."

"How?" asked Paris.

"The Little Lady," said Romeo, looking over Paris's shoulder at her.

And then he saw that she was no longer still; she was rescuing the other people who were trapped with Makari.

"I am your master's lady," she called to each one. "Come."

One by one, they came to her. They crawled up out of the mud, and she said to each, "I set you free." One by one, they shuddered, and the mud fell from their bodies, and they walked away. Until at last there was only a single trapped soul left holding up Makari in the boiling mud.

The Little Lady settled back on her heels. "If I call the last one," she said, "he will leave my beloved to drown."

"Can he drown?" Romeo asked doubtfully.

"No," said the Little Lady, "but he will sink for a very long time."

Even now, Romeo's stomach turned at the thought. But Makari deserved worse than this. Whatever last soul he had trapped with him deserved better.

He thought that, and then he realized: the Little Lady knew Makari's evil better than he did. And yet she hesitated. Perhaps because she longed for a way to love him still, as Romeo had once longed to love a Catresou girl.

"Can we pull him out?" asked Paris.

The Little Lady looked up at him. "You would do that?"

Paris stared down at the boiling mud, at Makari's gaping, helpless mouth, and the nameless creature who held him above the surface.

"I hate him," said Paris. "But I am Catresou. It is our duty to give rest to the dead. And Romeo loves him."

No, Romeo wanted to say. *You owe me nothing. I owe you everything.*

But Paris didn't hesitate. He knelt down and grasped Makari's wrist.

At the same time, the Little Lady seized Makari's last servant. She pulled him out, and said, "I set you free." But Romeo hardly noticed. He was staring at Makari as Paris hauled him onto solid ground.

Makari did not spare a moment for either of them. His gaze was all on the Little Lady as the mud fell away from his face.

"You are here," he whispered.

The Little Lady stood, setting her shoulders back. "Despite your commands."

"I loved you," said Makari.

"You commanded me to live," she said.

The grief on Makari's face was so terrible, Romeo could almost forgive all his crimes.

"I did," said Makari. "I regret it. And I have spent so many years seeking to undo the harm I did to you."

Romeo wanted to say: *What of the harm you did to Paris? To all the world? To Juliet?*

He wanted to demand, *What of the harm you did to* me? But the words withered in his throat, because Makari was staring at the Little Lady as if she were all the world, and Romeo knew his words didn't matter anymore.

"You undid my death and you condemned me to torment," said the Little Lady. "And you destroyed all that I loved."

Makari laughed bitterly. "What did you ever love, but the masters who used you as a slave?"

"I loved them," said the Little Lady, as righteous and as sure as Juliet. "And I loved *you*, who used others as slaves."

As she said the words, she stepped forward and took his hands. "I only wanted to be with you and do my duty."

"I tried to give you that," said Makari, and bent to kiss her, but she turned her face aside.

"You never understood," she said. "I must make you."

And Romeo knew, suddenly, what she was going to do. He nearly called out *Stop*—but he had no right. He was nothing to Makari and less to the Little Lady. He was no part of their doom.

He might have tried anyway, but Paris seized his wrist and held him.

"I will suffer anything," said the Little Lady, "that will make you understand."

Then she flung herself to the side, dragging Makari down with her into the boiling mud. Their figures writhed a moment under the surface of the mud and then were gone, sinking ever deeper, deeper.

Over them, the mud grew solid. As Romeo and Paris watched, the moss and the flowering vines grew across the raw earth, reclaimed it, made it whole again.

Makari is dead, thought Romeo.

He had already died twice. And yet Romeo felt like this was the first time Makari had been torn from his heart.

From this sinking, there was no return. Or rather, there was a return: but only once Makari understood *zoura* to the Little Lady's satisfaction. And Romeo knew that would take ten thousand years, and he did not know whether to be sad or relieved at that thought.

He would not see Makari again.

He and Paris were now alone in the land of the dead.

Romeo looked at Paris. He thought, *What do we do now?*

"I don't—I don't where we are," said Paris. His voice was small and lost. "This isn't the Paths of Light."

Romeo said nothing. His heart was breaking. He had never believed in the paths, but he knew what they meant to Paris, and he wished they were real for his sake.

"I suppose I could never have hoped to reach them," said Paris. "I wasn't buried like a Catresou, was I?"

Romeo wanted to lie and say yes, but he felt sure that Paris would know, somehow. And he wanted to say, *You deserve peace even if no Catresou muttered over your body*—but that wasn't comfort, that was spitting on what Paris had spent his life believing.

Instead he replied, "I don't know where we are either. But I can promise you this, you won't face it alone."

Hope startled onto Paris's face. "Really?"

"I swear by my name," said Romeo, "I will not leave you."

35

THE CRASHING CITY WAS GONE.

She was not dead.

Juliet thought that, and in the next moment remembered, *I
am already dead.*

She stood on a slope very like the one she first walked, before
she met the Eyes and the Teeth. Again there were pebbles and
moss, vines and little white flowers beneath her feet. Again the
sky was pure black above her, and the light came from little glowing motes that drifted lazily in the air.

This time, she was not alone.

There were hundreds of people about her; perhaps thousands,
if she gazed away into the distance. They walked slowly down the
slope, some alone, some in twos and threes. Some were silent,
some spoke—but their voices were only a faint, faraway murmur:

the cool air felt vast and open, yet it muffled sounds instead of carrying them.

The sight should have given her hope. She had been told that all the dead must descend, and here were all the dead descending; surely Death herself was near. Yet the quiet, inevitable stride of the dead souls filled Juliet with dread. She felt that if she joined their march, she would become one of them—not the Juliet, not the key to death, not anyone who could hope to bargain with Death and win.

But if she stayed here, she would not be able to save Viyara. Runajo would sit vigil until the walls broke and the white fog of the Ruining found her there at the Mouth of Death and killed her.

That image gave her the strength to walk forward. Juliet started down the slope, and after a little while, her dread began to fade. She still remembered her quest. She still had command of her own feet.

She still had a chance to keep her promise.

Not all the dead walked peacefully. Despite the strange, muffling quality of the air, Juliet heard an old man's raised voice. First it was just a garble on the breeze, and then she could make out words:

"Fools! They're going to eat you!"

She saw him: a withered old man crouched on the ground, gripping the delicate, flower-studded vines as if they were the only thing holding him in place. Perhaps they were, because the crowd flowed around him like a river, all staring but none stopping.

Juliet halted. She looked into the old man's wide, wild eyes—they were golden, bright against his dark skin: he had been Old Viyaran when he lived—and she said, "What do you mean?"

The old man's lips drew back from his teeth in a snarl. "I *mean* that everyone walking down this slope is a fool. There are monsters waiting at the bottom. They're going to tear us to pieces, and since we're already dead, we'll never stop screaming."

Juliet remembered the Eyes and the Teeth, the creatures by the riverbank, and fear prickled across her skin.

Somebody sighed behind her. She looked back, and saw a tall, lean woman with her arms crossed.

"That's just a rumor, you idiot," said the woman. "There's nothing at the bottom but the reapers, and all they do is snuff us out. Make us *nothing*, so we can finally rest."

A young man, who moments ago was striding eagerly forward, paused at the woman's side.

"Where do you hear these things?" he demanded. "At the bottom, we are all judged and rewarded according to the lives we have lived."

"Count me out if that's true," the woman replied. "I'm walking only for hope of an end."

But there was an affectionate curve to her mouth, as if she

knew this young man and cared for him. He slid his arm into the crook of hers, and they leaned toward each other as they continued walking down the slope.

It was a kindly sight, but it left Juliet cold. She realized suddenly that was all she could feel: cold, helpless fear as the currents of wandering dead shifted and rippled around her, all of them driven slowly, helplessly, inevitably down the slope.

She thought, *I must protect my people.*

She thought, *I must keep my promise.*

The words felt like they meant little now. But she clung to them, repeated them to herself as she started walking again, down the slope, surrounded by the muffled voices of the dead.

She wondered what they were telling one another, what stories and rumors, what hopes and fears.

She wondered what waited for them all at the bottom.

"Do you want to know what the dead find?"

Juliet looked back. The reaper was behind her, wings slowly stroking the air, hovering with its feet barely the width of a hand above the ground.

"I can tell you a story," said the reaper.

Juliet shuddered. She wished the reapers would fight her. She wished they would test her with any other torment except hearing tale after tale of mortals who challenged Death and lost.

Every tale drained a little more of her hope. Not just hope, but her will to fight. Every tale made her feel less like the Juliet and more like a nameless ghost, unable to save or remember anyone.

But she was not lost yet. She was the Juliet still, and while she was, she had a duty to fulfill.

"Tell me," she said.

And the reaper spoke, and the story wrapped around her:

There was a boy and a girl, and they saw their parents die in a flood. Together they sat in a tree for three days as they waited for the waters to go down. Then the girl fainted from hunger, and fell into the water. She struggled and choked and drowned, and then she saw Death, wearing her own face.

The tale was like a cold drop of water, trickling down her soul. Juliet waited for the next part of the story, the twist that would send a wave of despair crashing through her.

But there was only silence, as the reaper tilted its head, studying her.

"That's all?" Juliet asked finally.

There was an old man who had buried three wives and two children. But twelve grandchildren filled his home, and he was happy. When the sickness filled his lungs, his family wept. He closed his eyes, and he saw Death wearing his own wrinkled face.

There was a king who conquered all his enemies abroad, outwitted all his foes at home. His wife put poison in his golden cup, and he closed his eyes, and saw Death, wearing his own handsome face.

Juliet shivered. Everybody died; she knew this. She had always known it. But the quiet, inevitable way that the reaper told the stories stirred a deep fear in her soul.

"I don't understand," she said.

There was a slave who did not have a name, but could sing more beautifully than anyone who has lived before or since. One day her master's beating was too hard. She closed her eyes, and saw Death wearing her own bruised and battered face.

There was a baby whose mother feared shame. In the same night that she birthed that child, she left him in a drift of snow, and called herself merciful because she did not shed his blood. That baby wailed away his breath, and closed his eyes, and saw Death wearing his own face, grown to the adulthood he never had.

There was a boy. There was a girl. There was a man, a woman, there was anyone at all. For each of them, there is only one story. They close their eyes, every one, and they see Death.

And Death was the end of every story.

Juliet had walked into death, and so her story was ended. Why had she hoped to achieve anything after?

She realized that she was bowed to the ground and shaking. She realized that she was no longer the Juliet. She was a mortal like other mortals, and she was helpless. She was going to die.

She was dead.

Dead, and walking down to the final end, from which no dead soul returned.

How had she ever thought she was different from the quiet crowd around her? How had she ever thought herself special enough to outwit Death and heal the Ruining?

It was done before, she told herself. *It can be done again.*

But she could no longer believe it.

She thought of Runajo, who had fought so long despite believing all was hopeless. She thought of Romeo, who had walked into death, though he had believed all his life that the dead were only dust and nothingness.

She might be doomed to fail them. But she could refuse to break her promises.

Slowly, she raised her head. "If Death waits for us all," she asked, "then *where is Death*?"

The reaper bowed its head and folded its wings about it. "The dead keep their own calendar," it said from among its feathers. "You have hardly begun your death."

The feathers shivered and turned to smoke, and the reaper blew away on a silent wind.

The dead continued to walk past her. But Juliet was still.

If she wished, she could stay here. Perhaps she would turn into a monster, as the people at the festival had. But she would not have to learn what terrible truth waited at the bottom, the fate of all the world.

She was very much afraid.

And yet she turned, and began to walk farther down.

36

AT LAST JULIET REACHED THE end of the slope, and saw what lay at the bottom of death.

Dust.

An endless plain of soft, gray dust.

Some of the dead hesitated when they reached the bottom; they stood at the edge, among the last pebbles and dried-out moss of the slope, and turned themselves this way and that, looking for a path. But there was no path, only the flat gray surface stretching on forever.

Most of the dead did not pause. They did not speak, either; they walked forward, slowly, inevitably, looking neither to the right nor the left. The dust puffed up in little swirls around their feet, and settled back to fill their footsteps as if they had never been.

Juliet did not hesitate. She marched forward, step by step.

It was less crowded on the plain. Occasionally, two of the dead walked hand in hand, but most wandered by themselves. At first they strode confidently forward, eyes fixed on the horizon—or nervously, glancing side to side and over their shoulders. Whether fear or hope drove them, they were swift and full of will.

But farther out, the paces of the dead slowed. Their eyelids drooped low, their shoulders slackened. Their faces drained of hope and fear alike; and one by one, they knelt.

Juliet did not understand at first. She saw an old woman kneeling on the ground, and pitied her weariness. Then she saw a young boy drop to his knees, and she wondered.

Then she saw a man sink to the ground and begin to dig.

The silence and the vastness of the plain had numbed her at first, but now she felt a cold worm of fear, burrowing around her heart. She stepped closer to the man and said, "What are you doing?"

Softly, serenely, the man replied, "I am digging my grave."

The gentle words set her heart pounding in a sudden spasm of mortal fear. Wildly she looked around, and all around her she saw other souls digging into the dust with their hands. Some had been working awhile already; they knelt in holes, up to their hips or up to their chins.

They did not look at her. They did not speak. They were ready for rest and ending, and Juliet felt like her heart had turned to a cold stone in her chest, because she was not ready. She was *not*, and the simple peace in their faces was the most terrifying thing she had ever seen. How long until that peace overtook her as well, quenched her will, undid her?

Grimly, she marched forward. She had faced the reapers. She was ready to face this.

But here on the empty plain . . . there was nothing to face. Nothing but the flat gray plain that stretched infinitely onward, fading into shadows without even the line of a horizon. She walked ever forward; she saw no more wandering souls, only those who had turned to digging. She saw holes fully dug, with the dead curled still at the bottom. She saw the dust shiver, and collapse, and fill the holes. And the dead did not stir.

She walked on.

She was alone now. She saw nothing before her; when she looked back, she saw nothing except the same trackless dust.

"I am looking for Death," she whispered, then sucked in a breath and shouted, *"I am looking for Death!"*

But her voice was muffled by the everlasting stillness of the air, and there was no answer. No reaper appeared to tell her a story, and as she looked around at the darkness and the dust, she thought perhaps it was because this was the only story, this place where all stories crawled to end.

Perhaps *this* was the true face of Death.

Her feet and her eyes were heavy. She felt very tired, yet there was a strange energy to her hands. She realized she was constantly flexing them, that a strange hunger itched at her fingertips.

She wanted to dig.

The realization drove Juliet forward. *I cannot give up*, she thought. *I must not give up.* But every moment the hunger grew more acute, and her heart felt like the dust at her feet, dry and crumbling and helpless.

She wanted so very much to rest.

She thought, *Romeo*, but he was not here. If her journey had taught her anything, it was that even love could not turn Death aside. (Did he already lie buried in this plain?)

And then she realized that she had stopped walking.

Juliet looked down at her feet. She knew that she had to keep walking, that this was the last moment she could avoid this fate—

But she couldn't. She could only stare at the dust, and hunger for it.

Slowly, inevitably, she dropped to her knees. She swayed a moment, alone in the darkness.

Then she began to dig.

The dust was soft and silky between her fingers. She knew that this was her doom, that she was failing in her quest; but each handful of dust scooped aside was as helplessly satisfying as a yawn, and she could not stop herself.

She thought, *Perhaps I can rest*, and her eyes stung with tears as if she were alive. Even now, at the last abandoned moment, she did not want to give up. Here at the bottom of Death's kingdom, she did not want to die. But for all her love and bravery and weary, stubborn loyalty, she had found no hope. No answer.

Nothing but this gentle dust.

She dug. She remembered Romeo, who kissed her and swore that she mattered, even though she did not have a name. She remembered Runajo, who said that all the world was dust, and in the same breath swore to save it. She remembered Paris, who was nothing to her, and who was everything, because he was the kin she had longed to have.

She remembered Arajo's smile. She remembered Justiran dying in her arms. She remembered the crowds in the Lower City. She remembered a cat sniffing at her fingertips.

She remembered them all, and she thought, *I am sorry. I tried. I am sorry. Good-bye.*

Her fingers sank deep into the silky dust—

And it crumbled away beneath her hands. Drained, as if a hidden pit had opened.

Before her, in the dust, was a hole. Not a grave: a gap, and she looked through it, down and down and *down* into an infinite space full of darkness.

In the darkness, there were stars.

That was the only word she could think—the only thing remotely *like* she had ever seen—but these blooming, shimmering lights were not at all the same as stars. They were vaster and far-ther away, and small and close enough to cup in her hands, and they sang to her. Her heart turned over, and she wanted to smile and weep at once, and there was nothing, nothing, she desired so much as to fling herself down and be eaten up by their light.

She thought they might destroy her. She knew they would change her. And she yearned for it, because it felt like coming home.

But she remembered the light that was in Runajo's eyes, as she spoke about seeing a beauty at the heart of the world. She remembered Romeo's smile as he kissed her reverently, and kin-dled stars across her skin.

For their sake, she could wait a little longer to be consumed.

For the beauty unfurled beneath her, she could still bear to hope.

It was the hardest thing she had ever done, but she did not throw herself down. She rose.

And she heard a voice—so like her own—say, "Hail and well met, my child."

She turned, and saw Death.

37

"I DON'T KNOW WHO ELSE has gone so deep in my kingdom, and yet looked back," said Death.

Juliet couldn't speak. A cold feeling blossomed behind her ribs, and it was like fear, but she was too dazzled and surprised to feel true fear. The song of the stars beneath still echoed in her ears.

No longer was she on the endless plain of dust. Instead, she stood on a little island filled with blue flowers and broken white columns. Surrounding her was dark water, slick and reflective as a mirror.

Before her stood Death: a girl her own age, wearing a red Catresou dress, dark hair falling free.

But Death did not wear her face.

It was *like* her face, but there was a shape to the eyes and chin that was different. There was no mistaking one for the other, and she wondered what that meant.

"I suppose you've come to bargain," said Death. "Everybody does."

Juliet caught her breath, and *now* she was afraid. Because she knew this was the final moment, the only moment that mattered, when one mouthful of words could redeem the world . . . or just as easily lose it.

Everybody bargained with Death, and nobody ever won. The reapers had told her this, and she still believed them. But she had to find a way.

"No," she said.

"No?" Death raised elegant eyebrows.

Juliet bared her teeth. "Bargains are for equals," she said, "and I know that you can use us as you will. But I came to tell you . . . Romeo returned what was stolen from you."

"I know," said Death, and smiled in satisfaction. "Already my land is healing."

"Then why didn't you end the Ruining when he did it?" Juliet could barely keep the anger out of her voice. "You have no right to hate us any longer."

Death clasped her hands, pale fingers lacing together. "I hate no one. Do you not yet understand?"

"No," said Juliet. "I'm not clever. I'm only the sword of my people." She took a half step forward, feeling the terrible weight of the world swing upon her next breath. "And I only came to beg of you . . . let us go. You have us all in the end. Release the world from the Ruining, and let us live a little while before we come to you."

"Do you?" Death tilted her head. "Do you *beg*?"

The line of her throat was as proud as Juliet's father had ever been, and Juliet's body shook with bitter laughter.

"Yes," she said, and dropped to her knees. "*Yes*, I beg you. Do you think I would do anything less for my people?" She bent and kissed Death's bare toes; they were cold against her lips. "Please, *please* release us."

Death stooped to face her; she seemed taller now than she had before, less human. "Is that all you have to offer? Words?"

Romeo's words had been enough to crack her world apart . . . but she was not Romeo. And Death was not a lonely maiden.

"No," said Juliet. She drew a breath, remembering the tales the reapers told her. "I'm here to offer my life. And my death."

She did not want to say these words. Even now, when life was so far lost to her, she wanted to save herself. But there were people to protect. She had *promised*.

"Make me a tree," she said, "or a reaper, or a drop in the river of blood." Every word was heavy as stone, but she did not cease speaking. "For all eternity, if it pleases you, let me suffer anything you like. Take me, as you took that handmaid of the last Imperial Princess, and let me pay for the world."

There was a little space of silence where all she heard was her own heartbeat, her own desperate breaths. Then:

"That is not the bargain that I made with that girl," said Death. "And even if it were—I never make the same bargain twice. And even though it is not—your life, child, is not half enough to pay for Romeo, let alone the whole world."

Despair wrapped itself around Juliet's heart.

Then Death shrugged her shoulders. "But you have done what that girl did not. You have righted all the wrongs of your people."

Juliet stared at her. "*All* the wrongs?"

"Your people have been so reverent in their blasphemy," said Death. "I cherish them for that. It was a very great blasphemy nonetheless, to seize the sacred words for themselves. You cannot understand how terrible. But now those words have been borne back into my kingdom on a living body. And you, sword of the Catresou, will you now relinquish those words on behalf of your people?"

Juliet couldn't speak. She thought, *It cannot be that easy.*

"There will be no more Juliets," said Death. "There are only two Catresou magi left alive, and when they wake tomorrow morning, they will remember nothing of the sacred words. Half the rites and the magics of your people will be gone. Will you ruin the pride of your people, to end the world's Ruining?"

It should have been easy to say yes. Juliet had dreamed so long of finding a way to protect everyone. And this was not just protection: this was a new world, one not governed by the bloody, abominable equations of the Sisterhood. Where they could have a city that was not a charnel house, and their lives did not have to be bought in blood and murder.

And yet she was Catresou still. For one wretched moment she hesitated, remembering the prayers she had learned at her mother's knee, the pride she had once felt when she stood beside her father.

In that moment, what gave her strength was Paris, who had become living dead, an abomination in the eyes of the Catresou, and yet still done his duty to them. She could bear that fate. She could accept it for all her people.

"Will we remember *zoura*?" she asked.

"All people remember it," said Death, "unless they willfully forget. But that word your ancestors fashioned with their own tongues. So yes, you will remember it."

"Then," said Juliet, "yes. I yield the words back to you."

Death smiled and laid her palm on Juliet's forehead. Fire seared down Juliet's back and across her palm. Juliet gasped, and she knew without looking that the words had unwritten themselves from her skin.

"The Ruining has ended," said Death.

She spoke quietly, yet Juliet could feel the words echo through all of Death's kingdom; they made the ground tremble beneath her knees. She did not trust the words, because she simply *knew* that they had accomplished their meaning.

The Ruining was over.

Juliet stared down at the little blue flowers by her knees, and wanted to weep in relief. Not for Viyara. She should have cared for her city first, but in that moment, all she could think was that Runajo's vigil would not end in death. Romeo's sacrifice would not be completely in vain.

"And now I am prepared to be kind," said Death. "So I will grant you this. You may walk out of my land alive, as no one has before. You will never be Juliet again. But you will live in the world you have won."

You will live.

The words slid off Juliet's mind like water over glass. Life in a world without the Ruining, where she was not the Juliet any longer. She could hardly comprehend it. If she was not burned up and sacrificed for her people—if the world around her was no doomed—it was more than she had ever hoped for.

And yet.

"What becomes of Romeo?" she asked.

"He is dead," said Death. "Do you think that you, more than anyone else, deserve to have your true love back?"

Juliet remembered Tybalt and the river of blood, and all who had died by her hands or because of her.

"No," she said. "But I think that he deserves to live, and more than I do. He righted half the wrongs of my people, didn't he? And he wasn't even one of us. He deserves life far more than I do."

"Oh," said Death, almost laughing, "don't tell me you still think *deserving* has anything to do with who lives and who dies."

"No," said Juliet. "But once *you* start picking people to live, then it does. Why else are you letting me go?"

"Because you, of all the people who ever stole into my kingdom, did not come alone. Whose face do you think I am wearing?"

Juliet stared at her, utterly baffled.

Death rolled her eyes. "Surely somebody told you what happened in the marriage bed."

"Do you mean—"

"I mean you didn't come here alone, you simpleton. I wear the face of the child you carry beneath your heart, whom you conceived the night that Romeo married you before both your clans."

Juliet sat back on her heels. *A child,* she thought with dazed, terrified awe. *I am carrying Romeo's child.*

All her life, she had been a weapon: a thing to be used up and sacrificed for the protection of others. To think that now she was going to be a mother—that there was *life* within her, that she was person enough to grow another person in her flesh—she could barely comprehend the idea.

"As each soul comes to me, so I deal with it." Death's voice was sweet and heartless, like the moonlight. "Those with clever plans, I outwit. Those with noble intentions, I sacrifice. But you came to me with life, so I am prepared to deal it back to you. Just a little."

Death reached down, and took Juliet's hands, and raised her to her feet.

"I will grant you this much mercy," said Death. "If you can find Romeo among the souls in my realm, you may take him back with you, and he will live again. But know this: even if you do find him, and lead him back to the light of day, you will lose him. He will die before you, and no power in all the world can change that fate. Before the hair is white on your head, you will bury him. Is that a bargain you can bear to keep?"

Juliet stared at Death's serene face—the promise of a future she could barely imagine—and she remembered the drumbeat as she performed the sword dance to celebrate the Night of Ghosts, and the moment when a masked boy caught her sword out of the air.

She said, "I have never loved him except under sentence of death."

There were many islands. The water around them was black as the sky above, but the flowers that grew on every one were bright, bright blue, shining in the darkness.

Juliet wandered across the water; it cradled her feet and did not let her sink. At first she thought that the islands were empty, that Death had brought her to the only place in her kingdom with no souls. But then she realized that the shadowy lumps on the islands were not stones but sleeping people. Some lay alone, decorously laid out with hands clasped over their chests; others curled into each other, chins resting on shoulders and fingers gripping hair.

They were as still as the souls caught in the terrible grove of the Eyes and the Teeth, but they did not fill her heart with horror.

None were Romeo.

As she went farther, she saw some who were not asleep, who sat up half awake and drowsing, or whispering in quiet tones with each other. Then she saw an island with a looming, twisted shadow, and for a moment her chest clenched in fear—but then it shifted, and she realized it was a reaper, wings curving over a child it held sleeping in its lap.

Its eyes gleamed as she approached.

"What is this place?" she asked. "I thought everyone had to keep walking, or—" She remembered bodies absorbed into trees, half-animal faces, feet turning into stone.

The feathers in the reaper's wings stirred gently, though Juliet felt no breeze on her face.

"All must complete the journey or turn to rot," it said. "Some are allowed to rest first. This is their place."

"I am looking for Romeo," she said. "Is he here?"

Again its wings rustled. "Human names are not a thing I was made to remember."

It stroked the hair of the child in its lap, and lowered its head, and began to croon a wordless song.

Dismissed, Juliet wandered onward. Because she did not know what else to do, she began to sing to herself:

"What is love? 'Tis not hereafter;
Present mirth hath present laughter;
What's to come is still unsure.
In delay there lies no plenty,
Then come kiss me sweet and twenty;
Youth's a stuff will not endure."

She sang, and fell silent, and listened to the silence: the vast, sleeping silence that was only made emptier by the soft whisper of water against island, dead soul confiding in dead soul. She wondered if this was how Death would mock her, outmatch her: by saying that she could have Romeo if she found him, and leaving her in a place where she could never find him.

And then—beyond all hope—she heard his voice singing softly across the water:

"O mistress mine, where are you roaming?
O stay and hear, your true love's coming—"

She did not hear the rest, because she was breathlessly running, running across water and rock and infinite dark spaces—she thought she had been running forever—and then she skidded to a stop because there he was before her, there he was.

Romeo.

He sat on a small island, with his back against a white stone column. There was another soul cradled sleeping in his arms. He was waiting for her as he promised, and she had never felt so desperately relieved as when she knelt before him.

"I found you," she said, and suddenly could not stop smiling.

"Juliet," he said, staring at her in wonder and fear. "You—did you—"

"I followed you," she said. "I spoke with Death. The Ruining is ended."

He smiled, as beautifully as the first time she let him touch her face. "That's wonderful," he said, and then the smile dimmed. "But you . . . what did she ask of you?"

"She said that I could go back," said Juliet. "She said that I could take you with me, if I found you. And I found you."

But he did not smile again.

"I can't," he said.

She stared, her heart turning cold. "Why not?"

"Paris," he said, and for the first time she realized whom he held sleeping in his arms. "I found him, and I promised I would stay with him. He will wake eventually, and he'll need to walk farther, and—and even if he slept here forever, I couldn't leave him. I swore by my name." Romeo's eyes were wide with distress. "I'm sorry."

She thought this was what it meant to feel a heart break: to have it crack in two, between one beloved thing and another. Because Romeo was dearer than the breath in her mouth and the light in her eyes—but Paris was her kin, and he died for her, and she loved honor too well to wish that Romeo would break his oath.

She thought, *I cannot accept this.*

She said, "I'm glad I married a man of honor." And she stood. Her heart was beating very fast, and her blood was singing with a pristine fury that felt like peace.

In any other time or place, in any other way, she might have accepted Romeo's sacrifice. But not here. Not now. Not after all she had dared and done and suffered—not as recompense for Romeo's kindness and Paris's loyalty.

Those with clever plans, I outwit, Death had said. There was no trick or scheme that Juliet could hope to use against her.

There had been no hope for her to defy Lord Ineo, so she had turned her obedience into a weapon. If cleverness was always outmatched by Death, how would she treat faithfulness?

"Death," she called out, her voice filling the great silence. "You broke your promise to me."

"Did I?" said Death an instant later, from only a step behind her. "How rude of me. But what did I do wrong?"

Juliet turned to face Death, and stared fearlessly into those half-familiar eyes. "You said that I could bring Romeo back, if I could find him. And I found him, but he has vowed not to leave Paris here, so I cannot take him with me. Your promise is broken."

"And what would you have me do?" asked Death, grave and amused at once. "Send Paris back to life as well?"

"Yes," said Juliet.

"That is a very childish wish," said Death.

"Children," said Juliet, "believe their elders will keep their promises. I know my father was a liar. Tell me, are you one too?"

And Death smiled. "That is the right answer, my child. Take him with you, if you can rouse him from his sleep. And try not to let me see you again for a very long time."

In the next breath, she was gone, faded into the darkness of her kingdom. Juliet turned back to Romeo and Paris.

"I don't know if we can—" Romeo began, but she ignored him.

"Paris Mavarinn Catresou," she said. "I command you on your obedience, to me and to your clan, *get up and walk*."

And his eyes opened. He blinked, drowsily, and then he sat up. "Lady Juliet?" he said.

"Not anymore," she said, and hauled him to his feet. "But you're still mine. And we're all going home together."

When they returned, it was dawn. The sky overhead was pink and gold.

Runajo was waiting still. But she no longer knelt in formal prayer like a Sister of Thorn. She sat with her knees pulled up to her chin, hands twisted together. When she saw them, her eyes widened, but she didn't move, as if she could not believe they were real.

For a heartbeat, Juliet could not believe that Runajo was real either. She had never before looked on the other girl without feeling her mind as well, and it hurt to think she would never have that again.

But she had sacrificed that closeness when she gave up the sacred words of her people. And she had bought something far more precious.

Juliet let go of Romeo's hand. She walked forward and knelt before Runajo. She reached across the invisible chasm between them and cradled Runajo's face in her hands as she said, "I am no longer the Juliet. So I can finally tell you this: I forgive you."

38

THE DAYS THAT FOLLOWED WERE full of beginnings.

This was one: as they lay together in bed, she whispered to him, "I don't have a name anymore. I never had a name, and now I'm not even the Juliet. But I would trust you to give me one."

He brushed the hair away from her face, and then kissed her. "You nearly killed me. And you saved us all. What other name could I call you, except Juliet?"

They signed the new Accords in the Exalted's palace, before the Exalted's silver throne, beneath a ceiling carved into foamy swirls of white stone.

Runajo was not entirely sure why she had been summoned to witness it. She knew why Lord Ineo was there, and the new Lord Catresou, and Vai. They each had to sign on behalf of their people. And she could guess why Xu was there, no longer a sub-captain but the Exalted's right hand.

Officially, the previous Exalted had sacrificed himself out of grief for his people. But Runajo felt very sure he had died on Xu's blade, abandoned by his personal guard. She had read the histories of Viyara; it was a form of succession that was not unknown.

But Runajo didn't know why *she* was there. She was not Juliet, who had walked into death, and now people would try to kiss the hem of her dress in the streets. She was not Sunjai, who had died to save the Upper City, and now a statue of her was being carved in the Cloister.

In the end, she had done little besides try very hard and get a lot of people killed. And she was learning to live with that shame, but she didn't understand why Inyaan would offer her any favor for it.

"It is our command that these Accords supersede all previous bonds and ranks, and lay to rest all previous feuds." Inyaan looked very small, sitting on the throne, and her heavy gold collar and crown only made her look more delicate still. But she held herself with stiff, unyielding pride. "If anyone cannot abide these terms, then do not sign."

The words were clearly addressed to Lord Ineo, but his expression of calm respect did not twitch. "The Mahyanai have always been honored to keep the laws of Viyara," he said, bowing slightly. "We will abide by them still."

The new Lord Catresou's expression could not be seen, hidden behind a golden, full-face mask. But his voice was also respectful. "We will also abide by the new Accords."

"And we," said Vai, "have waited far too long to be allowed to keep them. You needn't fear *us* breaking faith." She was the only one of them wearing no jewelry or fine clothing, just a worn blue coat; but she held herself with a proud grace that put the others to shame.

So each one went forward in turn, accepted a tiny silver knife from Xu, and signed the Accords in blood. Last of all Inyaan signed, and Runajo thought she saw a slight tremble in her hands when she sliced her finger open—but maybe it was just her imagination.

They all signed the Accords in blood, but they promised none. There were no more walls to maintain. The Great Offering was over. For the first time in a hundred years, Viyara could be a city that sheltered innocents, whose lives were not bought in blood.

When the signing was finished, Inyaan told Runajo to stay. As the others filed out, Runajo felt a little trickle of fear. Xu had remained behind, to fill the role of bodyguard, but everyone else had gone away. If Inyaan wanted to punish her for anything she had done, Lord Ineo would make no protests on Runajo's behalf.

They stared at each other for a moment, Inyaan still sitting on her throne, Runajo standing before her. Runajo had never liked to apologize, and yet now *Sorry* was on the tip of her tongue. She wasn't sure for what. *I'm sorry that Sunjai is dead?* But that had been Sunjai's choice, and Inyaan's fingers on the blade. *I'm sorry that I sent you to your brother?* But that had been the one time she'd been trying to help Inyaan, no matter how badly it turned out. (And in the end, it had made Inyaan the new Exalted.) *I'm sorry that I hated you in the Cloister?* But their squabbles when they were novices seemed so insignificant now.

"I want you to return to the Cloister," said Inyaan.

Runajo stared at her. She did not miss the shift away from the royal *we*. This was not the Exalted's command. This was a request, from one former Sister to another.

"Why?" she asked.

"Because she wants the lot of you gone," said Xu, looking faintly amused.

"Viyara was never meant to be the home of all the world," said Inyaan. "It is a city for those who serve the gods with their blood. None of those who came here to escape the Ruining have ever done that except under compulsion."

Runajo could say nothing to that. It was true enough.

"No boats remain from the time before the Ruining," said Inyaan. "But I have spoken with the High Priestess. We do not have so many to feed now. If we adjust the water gardens to grow trees as fast as possible, we could start building boats in five years."

It had only been a few months ago that Runajo had last

climbed the central tower of the Cloister to inspect the wall, and had gazed across the water at the dead city of Zucra on the mainland. It felt like a lifetime ago.

"We need our best to make it happen," said Inyaan. "You are one of our best. So you will do it."

It was absurd to feel this thrill of pride, being told she was *best* by a girl she had always despised. And yet Runajo felt her spine straightening, her shoulders squaring.

Five years. A fleet of boats. And then—

All the world.

"I won't help sacrifice anyone," she said, "ever again. Will you let me back in the Cloister, on those terms?"

"If a sacrifice is needful," said Inyaan, "I won't give you a choice. Will you take that risk?"

Runajo remembered Sunjai's blood spilling across the sacred stone at the heart of the Cloister. She remembered Juliet returning to her, splattered in Catresou blood.

She would regret those shames forever. But she already knew her answer.

She said, "Yes."

All four high houses were required to help with cleaning out the Lower City and rebuilding it. But it was the Catresou who worked hardest, who walked into the depths of the Lower City first. Because they needed to retrieve their dead.

And then they needed to bury them.

Romeo walked in the funeral procession beside Paris. This was nothing like Emera's funeral, when the Catresou were fugitive. The Ruining was only five days ended, the Catresou had barely been granted their status again, and yet the procession and the veiled mourners were stately and sumptuous.

Meros was one of the first bodies they had recovered from the ruins of the Lower City. Romeo had found him, huddled by the walls under a pile of other bodies, fingers ruined from crawling at the gates. He had been cruel and worthless, and then he had died in fear, and he had become a revenant, who desired nothing but the flesh of the living.

Now he was being buried with honor, and Paris carried the jar that contained his pickled heart.

Juliet walked in the procession too, carrying Justiran's heart—Juliet, who had so much cause to hate everyone in her clan but Paris, and yet loved them—and now that Paris was her bodyguard, he would be walking at her side except for his place as Meros's brother.

Romeo was honestly surprised that he was allowed to participate. He would never be a devout Catresou. And yet Ilurio and Gavarin had demanded that he join the funeral. Paris had asked him. *Juliet* had asked him, and now Romeo carried the jar that held Meros's pickled brain.

The corridors of the sepulcher were just as Romeo remembered: pale stone walls carved into filigree, flickering lamps that cast dancing shadows. But this time he was not being dragged as a prisoner, about to be offered as a sacrifice.

This time, he was here to honor the dead.

Most of them were dead he did not love, did not regret. But the Mahyanai sat vigil even for the dead they did not love. Romeo supposed he could assist the Catresou in this.

He had to. They were his clan now.

After the funeral was finished, Paris lingered awhile before the coffins. Romeo stayed by his side—and he wished, suddenly, that the bond between them was not broken. That he could feel Paris's heart, and guess a little of what he was thinking.

"Amando isn't buried here," said Paris.

Romeo's first impulse was to say, *Who?* But then he remembered: Paris's other brother, who had died as a sacrifice for the Great Offering. When Romeo had failed to save him.

"I'm sorry," he said.

"He wasn't as bad as Meros," said Paris. "He deserved a Catresou burial more."

Romeo had nothing to say to that. They both knew how little a Catresou burial guaranteed—how little the land of the dead was like what the Catresou promised—but Romeo had no right to tell Paris that.

He wished again that he could feel what Paris was feeling—but slowly, carefully, he put his hand on Paris's shoulder, and he felt Paris lean into the touch.

"I still believe in the Paths of Light," said Paris, his voice low. "I don't know if they're exactly the same as I was taught. But I talked to Juliet. We both still believe."

Romeo had not yet asked Juliet to tell him all that had happened to her in the land of the dead. He had been afraid to trespass on something that she thought sacred. He had no right to comfort her, if she grieved the loss of her faith.

Now he said, "I am still under oath. I will follow you there, whatever it takes."

And Paris looked up at him, with a smile that was heartbreakingly beautiful. "Thank you," he said.

"There is something that I have to make clear to you," said Vai. "You can only be my consort."

"What?" said Paris.

It was midafternoon; the sunlight drenched the courtyard where they sat, burning through the fabric of Paris's shirt, and after he had spent the morning in the chill of the sepulcher, it was the most welcome thing he'd ever felt in his life.

His blood was red again. (He had checked. He had to, though Romeo was furious.) He no longer felt that horrible, restless tug of death. He was alive.

But sometimes—at night, in the still, dark hours, but also in broad daylight—sometimes Paris still felt the memory of that chill. Sometimes the whole world felt numb and cold, a foreign thing not meant for him.

He couldn't feel that way now, when the sunlight was so warm it felt heavy on his skin, and Vai was sitting beside him and smiling. Her head was shaved now, and it was a strange sight to him, but he loved the way the sunlight fell around her temples, and how clearly he could see the line of her jaw.

"It was the only way I could become a woman," said Vai. "I told my mother and grandmother that, as head of the family, I was using my power to decree that a woman could lead the family and produce heirs. As I was the man of the house, they had to obey me. But that means my children must be *my* children. They won't inherit anything from you." She paused. "Perhaps your eyes. I like those."

"I've been alive for five days," said Paris, "and you're making plans for our children?"

"Yes," said Vai. "What sort of girl did you think I would turn into? I created a fourth high house just to sign the Accords; of course I have to plan for the future."

And he couldn't help laughing, because of course she did. This was the girl he had fallen in love with.

"It's only," she went on, "I know what your people mean to you.

If you can't accept that your children won't be Catresou . . . well."

Paris sighed. Before his death, he would have said no. He would have thought he had no choice. But since then . . . he had walked the land of the dead. He knew it was more than the Catresou said, if not less. And while he was determined that his children would know *zoura*, he was no longer sure what that meant.

"Juliet made me her bodyguard," he said. "I'm not leaving her. Can *you* accept that?"

"Well, I'm planning to get my people out of this city as fast as possible and I know she is too. So yes."

Paris took Vai's hands. He tried to imagine the future they had been discussing, and he couldn't. He had been living dead for less than two months, but it was hard to remember the time before, when he could look forward to anything but death.

Even before that, he had been an outcast from his clan, with little hope of returning. And before that, he had been the useless son, expected to fail.

So he couldn't comprehend the days and months and years that were waiting for him. But he could understand this: Vai's fingers wrapped around his, warm and strong. He could remember this: Romeo waking him from nightmares, Juliet swearing to him that she would have no other bodyguard.

He could believe in this: his friends, willing to save him, against all odds.

433

"And if we do have any problems," Vai continued, "we can always fight a duel again. Though I suppose that's hardly fair, since so far I always win. Unless you've come up with some new tactics?"

"Yes," said Paris, and stopped her mouth with a kiss.

Runajo was not used to Catresou furnishings. But this was where Juliet lived now, among her people, and if she wanted to be part of Juliet's life, she had to sit on the hard, awkward chairs, and stare at the plaque of Catresou calligraphy on the wall as she waited for Juliet to return.

It still hurt, to think of Juliet and not feel her emotions, not hear her thoughts. To know that she never would again. But Runajo was growing used to the silence. And it was worth all the pain and more, to see Juliet smile at her without any pain or hatred.

There was a noise behind her, and she turned, hoping it was Juliet come back from a late patrol—but it was only Paris, his pale hair rumpled, his eyes shadowed.

They had not really talked since that day Runajo had used the Catresou sacred words to claim him and set him free at the same time. Since the day that Runajo had said, *I love a girl who loves a boy who loves you.*

She did not regret those words, and she still meant them, but when she saw Paris—when she remembered what she had said, so honestly, in those hours when they had all thought they were sure to die soon—

She couldn't help dropping her gaze.

Paris didn't seem to remember, or at least to care. He dropped down into the chair beside her and leaned forward heavily, against his elbows.

"Shouldn't you be sleeping?" said Runajo finally, after a long silence. It was very late at night.

"Yes," Paris said lowly, not looking at her.

The bond between them had lasted less than a day. Runajo had felt his mind only for a few hours before he died—and he was still not her friend, would probably never be her friend the way Juliet or even Romeo was—

But when she looked at the slump of his shoulders, she remembered the cold, aching gap in her mind after he died. Without thinking, she reached out, fingers stretched toward his messy hair to—

What?

She snatched her hand back. They were nothing to each other, except in that Runajo loved Juliet who loved Romeo who loved Paris. And that was a bond good only for saving each other, not making friends.

Soon she would be in the Cloister again, surrounded by women she did not love or trust, and any bonds she had with the people outside would hardly matter.

"It's cold," said Paris. "I can't sleep."

The night air was warm and balmy. Runajo opened her mouth to correct him.

Then she caught his eyes and remembered how long he had been one of the living dead, a cold corpse compelled to walk among the living.

Perhaps it was understandable that he felt cold even now.

Runajo knew hardly anything of Paris, had no reason to care for him, and yet the dead bond still echoed in her veins: he was hers. She had to protect him.

Hardly knowing what she was doing, she reached out again and put a hand on his shoulder.

For a moment, Paris tensed. Then she heard him sigh, and felt him relax under her palm.

He didn't look at her. She was glad of that, and suspected he was too.

And then, wordlessly, Paris leaned to the side and rested his head against her shoulder.

Runajo went rigid. Her first impulse was to shove Paris away, let him fall to the floor—

But he was still hers, in way. He definitely belonged to Juliet, and Runajo had to cherish anything that she did.

So she let Paris rest against her shoulder. She listened to his breathing grow slower, until he was asleep, half snoring against her collarbone. She felt a strange, stuttering wonder, that anyone could find comfort in her. And still she waited.

Until the door of the house opened, and Juliet and Romeo returned together.

Runajo mouthed, *Help*, silently at Juliet, whose mouth quirked in amusement. Romeo hastened forward, and pulled Paris to his sleepy feet, threw an arm over his shoulder. Together the two of them went up the stairs, and left Runajo alone with Juliet.

"I've heard you're going back to the Cloister," said Juliet.

"For a few years," said Runajo. "Until the boats are finished. And they say I can leave sometimes to visit."

"And after?" asked Juliet.

Suddenly Runajo couldn't look at her any longer, the same way she couldn't look at Paris. There were so many Catresou she had wronged.

"Then," she said, "I suppose Lord Ineo will find a use for me."

Juliet leaned forward, her hands resting on the table. "I am no longer the Juliet," she said. "But I still consider myself the justice of my people. And I forgive you the debts you have not yet paid. When we finally leave Viyara . . . I would like you to come with us."

"Which *us* would that be?" asked Runajo. "I don't think Lord Ineo wants our peoples tied together any longer than he can help it."

"And not all the Catresou want me back as part of their clan," said Juliet. "I don't know what's going to happen. But I'm going to make a future for us." She held out a hand. "And I want you there for it."

Her eyes were steady and unyielding, and Runajo remembered when she saw those eyes amid the procession of dead souls. And she reached out, as she did then, and took Juliet's hand.

"Yes," she said.

Epilogue

IT WAS SUNSET. ROMEO AND Juliet had slipped away from both their families, and they sat together on a rooftop, watching the red-gold light of the setting sun gild the water. Beyond the shining water, the mainland was made of shadows. But it was no longer a place of death, and they talked together of what they might find, when the boats were finished and they sailed across.

After a while, they fell silent. They no longer needed to talk and kiss in every moment; not now when their time was not stolen, when they knew they could fall asleep and wake up together, night after night, day after day.

Juliet thought of those nights and those days, and she thought of what would come after. At last she sighed, and came to a decision.

"There is something I must tell you," she said.

Romeo waited, his dark eyes attentive, and she loved him more than ever.

"When I bargained with Death, she said I could have you back. But there was a condition: that you would die before the hair was white on my head. She swore that no power in the world could change that fate. I brought you back anyway, but I—I thought you should know."

"Is that all?" he asked her, after a moment.

"All?" she echoed.

He smiled faintly. "Didn't we always know that you were stronger?"

It wasn't a matter of strength, she wanted to tell him. And in all the ways that were not to do with swords, he was already stronger. He had loved her when she was nothing but the weapon of his enemies, and that was a grace that she never could have had.

"I'm sorry," said Romeo. "I was selfish, and now you're the one who has to pay, and that's not fair."

"It's not fair that you're going to die young," she said.

He shrugged. "Keep your looks, and I could live a few decades still."

Then gently, reverently, he touched her stomach. He said, "At least I have a chance to see our children."

Children. A future. It was a terrifying thought. Juliet didn't know what they were going to find on the far shore of the world that now lay empty. She didn't know if both their clans would leave Viyara, and how they would balance the duties they both now bore. She did not even know if they could keep the peace they had bought with so much suffering.

All Juliet knew was this: she had one husband and several friends, and none of them were willing to abandon each other, or forsake their peoples yet.

"But you," Romeo asked gently, "will you be all right? I know you're strong enough to live without me, but . . . I can't bear to think . . ."

His voice trailed away, but she knew what he was asking. She remembered the dry, hopeless shadow that lay on her heart, in those first days when she had thought that he was dead.

She remembered darkness and despair and the infinite, lonely dust at the heart of death.

She remembered the light singing underneath.

First she kissed him, slowly and reverently: her miracle, her Romeo, who stole her name and gave it back to her.

Then she took his hands. "Journeys end in lovers meeting," she whispered, pressing her forehead to his. "Every wise man's son doth know."

Acknowledgments

By the time you're writing acknowledgments for your fourth book, you start to feel like you're a repetitious bore—but some people always have to be mentioned. So: Megan Lorance and Sasha Decker are the lights of my life. Hannah Bowman is a fantastic agent, and Kristin Rens is a supremely patient editor.

Bethany Powell and Rebecca Anderson are not only excellent beta readers but A+ friends. I don't know if I could have finished this novel without them.

I also want to thank everyone who read *Bright Smoke, Cold Fire*, and especially every person who took the time to tell me that they loved it. Stories are meant to be heard, and your willingness to listen means the world to me.

I've wanted to write my own katabasis for a very long time. In constructing my land of the dead, I drew inspiration from a huge variety of sources, but I must particularly acknowledge: Dante's *Divine Comedy*, "When I Watch the Living Meet" by A. E. Housman, "The Garden of Proserpine" by Algernon Charles Swinburn, *The Farthest Shore* by Ursula K. Le Guin, *Abhorsen* by Garth Nix, *Passage* by Connie Willis, the ballads "Thomas Rhymer" and "The Unquiet Grave," and the legend of Savitri and Satyavan.

Finally—as always—I am forever thankful to William Shakespeare.